VISIT TO THE CIRCUS
CIRCUS
OF
FOOLS

Charles E. Schwarz

VISIT TO THE CIRCUS OF FOOLS

iUniverse books may be ordered through booksellers or by contacting:

iUniverse LLC
1663 Liberty Drive
Bloomington, IN 47403
www.iuniverse.com
1-800-Authors (1-800-288-4677)

ISBN: 978-1-4917-4786-5 (sc)
ISBN: 978-1-4917-4787-2 (hc)
ISBN: 978-1-4917-4785-8 (e)

Library of Congress Control Number: 2014917492

Printed in the United States of America.

iUniverse rev. date: 11/04/2014

Dedication

To the women most helpful for this work
mother, Agnes
wife, Emily
Our Mother, Mary

CONTENTS

PART I: COME WALK, TALK IN SUPEIOR LANDS
1. Getting into the IV 1
2. Visit to the Restful Room 4
3. Morning Before—Meeting The IV Coworkers 9

PART II: INTELLECTUAL LANDS
1. Scientific Land 15
2. Psychiatry Land 33
3. Education Land 54
4. Communication Land 86

PART III: LANDS OF JUSTICE
1. Legal Land 131
2. Rights Land 166

PART IV: HAPPY LANDS
1. Acceptance Land 197
2. Feminine Land 236
3. Health and Beauty Land 253
4. Compassion Land 289
5. Kumbia Land 320

PART V: MISCELLANEOUS LANDS
1. Entertainment Land 337
2. Green Land 358

PART VI: THE IV ENDS

1. Back Home 395
2. Restful Inn Again.. 399
3. Climax 405
4. Anti-Climax.. 410
5. Just for the OPs 414

PART I

COME WALK, TALK IN SUPEIOR LANDS

1

Getting into the IV

In a grand government corner office occupied by Ignatio Hoar, the head of the Secretariat for Technical Development Department, aka STD, Edmund Peoples stood respectfully silent. Midway between the door sill and desk's edge he waited for the departmental head to look up from his perusal of a single paper containing one paragraph holding four lines.

Dealing with a subordinate whose insignificant pay grade makes him invisible, a low to your high, Hoar enjoyed the pantomime paperwork; such are the joys of little men in high places. With a slight theatrical start, noticing Peoples standing in front of him, as if an unexpected apparition suddenly had materialized, Hoar said, "Oh, Peoples," (talking high to low, you can misplace low's Mr.), "I called you in to give you an important assignment. You haven't any idea?"

"No sir, I don't," Edmund said.

This type of petty belittling was Ignatio Hoar's favorite modus operandi.

"Success with this assignment could make the STD stand out. Do you understand that?"

Peoples understood the 'that,' but was totally mystified as to understanding the what of the 'that.'

Leaning forward, adjusting his empty Moroccan leather in-box, Hoar asked Peoples if he knew how hard he had to fight to get him this important appointment.

Knowing nothing, fearing the nothing, Peoples said nothing.

Pausing in the manner of an Evangelist announcing 'you're saved,' Hoar told Peoples, "You've been appointed as the STD's representative on the IV Commission. What do you think of that?"

Never expecting it, never thinking about it, Peoples thought nothing about the 'that,' yet sensing from the announcement's momentous delivery it demanded expressions of happiness and gratitude over the 'that,' Peoples delivered the expected response. "I'm certainly happy at the appointment and grateful for all your efforts on my behalf."

Smiling at the offered gratitude for his benevolence, Hoar went on to amplify. "This is a very responsible assignment. Being one of three appointed to the Investigator Visitor's Commission, I feel totally confident in your capabilities to be successful as the STD's representative on the IV. Remember, you'll be representing the Secretariat for Technical Development. The entire STD is counting on you."

Peoples didn't feel confident, didn't feel all that capable, but mostly didn't want to represent the STD. In order to get a grip on all the oil Hoar was spreading, Peoples diffidently asked, "Sir, about the Investigatory Visitor's Commission, I—"

"You'll travel to many lands and it's all on the public's dime." The dime brought out Hoar's conspiratorial wink. "Just write a brief report on your findings after each visit. "Do you know why these lands were chosen?"

A confused Peoples issued a pausing, "Er ...."

"Yes, exactly. You don't. These lands were carefully and particularly chosen because each contains a specific public policy more advanced than ours. I'll need an honest appraisal submitted directly to me immediately after each visit." Hoar decided to continue enjoying his hi to low conversation. "I trust you're an OP man, not a PP wimp."

"Sir?"

"Optimistic person, not a pessimistic person."

"OP sir, definitely OP. Never a PP."

"We at STD don't like PPs. It's all OP for us or nothing."

After a slight pause Hoar continued. "Peoples, you'll be on the road for a long time. It could be very lonely even though you'll be accompanied by two other visitors chosen from other departments."

Being a disconnect, Peoples waited for the connection to be made to Hoar's solicitude.

"Guess you'd like to take my secretary with you. Aren't you and Miss Pru Trubody in a relationship?"

With the thread of each sentence remaining unstitched, Peoples mumbled a hesitant 'yes,' waiting for a connector.

"You're a lucky man. Miss Trubody is a beautiful woman."

Another thread. No cloth in sight.

"Yes sir," Peoples answered.

"One hell of a great secretary. A beautiful mind. Will hate to lose her," Hoar said.

More thread, possibly a patch is in sight. Peoples waited for more cloth.

"Suppose you'll want her to stay home if you marry and have children, although today marriage is optional." Hoar gave 'optional' a leer.

"Sir?"

"No need to rush with the children, but remember, day-care starts at one year olds, even earlier," Hoar said.

"Yes sir." *Shit, is he trying to keep her as his secretary?*

"Know who will be the other Investigating Visitors, the other IVs?" Hoar said.

Still looking for some cloth, Peoples responded with a stupid look.

Satisfied with the response, Hoar grandly announced that the PIS, Psychological Investigative Secretariat was sending one of their best people. "Know who? Of course you don't. Well it's Sunni Childless," and laughing a sly salesman's laugh, Hoar assured Peoples that Sunni was a looker. "The third IV member is from the SSS, the Secretariat for Sociological Success, Omar Hinki. A young man like yourself who's on his way up."

Confused but happy, excited by the future, but unsettled over its uncertainty, Edmund Peoples took his leave of the great man, who picked up and contemplated the paper holding a paragraph formed with four sentence lines.

3

2

Visit to the Restful Room

A Warning To The Reader

In the Restful Room Cocktail Lounge, my love Pru Trubody, my best friend Rudy Truman and I were celebrating my unexpected appointment as one of three Investigative Visitors. The other IVs were Sunni Childless, a 29 year old attractive female representing the Psychological Investigation Secretariat, aka PIS, and Omar Hinki, representing the Secretariat for Social Success, aka SSS. I represented the Secretariat for Technical Development, aka STD. We were chosen to undertake extensive separate investigations of lands noted for being particularly successful in social areas and were to submit reports after each investigative visit on how our country could profit by adopting each land's successful methods so we can achieve social betterment.

Seated at on a barstool facing me, with love in her eyes, with worry in her voice, Pru Trubody told me to be very careful. Her anxiety for my safe return was so intense she swore her sleep would be restless, her appetite distracted, and her mind distraught with dire thoughts of the dangers I'd be facing in traveling to strange and exotic lands. Touching my hand she again begged me to take care and return to her safe and sound. Moving her hand to my forearm, Pru said she wouldn't breathe easy 'til she was holding me in her arms. Patting my chest, Pru sincerely confessed to loving me more than herself and said that what happens to me happens to her.

Though her words involved the usual feminine dramatic exaggerations, her real meaning, speaking of sincere love and concern for me, elicited my warmest feelings for her.

Rudy Truman, my best friend and coworker, stood next to us, interjecting his personal thoughts into our increasingly exclusive tete a tete. His insertions checked her hand from reaching for cheek caresses to be followed by the meeting of lips. Rudy said, "Ed, you're the luckiest guy, and honestly I've got to confess I'm envious. Fantastic exciting adventures await you, and at the end of your mission, promotions. And having Pru in love with you; a girl whose beauty is without equal—what more can a guy want?" Rudy emphasized his congratulations with a hard backslap and a call for another round.

In the Restful Room's soft-lighted lounge, warmed with Pru's shower of love and concern, basking in my true friend Rudy's acknowledged envy at my success and his sincere good wishes for me, all validated my good fortune and filled me with love and good fellowship. Of course the cocktails must also be mentioned and I must give them due credit. I mentally resolved to marry Pru on my return, and to my utmost ability, assist Rudy to get his own deserved promotion.

Another round came and I proposed a toast. "To Pru, my true love, and Rudy, my best friend." They felt the same pleasurable affection upon hearing my words as I did while expressing them.

Fearing Pru, in expressing her affection toward me, would turn our threesome into a twosome, Rudy moved closer to us and continued talking, addressing his remarks to Pru but for my ears. "Pru, can you imagine Edmund here getting picked for this fantastic assignment? Everyone in the STD was trying to get it, even yours truly, and who gets it? Edmund. No one can figure out how he got the appointment. Possibly slipping the old man Hoar a couple of bucks, or laying a few kisses on Hoar's ass," and he laughed at his mean-spirited witless wit. As they say, 'In vino verritas,' and as Rudy Truman was feeling no pain, easily seeing the stark truth in his previously veiled envy, I easily forgave his back-handed meanness; if positions were exchanged, so would our emotions be exchanged. You can't realistically expect more from a friend than from yourself, though of course you always do and are always disappointed.

Rudy continued his annoying ramblings about his amazement at my appointment to the extent that the depth and honesty of his remarks were becoming unflattering, even harsh. However, in truth, I also wondered about my appointment. From among the well-populated Secretariat for Technical Development senior researchers—each one thirsting for the appointment, each one my superior in practicing the nuances of office politics, each one's ego surpassing my own—from such a ravenous pack I had been selected.

In truth, I only threw in my application because everyone else was doing it, along with everyone lying loudly, proclaiming how disinterested they were in receiving the appointment. Individuals had come up to me encouraging me to show more strength of character than they showed by not submitting my application.

To everyone's wonderment, most of all mine, I won, and I felt a lottery winner's surprise. The fact of the matter was, some of my enthusiasm over my appointment was the result of everyone's marginally hidden envy and their evident disappointment when congratulating me for getting what they had wanted. Although I'm as ambitious as the next person, in honest modesty, suspecting my abilities and temperament didn't support such a promotion and fearing failure, I didn't welcome the gift with unrestrained joy.

Also, leaving Pru at this time, in the season when our love was coming to full flower, I was reluctant to accept the promotion. Yet, if such a crowd of coworkers so eagerly wanted it, could I, standing alone, deny their reality and deny my appointment? For such petty reasons, and from the knowledge in thwarting superiors, my denial would result in my professional disaster? I especially feared refusing the fortyish Ignatius Hoar, my department head, who was reputed to be devious, politically adroit, and well connected. He viewed himself as benevolent in extending the offer to me, so it would be suicide for me to refuse. Finally, letting the department's ardor buy mine, I soon was convinced of my own ardor's genuineness.

With a drink in hand, with several within me, blessed with Pru's adoring love and Rudy's convivial chatter, I stood between them, a hero about to seek the Holy Grail of bureaucratic success and possibly change my land for the better.

Rudy asked, "How many lands will you visit? I've heard as many as seven."

I answered, "At least ten."

"Wow!" Rudy gasped. "As many at that? And all on the expense account. Hell, the next round is yours."

"You'll write," Pru begged. "Please Edmund, promise me, and I promise to write each day."

Being drunk enough to be truthful, sober enough to still think, and innately honest, I told her that letters from her would be heaven sent, but what with writing all my reports I doubted the feasibility of writing daily letters to her, but I solemnly vowed to write as frequently as I could.

Reiterating her letter promises, sealing the promises with concerns for my safety, Pru begged for as many letters as my time permitted, then added her understanding that I'd be very busy and heavily burdened by my work.

To Rudy's annoyance I leaned over and gave Pru a long kiss: a symbolic reward for her love, a gesture of gratitude for her words of love, a sign of my love, a promise of our future love, and not the least a very meaningful expression for my desire for her, all buoyed up by alcohol.

With all of our letter promising, Rudy promised to keep me informed as to what was happening at the office and how my reports were being received. He would be my eyes and ears and report on what was happening in my absence.

With each round, with each toast, with such warm love, with steadfast friendship and expansive goodwill, my confidence increased. No longer apprehensive, I was eager to begin my journey, envisioning a triumphant return to Pru's loving soft embrace, to bask in the hoorays from friends, to possess my enemies' respect and envy, and receive the deserved promotions from Hoar's hands.

It's human nature when at the pinnacle of your happiness to naturally view the future as a series of stepping stones leading to even greater happiness, where from such heights, leaving the crowd, you become fortune's favored one standing above all others less blessed.

At night's end I stood at such a cusp, not realizing to be at a vertex is also to be surrounded by sharp, dangerous precipices. That night was my last happy night. If I'd had knowledge of the future—the pain and danger I would soon encounter, the stressful insights I'd gain of fraudulent stupidity, and illusional madness—I would rather journey to hell than have set out as my country's IV.

I had won, and was one of three investigating visitors to travel to strange lands of great promise. Unfortunately at my journey's end I managed to survive, just barely, but with a permanently scarred mind, with destroyed faith, and with memories mocking my past confidences. If you are optimistic about the future, an OP who believes in man's rationality and in knowledge, progress, love, and friendship, and greets his mornings with smiles and puts evenings to bed with hopes for tomorrow, do not read further for I was just such a fool. Now disillusioned, I am wiser and so much sadder. Better to stay the happy fool than the disillusioned sagacious cynic. Possibly that's why fools are so numerous and everyone enjoys and applauds their happy talk and their tenacious belief in foolish concepts.

If despite my caveat you continue to read, then come, join me on my journey to lands that are strange, frightening and laughable.

3

Morning Before—Meeting The IV Coworkers

On the morning of our first visitation I met the other two IVs in the hotel lobby where we agreed to separate and investigate each land alone, and from our own perspective submit our reports. Being loath to work in a threesome, I enthusiastically agreed.

The SSS, the Secretariat for Social Success, representative was Omar Hinki, a thirty year old. Given his appearance and his personality, I'm sure it took all his mother's love to nurture him to maturity, and once there, the expenditure of all his father's forbearance not to show him the door. First impressions of Hinki could be more favorable if he possessed six inches more in height, and a hundred pounds more in mass. His facial features could have compensated for his body's deficiencies if he possessed a chin. His chin, unfortunately bashful, had receded to the friendly confines of his Adam's apple. An inch of sparse upper lip hair emphasized the lack of land below. His eyes, which I suspect were brown, were inexplicably hidden behind light-sensitive brown-tinted granny glass, whose lenses, from defect, never turned completely clear. If his height, weight and facial features were deficiencies, his concave chest suggested a careless adult may have stepped on him during his infancy.

These enumerated defects could be overcome if Hinki remained silent, a virtue he sorely lacked. His nasal, grating voice was always on

9

display. Not a believer in the axiom 'wise men listen, fools prattle' he was overly generous with his thoughts. On continuous display they could easily be evaluated as mundane and predictable. He was a person who, on a rainy day would tell you with complete assurance it was raining. The only escape from his platitudes was when he dragged 'I' into the conversation: 'I plan to accomplish a lot on my visits,' 'I know people will be astounded when they read my reports.' The only respite from his 'I's future success was his 'I's' past success: 'I went to the best university,' 'I never took easy courses, only the most difficult', 'I had the greatest teachers,' 'I got all As,' 'I graduated with honors.'

His 'I' didn't ignore the present with, 'I'm really excited about this commission,' 'I expect to learn a lot about the various lands' diverse cultures,' 'I can't wait to get started.'

As an indication as to how the 'I' was benevolent, the 'I' expressed pleasure to be working with us, and his 'I' offered me assistance if I encountered difficulties. Implicit was the condemnation that if I didn't seek his assistance, my resulting failure would be deserved.

To say I disliked him within the first five minutes would be to refer to a black hole as airy.

Sunni Childless, representing the Psychological Investigation Secretariat, PIS, was a twenty nine year old looker who immediately demanded we call her Ms. Childless. Her justifying explanation for the formality was a cryptic 'it's who I am.' Unlike the brown granny glasses hiding Hinki's eyes, Sunni's green eyes, outlined in dark purple and surrounded by two inch eyelashes that constantly waved for your attention, were a strong enough attraction to pull your attention up from her prominent fullness, and pass by the straight white teeth that separated her full crimson lips. All this beauty lay under a tangled mass of sunburst yellow hair. In her presence you stood straight, desperately trying not to stare, eager to assist in any way she wished, hoping to be favorably noted by her, desperately trying to attend and respond to what she said while being distracted by her various picture-perfect parts.

Her glaring presence placed her stage front, regulating me and Hinki to the wings, if not to the theater lavatory. Her role in life was to play the lead. A fluttering hand continually moved here, there, trying to touch you, trying to assure herself you were actually there to hear her joy, to believe in her joy, to share in her joy in your discovery she was there with you. Her finger, if not tickling the air or lightly touching you, was patting her hair. Often her hands cutely covered her mouth as if hiding her words, or gripped her left breast as if holding her heart, or clutched both pancake cheeks as if she couldn't believe she was so reckless to say whatever she had said. Her hands succeeded in holding your attention, dragging your mind from her verbal ramblings to accompanying her hands' travels from here to there on her body.

She and Hinki dueled with smiles, similar words and sentences. The only difficulty was who got to say it before the other. If Sunni commented on how making these visitations was a good idea, an agreeing Hinki said it was a fantastic idea. If Hinki commented on how we were going to accomplish great things, Sunni seconded the sentiment mentioning we were going to change our world, and wasn't that just simply fantastic. When Hinki mentioned how proud he was to have been picked over everyone else in his department, Sunni expressed humility. She wasn't surprised at being picked, she was an absolute dumbfounded Cinderella at her selection.

Between Sunni and Hinki, I was a bridge to normalcy. All I could wedge between their verbal struggles for supremacy was, 'Really?' 'Not really!' 'Yes,' and 'No.'

PART II

INTELLECTUAL LANDS

1

Scientific Land

It had been decided Scientific Land was a logical choice for our first visit as people believed it would provide important insights and the scientific perspective we would need in evaluating the remaining lands. I was definitely optimistic that listening to great minds, hopefully conversing with people who really knew what there was to know, would excite my mind and increase my knowledge of the world and how it functions.

My guide in Scientific Land, Isaac Newt, approached me, extending warm greetings. He was an intellectual giant, well respected not only for the depth and breadth of his knowledge, but was equally honored for his humility and self-effacing attitudes toward his many intellectual accomplishments. As we strolled to the hub of the land's intellectual activity, its university, simply referred to as Ivy, Newt demanded I ask questions. "Only by questioning even the most sacred tenets does mankind achieve true understanding of his world."

Blue eyes twinkling under a thick lion's mane of white hair, the intellectual elder statesman asked, "Edmund Peoples, are you afraid to question?"

"If one pops to mind I usually spit it out."

"Don't be flippant. Again I ask, do you fear challenging popular beliefs?"

Chastised, I gave him a humble, polite, "Yes... er, no... er... well, I do question, but from my experience I discovered the questioner is often disliked, even hated due to people, in identifying themselves with their beliefs, inevitably view questions about their beliefs as personal attacks. Filling their personal emptiness with beliefs, the individual's self treats challenges to their beliefs as malicious attempts in diminishing their self, assaults against their very existence."

"Small minds. Ignore such people. Here in Science Land the glorious search for knowledge transcends the petty, egotistical concerns of petty people. We in the scientific community, working together and respecting each other, are a brotherhood if you will, a cloistered community of truth seekers.

"Now Edmund, here we are, the buildings and quadrangles, the lecture halls, the labs, the offices of Ivy U. Isn't it impressive?"

Impressive was too poor in syllables to describe the number and height of modern glass windows and chrome buildings intermixed with ivy covered red brick Victorian edifices. The scattered stately majestic oaks imprinting circles of cool shade on manicured green lawns lent a monastic, quiet aura to the extensive campus. In the center of Ivy was a one hundred-foot marble replica of The Thinker. Around the base students lounged, eating lunch.

Gradually taking it all in, all I could return to him was a mute, emphatic nod. It was certainly impressive and much more.

Newt said, "We'll visit the Science Building first. It's the ultra-modern black marble building in front of The Thinker. Doesn't it look like The Thinker is looking at our building and thinking we're thinking great thoughts?"

Confused, I thought there was a lot of thinking going on here.

Walking the corridors, we passed labs, lecture halls and veritable warrens of secretarial offices guarding the access to great scientific minds. To say I was intimidated is to say too little.

"Here's Al Einstol's office, the foremost physicist who has revolutionized our knowledge of the world."

The man was a disheveled sixty year old reminiscent of a family's elder uncle with either a fondness for drink or pre-teen girls or both.

Newt whispered, "Here's a man you need to attend to carefully. You can learn a lot from him; he has both special and general theories."

Al was on the phone cursing someone called Plank. "Maxi, you're an idiot…. You're wrong and I'll prove you're an ignoramus…. Screw you, Maxi! Don't call me again…. I don't care what your BS experiments' results are…. Yeah, you only wish you could do that to me!"

Slamming the phone down, glaring at us, then pointing to his desk lamp Einstol shouted, "Tell me, are light waves wiggling here and there, going up and down, or are they like bullets, fast discrete pieces of energy shot right at you?"

I foolishly guessed they're pieces and was soundly cursed by an irate Al who, jumping up to the blackboard, put several indecipherable formulas on it. "There, now you see your error? You're wrong! Admit it!"

Standing in the office looking at strange symbols reminiscent of Egyptian hieroglyphics I was more than impressed; I was once more intimidated.

Constructed of sterner intellect, my guide Newt wasn't impressed, not a jot, not a blackboard stroke. He started to argue against Al's theory of gravity with all its bowling balls rolling around a mattress. Newt vigorously put forth his clock maker and falling apples. Both agreed Maxi was an idiot, the discussion becoming so heated Al told us to get the hell out.

On our way to the next office Newt told me not to listen to Al, he was a crackpot. Apropos of nothing Newt ordered me to remind him to give me a prism as a parting gift.

The next office was Dr. Maxwell's. Dr. Maxwell was a man whose amble girth squashed his height down to five feet. A foot shorter than I, he was still able to effortlessly look down his commodious red nose at me while continually addressing my belt buckle. With his bent head studiously studied my shoes, he asked my shoes, "Do you have paper for note taking?"

To my 'no' he scolded me. Apparently note taking was essential to asking questions. He told me to call him Dr. Maxwell as if it were a nickname.

"What's electricity?" he asked. I suppose it was an appropriate question in intelligent land but I took it as a putdown because I didn't know and he knew I didn't know.

"What's magnetism?" he asked, and again I felt the same annoyance in being forced to give the same 'I don't know' answer.

"They're the same," he shouted to my shoes. "Magnetism creates electricity, electricity creates magnetism," he said, as if it explained something and my shoes understood.

"Er," I timidly ventured, "but what *is* electricity or magnetism?"

"Forces," he told my left shoe.

Still confused I continued. "But what are these forces?"

"Invisible waves," he told the right shoe, as if the right wasn't quite as swift as the left.

With some annoyance I persisted. "What are these waves?"

"Are you just stupid or being sophomorically perverse?" he accused both shoes. "Waves are forces and forces are waves. They're the same, and I'll prove it."

Here he jumped up and started to write unintelligible formulae on a huge blackboard behind his desk. We left him there, perched atop an empty soda crate, ambidextrously, frantically writing with his right hand and vigorously erasing with his left.

On our way to the next office a passing malicious student stopped and told Newt, "Al Einstol said you're full of it and he says he's going to prove you're just a limited-minded BSer past his prime, dealing with only what he can see and feel on earth."

Shaking his fist in the student's face, Newt yelled, "Do you see this!" and before any response could be given Newt gave a good hard blow to the student's ear asking, "Did you feel that?"

As the student holding a red ear ran away, Newt yelled, "I guess you saw and felt that. I still rule where it counts." And without further explanation Newt ran back to Einstol's office with me following.

Blasting into Al's office Newt yelled, "Al, you smart ass bastard, what crap are you saying about my theories? Shit, theories? They're *laws!*

Shit, laws? They're *divine commandments* from the big clockmaker in the sky!"

Brushing pipe ash from his vest Al dogmatically stated, "Wrong... they're all wrong."

"For someone who ridiculously maintains that matter is not matter but energy, and energy is not energy but matter, how dare you question my... er, His laws?"

Al growled, "Look Newt. For the last time, energy is equivalent to mass and vice versa."

Newt yelled, "Energy is the ability to do work."

Confused I asked both of them, "What's the matter?"

"Energy," Al triumphantly yelled. "Matter is energy!"

"Matter is something that occupies space!" Newt yelled louder.

"Ah, I see," I whispered to myself, and with each of the intellectuals satisfied in feeling he was right and victorious, Newt and I left.

The next office we visited was that of the famous cosmologist, Steve Hawk, who due to a speech impediment could only mumble. Constantly standing by the great Hawk's shoulder was an interpreter who was able to translate the Hawk's mumbles into intelligible words. The first thing Hawk mumbled and was interpreted for us was his complaint. "You're late, Newt. Scientists should always be conscious of and precise about time."

Replying, "My fault," Newt accepted responsibility for a quick second, before excusing himself by accusing me. "But our IV visitor was late."

Hawk mumbled and the interpreter chastised me. "Late will never do."

Defensively I assured him and the interpreter that I was on time.

"He's wrong. He was late!" Newt shouted. "By my watch he arrived at 10:01, a full minute late."

Defensively I countered, stating by my watch I actually arrived at 9:58, a good two minutes early and now I have 10:58. I then asked, "What time do you have?" That was a mistake.

Immediately everyone exposed their watches. Hawk and his interpreter had several watches on each wrist as well as desk and wall clocks. Some timepieces stood on my side of eleven, some stood on Newt's side, and with all the watches having different times, a good half-hour was spent trying to synchronize all the timepieces. This proved difficult for if one said my watch has 10:51:03, during the time it took in saying it, it was no longer 10:51:03 but 10:51:04. If all this wasn't sufficiently difficult each wanted his watch to be the frame of reference and continually shouted various times for the others to mark. All were shouting except the Hawk, who loudly mumbled. None were marking the other's time and so time passed and tempers rose.

Newt, red in face and loud of mouth, was in the process of shoving his wrist watch up the interpreter's nose as the interpreter was responding by trying to insert his pocket watch into Newt's ear. Then Hawk slammed a heavy book down on his desk and excitedly mumbled. Newt asked, "What was that noise?"

"Sure startled me," I confessed.

The interpreter with ear so close to Hawk's mouth he had to continually dry his ear, shouted, "It's the big bang. The universe started as a single point that went bang, though it didn't make a sound."

Between mumbles and drying his ear, the interpreter shouted phrases.

Mumble, mumble.

"It's called a singularity."

Mumble, mumble.

"The point exploded."

Mumble, mumble.

"It's an expanding universe."

"No," Newt said. "It's an oscillating universe, the power of gravity."

Curious, I asked what existed before the point exploded with a big bang.

Mumble, mumble.

"Forget before. There was nothing before. Think after."

Confused, I asked again. "What did the point, this singularity containing the entire universe, look like? Was it an abstract mathematical point having no dimensions or did it have depth and breadth? Could it have been a simple idea in God's mind?"

Mumble, mumble.

"Not important. Don't get bogged down in the trivial."

I persisted. "What did this magical point look like?"

Mumble, mumble.

"Energy... maybe energy. We don't know. Have faith and trust me. I've got the theory; you only have to believe."

Suddenly the Hawk jumped up and started drawing swiggly, wiggly lines on his blackboard.

As he incessantly mumbled, noting an inflated red rubber donut on his chair, I sympathized.

Pointing to the wide array of drawn wavy lines, the interpreter excitedly yelled, "String! It's all strings! It's all about strings, a new intellectual breakthrough, a brilliant theory that explains the universe! The explanation only requires a few parallel universes containing a mere 22 different dimensions. A hell of a lot better than Einstol's paltry four dimensions."

"Ah yes" popped out of my mouth. Damn. That annoying phrase would become habitual as my visits progressed. Listening to these men made one's belief in God an easier, simpler, less exotic act of faith.

We left them, the Hawk again squatting atop his donut excitedly mumbling into a moist ear. Ungraciously Newt yelled back, "It's now definitely 11:32:02!" and slammed the door.

Walking to the next office Newt bitterly complained how listening to these cosmologists was enough to make you lose your faith in science.

The next scientist, Charlie Darlin, was a burly bearded man with very unattractive features. We interrupted him—well, surprised him— tutoring a student: a coed student, an attractive young coed, a well-developed attractive coed whose intense interest in Charlie's bon mots of wisdom had her perched on his lap, fearful of missing even the slightest mot he tossed out at her.

When we entered she jumped up squealing while pulling down her blouse and skirt. Charlie Darlin shouted, "Damn you, Newt, knock next time! Bambi and I were at an intense critical point in her intellectual development. She's evolving very nicely into the best co-ed I've ever had."

Embarrassed, Newt apologized as I mumbled "Ah yes" under my breath.

After introductions, the coed started to leave, suspecting her educational evolving was at an end for the day.

Darlin yelled, "Bambi, where do you think you're going? I'll get rid of these two and we can continue. I've got some startling information about the cute platypus that will simply amaze and thrill you, while simultaneously arousing in you the warmest feelings toward nature."

"Let's all sit down. No Bambi—not on me, you silly little dear—on the chair."

Once we were all seated Charlie said, "I guess you want to hear all about the beagle."

Surprised, I told him I thought he had something to do with biological theory, not dog breeding.

Picking up a massive tome containing a multitude of polysyllabic words hiding in taxing sentences Charlie exhibiting felonious throwing intentions yelled, "Damn you! Are you trying to make fun of me!"

Newt interrupted, "Darlin, no one is making fun of you. After all, you're tangentially concerned with dog breeding."

Bambi also tried soothing Darlin with many 'Charlie darlings' with many ambiguous meanings.

Mollified, Charlie mumbled, "The beagle was a boat. Everyone knows about my boat. Now, forget the beagle. Let me give you the gist of my brilliant theory so I can get back to Bambi's private tutorial session." Then he shouted, "Where's your paper and pen?"

Both Bambi and I looked guilty.

"No, not you, my beautiful mind. My question is to my unexpected, unasked-for visitor from heaven knows where. How can you learn my theory without taking the minutest notes of all your observations about my theory?"

"I'll buy the book," I said.

"Yes, do so. I need the royalties as Bambi and I are planning a field trip to a deserted south Pacific Island to intensely study the evolution of the three-eyed squid. Now, where was I?"

Newt hinted. "Your theory, Charlie."

"Yes, the theory. Everything evolves, that's why I call my theory Evolution. Remember that. And I ask you, what's the impetus to evolve? The instinct to survive – it's all about survival. Write that down."

He didn't wait for an answer. In fact he was the type of teacher who never waited, being anxious to be the first to shout out the correct answer to his question and thereby impress himself.

Charlie asked, "Now, what is the threat to survival?" and quickly said, "It's environmental changes which threaten survival and the survival instinct is the impetus bringing about organic changes in order for the orgasm—whoops, I mean organ*ism*—to successfully adjust to environmental changes. Are you getting this, Mr. IV Visitor? It's heavy stuff. Not like Bambi here, light as a doe."

Bambi giggled. "Oh Darlin, you're just too much!"

Of ample proportions, he certainly was. You could truly say, 'just too much'.

I inserted into their cute flirtatious asides, "So the goal of life is to survive."

Leering at Bambi who returned a giggle, Darlin said, "And to reproduce. Can't survive without reproducing."

"Where does this instinct to survive originate?" I asked.

"Huh, the instinct— well, it's just there, you know? Who cares how it originated? It's just there, like sex."

Leer.

Giggle.

I persisted. "If the goal of the entire biological spectrum is to survive, are any means permissible in achieving survival?"

Again reaching for his heavy beagle book to throw at me, Darlin shouted, "You're trying to be a smart ass! You're trying to bring ethics into evolution! You're a wimp, a nancy boy, not a real man!"

Bambi giggled again. "Not the man you are, darling Darlin." She got back a leer.

"The weak gotta go. The dumb gotta be dropped. The helpless needing help to get through their pathetic lives gotta go. Same as with the stupid elephants, tigers, deer. They've gotta go. Unable to evolve, can't survive, then goodbye. You can't get all maudlin like a girly man."

"Oh darling, not the cute deer… save them."

Winking at us and leaning over to pat Bambi's worried, dimpled cheek, Darlin said, "My dear, the deer can stay."

I then asked to survive for what.

"For what! You trying to be an obstinate obstructionist by continuing to try dragging ethics into science. Damn it, I don't know, and I don't care! If you want to have a goal, then the goal of survival is to survive. The most important thing is for you to survive and reproduce."

Giggle.

Leer.

Partly to annoy him, partly to show some intellectual credentials, I continued. "And so I can use any means to achieve survival; my society can do anything, my race, my economic group can do—"

Throwing his beagle book at us, Charlie Darlin yelled, "Out, damn it, get out! You're a trouble maker!" Fortunately the book missed us. Unfortunately in his follow through he hit Bambi's perky breasts too hard. During the ensuing cursing, yells, apologies, slaps and pats, we were able to make a dignified exit.

"Where to next?"

Walking down a long hallway barely lit with dull red lights, I asked Newt why the shift to red. His only response was to warn me to stay close and not be afraid. Before I could ask 'Afraid of what?' the 'what' jumped out, clothed all in black with a black ski mask and a black cape with red lining.

"What the hell?" I exclaimed, and so surprised was unable to resist being pulled into a totally black room. Within the room, feeling this was all theater, I wondered whether the black apparition took himself and the room serious.

"Hold tight to my arm," the black figure whispered. "Do you believe in what you can't see?"

"Yes, I believe in God."

"In the black room there is no God. Other than believing in Him, must you see to believe or can you believe without seeing?"

Feeling my intellectual sophistication was being challenged I said, "Certainly I can believe in what I can't see."

With his repeating his question of my ability to believe in the unseen, I thought a little give back was warranted. Pointedly I told him I didn't believe in psychic powers, levitation, palm reading and mind reading.

Not seeing him, observing nothing in the black room, if one could observe nothing, I told the unseen blackness, I'm in a room where I can't see, talking to an unseen person who believes in the unseen.

As if I hadn't said anything he whispered, "Do you believe in negation?" The hoarse whisper spraying spittle on my nose made me take his question seriously and made me seriously wonder about him. I became fearful for my safety and wondered where Newt was. "Newt, are you here? I can't see a damn thing."

The stranger whispered, "We left Newt far behind and even though you can't see me, you believe I exist."

"Shit, I can hear you."

Suddenly he stopped talking and then I didn't hear him. Thinking, *Where is the damn exit?* it took several repeated 'Are you there?' each successively raising in volume and desperation, to get him to speak..

Finally the weirdo answered. "You repeatedly asking 'Are you there' says you believe I'm here, even though you can't hear me, as well as not seeing me. If you didn't believe I'm here, even though you can't see, touch or hear me, you wouldn't be asking if I was here."

"Look, who the hell are you? And why is the room black, and where is the exit?"

"Manny Factoid is my name. Now Mr. Peoples, I ask again, do you believe in the existence of the negative?"

Not too sure but thinking of positive-negative statements, like two plus two doesn't equal four, I said, "Yes."

"Good. Now, do you believe in darkness?"

"Certainly. I'm standing in it."

"Excellent. You have made the great intellectual leap in confessing you can believe in things you can't see and believe in darkness. Now, are you ready for the darkness?"

"This room could use a little light."

"Don't be fractious. I'm talking about dark matter and the forces of darkness."

Shit. Is this guy going into race relations? I asked, "Dark matter?"

"Yes, it's matter you can't see. It's dark matter."

"If you can't see the matter, does it matter?" I joked. Its humorous value, unseen by Factoid, died in the darkness.

"Matter, dark matter, fills the universe. You can't see it or feel it or weigh it, but it's out there holding up the galaxies," Factoid said. Close to me, he whispered, "There is more dark matter than light matter."

I couldn't resist. "Then is light matter lighter?"

Missing my pun, Factoid whispered as if sharing a confessional sin, "What is matter?"

Remembering Einstol I quickly answered, "Energy!"

I got back a whisper containing garlic molecules. "Now if light matter converts to light energy, what will dark matter convert to?"

Feeling foolish, wondering if palmistry wouldn't make more sense, I guessed, "Dark matter converts to dark energy."

He—I think it was a he, it sounded like a he, and hopefully he wasn't some dark matter gripping hard my shoulder—observed, "Now you've got a grip on darkness. The room has to be black so we can investigate dark matter and dark energy, in total darkness, you understand."

Taking a few steps back I banged my leg on something hard. Angrily I told the whisperer, "Turn the damn lights on!"

"If you turn on the light then you can't see what's happening to dark matter because of all the light energy and positive matter. Now, in a black room we can see what's really happening with dark matter. Now be careful. You may easily run into some anti-matter."

"Anti-matter! What the hell's the matter with you?"

"Anti-matter is more abundant than matter. It's what's happening in the universe."

"I can see what's happened to you. Now I'd like to be let out of this blackness and anti-matter and into the light and real things."

Manny Factoid screamed, "You don't understand! There's tons and tons of anti-matter making the universe vibrate with dark energy."

In the darkness I could sense he was wildly vibrating with excitement. For myself, feeling there were numerous vibrating strings from the 22 dimensions reaching out and grabbing hold of Manny, I demanded to be let out of this dark room of the bizarre.

Newt was waiting for me in the red lit hall.

"Let's get out of here," I pleaded. "What's next on the tour?"

Newt said, "Psychiatry," as if spitting out some phlegm. He stated he couldn't continue being my guide as in Psychology Land, given that he seriously doubted their sanity.

"Wait!" I exclaimed. "What about that tiny black door over there? Why is everyone giving it a wide berth as if afraid of the darkness?"

"Shit! Stay away from that entrance!" yelled Newt. "It's the last place you'd want to visit. Neither Einstol nor myself would dare go through that black door of the damned."

Intrigued I asked what was behind the door and why it was so frightening.

Shaking his head, Newt explained. "People who go through that door never come out. What goes on behind the black door is a horrible mystery. We suspect ugly things happen behind that blackness."

Curious, I started to approach the black door. When Newt screamed, "Mr. Peoples, don't cross that red boundary line. It's the event horizon. Step inside the event horizon and you're dragged through the door by unseen hands, never to return."

"So it's a total scientific mystery as to what goes on behind the black door?" I said.

"Certainly we men of science have numerous theories of what goes on behind the black door, and since no one knows what happens in there, no theorem can be proved wrong. Since no one ever comes out, we believe it's damn crowded in there, but like a filled rock concert there always seems to be room for one more. Here, let me show you. Do you have a coin?"

I passed Newt a half dollar, and he tossed it over the event horizon line. Magically it swirled around in ever tightening concentric circles, a leaf in a whirlpool 'til it was silently sucked into the black door and disappeared.

"Amazing," I said, then asked if I'd ever see my half dollar again.

Newt said, "Not any time soon. In fact, speaking of time, rumor has it that beyond that door there is no time."

"No time?" I said.

"A theory, like I said. Since no one comes out of the black door, all scientific theories can be right because they're never proven wrong. In fact, some great minds maintain that once you enter the black door you fall down a worm hole and come out at a different time and a different place... even in a different universe. When talking about the inside of the black door, you have poetic license. Einstol says, in the middle of his mattress there's a big black hole.

"If you want to play the advanced black hole science game, publish a theory and enjoy all the deep scientific thinkers proving that you're wrong and their theory is right. It's all very exciting. At conventions it can become quite physical: beards are pulled, glasses are tossed, tweed coats are torn, fists are shaken, and people are pushed hard in the chest."

We were leaving the black hole when a hippo inadvertently passed across the red event horizon. With a loud sucking noise the animal was gone.

"Did you see that?" I exclaimed.

"Yeah, one less hippo, but one theory says he's now the size of a mouse traveling through the worm hole and coming out the other side of space is now grazing on a field of cheese. You've got to love what you don't know."

Walking farther down the corridor we approached a green door that suddenly disappeared only to reappear some yards distant, half the size, and purple.

"Newt, did you see that? Are my eyes at fault?"

"Mr. Peoples, avert your eyes. Don't look over there, but keep your mind open. That's the door leading to the Quirky club room. Only those who have the greatest mental fortitude can enter. If you value your common sense sanity, don't go in there."

Just then two men in polka dot suits came out carrying a screaming man on a stretcher. In a purple straight jacket and foaming at the mouth, he kept yelling hysterically, then laughing about how up is down, left is right, it's there and it's not there, it's here and not here.

Curious, feeling I had an excellent grip on my sanity, never having had a questioning mind, never having devised a theory, and possessing normal curiosity, I told Newt I'd like to peek in on the Quirky club room.

We entered through the purple door, which unexpectedly turned yellow, and found ourselves in the office of the great Hersenbigger. Looking over his desk without a greeting he asked, "Are you really there in front of me and if you are, will you stay there or are you going to appear behind me?"

I answered, "I'm in front of you and I will not move."

Pulling on his hair, Hersenbigger cried out, "I've proven my theory! If you're in front of me, I can't tell if you moved, and if you moved I can't tell where you are. It's all very uncertain. That's why I call my theory the Uncertain Theory."

Clutching a fistful of hair, Hersenbigger demanded, "Can you tell me, are you coming or going? Are you going up or down? Left or right? Are you going fast or slow?"

Patiently, as one might speak to a disturbed child, I explained I was still in front of him and if I decided to leave he would be able to see me go.

Suddenly Hersenbigger jumped on the top of his desk and demanded, "Peoples, did you see me move?"

"Yes."

"No, you didn't. Due to my Uncertain Theory, you can't both see me and see me move."

"But I do see you and I did see you move," I said.

"Impossible. My theory guarantees you can't do both, so don't lie," he said.

Discourteously I told him it was certain that all the uncertainty was in his mind.

Ignoring my comment Hersenbigger yelled, "Did you see it move?" and pointed to something behind me.

Looking behind me I told him I saw nothing.

Hersenbigger joyfully announced, "You can't see it because it moved, proving once again my theory. If something moves you can't see it move and still see it. Look, now it's not moving, so now you can see it."

I noted a spotlighted bronze stature of Hersenbigger poised as a prize fighter with arms upraised in celebration with an inscription that read *In honor of Hersenbigger and his Uncertainty.*

I told him I saw it.

"Can you see it move?" he asked.

"No, it's not moving," I said.

"Eureka, my uncertain theory is proven once again. You see it and you can't see it move."

Being completely uncertain as to what he was talking about, I just gave him a 'whatever' shoulder shrug.

Suddenly, from an adjacent room, loud hysterical laughter and screams cut through all the uncertainty.

Ducking into his desk well, Hersenbigger shouted, "You can't see me, but you know I moved."

Ignoring him I asked, "What is all that yelling about?"

An unseen voice from the well said, "It was the Quirky comic club. Neils Boor is the headliner act. Things can get pretty wild in there. If you enter the club be careful. Don't let them sweep you away with all the craziness going on in there. Neils goes wild in there."

Feeling I could use a good laugh just then, especially as Hersenbigger's grinning head had just surfaced from the desk's well and he'd challenged me to say whether I saw him move.

I entered a large, almost empty auditorium with only a few individuals dressed in different colors trying to bounce off each other. A laughing Neils Boor, a small rotund master of ceremonies, greeted me and asked if I was ready to get crazy.

Being uncertain, I gave him a qualified, 'Yes.'

Giving a belly laugh—and he had the belly to do the laugh justice—Neils announced he had discovered six new flavors and I could be an apricot flavor.

Suspicious, declining the apricot flavor, I observed the auditorium participants jumping up and down, twisting left and right, bouncing forward, hopping backward, falling down, springing up, all in chaos. Each dancer was dressed in gaily colored flavors with vanilla most prominent. Except for the great expanse of space surrounding each dancer it was similar to a modern rap dance concert.

I asked Boors what were the dancers doing.

To control his jiggling stomach Boor told me, "It's the newest dance craze, called the Quirky Rag. You do whatever your energy says you're to do."

To my puzzled expression Boor explained, "It's all about attraction and repulsion. Don't you feel it in the ether?" Then, "Wait!" Boor yelled. "I feel a wave coming," and everyone started waving back and forth, and it all became blurry.

Excitedly Boor cried, "Feel the energy in my Quirky Comic Club room. It's all around you."

Confused, suspecting the inhabitants' sanity, I asked about the laughing, crying, yelling and general bedlam going on in a black corner of the auditorium. "I can't see what they're doing in the darkness."

"Oh," Boor said, "that's the anti-party. They party in the dark so you can't see what they're doing. If you listen, you can hear them, and you've got to suspect it's an orgy, what with them staying in the dark. Whatever is going on in the dark party, you have its opposite in the Quirky Club's party.

"Oh dear, here comes another poor soul who can't take all the energy generated in the Quirky Comic Club."

Being carried out by pink and blue flavors, he was a drooling mess, uncontrollably giggling. He asked as he passed, "I'm here, so I'm there; I'm not real, so I'm real. I jump and don't know where. I attract yet never get connected; I feel energy, then am de-energized and never know why."

I followed the poor suffering man out of the Quirky Comic Club and watched the poor soul being placed into a decompression chamber, where movies of summertime apples gently falling was the accepted therapeutic treatment.

2

Psychiatry Land

Stumbling and disoriented, Newt and I left Scientific Land and entered Psychiatry Land. The Psychiatry building consisted of dark-tinted glass grafted together by straight stainless steel lines. Innocent of any hidden mental significance, I told Newt that with its geometric lines and darkened windows, the building resembled a nightmare on graph paper.

"Careful," Newt said. "Don't use metaphors, analogies, similies, or any other comparative descriptive speech. In that building all such figures of speech are taken seriously. Words you use do not mean what you think they mean; they never do. They mean what you don't want them to mean. They mean what you're trying to hide, not from others but from yourself. A slip of the tongue will supply these people with sufficient material to construct numerous different contradictory books all revealing your real self, whom you didn't even know. In these books you'll find yourself as a bizarre self, a sexual-deviant self, a person you don't recognize but in reality is more you than you are. But not only that, the words you *don't* speak are more revealing about your hidden self than words you speak. Unspoken words you can't hear are words that will frighten and scare you. Always remember, spoken words don't mean what you think they mean and words you do not say tell everything about you."

"Ah yes, very complicated," I said.

Newt's last words were, "Be forewarned," as he introduced me to my new guide, Dr. Fruit. Newt left us to return to Scientific Land, giggling to himself as he waved goodbye.

Dr. Fruit was a small, bearded gentleman with a cigar planted in his mouth and ashes falling on his vest. I asked him who we were to visit first. He didn't answer and appeared not to have heard me, but I know he did. I believed he was wordlessly telling me he was immersed in his great mind's thoughts, which were too deep and opaque for my words to penetrate.

Passing a large secretarial area where numerous women were typing, sorting, and folding, but mostly gossiping amid stacks of paper, journals, and books all carelessly tossed atop every horizontal plane, we entered a large room cut into cubes. Some cubes housed male college students watching pornographic films, pressing a buzzer whenever they felt aroused. It sounded like a stockbroker's office on a very high-volume buy day. With pride, Fruit mentioned they were all selfless, payless, eager volunteers advancing the frontiers of psychology.

In other cubes, females were trying to guess the shape on hidden cards, crying in despair at their lack of ESP. In some cubes, strange, unintelligible inkblots were being analyzed in depth for hidden meanings, usually very ugly sexual meanings. In one large cube several individuals were trying to bend various cutleries using mind power. Every spoon, knife and fork appeared straight, so either there had been no success or they had been successful in restoring the pieces to their original shape.

In the next laboratory, a dark candle-lit room, in a circle, several women were holding hands and looking to the ceiling, to the floor, and to the corners, all asking in guarded, hopeful whispers, "Is that you, Daddy? Have you come back? Where is the jewelry? Are you happy? I can't find the will."

Suddenly someone yelling, "I see Elvis, a young Elvis," brought numerous questions: "Is he singing?" "How is he dressed?" "What's he saying?" It all ended with some middle-aged woman shouting, "He just kissed me! I felt his lips, his hot breath on me! Someone hold me; I'm going to faint."

Another woman yelled she was beginning to levitate. Her left foot was off the floor. "I feel my right foot is beginning to rise." Suddenly there was a large crash and the woman was yelling, "I was levitated for at least three seconds!"

Warning me never to have a closed mind in Psychiatry, Fruit explained, "ESP, got to be open to all ideas, no matter how strange or how sexual and only by careful, controlled experimentation can we verify or debunk them." He flicked an ash from his cigar to his vest for emphasis.

I asked Fruit what great mind we would visit first.

He answered, "Skin."

"Skin?" I repeated.

"His name is Skin and he's done great things with electricity. Now remember the three maxims in Psychiatry Land: take notes, never argue, and pose only relevant questions to these great men."

Skin's large office was filled with an array of caged animals with their corresponding nasty smells, reminiscent of subway lavatories. After a brief cursory introduction, Skin, tall, intense, and bald save for some thick gray ear fringe hiding his ears, excitedly told us that we were in luck; Pricilla had just experienced a learning breakthrough.

Innocently I expected a female student. I was dumbfounded when Skin proudly picked up a fat hen and presented her to me. "Meet Pricilla."

Between Pricilla and me, she alone kept her aplomb. I was so surprised, I impolitely back stepped when he thrust her at my face.

"Don't be afraid. She doesn't bite," Skin said. After giving her a peck on her beak, Skin placed her down on a miniature dance floor.

It was only then that I noticed the wires connected to her butt.

"Watch this!" he exclaimed. "And I've only been teaching her for three weeks! He turned on a rap music CD, and Pricilla started to do some serious rap dancing, energetically hopping up and down, excitedly flapping her wings to the music's beat, a feat not that impressive given rap music's moronic monotone beat.

Except for the one time she stopped, forcing Skin to give her butt a jolt of volts, she did admirably, even better than most frenzied teenagers at an MTV concert.

With a rooster's pride, Skin rhetorically asked us, "What do you think of that? Did you ever see a hen dance like that? And note, only three weeks training."

Ignoring the hen's dance, a suspicious Fruit asked why had Skin kissed the hen, observing, as a world-renowned psychiatrist, that he found the hen-kissing behavior disturbingly sexually bizarre, fraught with hidden sexual abnormalities.

As an aside Fruit told me, "Ignorant lay people wouldn't notice the nuances and ramifications of that kiss, but with my brilliance and experience, by employing my breakthrough theories I'm able to pick up on serious latent sexual bestiality."

Defensively Skin countered that any normal person intensely working for three weeks in training a student to rap dance would normally bond with his student. Skin went on. "What is strange, Fruit, is your blindness to the fabulous implications of Pricilla's dance in the field of human behavior modifications. Seeing an innocent, meaningless, affectionate kiss between teacher and student you misinterpret the normal peck for a hidden, revolting something. Her learning to dance is an exciting intellectual breakthrough. Pricilla dances just like a normal teenage girl and likes to receive as a reward a small token of affection."

Fruit pointed. "You said teenage girl! That's very significant!" He jotted vigorously in a little black book.

Trying to ignore the butt wires I asked, "How did you teach the hen to dance?"

"Conditional behavior modification—it's my stimulus-response theory," Skin answered. "Look, here's Pricilla's rehearsal room." He pointed to an enclosed chicken coop. "See the 16 volt car battery? See the wires attached to the rehearsal hall's floor? See the switch? See Pricilla dance like an excited pre-teenager attending a Michael Jackson retrospect concert? Sometime she does the Moonwalk. Right now I'm—"

"Pre-teen girl you said!" Fruit said. "I find that slip of a tongue very, very revealing," and again he frantically jotted in his black notebook.

I asked, "You mean you—"

"Yeah. When Pricilla's little feet are kissed by Sparky, she's stimulated and quickly learns the complicated intricacies of rap dancing."

"Kiss her feet!" Fruit mumbled, and while scribbling was starting to salivate.

Seeing my shocked expression and possessing a subtle mind, Skin deduced, "You're thinking it's cruel... that I'm cruel."

"Sadism," Fruit said, but more to his note book than to us.

"Well, I—" I started.

"Answer me this. What chicken can dance like Pricilla? You know the saying, 'No pain, no gain' is true."

Fruit mumbled to his notebook, "Masochism," then, looking up, started to ask, "Skin, your relationship with your mother... can you tell me—"

Ignoring Fruit, Skin said, "Now, the key is the music. When Sparky is singing and the music is playing Pricilla makes the mental connection and you get a dramatic intellectual breakthrough. Pricilla is conditioned to associate the stimulus with the learned response to the music. Get it? The stimulus-response learning theory. It's very deep."

"Ah, I see," came my socially conditioned ambivalent response.

Fruit wanted to discuss Pricilla's relationship with her mother during the first few days the child was out of her shell and whether it had been a difficult birth.

Totally ignoring Fruit and mistakenly viewing me as an appreciator, Skin continued talking to me. "The trouble is in varying the dance steps. Pricilla is slow to learn different steps. She continuously does the same rap dance to foxtrot music."

Fruit asked, "Did her mother have a difficult time during Priscilla's incubation?"

Skin was excitedly talking about starting young Rosie, currently still in her shell, to listening to waltz music through ear pads connected to her shell. He promised that when she hatched, instead of pecking Rosie would be doing a waltz and looking for a partner.

Again I said, "Ah, I see."

Fruit requested Skin to video record Rosie's mother giving birth.

"You mean laying her egg," I suggested.

Fruit, looking intently at me, said, "Well, that's interesting. You use the suggestive word 'lay' in relationship to giving birth," and he started a new page in his notebook.

Oblivious to us, Skin said, "If only I could get a government grant I could put a group of pigeons in the rehearsal hall and see if I could condition them to dance in a synchronized line, like the Rockettes... or maybe by grasping a rooster's wing they could tango about the electric grid."

"Dance the tango?" Fruit shouted. "That's a sexually loaded dance! Skin, you've got deep sexual problems, wanting to watch pigeons dance sexually. Hell, in addition you're a sicko, torturing animals for sexual gratification."

"Fruit, you're stupid and closed minded, and definitely not an intellectual," Skin responded.

Unperturbed, Fruit said, "Skin, you're closed minded, and although you're suffering from gross sexual problems, if I treat you, if I can talk seriously with you, with your hidden, sick self, I could cure you."

"Well," Skin heatedly retorted, "I'll change your behavior if I can get you onto my dance floor. In a month I could have you tap dancing with Rosy on America's Got Talent."

And with that promise a scared Fruit rushed out the office. Before I could leave, a worried Skin asked, "Look, like Vegas, what happens here stays here. Don't tell anyone. If those PETA nuts ever find out about my rehearsal hall... well, with their irrational group conditioning they'd go berserk and my research is too important. Just think, if schools wired students' chairs, inattentive students would soon be a thing of the past. And prisons—if they'd let me wire their cells' floors, I'd cure their recidivism problems damn fast."

As the office door closed Skin was on the phone ordering a gross of Tasers.

In the corridor, Fruit summarized. "That sexual degenerate needs extensive, expensive psychoanalysis. Hopefully he'll make use of my business card, which I slipped onto Priscilla's dance floor."

"Ah yes," I said.

Fruit announced the next psychiatrist. "Here's Piget's office. Now remember, take notes, never argue and always ask relevant questions. You'll never learn unless you question great minds and elicit their great answers."

Small, rotund of stature, with full, ruddy cheeks striving to contain a perpetual happy smile from reaching his ears, Piget greeted us with little hops and skips on petite feet that women would die to possess. "Just in time," he gaily announced. "I'll be able to show you several important ongoing experiments."

He held out his soft hand, knuckles up so I would have to rotate it 90 degrees to shake it. I decided it wasn't worth the effort.

As we passed through his office, the walls were covered with a profusion of infant and children's pictures, reminiscent of a pediatrician's reception room or a pedophile's bedroom.

The first room Piget took us to had a one-way mirror through which we could look in at a nursery with a young, perky mother nursing a newborn from breasts that were firm, full, and definitely without sag.

"Notice the video cameras are recording the event," Piget needlessly said.

Fruit suspiciously asked, "Why are you recording it?" in a tone indicating he suspected why and the why was a nasty why.

"It's a daring experiment. I've found that babies learn to instinctively suckle immediately after birth." Turning to me, Piget commented, "Admit it, you're startled by my recent findings."

I asked, "Why are both breasts bare?" as Fruit noted something in his notebook and mumbled under his breath either about my observation or about why Piget was recording the feeding.

"She doesn't realize we're watching her. Remember, she can't see us," Piget whispered.

"Wait," I said. "She's in a lab in front of a hundred square foot dark mirror, behind which is a bank of cameras and she doesn't realize people are watching?"

A surprised Piget asked, "Do you really think she knows? No, I don't think so. Besides, she's getting paid to advance scientific knowledge."

Mumbling "exhibitionism" and "voyeurism of the most perverted type," Fruit continued his furious note taking as we all watched in the scientific spirit as the woman switched breasts.

Piget asked if we wanted to see his video of the mother lathering and washing her breasts preparatory to breast-feeding.

I quickly declined, but Fruit's "No," was definitely ambivalent as he feverishly made notes.

In the next lab room, through its one-way mirror, we saw a pre-school playroom with two and three year olds wandering about, oblivious of the six cameras stationed about the room. "We're studying early childhood behavior," Piget needlessly told us, then excitedly exclaimed, "Look!" pointing to a little boy who was energetically trying to wrestle a Raggedy Ann doll from a little girl's tight grasp. Like two puppies tugging at a bone, they went back and forth until the little girl fell and the boy, successful and triumphant, started to bang Raggedy Ann's head on the floor.

"Do you see?" Piget asked. "Children exhibit aggressive behavior at an early age. Another breakthrough in my early childhood behavioral theory."

Fruit added that he saw sexual aggression in the male's id as he acted out his ego's attempts to sexually dominate the female.

Piget and I look at Fruit as if he was more than just a little strange.

"Take note," Piget commanded, pointing to two boys fighting over a plastic fire engine. "You have children at an early age seeking to possess objects. They seek to augment their selves with external objects. This behavior is definitely not learned but acquired through maturation."

Fruit found Piget's interest in little boys very disturbing, and by observing that the fire truck represented a penis, he theorized the boys fighting over it were indicating deep-seated castration fears.

"Were they circumcised?" Fruit asked, and when Piget said "Yes," Fruit cried out, "That explains it all! I'll need to see the little boys in my consulting room to intensely psychoanalyze them back to the day of their birth, even before. As for the boy banging the Raggedy Ann doll, he needs serious counseling. He's a potential wife beater, if not a future serial rapist and murderer, or on the other hand, he could be fighting against latent homosexuality. The little girl, of course, needs help to overcome her penis envy. She's definitely on the road to promiscuity and drugs without my penetrating her subconscious, pre-conscious, and unconscious, making them all conscious."

He received our looks, but leaving them unopened he was happily unconscious of their import.

In the last room, peering through one-way mirrors, we saw a kindergarten class where a healthy braless teacher named Trudy, over eighteen and definitely less than twenty, was trying to teach the alphabet to four inattentive children. They were repeating each letter as the teacher, in a tight, low-cut silk jersey and tight black short skirt held up a letter card. The little girls repeated "R" while the boys were picking their noses and tossing the results at each other. Several white coats were intensely observing through the one-way mirror. The intensity became keen as the teacher hitched up her tight skirt to sit atop her desk, then crossed her legs, revealing pink bikini briefs. While all white coats stooped to closely observe scientifically, Piget informed us that the little girls' learning behavior was better than the boys' behavior.

Fruit, finding his notebook filled, pulled out a new one and said with finality, "The boys are exhibiting the classic symptom of major future sexual frustration, possibly maladjustment, indicated by throwing their snot, which represents their sperm, at each other. Did I mention I see potentially gay boys subliminally acting out?"

With stupefaction, I exclaimed, "What?"

"Only a highly trained psychiatrist can recognize the subtle but all so evident hidden symptoms. Peoples, seeing you're a lay person, I don't want to get too technical, but doesn't the finger going into a nostril suggest anything sexual to you?"

"That's sick," I said to him, about him.

Ignoring my real meaning and unconsciously misinterpreting my meaning, he chastised me. "Sick! The young boys aren't sick! Nothing is sick! Maybe maladjusted or dysfunctional. And note the nose, the penis of the face, and the toes, the penis of the foot, and the true penis is roughly equally distant from each other on the body. I'll say no more on the subject, as I'm writing a groundbreaking article for the *Journal for Psychiatrists* in which I'm proving—"

Piget excitedly interrupted. "Look, teacher Trudi is picking up another letter card."

With her back to the glass, slowly swaying, Trudi bent from the waist, establishing for the scientific observers that the pink briefs were definitely string bikinis. Turning to face the class and our glass, she foolishly dropped the letter. She wiggled everything on top in her struggle to pick up the letter. With a sexy pout, she brusquely shoved aside a helpful boy. Unfortunately, not realizing her foot had pinned the letter to the floor, she was forced to shake her body in her intense struggle to retrieve it. With her unfettered, hanging fulsomeness swaying to and fro, she moaned in her efforts. In unison the white coats sympathetically groaned, then cursed aloud when a little boy pointing a snotty finger at her shoe caused her to exhibit appropriate surprise. With girlish delight and gratitude she squashed the little boy's head between her fulsomeness, depriving him and her audience of breath. Finally she straightened up and every white coat leaned back. The sole white coat woman, with a very short haircut, commented how Trudi was the best children's teacher they'd ever had and worth every penny the Foundation was paying her.

The little boys, out of snot ammunition, started tossing spitballs at the girls. An astonished Piget announced, "Look everyone, the first sign of cooperative activity. Make notes. The boys are working together for a common goal, trying to attract the girls by attacking them. Note the average age is four years, two months, and six days...." He checked his watch and added, "Ten minutes, seven seconds. This breakthrough observation will be an expanded chapter in my new Childhood Development textbook."

"Fool!" Fruit cried. "Look at the new letter she's holding. It's the letter S. Don't you see the subliminal message? Can't you grasp its significance?"

Knowing Fruit's mental predilections, I guessed. "Sex?"

"Exactly. The young boys, unconsciously sexually active, are subliminally and unconsciously stimulated by the letter's hidden message and now are unconsciously trying to impregnate the girls with spitballs."

The girls, trying to defend themselves, were pinching the boys at any soft flesh they could get between two fingers.

Piget shouted, "Look, by the age of four, girls group together for cooperative defense. I've got another breakthrough chapter. I've got to call Dr. Phil for a TV appearance, and I know Dr. Oz will be stupefied."

Furiously jotting in his notebook, Fruit shouted, "Piget, you're totally wrong! The girls, sexually threatened by spitball impregnation aren't trying to defend themselves but are trying to stimulate the boys by pinching them. All this sexual activity is unconsciously ignited by the letter S. Damn your chapters, Piget! I've got a book here, hell, a best seller! Shit it's Hollywood bound. *Oprah* and *The View*, here I come!"

Piget said, "Don't kid me, you pervert. Your book is sick intellectual kiddy porn, intellectual land's greatest malediction. And you're closed minded."

Fruit countered. "You're closed minded and unconsciously you suffer from gross sexual problems and I refuse to treat your difficulties 'til you apologize."

Suddenly standing behind us holding a car battery, Skin yelled, "Both of you are stupid and closed minded, definitely not intellectuals and I'm sure I can change your behavior if I can get you two on the dance floor. I'll have you dancing the Can Can with Priscilla and Rosie."

Suddenly an excited white coat yelled out, "Trudi is going to demonstrate how to exercise and play All Fall Down on an air-filled rubber mattress."

Every scientific observer crowded against the one-way window, with elbows thrown and accompanied by vicious pushes and pulls as faces pressed against the glass to attend to Trudi's hands, which she was waving high above her as she bounced and somersaulted in teaching physical exercises. When it was time for Trudi to teach her students how to play All Fall Down on an air mattress, the press against the glass was reminiscent of the crush at Titanic's last lifeboat

A little girl came up to Trudi asking if she could fall down. The little girl, blocking our view, brought numerous energetic curses, except from Fruit, who was furiously making volumes of notes.

After we studied a series of provocative yoga contortions by nimble Trudi, Fruit suggested we visit Dr. Ruby Horny next, mentioning he had planned to visit Adler, but for some reason now had decided to visit Ruby Horny.

"Horny?" I exclaimed.

"That's her name. Does it suggest some hidden meaning to you?" Fruit excitedly asked.

"Well it's er... well, possibly suggestive."

"Of what? Tell me, what are you trying to repress?"

"Well, er... just forget it."

"That's what repression means. You'll need intense analysis at my clinic. For only two hundred dollars an hour, I'll get you talking to your hidden, repressed self. Hell, you'll be having a no-holds-barred conversation with your unknown self 'til finally, before you know it, the two of you will be good friends."

Thinking six margaritas could make my hidden self and me lifelong buddies, I said "Maybe later," by which I meant, "Never."

On leaving Piget's One-Way Mirror Land we were knocked aside at the doorway by an entering group of white coats, digital cameras in hand, worriedly shouting, asking whether they were too late to observe Trudi teaching her students how to jump.

Picking up several of his full notebooks, Fruit, observing that the rushing group had sexual problems with children, mumbled he'd have to do a lot of heavy psychological healing with that lot.

A frantic white coat running out the door almost knocked me down, shouting, "Emergency! Emergency! I've got to go home and get to my wife!"

Before Ruby Horny's office suite, Fruit warned me that putting off important things like my analysis was another form of repression. I was repressing my need for analysis to find out what I was repressing and why was I repressing my need for analysis. With my serious need of therapy, with two intense hours a day, every day, for at least six months, he promised he'd begin ripping my sick hidden self from its dark, unconscious hiding place so I, standing face to face with it, could slap that dirty ugly self silly.

Before I could tell him to forget about my repressed self, we were in Ruby Horny's conference room with ten or so women ranging from college babes to moms to grandmas, all searching for a suitable daddy.

In a serious business suit, a white shirt, and short, dark, combed-back hair Ruby Horny was standing at the conference table's head. Wearing a gay, colorful scarf to soften or hide her sartorial masculine message, it unfortunately said yes rather than no to your not so repressed sexual questions. Short, stout, the thumb on a feminist hand, her voice was deep, her manner brisk in introducing us to the conferees. Fruit started to explain why I was visiting her student conference when she abruptly cut him off. "I'm head of the women's psychology studies and just as good as any man, even better, so I don't need you. If you've got some troubles with them, deal with them."

When we both admitted to being trouble free she pointed a stubby finger at Fruit, accusing him of being sexist.

Silently I agreed. Fruit certainly was absorbed by sex.

With pride he responded, "Certainly I am. The instinct to procreate is paramount in my theory. I feel—"

"You took him," and she tossed as much of her hair as was there at me, "to see Skin and Piget, both male psychologists, before me. Why?"

"Well, they were closer to the entrance and—"

"And why do men have offices next to the entrance and I, the only woman, who is as good or even better than any man, am told to sit at the back of the bus? It's the glass ceiling all over again."

"Surely, Watson's and Roger's offices are after yours and—"

Pointing above she angrily shouted, "Glass ceiling!" so loudly that I looked up at acoustical tile. "You're afraid of a strong woman who refuses to sit in the bus's back."

Turning to me she held out her hand, not to shake but to ask, seriously, "Want to arm wrestle?"

I declined even after she offered to simultaneously arm wrestle Fruit left-handed and me with her right.

Both Fruit and I, dubious of the outcome, declined. Then Horny, picking up a laser light pointer, sent the light to my crotch and asked the class, "What's that?"

Everyone turned, the babes foolishly giggling, the grandmas politely smiling, the mamas smiling nasty smiles, while the lone man in the group gave the widest welcoming smile.

I demanded she turn the laser off as she repeated, "What's there?"

No one answered, yet they all knew the answer. Apparently Horny, feeling no one knew, announced, "Hidden under cloth, available, an easy zipper escape, is the penis." Turning the light on Fruit's privates she shouted, "We spit on your penis envy!"

I thought, Shit. *This is one mean, nasty broad. She acts like the dominatrix role would not be all that foreign to her.*

Continuing, she informed the class, "Fruit, with his old shriveled up one, thinks we're interested in it. Women, are we interested in it?"

All the women shouted, "No! Never!"

Only the guy said yes.

"What interests us is righting social inequality. Women labor under male domination. It's time to break the glass ceiling. Now, do I hear a 'right on?'"

She heard it, as did all the adjacent offices.

"We need to be free from males' definition of what a woman should be. Do I hear a—"

The building shook with "Right on!"

One granny yelled out, "Go sister! Don't hold back! Give it to them hard in the crotch!"

"We aren't as good as men?" She paused before shouting the expected correction. "We're better!"

Wild excitement bounced from walls, ceiling, and floor as Fruit whispered, "Typical repression reaction, attacking the cause of their repressed fears instead of facing them."

I didn't say 'Ah yes' this time, being too busy watching one of the young babes who was so excited she had to take off her sweater and wave it over her head, revealing a push up, shove out, squeeze together, generously filled out purple half-bra.

"Are we smarter?" Horny shouted.

She was greeted by hysterical shouts of "Right on!"

"Are we braver?"

Their "Go sister!" went right through adjacent offices and into fresh air.

"Are we more sensitive?"

"Right on!" and a blouse came off a middle-aged matron, revealing some serious, heavy, unappetizing chub barely encased in pink lace.

"Do we envy their ugly, dirty thing?"

Amid shouts of "No! No!" the sweaterless babe was jumping up and down and vigorously shaking her head, her bottom and everything in between.

I tried to look away but was locked on each wiggle.

"We are women! Let me hear you roar!"

And immediately, the room was filled with high-pitched grating screams.

In the excitement, two had fainted—a looker and a granny—while the guy somehow was now standing uncomfortably close to me. I nodded to Fruit, indicating I wanted to leave.

As we left I heard calls for a free universal sperm bank where successful, strong, intelligent free women could make beefcake withdrawals as needed.

Outside, after telling Fruit my observations concerning the guy's inclinations as well as Horny's, he told me I was repressing my own homosexuality and needed at least six additional months of treatment for three hours daily. Repressing my true feelings, I didn't answer, not even an 'Ah yes.'

Walking down a long corridor, we passed many treatment rooms. One had a woman crying on a therapist's shoulder. Fruit said, "Crying therapy."

Another room had a woman in a fetal position clutching a pillow to her stomach and screaming uncontrollably. Fruit said, "Screaming therapy."

Another room contained several women in a circle loudly screaming at each other. Fruit said, "Group therapy."

At a room with several people industriously writing in journals, I successfully guessed "Writing therapy." Passing a room filled with people laughing I was right again, saying, "Laughing therapy." And at a room filled with nude people who were entwined and entangled, I guessed, "Orgy therapy." I was wrong.

Fruit said, "Touching therapy, whereby through touching others one gets rid of repressed fears of being close to others, and by being touched by others, you become open to others. Peoples, you must realize, clothes are unnatural and an artificial barrier to intimate contact, interfering with meaningful, honest, interpersonal communication."

"Ah yes."

In the next room through a one-way mirror I saw two women who were oiling each other as well as a smiling guy. I correctly guessed, "Sex therapy."

"This is Jerry Kinsi's sexual clinic for the sexual dysfunctional. This man is coming to grips with his sexual dysfunction. Shall we stop and say hello? The sex therapists, Mandi and Randi, in helping numerous men with their repressed sexual dysfunctions, enjoy an astounding success rate of 99%."

Looking at Mandi and Randi working on the smiling patient, I wondered why there was a 1%; then remembered Horny's guy.

"Shall we stop? Shall we go in and say hello?"

"Shit no," I automatically responded.

"You're repressing your fear to face your deep sexual questions, possibly repressing your homosexual tendencies. Tell me, was your mother a dominating or submissive factor in your life?"

To stop him I entered Jerry Kinsi's office. He was middle in age, weight, height and looks. On one office wall were provocative erotic pictures of women. On the opposite wall were men in bikini briefs. On the adjacent walls were graphic pictures of what happens when one wall meets the other wall.

After perfunctory greetings, Kinsi asked whether we had seen his sex therapy in action. He followed this question with a wink and then offered me a special introductory rate for Mandi and Randi's treatment for any impotence problems I was experiencing, promising after Mandi warms the oil and Randi pours the oil I'd be a new man.

I declined impolitely, saying it seemed to be sex for money.

"This is an Institute," Kinsi haughtily said. "This is medical stuff. The rules do not apply. We make the rules—in fact, we're above the rules—and I sense you seem closed minded, and even threatened by scientific medical advancement in treatment of human sexual problems. Your declining suggests you have serious sexual problems. My institute has a sensational cure rate for erectile dysfunction. Don't be ashamed to admit any sexual difficulties. Remember, sex is good. It should be seen in the light of day and not hidden like something you're ashamed of."

Writing in his note book while glancing at me, Fruit eagerly diagnosed, "Yes, suffering from repressed sex," and prescribed an additional six more months of treatment, five hours in length.

Kinsi suggested a session with Barry to allow me to get in touch with my feminine side, mentioning his statistical data gathered from a random sample of San Francisco male fashion designers and hair stylists prove 95% of all men are really homosexual.

Fruit seriously asked me, "Are you sure Barry couldn't help introduce you to your real self, your repressed self?"

"Ugh, that's disgusting," I simultaneously said, thought and felt.

Kinsi diagnosed fear of sex, while Fruit, sadly shaking his head, said my repressions were so numerous and so deep I would require at least five years of treatment eight hours a day and he wasn't giving guarantees.

Pulling out a journal article he had written showing in an unbiased survey of NOW leadership, 57% of all women were lesbians, Kinsi offered to introduce me to Buster Babs, a sex expert in that area, mentioning that many men searching for their feminine sensitive side found being rump thumped by Buster Babs worked wonders. Apparently Buster Babs specialized in men and women suffering from deep-seated sexual guilt that needed release through well-earned pain.

Suddenly a young couple entered. The young man introduced his girlfriend as Hillary, saying she was interested in becoming a professional sex therapist at the Kinsi Institute. When told she had no license as a therapist, Kinsi asked if she had studied for the profession. With pride she admitted to home study since the age of fourteen and said she had continually engaged in intensive, extensive fieldwork to expand her knowledge.

With such extensive experience, Kinsi decided all she needed to do to gain her license was to pass the Institute's stringent exam. Noting the bedroom exam room was empty, he suggested Professor Bruit Bruno administer the exams.

With perky confidence, Hillary entered. "I'm ready for anything."

After she departed, Kinsi started to comment on her boyfriend's good looks. I took that as my cue to leave, especially as Fruit was mentioning some personal sexual repression of his own and wondering whether possibly Mandi and Randi, with an assist from Buster Babs, might bring things to a head, but only if he was accorded a professional discount. Unfortunately Kinsi was adamant concerning the full rate even after Fruit offered Kinsi a week's counseling treatment on the couch in exchange.

AFTER PSYCHIATRY LAND

At day's end, in a five star hotel and resort, after enjoying a lobster dinner with Hinki and Sunni, accompanied by several bottles of white wine (on your dime), I escaped the two who were energetically engaged in talking about themselves to themselves, much to the satisfaction of each. Connoisseur Hinki was telling himself and the silverware (between bits of lobster dripping butter) how inferior this lobster was compared with other lobsters he had encountered. Sunni was amazing her china setting with all her fabulous dinner dates where succulent lobster was flown in from Maine, shrimp the size of your forearm, and sushi to die for, all of which swam around her and her companion, a handsome dynamic CEO or a brilliant author or a powerful political leader. Her companions' occupations often changed without any worry on Sunni's part.

Each energetically speaking only to plates and forks, their respective conversations unnoticed occasionally bumped into each other's respective soliloquy to miraculously emerge unhurt.

Gratefully retreating to the hotel lounge, I contemplated the letters I had received from Pru and Rudy. Pru's letter, between exaggerated but welcomed promises of undying love, indicated that my reports on Science and Psychology Land were received with disappointment. Querying Hoar over an afternoon coffee break, she had learned my pessimistic tone was viewed with distaste. Hoar thought I was going PP and should be more OP in my report. I didn't care for them having coffee together, but she was trying to be helpful. However, hearing my report was unfavorably received did hurt my ego.

In contrast, Rudy's letter conveyed the opposite reception to my report. His careful reading of the department's higher ups indicated my report had been enthusiastically received. My honest, hard-hitting evaluation viewed against the ridiculous Pollyanna account submitted by Sunni and Hinki stood out in favorable relief. My realistic, critical report was greeted with the joy of a cold shower on a hot day, with Rudy mentioning that Pru and he had shared information over lunch. The apparent dichotomy between the two letters was confusing.

Joining me, my fellow visitors plopped down in the lounge's soft leather easy chairs and ordered brandies (your dime). It took three minutes and three deep brandy sips for them to talk about their observations, but only after declaring the brandy's inferiority.

Sunni, taking smaller sips, was able to begin first, congratulating herself in her perception in seeing the importance of the land's commitment to psychological studies. "Hinki, did you see Skin's amazing gecko strutting through the maze without a false turn?"

"Yes, Sunni, but I think you missed the ten squirrels climbing on each other's shoulders to open a six foot high door, or the frog doing back flips on the high wire. And didn't they all look a little frightened? Maybe more like terrified," Hinki said.

Sunni was impressed with the important role women played in Psychiatry's investigations. "Yes Hinki, it was amazing, but what impressed me most was the important role women play in the Land's psychological investigations."

I had to ask Sunni if she was referring to Trudi or the sex therapist oil girls, Mandi and Randi.

"Certainly not. You must be impressed with the psychological work Ruby Horny is doing for all women. My only fault with her was her aggressive nature. I couldn't get rid of her. She kept inviting me to her apartment to do an in-depth analysis of a Girls Gone Wild DVD."

Hinki, in ill grace, brought up the wonderful artistic elephants, painting abstracts with their trunks to disco music. "That shows animals possess great intelligence," he said.

Before Sunni could top his story, Hinki went to the ice. "Did you visit the Environmental Land where ice is melting? We'll all be under a hundred feet of water and drowning. Now that was really scary."

"True Hinki, but you had to cry for the poor baby polar bears starving and drowning without their ice."

Between debating whether to order a highball or not, my nasty self inserted, "But imagine the seals' joy."

Ignoring me, Hinki said, "Sure the flooding scenario was bad, but even worse was the heat, turning everything into deserts. And the hurricanes and the earthquakes. Talk about your disasters."

Leaving my comfortable chair, I left as Sunni was relating how Piget offered her a prestigious appointment at an enormous salary to work with Trudi, teaching two year olds how to jog in place. I didn't hear the rest of the conversation, save Hinki mentioning Kinsi offering him a job in the Kinsi sex institute.

3

Education Land

After enjoying a fulsome breakfast alone in the hotel dining room—eggs Benedict, lox, Belgium waffles, juice, espresso (your dime again)—I wandered into the lobby, waiting for my guide. Satiated from breakfast I sat dumbly watching a TV show: a cartoon with the alphabet dancing in circles singing songs telling everyone to love everyone, especially those who are different letters.

After the tots' program, a junior high school show came on entitled *Sex Education Appropriate for Jr. High School Students*. It consisted of four serious teenage girls and a middle-aged teacher learning safe sex (never too young) by putting condoms on bananas. The teacher solemnly told the girls not to be pressured into having sex, but wait for the right time. I suspected the 'right time' would be right after the class.

With wide-eyed disbelief at what I was watching, my guide showed up and introduced herself as Candi Wright, a matronly forty-plus with a welcoming smile as lavish as her greeting hug. I said, "I'm here to learn some of your land's educational secrets."

She pompously said, "In Education Land no child is left behind."

Being slightly obnoxious I asked, "Behind what?"

Ignoring my inane comment, Candi Wright said, "A mind is a terrible thing to waste."

Tempted to ask where they disposed of wasted minds, instead I said, "So true" with a touch of irony.

Ignoring the irony, she continued spouting their educational secrets. "Interest is our watch word. Do you know, not only do all our students graduate from high school, but they go on to advanced degrees at our University. It's all due to interest in education."

With sincerity I responded. "I have been told of your educational achievements by our teachers, and we are eager to adopt your successful pedagogical methods. My sole purpose is to observe and report on how you have achieved the results that we have been energetically striving for and continually failing to secure. If we can instill a love of knowledge and the joy of learning in our students, it will lead to academic success, successful careers, and a self-satisfying life of accomplishments."

Confidently she said, "I promise you, you shall see and learn. Our school is just a short pleasant downhill walk. We can converse as we walk."

Proceeding downhill, I noticed the abundant, disgusting garbage and filth adjacent to the path and that the surrounding fields were covered with waist-high weeds. As a guest, I refrained from giving voice to my negative observations.

She began her instruction. "In Education Land our philosophy is first, you must love children, all the children. Do you love children?"

Could anyone say "No, I do not love children?" Certainly not, although I've never met 'the children'. On reflection, you may love a child you know, but for abstractions, I don't know how to love airy words and airy children, and neither does anyone else, despite their optimistic belief they can and actually do. However, with a nod I let the banality roll down the path in front of us.

Candi continued. "It's essential in educating children; you must first love them."

When people utter abstract nonsensical hot air you can only utter similar affirmations, hoping that when the dirigible balloons land, their baskets won't be empty.

"We love our children and out of our deep love have committed ourselves to their education, resolving not to rest until each child totally fulfills his or her potential." She said that as if the cliché profundity was unique to Education Land and no other.

I thought, *As opposed to people believing they* didn't *want students to achieve their academic potential?*

With her, a firm believer in speaking both vague, abstract words and the even more vague, abstract ideas they carry as if they were heavy with meaning, and looking like the aunt you'd like to have had and never did, I decided to massage this imaginary aunt. I said, "Your commitment to education is admired the world over." But I was thinking, *Yeah, I know... you love children and want to educate them. Deep.*

Passing a group of bearded men dressed in tatters and feverishly drawing figures in the dirt, I glanced at them before quickly looking away. Still, they started to beg for money in the most pitiful manner.

Quickly leaving them behind, Candi told me to ignore them, explaining they were mathematicians and physicists, as if somehow that completely explained their sorry state and nothing else need be said.

I protested. "But they're in dire need. Surely society should reward such abilities."

"Their reward is being happy doing what interests them," she exclaimed, and continued with abstract and undefined concepts. "Tell your people, for educational success it's interest, interest, and again interest."

Facetiously I couldn't help myself. "Can all this interest be withdrawn?"

I doubted Candi heard my silly sally as she continued. "Interest is the key to education. All children, naturally inquisitive, are filled with questions of how, why, and what. This natural curiosity is the touchstone of our educational philosophy. If you wish to educate, if you hope to guide, to lead a student to drink from the springs of knowledge, the student must want to imbibe. You cannot force the child to learn. Forcing a child to learn only teaches him to hate and avoid all learning. Remember the great pedagogical axiom: you entice the child to learn by leading him through his interests and curiosity to knowledge. And the negation is just as true: you cannot force-feed learning. By taking advantage of the child's natural curiosity, discovering his innate interest and utilizing those interests, you educate the child. Because you're educating the student by using what interests him, learning is enjoyable for him and he quickly becomes self-motivated. The teacher and the school environment then becomes resource aids to facilitate and forward the student's self-directed learning process."

It all sounded wonderful—possibly a little too wonderful to be real. Were the balloon baskets empty? In my land, each year the hard hand of having to learn this or that fell on all students, letting its bite be a lesson learned, requiring the expenditure of mental energy. Learning is hard work.

We walked past several old hags industriously making pie crusts in front of a dilapidated shack while other crones were making stirring motions over cracked pots filled with disgusting chicken remains. Seeing us they stopped their labors and began begging for food while offering to sell us their thin gruel. Before they could encircle us, Candi hurried me past them, telling me to ignore them, as they were neither as distressed or as miserable as they seemed. In fact, they were all Cordon Bleu gourmet chefs.

Noticing my puzzlement, she amplified, increasing my confusion. "They're cooking," she said, as if that explained their begging for food and excused the proffered revolting watery gruel for sale.

Labeling Candi as simple-minded and the chefs as mentally disturbed, I listened as she continued my education by rhetorically asking me, "Doesn't everyone enjoy doing what interests them?"

"Certainly." I wondered about the meaningless tautology: people enjoy doing what they enjoy doing.

"Doesn't everyone shun doing what is uninteresting or boring?"

"Without a doubt." More nonsense—people don't want to do what they don't want to do.

"So happiness is working at what interests you and unhappiness is being forced to do what is uninteresting to you."

I let her sneaky 'forced' go by, and when it had gone, I allowed Candi an assenting nod. Continuing, she explained. "And what is interesting to you is important to you, and what is uninteresting to you is unimportant to you."

If I were in a classroom and wrote that down I'd feel foolish.

I wanted to pause and argue the point but held my tongue when, startled, I beheld a group of filthy men and women dressed in rags parading about each other, placing small patches on each other, only to have others remove the patches and initiate excited arguments accompanied by gesturing hands, stamping feet and obscene shouts.

Seeing us, they enthusiastically beckoned us over. Fortunately, being some distance away, we were able to easily evade any contact as Candi described them as haute couture designers, whose creations rival those of Paris, London, and New York. After several paces she said, "Where was I? Ah yes... given all the salubrious advantages of allowing students to pursue what interests them, you simply can't stop the learning process at a graduation. We must be able to allow them to continue their education throughout their life. Now with everyone in Education Land doing what interests them, can anyone realistically expect monetary rewards for doing what interests them, what they enjoy doing?" She paused expectedly for my amen.

I just couldn't be that dishonest, so I tickled her. "So by the same reasoning, I'd bet you don't assign grades to students since they're studying things that interest them."

"Certainly we don't. It's hurtful for the student to fail. If they sense failure, if they receive negative feedback in pursuing their interests, they'll become discouraged and leave the learning process, by which I mean drop out of school. Besides, it teaches students the wrong motivation. Instead of pursuing their interests and being happy, they'll pursue grades, pernicious artificial rewards, and rather than being self-motivated, they'll become puppets manipulated by others to do what they aren't interested in doing. With grades, students will be seduced from pursuing their interests into areas they're not interested in, and that will result in—"

"Learning?"

Candi corrected me. "It will result in unhappiness, frustration. It's all so simple. Interest leads to learning, to success, and eventually to a happy life."

"So the final goal to your educational system is happiness."

"All our students are happy, and that is why we decided to make the Interest Theory of Learning the cornerstone of our educational system."

Thinking it was certainly a pompous name for such a simplistic idea, I nodded as a tickle for her to move her forward, which she did. "Equality—all children are equal," was her non sequitur scratch.

Dumbly I said, "Amen" to that bland, nonsensical tripe as I wondered, *Equal in what way?* In truth, no one is equal to anyone else in any way.

Candi said, "Aren't all children born with blank minds, and the only difference between children is their parental circumstances?"

Being her guest, being there to learn, not to dispute, and ignoring DNA, I gave the conjunctive 'and' holding together the nouns 'blank mind' and 'circumstances' a pass.

"Given the children's initial equality, their blank mental slate, and the differentiating effect of parental circumstances, if you love children, want them to learn, to be happy in learning, and lead a happy life, what is to be done?"

"Just a moment," I said, pointing to a lean-to where several people holding down a screaming man were allowing another to cut him. "Look; they're murdering that man."

"Of course not. They're doctors doing a delicate operation."

Dumfounded, I said, "Without being anesthetized?"

"Unfortunately we don't have any anesthetic products in our country."

"Why?"

"No one is interested in producing it."

"That's ridiculous."

Ignoring my comment, she pointed to a huge building covering many acres some distance away, Candi said, "And there it is." It was a school, a building, once a magnificent edifice set in beautiful, landscaped acres, now looking tired and woe begotten, with graffiti decorated walls, broken windows, and litter and weeds scattered everywhere.

Apparently blind to the building's seedy tenement appearance, Candi spread her hands grandly, announcing with genuine love, "Our school!"

Could I, a visitor, say *It's a dump, I wouldn't board pit bulls in it?* Forced by my circumstance I said a noncommittal, "Ah, yes." Then, seeing a disorderly crowd yelling, pushing, shaking their heads and fists at each other I hazard a guess: "Angry parents?"

"Teacher meeting," Candi said.

I said, "Ah, yes," which she could take as a period or a question mark.

Grabbing the question mark, Candi amplified. "They often meet to discuss the latest, most exciting innovative pedagogical techniques for engaging students' interest.

"Ah, yes."

Again ignoring the potential period and grabbing the mythical question mark and tossing aside the angry, enraged teachers, Candi continued. "Every student is a unique individual and as such has unique interests which must be respected and nurtured, and it's the sacred task of teachers to discover each child's unique interest and to creatively devise exciting pedagogical methods to direct the students' natural inherent interests toward learning more about what—"

"Interests him," I finished for her.

"Or her," she said.

I didn't bring into the open the unique interest, the blank mind and all the sameness difficulty. Instead I said, "Ah yes."

She ignored the now emphatic, unambiguous period.

"Remember, teachers are teachers because they are interested in being teachers and educating others. So at these teacher conferences there's always an energetic enthusiastic exchange of ideas concerning the efficacy of different teaching methods to uncover, nurture and develop interest in studying. Teachers who have devised new successful teaching methods are always generously anxious to share them with their colleagues, who in turn have created their own newly minted successful teaching methods."

"Look!" I shouted. "Two women are fighting."

Calmly Candi explained. "Totally committed to successfully teaching all our children, and adamantly refusing to leave any child behind, from deep commitment to education, teachers may engage in strenuous energetic physical debate."

"Wow!" I said, implying an incredulous *holy shit* at the ongoing combat before impishly asking, "So is any child left behind?"

Quickly Candi answered with a proud, emphatic, "None. Not a single, wonderful mind is wasted." Then she asked out of the blue, "Does your country have a dream?"

Still of an impish mood, I said, "Certainly, when people sleep."

"You misunderstand. Here everyone has the same dream, and the dream is to have every child achieve his dream. They're dreams within a dream."

"What's all this dreaming? I'm confused. I don't understand."

She graciously amplified. "Yes, the complexity of our educational theory has confused a lot of the uneducated or closed minded." Candi graciously amplified. "It's a beautiful sentiment, our wonderful promise. We promise our youth they will achieve their dreams and in doing so will fulfill our country's dream."

I asked, "What are the contents of all these dreams, the contents of all these promises? It's all so airy and illusionary. Can you anchor it by illustration?"

"We all have a dream of a better tomorrow."

"Wasn't there some stupid musical song about a little girl called Annie singing about tomorrow?"

Ignoring my nonsense, Candi continued with her own. "To continue, every person wishes to be happy. True?"

Thinking, *As opposed to wishing to be unhappy*, I replied, "True."

"Well that's the promise we make every child. They will be happy because doing what interests you makes you happy. Children will be happy not only in the future, but in the present."

"An impossible task. How can anyone—"

"Please, IV Peoples, stop your negativism. Here in our land only optimism is allowed. There are only OPs here. One should never utter a 'not' to a person's dream of happiness, never argue against the promise of a better and happier tomorrow for our children, never point out the pitfalls or shortfalls and any other type of falls when new, quasi-new, or reconstructed avenues of educational theory and pedagogical techniques are discovered through which our Land realizes its dreams: a world where all people are successful, healthy, caring, educated, but most of all, happy. That's our dream, that's our promise, that's our commitment, and we will leave no child behind in our or his dreams, nor outside our promises, not to leave any potential unfulfilled. PP thinking is not allowed here."

Candi began to mist up at her imaginary child: definitely a poor child, most probably a minority child, must probably a female minority woe begotten child, with her brilliant mind desperately starving for book food, standing by the side of the road as the great glorious parade of happy, successful, healthy, wealthy, most probably men, definitely white, pass by the little crying girl.

To forestall Candi's continued uncontrollable emotional responses to her own images, I surrendered. "Yes, Candi, you, your children, your country have dreams, beautiful dreams, precious dreams of a happy life for every child and you made a solemn promise that every child shall achieve that dream. My one question, picayune in substance, is this: how does your system work?"

"That's a great question. We have a three-prong attack. Do you want to write them down? It's the core of our complex educational philosophy."

Suspecting what was coming, I told her I'd memorize them.

"Well, I hope so. You really should take notes of all we're discussing. Our educational philosophy is an extremely difficult concept to fully grasp, especially for the non-professional. Sure you don't want to jot down an idea, or make a mark or two?"

"Not interested in note taking."

"Well, if you're not interested in note taking, then it's all right, because note taking doesn't interest you. Well, it all starts with caring. In our caring society you won't find a person who doesn't care about our children, and being so caring, everyone is totally concerned about their education and happiness.

"Peoples, tell me honestly, do you deeply care about children, their health, their education, their future, and their happiness? Tell me honestly."

"Oh, I deeply care," I said, then underlined my lie with, "Trust me, I sincerely, deeply care."

"Good. Now the second prong of our system. If you care, if you're committed to education, you'll gladly spend the money necessary to give every child the opportunity, time and tools to achieve their self-directed goals."

"Caring and opportunity. I got it. But er, how much money and from whom?"

"How much money?" a shocked Candi repeated. "Just to ask the question suggests a mindset that puts money before children's happiness and education. I certainly hope your land doesn't put money before a child's education and dreams."

After my repeated vows of my country's love of children and our total indifference to the expenditure of money for education, Candi relented sufficiently to give me the third prong.

"We come back to interest. It all revolves around interest. Find out what interests the child. Remember, doing what's interesting to you is not work, but a joyous time spent in happy pursuits. The child is caught up in our educational system because we appeal to his interests."

Apparently Candi felt she had closed the circle: caring, money and interest yields the love of learning in the child and fulfills both society's promises and the child's potential. Like an inflated rubber tube, the educational circle serenely floats atop an ocean of happiness and love.

Walking past the pugnacious teachers, I noticed one with clenched fists was maintaining that multicolored pop-up pictures were the key to educational success, while another shaking a middle finger in fist's face maintained the key to educational success was larger print and larger margins with a multitude of colored diagrams. A third teacher vigorously yelled at the middle finger his 750-page six-pound text was too big and the only true answer was to reduce the subject material covered. He maintained that books should only be 10 pages with lots of transparencies, schematics, color inserts and pictures of Big Bird and Oscar the Grouch walking across the pages instructing children out of cartoon balloons.

A fourth put forth electronics, computers, and tablets as the technological innovation were best for teaching. Books were obsolete, students would love to read from a tablet or a computer monitor.

The fist bit the second's middle finger, who responded by kicking her, while the third gave both vigorous hair rearrangements.

I was fascinated watching the bizarre teacher conference. Misinterpreting my opened-mouth stare, Candi joyfully told me I was in luck as I had an appointment to visit not only the student science fair and a spelling contest, but also a student musical production of their own composition.

This time my "Ah, yes," was one of dejection. Having walked through, sat through, and listened to such student endeavors in the past, I knew boredom was waiting for me. However, in the land of successful education I hoped to still be pleasantly surprised, and wonder of wonders... I wasn't. I was horrified.

On the way to the school auditorium where a musical was being presented we passed a classroom filled with fifteen or so co-eds busily shouting at each other. Sharing lipstick, eyeliner, and blush, the shouts were accompanied by high squeals underlying their joy in discovering various cosmetics' ability to enhance their faces, as well as strenuously debating the best methods for bust enhancement for display.

To my quizzical look, with no shame Candi said, "Developing language skills concomitant with interest in cosmetology."

Passing an unsupervised cafeteria I'm glad to report the students were not engaged in food fights, but rather were fighting each other for food, for the few carrots and stale crusts displayed.

Again ignoring my quizzical look, Candi hurried me past the starving students, commenting on the school's all-out assault on childhood obesity.

We encountered an ongoing parent/teacher conference in which a parent was angrily saying, "My son is brilliant. He's failing because he's not being challenged. He's bored in class."

The teacher abjectly confessed, "It's my fault, but I can't seem to find any way to interest and stimulate him in school work." She then asked the parent, "Do you have any suggestions?"

"Hell, no! You're the professional! You should do your job and make my son interested in school work so he'll realize his fantastic potential."

To my quizzical look Candi explained, "Often it's difficult to find that particular key to unlock each child's unique interest in order to open the child's mind."

"Ah, yes." It was an 'ah yes' echoing my fond memories of the three 'R's and rote learning.

Leaving the parent/teacher conference we heard the teacher lamenting if only she had the money to buy more supplies: mobiles, construction paper, videos, slides, and movies. If only she could devote more one-on-one time with the student, but coping with as many as five students in the class and allotted only three teacher aids, well, what could she do?

Candi apologetically commented on the teacher's complaint. "We're still working on reducing class size, but there never is enough money to pay for quality education. In fact, in education, it's axiomatic. There can never be enough educational money."

"Isn't your educational system totally successful?" I said, hopefully keeping the sarcasm from my voice.

"In education, even after achieving great success there is always and will always be the need for greater success and therefore more money. Remember, education is an ongoing, ever-growing organic process. Ah, here we are, at the students' musical presentation."

As she opened the double doors to the school's auditorium, a cacophony of ear grating noises filled the hall. On the stage were a hundred or so student musicians who apparently were tuning their instruments, each running up and down the scales, while in front of them twenty or so students were frantically waving rulers in the air. Positioned at the stage's apron, thirty or so boys and girls of all ages were each singing different songs in different keys; a pessimist might characterize it as yelling. Candi commented how wonderful it was that the singers could project their voices to the rear empty seats.

"When will the production begin?"

"It's in the third act now."

"Ah, yes," was my confused assent.

"Look, here come the dancers."

And yes, on the stage came students, dressed in all sorts of grubby attire, gyrating, jumping, tumbling, shaking hips provocatively and pirouetting in all directions, often colliding with musicians and the ruler people.

My surprise was such that I couldn't refrain myself. "It's all just chaos, certainly not the third act of any musical presentation I can recognize."

"Your eye is not trained to see the beauty of it all, nor your ear conditioned to hear the complexity of it all, nor is your mind sufficiently educated to put each students' diverse pieces together to form a magnificent ongoing, unfolding educational musical mosaic."

Visitor or not, diplomacy be damned. Forcefully I told her there was no harmony, no melody, no cohesive plot, no unifying direction in all this disorder. "It needs discipline."

"There is discipline. The greatest type of discipline, self-discipline, the discipline an individual imposes on himself when he's interested in what he is doing. In the land of educational success, we abhor discipline imposed from without. It can lead only to rebellious conduct against the school, to a hatred of learning, and to a disruptive internal conflict in the student between what is being imposed from without and what is the students' true motivating interest emerging naturally from within the student."

"But you have to have a conductor in authority. It needs a score, a choreographer, a—"

"You miss the intellectual depth of interest learning. See the students with rulers? Their interest is in being symphony conductors. The dancers are interested in ballet or ballroom or rap dancing, while the musicians are showing their devotion to their instruments and the singers are hoping to develop into operatic, country or rap vocalists. As proof of our success I'd like to point out we have had some very successful rap singer graduates and our Zumba dancers are world famous."

Looking up at the stage I persisted. "But it's all noise, it's all nonsense, it's all asinine, it's all—"

Candi warned me. "Careful, Peoples... you're being very negative. Hopefully you're not a pessimistic person, a PP. I've heard of such destructive people in other lands." She then patiently explained, "If a student expresses an interest in doing something, we firmly believe optimistic evaluations should be given in order to encourage the student to continue his passion. To say to a student 'that's wonderful' not only encourages him in his interest but makes him happy. To pessimistically say what he did was terrible or wrong is to discourage him from pursuing his interest and more importantly makes the student unhappy, unhappy enough not to try again, to turn away from education, to—"

"To stand on the curb watching the happy parade of successful others pass by," I added.

Sensing a dollop of sarcasm, Candi was suspicious. "Exactly, but perhaps the arts are not the area best suited to illustrate our progressive interest learning theory. Let's go to the science fair, where empirical study imposes its discipline upon the students."

Out of the auditorium and walking down a litter-filled corridor we passed many classrooms filled with students of both sexes, laughing, pushing, groping, kissing and fighting with each other, while the teachers were yelling various praises and encouragement to them to continue doing whatever they were doing as long as they liked what they were doing.

We stopped at one chaotic classroom where pre-teens were being energetically prodded by their teacher to consider careers as astronauts. After they'd been shown *Star Wars* and *Star Trek* movies and were playing computer games involving shooting at meteorites and aliens, I had to confess the students seemed more than interested. In fact, they seemed excited while making zapping noises at each other. Unfortunately the teacher tentatively whispering about the possibility of a few moments of Physics and Mathematics acted as a sieve, straining out student excitement and interest and leaving a watery substance consisting of boredom and disinterest, occasionally broken by a half-hearted zap at an alien.

Candi remarked that when classroom's interest wavers and wanes as in this case, the teacher will employ different creative devices to restimulate the students' interest.

True to Candi's prediction the teacher suggested they put on *Star Wars* costumes and have some Darth Vader ice cream cake. This immediately restored both the class's enthusiasm and renewed interest in careers in space exploration.

Leaving the class, noting my bewildered head shaking, Candi said, "A noisy, chaotic class is a class interested in, and busily engaged in, the learning process. A silent classroom loudly says bored, uninterested and worse, unhappy students.

Passing another open classroom door I saw students watching *The Untouchables*, I guessed aloud, "Interest in police work."

"Law enforcement," Candi said.

"Ah, yes," I said, having no other reply in mind.

Finally, reaching a huge all-purpose hall, Candi told me we would see the results of students' scientific interests as shown in their exhibits. At the elementary grade exhibition tables I saw potato men, live cute baby rabbits, and finger painting smears. Unfortunately several finger painting artists were energetically engaged in throwing paint at each other or smearing it on themselves, an obvious precursor to interest in either military careers or tattooing.

Candi hurried me to a table of plastic volcanoes spawning obnoxious liquids. Holding my nose with one hand and shielding my eyes with the other as one volcano suddenly exploded with real fireworks. I suggested we move on. A coughing Candi agreed, mentioning future volcanologists.

Passing to an exhibit where several groups of enthusiastic students huddled on the carpeted floor were shouting and exhibiting admirable focused concentration, I thought, *Ah yes, finally this must be real interest learning at its purest.*

Bending over, peering at the center of one excited group I was surprised to see they were busily tossing money down and rolling dice. Shocked, standing up, I exclaimed, "It's a crap game!"

"Interest in studying the laws of probability. We encourage mathematical interest," retorted Candi in countering any possible negativity.

"Ah, yes."

Pointing to several tables where poker was being played, I ventured, "More probability?"

"Certainly, as well as honing important decision making abilities."

"Ah, yes, what else?"

Near the exit was a race track where several students were racing remote control cars, and when I pointed at them Candi said, "Automobile technology."

"And the eight ball pool game over by the window?"

"Either Newtonian Physics or Astro Physics. It's hard to tell from here."

"Ah, yes."

"You want to see more science projects?"

"No, I've seen enough. Can we leave? The noise is giving me a headache."

"To repeat," Candi shouted, "noise in the learning process is a good sign, indicating significant students' enthusiastic interest in learning and their energetic exchanging of shared knowledge."

"Ah yes."

"And our educational system fosters democratic attitudes."

"Really!"

"Certainly. Working together, through shared common interests, students come to understand the benefits of working and cooperating together to achieve goals."

"Ah, yes, and I suppose the goals are established by the students."

"Definitely, the goals arise from the students' natural curiosity and interest. Of course, molded, fostered, encouraged by their teacher. The student's interest is within the student and only needs a teacher's gentle creative stimulation to burst forth."

"Ah yes!"

"And the teacher is not an authoritarian figure, but a resource person."

"Ah, yes."

"The teacher respects the student and as a result the student respects the teacher."

"Ah yes."

"You know, every individual is different and different individuals not only have unique interests but learn in different ways at different speeds."

I couldn't hold it in any more. "All I see is chaos, noise, mayhem, and directionless activity squandering school time with no profit."

"The noisy, disorganized activity you perceive is from you educational ignorance. You see only the superficial surface. If you were pedagogically literate you'd be able to penetrate beneath the surface and celebrate all the movement and shouting as visual manifestations of serious learning."

"Ah yes."

"I don't want to be critical, but you say 'ah yes' quite often and sometimes it sounds like you're not convinced, like it's a negative comment. Now, don't be a closed-minded pessimistic person, a PP. Open your mind to the educational revolution successfully going on before your eyes. For the first time in the history of teaching we have made learning fun, made teaching exciting."

"Fun? Isn't learning a difficult endeavor requiring mental discipline and necessarily enduring mental pain and the ensuing mental fatigue in its pursuit?"

Shaking her head, Candi asked, "Are you a naysayer? Are you a PP? Are you afraid to escape past theories and plunge into new exciting theories whose success you can see for yourself in our schools?"

To appease her I said, "I'm learning and am thankful for all I've seen so far." I tried to pin a badge of sincerity to my words and since I was learning, they were sincere. Yet implying polite counterfeit sentiments, I required effort to keep from smiling at their dual mirages.

As we passed a class in sewing, a group of girls were busy making a school quilt as an AIDS project. Apparently the girls were divided into several warring groups as to whose patches should be centered and which patches were to be placed at the borders, while a teacher was shouting they should take a vote.

"See? Democratic learning," Candi joyfully said.

"Ah, yes," I said, as the two groups were now going at each other with scissors, with a few less-combative students walking out of the classroom in hissy fits. Some unknown hand in a temper threw her scissors, thankfully closed, and hit me in the chest. While rubbing the tender spot, Candi said, "Note how energetically enthusiastic, how deeply committed, how intensely interested the girls are in their sewing project, and indirectly in the process of learning how to sew and to work together democratically. It's all so wonderful."

Massaging my chest, I asked if we could please leave the school.

"You haven't seen the spelling bee competition in the auditorium. We must just peek in and see all the wonderful children spelling."

Unfortunately we were at the auditorium door and before I could say no she had me inside. Looking about the auditorium I ruefully thought being a IV visitor wasn't really very exciting and wondered about how my comrades Sunni and Hinki were making out.

The stage was filled with fifty or so eighth-grade students, sitting, talking, or walking about while waiting their turn to spell. The audience section was sparsely filled with, I thought, parents. A rather fat, nervous boy sniffing loudly into the microphone announced he was Jerome from Miss Gladys's Advanced Language Arts Class.

Candi whispered, "Isn't this so very nice? The students are so self-motivated, they're willing to undergo the intense anxiety of a spelling bee competition."

Seeing the crowded stage I observed that the competition must have just started since so few had been eliminated.

Glancing at her watch Candi told me the competition was nearing completion.

Saying nothing, I wondered at the large amount of students not eliminated.

Jerome, after giving a last forceful nose inhale and swallowing the results was ready for his first word. The moderator, speaking very slow, enunciating with deliberate care, asked Jerome to spell 'would,' as in 'I would do my homework.'

Jerome's brow wrinkled, his eyes searched the auditorium, left and right, until suddenly with a triumphant smile he said, "W o d."

It was the turn of the moderator to frown. After his eyes going down to his papers then up to Jerome, he decided to give the boy a second chance. "Listen carefully to the word used in a sentence. I would like some ice cream."

Smiling Jerome answered, "Yeah man," and after he after spelling out "w o d," added, "I dig ice cream."

An irate woman in the audience yelled to the moderator. "You're confusing the poor boy by using a homophone. That's totally unfair."

"Jerome's mother? " I whispered to Candi.

"Oh no. She's his teacher. Parents have lost interest in spelling bees ever since we decided to have all the students be winners. We're adamantly against competition. A student who loses, loses interest, and you can't have that."

"Well, obviously Jerome's teacher takes it seriously, which I suppose is a good thing."

"Seriously? Maybe too seriously. She's interested in teaching, but she must remember not to have her interests implicitly hurt others. She should be interested in teaching but not so personally committed to her students doing well that it hurts the growth of their interest. If students are interested, they'll do well, and if she's interested in teaching she'll devise interesting ways to appeal to Jerome's interests, leading Jerome to learn. Then everyone is happy."

Noticing Jerome stayed on the stage, I asked Candi why Jerome wasn't eliminated.

"In Education Land, no one is eliminated. To eliminate is to discourage. To discourage is to kill interest. Remember, interest is the key and— Oh listen! Lucy, the next student, is about to spell."

Lucy, a very well-fed student, standing at the stage apron was asked to spell 'ask,' as in 'I ask you a question.'

Giving a smile that pushed both chubby cheeks so far out her mouth almost disappeared, she confidently answered, "Dats easy. A x ax."

As the moderator was about to say something negative, another frantic woman shouted from the audience. "Dats Black English. Lucy is correct."

"Teacher?" I asked.

"A dedicated teacher giving encouragement," Candi corrected.

Lucy wasn't eliminated and was replaced by a surly boy who glared at everyone. Sizing up the youth's minimal interest in spelling, the moderator gave him, 'the—the chair is there."

Only after digging into his nose, only after minutely examining the mined ore, and only after rubbing the precious finding on a pants leg did he say "D A, da chair is dar."

"Great Arnold," some woman shouted, you nailed da sucker. You da greatest."

"Teacher?" I asked.

"Dedicated, one of the best," was the answer.

I pulled Candi out of there before I started spelling cat with a 'k'.

"Well, there is one more area you just must see so your report back to your country is complete. It's outside the school building."

Standing outside, deeply inhaling fresh air, I pessimistically asked, "What is it?"

"It's an area set aside for individual contemplation to enable a person to discover one's interests."

It was a huge park area filled with students up to and past the age of senility milling about, laying about, standing about, and passing among themselves smoking instruments containing many types of vegetation and bizarre chemical concoctions. In a separate group paper bags outlining bottle shapes were being passed from lip to lip. Other groups suffering acutely from allergies or troubled sinuses were sniffing restorative white powder. Between these groups were several somnolent most probably diabetic students injecting themselves hopefully with insulin. I won't make any salacious references to the various copulations going on behind bushes and under trees. Looking at the sight I exclaimed, "They're druggies and degenerates!"

With motherly patience Candi said, "Oh, no, merely students who have yet to discover their interest in life."

"Their interests are drugs, drinking, and sex."

"Don't be so judgmental, so quick to damn. Don't be a PP. Many are in training to be drug, alcohol and sex counselors and therapists. As everyone knows, or should know, you can't effectively counsel addicts until you've been there, smoked that, sniffed that, drank that, injected that, which then enables you to relate to those you are counseling."

"Ah, yes."

With my 'ah yes' carrying no conviction, Candi felt impelled to amplify. "Of course, some are involved in drugs in the interest of expanding the frontiers of their mind."

"Ah, yes."

Candi complained, "I'd prefer if you'd stop saying 'ah yes'. Don't close your mind to new educational ideas. I'm beginning to suspect you're a PP. Now note, some students over in the bushes are enrolled in the Hugh Hefner Institute for Advanced Sexual Studies. They are currently engaged in the demanding work of expanding the boundaries of sexual behavior and ridding themselves of any puritan sexual hang-ups. The Hugh Hefner Institute has been very successful in evoking student interest in the study of human sexuality. I'd like you to notice the threesome rolling about the lawn; they're making a serious statement; you don't have to be ashamed of the sex act. It's all very courageous. Our *Playboy* and *Playgirl* educational textbooks are bringing sex out of the shaming shadows of taboos. We're trying to overcome any inhibitions regarding a very natural act. Our students have shown exemplary interest in advanced sexual studies."

Suddenly a thirteen or fourteen year old girl came up to us, pointed to an unoccupied bush and propositioned me, Candi, or both of us for ten bucks each, or for a Happy Meal.

We declined.

After cursing us as frigid, uncool, uptight, and definitely not *Playboy* or *Playgirl* educated types, she damned us in bold, explicit language as holding repressive, puritanical, ignorant views. As she left, she waved many energetic finger signs at us.

My habitual, "Ah, yes," escaped just as easily as breaking wind.

Unnoticing, Candi happily exclaimed, "Do you see, can you see, no destructive sexual repressed attitude. She's free. No more under man's control, but free to express herself, to have complete control over her body. Can you grasp the gain women have made through enlightened sex education at the Hugh Hefner Educational Institute located on the Playgirl Campus? And what is really most important, did you notice she had condoms? She's practicing safe sex in doing what really interests her. Look over there... some future elementary sex educators are doing research."

"Where?"

"In those bushes, see the feet sticking out? See the leaves shaking? See the branches vibrating? Let me tell you, when those future sex teachers get into the classroom to give a sex education class to elementary students, they'll be experts with advanced degrees in their subject."

"Ah, yes."

Not hearing the sarcasm, Candi added with pride, "In our schools every girl takes the pill and always carries a condom. Now you can't deny, that's great progress for women."

Suddenly at our feet a gray haired granny collapsed, dead drunk.

Jumping back I asked Candi if the granny was either a wanderer searching for educational goals or a motivated neurologist researching the effects of drink on the human mind, or was she interested in planning to become an alcohol counselor.

Stepping over her, Candi seriously said, "Can't tell by looking at her. We'll have to ask her teacher and mentor. He's over there," and she pointed to a straggly bearded dirty rag clothed individual clutching a brown bag in one hand and a strange looking pipe in the other, alternately putting each to his mouth. Candi asked me if I wanted to go speak to him to find out his pedagogical insights and interests.

"Never! Er... Candi, it's not necessary."

After a few steps Candi reminded me, "Education Land's motto is Leave no child behind."

"Ah, yes?"

"We don't let a child's age determine how much education she or he should receive. Age cannot limit a student's learning process. All children are born equal, save for economic and social circumstances at birth. Only by giving equal and unlimited access to our educational institutions can we overcome economic and social inequality."

"Does your 'all are born equal' refer to mental ability?"

"Everyone has different ability that must be nurtured and we must not discriminate against different abilities. Remember, you must be mentally flexible, hold no preconceived principles in your pursuit of knowledge."

Although feeling I could enumerate numerous principles that could dig serious wormholes in her dogma, as an IV visitor I felt it would be impolite to become argumentative.

Refraining from issuing another 'ah, yes,' I let the emptying pause of silence grow, knowing Candi would quickly splash the silence with pails of words. She waded in, repeated, "You cannot expect a student to learn things that do not interest him, boring things, rote learning. Memorized knowledge acquired through pain is quickly lost. Are you following me?"

"I'm right behind you."

"So if some student doesn't attain his life's core interest early in life we must be patient and supply different educational opportunities and experiences to help him discover his true interests regardless of age. Still with me?"

"Don't stop or I'll bump into you."

"Unlike some barbaric systems we don't throw students out of our educational system merely because they've reached some arbitrary age or fail to pass some ridiculous test on abstract concepts that do not interest the student and thereby destroy the individual's freedom and his inherent interest. Who is best to judge a student's progress? Some institutionally generated test or the student and the teacher cooperating together?"

"I don't understand."

"In our grading system, in a student/teacher conference, the teacher requires the student to honestly evaluate his progress, especially the degree to which his interest has been stimulated. The student, looking deep and honestly into his educational accomplishments, gives himself a valid evaluating grade."

Suspecting there were a lot of self-evaluated geniuses getting A pluses, pointing to a nearby group I commented as politely as possible, "So those forty year olds sitting on the grass passing a bottle back and forth, are still searching for their interest."

"I've been talking to their counselors," Candi explained, "and they feel they're only a year or so away from a breakthrough in discovering their life's interest. It just takes patience and caring, although some there are doctoral candidates studying methods of curing alcoholism."

"Ah, yes."

Sensing the possibility of disbelief hiding between the A and the S in my ah yes, she said, "Certainly we believe every student has the right to pursue, tuition free of course, their educational interest to their highest level. There are no arbitrary restrictions to how far you can develop your interest, as long as the student is interested in developing himself. We feel—"

"Damn it! Candi, look, isn't that a group sex orgy over there, with a crowd of people watching them? Ugh, what degenerates!"

"Degenerates? I hardly think so. The ones watching are studying to become sex therapists and the participants are working out personal problems in their sexual lives. It's all progressively educational. All so avant garde. Remember, shun closed mindedness. Don't be a PP."

"It's revolting."

Angrily she chastised me. "Well, of course that's your opinion, and I respect it, but you're too judgmental; you shouldn't be judgmental. You shouldn't express judgmental opinions. You should fight against having judgments. Always remember, judgments hurt people's feelings. In fact, you should make the conscious judgment about yourself on how you're too judgmental, possibly judging yourself as being negative, destructive, bigoted, closed minded, and a PP. I'm sorry I said that, but I did feel your negativity. Now, let's move on,"

As we left, bewildered, I glanced back at the ongoing orgy. It was like watching a horrible accident and just as hard to look away.

Suddenly one of the observing sex therapists tossed off her clothes and shouted, "That's not how you do it. Let me show you." Energetically she threw herself into the tangled melee of arms and legs.

One of the forty year olds clutching a brown bag bottle unsteadily made his way toward us. Without preliminaries he demanded to know who I was, who I thought I was, and he thought I definitely wasn't any better than he was. In fact, I was beneath him..

Candi, telling him my IV status, for some reason angered him.

"I could be a shitty IV visitor, but I wasn't interested. Could have been an inventor but I wasn't interested.

"Know what I'm interested in?"

Getting nervous over his belligerence I said, "No."

"So you're not interested in what interests me? That's hurtful. Do you think your interests are better than mine, think you're better than me?"

"No," I said, knowing damn well I was a hell of a lot better.

"Well, I'm interested in bashing in your head. Does that interest you Mr. high and mighty IV visitor?" And with that he brought the bottle over his head, planning to follow his interest. Fortunately the bottle was cap less, allowing the cheap booze to flow over his head.

"Shit!" he cried. Looking up, he opened his mouth, trying to capture the liquor 'til he realized he was spilling it and brought his hand down. "Stay right there 'til I empty the bottle. I'm still interested in your head."

Quickly leaving him, I followed Candi, feeling very few back home would believe this report, though I knew it would become a best seller, given the universal amount of human interest in sexual learning and its manifestation of degeneracy.

We found ourselves in a huge lecture hall with a formidable woman. This was the professor of education teaching hundreds students sitting, lounging on the floor, or propped up on randomly grouped desks. Obviously oblivious to the teacher, all were laughing and joking while busy making things out of construction paper. One group diligently making a mobile of the solar system was unaware they were three planets short and had located the earth in the center.

"The students aren't paying any attention to the teacher," I said.

"Oh, they're interested. This is how they show their interest in her lecture."

"Ah, yes," I whispered to myself, then said, "Enough... I've seen enough. I've seen more than enough."

On my way out of the Land of Education, Candi anxiously wanted me to ask her questions, saying, "Remember, it is only by asking questions that we learn."

Being so prompted, I complied, "Well Candi, I was confused by the pitiful state of your engineers, scientists and doctors that we passed walking to your school."

Sighing she answered, "Interest, and the lack of interest. We have a surfeit of students interested in being scientists and doctors, but currently no one has shown any interest in cutting wood, digging foundations, laying bricks, and working in factories. So until people show an interest in those activities, nothing gets built." Reluctantly she admitted, "The truth be known, we are experiencing a temporary housing shortage, as well as shortages in food and clothing but we're hopeful some students will soon be interested in laying roof tiles, pouring cement or tilling the land."

"Ah, yes."

"Peoples, I'm getting sick and tired of your ah yesses. Once our teachers, employing the newest creative innovative pedagogical techniques, are able to stimulate the students' interest in the joys of roofing, the excitement of asphalt paving and the allure of installing toilets, we are sure to experience a building boom."

Stifling an 'ah yes' I asked about the Cordon Bleu women cooking watery gruel made from the entrails of diverse animals who had expired on the roads.

"Interest. Many of our students are extremely interested in becoming chefs: to devise new and exotic dishes to tease the palate, to tempt the eye, but primarily to wear the chefs' hats and have TV cooking shows. However, in the interest of truth, I have to confess few of our students have shown interest in planting, picking, cleaning, sorting, processing raw food products, and that has resulted in a temporary food shortage.

"And Peoples, I repeat, it's only temporary because as I speak we have several elementary teachers developing pedagogical innovative techniques to interest their students in the joys of working under the sun in the fresh air, close to nature, picking tomatoes. Let me tell you, when the students see tomato slide presentations, draw pictures of tomatoes, grow a tomato in their classroom, do committee reports on the life cycle of the tomato... well, I don't have to tell you how much interest will be developed in growing and harvesting tomatoes on actual farms."

"What about those clothing designers? They're dressed in rags. How can such pathetically dressed people be fashion leaders?"

"Interest."

"Interest?"

"Certainly. Many of our female students have shown an interest in becoming creative fashion designers, creating beautiful original garments out of revolutionary new materials."

"But they're in rags."

"Factory workers. Somehow students seem disinclined to be interested in the manufacture of cloth. In fact, for some inexplicable reason, interest in any factory work is currently at a low point."

Commiserating, I said, "Ah yes, 'tis a mystery. And the filth and litter along the streets, on the school grounds, in the halls, the classrooms—a current lack of janitorial interest?"

"Exactly, but this will be easily corrected when we discover the correct pedagogical techniques to stimulate latent student interest in picking up trash."

As we reached the land's borders she happily said, "I'm sure you've experienced a deep understanding of our educational secrets, and I hope you've learned how to teach by maximizing student voluntary participation in the learning process through evoking and engaging his or her latent interest. I only wish I could have shown you all our judges, professors, astronauts, fire and police chiefs, race car drivers and CEOs, but I've an appointment to show our success to a gentleman from Singapore. Do you realize we have a glut in high achieving video game players and they don't have any? Isn't that simply bizarre? Shows what interest learning can achieve."

Leaving Candi at Education Land's border I shouted back to her, "It certainly has been very enlightening."

AFTER EDUCATION LAND

We were sitting together in a hotel lounge located outside Education Land, enjoying an after-dinner drink when I foolishly tried to summarize my report to Hinki and Sunni. My first words, "I found Education Land to be—" were cleanly sliced and left dangling and dying by Hinki's annoying pontificational, "What was most important was the absence of government compulsion to get people involved in the learning process. They were self-motivated."

Agreeing and reaching out, holding Hinki's arm as if to hold him back from speaking, Sunni said, "I was surprised to find—"

Ignoring her, Hinki continued his heavily delivered report on his light observations. "Yeah, Sunni, you also noticed the really important

Land's characteristic; the absolute disinterest in money. Something we in our land could copy with profit. It could revolutionize our society. I see—"

Gripping Hinki with both hands, once again Sunni tried to insert herself. "Not only that, but I believe—"

Hinki shook off her belief as easily as he freed himself from her grip. "Can you imagine a society not governed by corrosive modern materialism? This visit has been a revelation and I can't wait to write my report."

Trying to stop him from sharing his revelations, Sunni sought me as an ally. With a gentle touch as if her very soul depended upon my sharing with her my observations, she asked my views. I was unclear as to whether she wanted my opinion about Education Land, my view on Hinki's excited revelations, or Hinki's trying to monopolize the conversation.

Previously having made my own private evaluation of his mental depth, I had been sitting relaxed, sipping a Manhattan, letting Hinki's excitement flutter past me, finding my Manhattan's cherry more engaging.

Startled out of my revelry, I asked, "What's this shit about doing away with money? Sounds like a stupid idea."

With a pitying tone Hinki addressed me as one who doubted global warming. "Didn't you notice their commitment to interest? Doing what interests you creates happy people."

I retorted, "Yeah, interest... it was hard to miss, so what's the big deal?"

Teacher to the ignorant, Hinki patently explained. "When people do what interests them, being internally rewarded, they don't need any external artificial stimuli, specifically money."

With the guy flying way above me dropping bags of ignorance on me, defensively I tried to shoot him down. "Notice there wasn't much interest in picking tomatoes or laying asphalt."

Once an idea is adopted due to its conformability to one's self, it must be defended to the last as if protecting the very self, so it wasn't surprising my anti-aircraft shots bounced off Hinki's blimp.

Sarcastically I said, "Of course, there are some areas where their educational system has yet to discover ways to stimulate interest."

"Peoples, that's no reason for one to be negative and adopt a petty attitude in trying to bring down exciting educational ideas. Such criticism is PP-frothy negativity, the product of a small freighted mind, fearful of new ideas."

Never being high in Hinki's opinion, my current negative smallness dropped me into his mental sub-basement. If expecting support from Sunni I was disappointed, yet not surprised.

As Hinki paused to sip his Perrier she took the opportunity to finally spend her two cents. "Peoples, you're missing the big picture; you can't concentrate on minutiae. Didn't you realize their educational success rate. Talking with the superintendent of education I spent the whole day going over his figures showing student progress"

As if telling me to realize the world was round she informed me they have 100% retention rate. There are absolutely no dropouts.

I couldn't help myself. "If they say the student didn't drop out, then no matter how far out he is, he still must be in the system."

Hinki said, "Negative, Peoples, too PP, you've got to try to be more positive." That made me feel unfairly outnumbered. Hinki continued. "Like I always say, the glass is half full."

Noting mine was empty I waved to a waiter for a second Manhattan. Sunni gave Hinki a smile and a hand touching: the smile an appreciation reward for his support; the touch to keep him in check.

She said, "Peoples, do you realize they have 100% high school graduation rate, no child is left behind, no mind wasted. In addition for their educational system has awarded an absolute phenomenal number of advanced degrees."

Briefly escaping from Sunni's touch, Hinki added, "Shows the power of interest learning."

Sunni said, "Yes, Hinki, interest is the key. Encouraging and stimulating students' inherent interest allows their educational system to—"

Hinki finished for her. "To do away with pernicious competitive systems using external rewards like money and grades."

Annoyed, Sunni corrected him. "They *do* have a grading system, but it's on an optional basis, and it's self-generated."

With Sunni and Hinki industriously massaging each other's opinion I struck out at them, "Grades can't be optional. They're essential to the measurement of scholastic progress."

They looked at me as if I was drunk, to be pitied and placated.

Patting my hand Sunni said, "Grades are subjective, not objective. Who is in the best position to evaluate a student's progress if not the student?"

"So no one fails," I said.

"Certainly Peoples, no one fails! Given students study what interests them, it can't be surprising everyone gives themselves an 'A' and most important everyone is fulfilled, happy and enjoys strong self-esteem."

In Hinki's mind she spoke too long and the conversation desperately needed his input. "My report is going to concentrate on freedom from coercion, the self-motivation educational system."

"Yes." Sunni agreed. "Free from class competition, the system fosters a non-competitive cooperative fellowship, a democratic society which creates a happy society."

Manhattan and I felt it was incumbent to expend my two cents. "An educational system designed to make learning interesting and fun succeeds in creating a farcical community where misery abounds and failure is labeled success. To succeed, one must learn to do what you don't want to do. That is the purpose of education, to develop the habit of working hard."

I accepted my new Manhattan as they blithely continued. Sunni told the Manhattan as well as Hinki, "And did you notice the curriculum? It was breathtaking in its vigor: sixth-grade Calculus, seventh-grade Differential Equations and in eighth grade, Non-Euclidean Geometry with an in-depth study of Einstein's Relativity. I have to confess the titles for the higher grade courses were beyond my understanding, and they have one hundred percent student completion, all receiving A grades."

Hinki came back with, "And I found out the sophomores study Plato's *Republic* in the original Greek and Cicero's *Oration* in Latin. Now that's an unbelievable achievement!"

I added, "It certainly is unbelievable," but I didn't believe my doubt had registered as I hoped it would.

With Plato and Cicero entering the conversation I picked up Manhattan and left. The last words were Sunni extolling Education Land's twelve years of intense study on having safe sex.

4

Communication Land

Obeying the directive we received from Communication Land, Hinki, Sunni and I again split up, each instructed to wait for our guides at a separate locations. Following my instructions I waited for Cindi, my guide, at the designated train depot, sitting on a hard wooden bench.

I noted a huge digital clock with numerals a foot long on the wall. Above was a thermometer, a barometer with digital readouts, according to which it was 37 degrees. The F or C was not indicated. According to the other gauges it should be foggy and raining. Looking out the depot door I saw it was sunny and in the seventies. I amused myself by studying the huge video display of various train arrivals and departures to and from various cities. Flashing lights warned of delays in a city whose name was blacked out due to an electric malfunction. At 4:21:00 a train was due to arrive at this depot. Checking the digital giant, it was 4:15:46 so I looked forward to the diversion of the train's arrival.

Over the depot's entrance were an additional array of clocks giving the current times in the world's major cities, and above them the appropriate weather digital reports. It was interesting for a nanosecond or two to note the 92.761 temperature in Bangkok with an impossible barometer reading of 60.012. In one corner a TV was turned on to CNN. Unfortunately the volume was broken so serious faces of men of deep and profound mien were mouthing silence at TV's ubiquitous women: young, blond, good-looking, well-stacked babes who gave lots of eye rolls under penciled-in eyebrows, and whose glossed lips moving up and down kept pace with various rapid expressions from pancake faces. They talked at each other, then turned to talk to me. Their frowns came before and after sad pictures of hunger and fighting, their smiling laughing faces at happy pictures of people receiving awards. Another TV was tuned to a twenty-four hour weather station from which I learned it was snowing in the Rockies, hot in the Sahara, freezing in Alaska and rainy in the Amazon. Suddenly the digital time giant inexplicably jumped from 4:18:07 to exactly 4:21:00, but I heard no train arriving.

Checking my watch, which said 4:38, I adjusted it. The bank of TVs announcing train arrivals and departures told me the 4:21 had arrived on time. If it had, it was a silent empty ghost train as the only activity outside was a dog with raised rear leg saluting the country's rail system.

My guide was late, the CNN talking head was saying nothing, and knowing the time in Nairobi wasn't all that interesting. Suddenly from an empty train information booth a ghostly voice announced to the empty depot the 4:21 ghost train would depart on time at 4:53:04. The train's departure, I suspected, would not disturb the dog now sleeping on a railroad tie.

Where was the guide? The delay was getting annoying, even worrisome. Where were the people? Did I get off at the wrong station, a ghost station? Between reading the weather report from Tierra del Fuego, cold and rainy, and the talking heads looking out at me telling me nothing from busy lips and worried faces, I was feeling lonely and lost. The train information booth's mechanical voice reported the 4:53:04 train was leaving; all passengers must quickly board. Looking at the deserted streets and deserted rails, save for the sunbathing pooch, I experienced increasing tension, worrying if someone would be coming. Did I get the time right? The date right? The place right? The week right? Was I even in the right country?

Noting the digital's foot-high minutes were turning with the fleetness of seconds, while the seconds had gone on strike and refused to move a digit, I realized by changing my watch I had lost time.

I stood, I paced, I sat, I felt familiar hunger growing as the train's snacks I had consumed on the trip here had long-since left my digestive tract and with increasing discomfort were now making themselves felt in the colon area. The train station facilities? I think not. Better to follow the dog's example. I tried the candy machine. Placing a dollar bill in, pulling my selection knob I was electronically informed, 'Empty. Try another selection.' I did and apparently it malfunctioned as nothing came out and I was needlessly electronically informed it had malfunctioned. I tried to get my money back but the electronic scroll told me the machine had no change.

I tried to call my guide on my cell phone but couldn't get a signal.

Giving up, gazing at the weather monitor, I saw it was now snowing outside, though the sleeping dog would argue the point. The train's monitor informed me the Bullet Express had just left the depot, apparently without waking the dog. Suddenly for reasons only an in-depth analysis of a TV set's nervous system could explain, the sound of CNN came on. A duo, consisting of a blond, blue-eyed, deep-cleaved babe in her mid-twenties sitting across a somber, blue-suited white-haired man thrice the blond's age, were discussing economic matters. She told me unemployment was up. He explained it was the lack of jobs. Both agreed it was the greedy corporations' fault. Frowning, she said consumer confidence was low, to which he, sadly shaking his head, explained it was because of high unemployment. Both agreed it was the corporations' fault.

To keep to the gender sequence, he announced consumer spending was down, to which she, pursing glossed lips, told America its cause was the lack of consumer confidence. Professionally, she explained, "You see, if people lack confidence in the economy, they won't spend." Then with a glad face she told me the stock market had risen for the fourth straight day. Turning, she asked her senior citizen counterpart for the reasons for the rise, given the sorry state of the economy.

Looking intently at the teleprompter, he read, "Candy, without doubt it's because more stocks were purchased than sold today."

Suddenly the fantastic financial duo was interrupted by a black head yelling about a political revolution occurring in a vague African region caused by some dissatisfied people and instigated by undefined causes. The outcome was in doubt, and the combatants were unknown. The only certain thing known was that it was the fault of rapacious oil corporations.

After a film of third-world types running about burning, shouting and inexplicably holding signs in English saying down with somebody, a round table consisting of a black, an Asian, a woman, and a Hispanic, all of serious demeanor, began an in-depth discussion. They were conversing under the Indian moderator. Fortunately the sound again gave out and as the sun was setting, I noted the wall clock was now reading 1:32:04 p.m.

It was almost three hours before a perky, attractive, eye-pleasing young girl—well, she would have been all that if I had not been out of temper, in colon discomfort and hungry—in her mid-twenties ran up to me with laptop briefcase in one hand, a cell phone in the other, and a pager bouncing from her trim waist. She yelled, "I'm Cindi, with an I!" and tried unsuccessfully to give me a hug. Unsuccessful due to my sidestepping, and her having her two hands occupied, she settled for gushing, "I'm late. I know I'm late," as if I didn't know. Her announcement was made as if I hadn't realized I had sat on a hard wooden bench watching the wrong time fly by, invisible trains come and go, and pompous talking heads saying nothing. Her confession of being late was said in the spirit young perky attractive girls employ. With her perkiness she knew I wouldn't want to argue against her being late and even if she was late, somehow it was all right.

Without a smile I pointedly informed her she was two hours and fifty-four minutes late.

With a smile she exclaimed, "Really? That long?" with all the ingenuous surprise of a perky young girl finding she overcharged her credit card and by so much. "I had no idea. Time just flies."

"Only when you're moving. When you're standing still, time stands with you."

"Really?" she said, frowning at my inexplicable behavior of not bestowing forgiveness and blessings upon her generous, gaily given confession in her cute perky manner. "Well, I had so many incoming calls and text messages."

Was I to sympathize with her? Was I to marvel at her busy life? Was I to feel bad at being angry over my wait of hours? Whatever I was expected to express, I firmly told her, "I waited here for three hours."

"Let's not exaggerate," she said, "it was less than three hours."

"For almost three hours I sat, stood, and paced, going crazy looking at those TV monitors."

"You know, you were on video," and she pointed to a provocative—hell, erotic... hell, pornographic—bikini ad hanging between the London and Paris clocks.

"The camera lens is in the navel. Hope you didn't do anything embarrassing."

"I picked my nose and scratched my crotch," I angrily confessed. "It was my only occupation during the three—correction, *almost* three—hours. I've—"

"Well, now I'm here. Are we ready?"

"I've been ready for three—"

"Get over yourself. I've apologized. Now let's get started."

Suddenly a loud buzzer went off, almost scaring out of my colon what I had been holding in till I could find a clean, comfortable place to leave it.

Cindi, looking at her pager, smiled and dialed her cell phone.

Hoping for the best in train-station lavatories I left her, visited it, left what I was holding and came back to find her still on the cell phone, giggling. Waving me away she turned her head, signaling for privacy.

I watched the TV monitor showing a bronzed, buff couple jumping on and off an exercise machine with ecstatic smiles as if they were jumping on and off each other.

On another monitor some fat guy in a chef's outfit was cooking one hell of a great mouth-watering roast in front of an amazed, openmouthed, drooling audience. When he slammed a pinch of salt, the audience applauded. A toss of garlic brought them to their feet in ecstasy.

Suddenly a train roared by the depot, rattling windows, setting the dog to barking and sending scraps of paper zigzagging high in the air. No one was on board the train. The monitor informed me the train was three hours away from the depot and on time.

Enough! Damn it, enough. Waiting here so long I not only was acquainted with the debris outside the depot windows but also had memorized the fingerprints on the dirty panes.

Going up to her, I said, "Cindi, let's get on with my tour of Communication Land, and the first place I'd like to visit is an up-to-date restaurant with clean, modern facilities."

"Excuse me," she said to the palm of her hand.

Only by the most energetic peeking was I able to see a blue neon picture of someone talking on a cell phone the size of a half-dollar.

Frowning, she turned to me. "Please, can't you see I'm on the phone talking to someone?" Then to the palm, she said, "Mother, it's just a guy I've got to show around. Now who's going to be there?... No, not her! ... Don't tell me he's not coming! ... What about the sisters? ... Really? I can't believe it!"

I walked over to the monitors. Closer, they seemed more personal, talking to me, very interested that I hear and like them, and I understand and appreciate their efforts to inform and educate me.

The exercise people were gone but certainly not forgotten, especially the girls' healthy bodies and beautiful smiling faces. In their place were two sour, somber, snobby-looking characters sitting so the camera formed the triangle's third vertex. One was holding a book to the camera, the other, reminiscent of a devoted worshipper, was nodding reverentially at it. Apparently one of them had spent ten years researching and writing the tome, and the other was in awe either at the ten years or at the size of the product, probably the former. The book was selling in the millions. It was on CDs and in the theaters, soon to be on DVDs for home viewing. Apparently it was a thousand pages of an in-depth exposition and explanation of Madonna's impact on the fine arts as well as her contribution in elevating social mores and extending sexual freedom, and in her deep concern for addressing social problems, particularly starving children.

"I see you've devoted a chapter to her charities."

"Yes, I've included several chapters on her visits to Africa to talk seriously about health problems they are experiencing, to raise awareness of children starving, and to hold and hug cute black babies. She got the UN Humanitarian Award for all her work."

"Well deserved."

"The book wouldn't be complete without exploring how her past and current loves have impacted on the philosophical meaning of her exciting art, especially in the deeper sensual meaning her erotic videos express."

"What crap," was what I said to the tube and went with determination back to Cindi.

She was saying, "Roberto, you shouldn't say such things on the cell phone. What if someone was monitoring— You'd shout it where? ... Oh, you're too, too much."

Exasperated, I yelled, "Cindi, stop that stupid dribble and let's get out of this ghost depot."

"Excuse me, Roberto. I've got a call waiting and— What? No, I couldn't. Ha ha, you're just too, too, too much. That you, Daisy? I'm talking to Roberto. He's just too, too much."

I said, "Cindi, if you don't put a sock in it I'm going to hang up for you."

Just then a train pulled into the station and a black conductor stepped down holding a computer printout yelling that the twenty people getting off at Communication Land must exit now.

There was no one on the train and so none of the twenty computer printed people exited.

Opening the depot door, in a rich baritone he requested the fifteen people listed on his printout could now board. He didn't seem worried nor surprised that only Cindi and I were in the depot, but taking out a pocket size computer he busily tapped on its screen with a stylus, then looking up went out with a loud, "All aboard! Last call. All aboard."

I was tempted, very tempted, but refrained from boarding the train, being fearful of this ghost train. Who knew where it came from or where it was going? And thoughts of the Flying Dutchman train traveling the rails forever held me back.

The train left as empty as it arrived and as I approached Cindi I heard her complain to Daisy that Roberto was just so unbelievably fresh, followed by a series of, "Yes, he is," in raising crescendo ending with a screaming, "No, he didn't! I absolutely can't believe it!"

Standing one foot from her and one foot inside her space, I shouted, "Damn it, Cindi, let's go! Enough of this bullshit!"

"Daisy, I've simply got to go. Job, you know. He's right here. You're right, he is, but be careful. He might be able to hear you. Yes, you're so right."

Grabbing her hand, twisting it, I pressed every button till the red light went out. The screen went blank and the blue neon turned a sickly green.

An indignant Cindi told me an astonishing fact. "Hey, I was talking to Daisy."

"Shit on Daisy, shit on Roberto, shit on Mom. I'm hungry. It's late. Let's get the hell out of here, now."

"Calm down. Don't lose your cool. Now, if you're ready, let's go to my car."

It was a keyless model where you punch a code to open it. She nail punched, and nothing. Laughing, she punched again. Again nothing. Again a laugh, but she also gave a little bite on her gloss lips. She pushed a final time. Again nothing, and we stood looking at the car door's keypad. Turning to me with a little girl smile, which again was meant to elicit forgiveness because she was cute, she announced the obvious. "There are so many code numbers to remember, I simply forgot the car code."

My, "Use your key," advice was ignored as her cell phone came out and her mom came on.

"Mommy, you just wouldn't believe it. Couldn't guess in a million years what just happened. I— Yes, yes... oh yes, that's the code. Look, while I've got you on the phone, I'll be home late. Yeah, got a late start. You know the fax machine broke down, the text message was wrong and— As soon as I can. Oh, by the way, did you know what Roberto said?"

My anger and my threatening pose left what Roberto said unsaid.

Poking the car's code in she moved her ass so as to block my view. I thought it was to protect the code but when she announced the code was her birthday, I realized it was more a matter of preserving the number of birthdays.

The car's dashboard communicated to us: it told us the doors were closed, the doors were locked, then warned I wasn't wearing my seat belt, and informed us we were traveling south-west. If this wasn't enough an illuminated map and a dot showing where we were appeared. She pressed a button and a radio came on and a monitor informed us it was an all-day musical tribute to Britney Spears on WKK 9.65 FM. The dashboard informed me the weather outside was 72, inside 75 and inside the engine, 210. I ignored the oil pressure, engine revolutions, speed, total mileage, trip mileage, current miles per gallon, fuel used, fuel left, verbal and digital messages.

Suddenly a disembodied voice from the passenger door scared me when it asked if I wanted my seat heated. For a moment I thought my butt was being threatened, till I realized the car's door was concerned with the car's seat.

Talking to the door, I said, "No."

The door asked if I wanted more lumbar support.

I told it no.

The dashboard told me again I should buckle up, that it saves lives and that not doing so could result in a police citation.

Ignoring it, I asked Cindi if we were going to a restaurant.

With left hand on the steering wheel, holding her cell phone in the right hand, she told me to be quiet. She was making reservations.

"Jorgi, this is Cindi... Cindi Post. Post, Cindi. No? Well, anyway, I'd like to make reservations for two for eight. Okay? Great." Leaning to the right toward her phone as she spoke, she slowly dragged the car in the same direction. She had barely ended the call, phone still in hand, when it rang.

"Jasmine, is that you? I can't believe it."

I believed it as I nervously watched the car nearing the curb.

"Driving to dinner. Who? I'll tell you all about him later. I can't right now. He's sitting next to me. What? You're telling me Roberto spoke to you and said what? I can't believe it!"

With increasing anxiety I saw the right front tire was only inches from the curb.

"Cindi," I said with as much calmness I could muster, "you're drifting off the road."

She made the correction while saying, "And Roberto told you that? I can't believe it!"

The drift started again.

"Well, I was just speaking to him and I just can't believe he'd do that."

"Cindi, you're drifting again."

No correction as she exclaimed, "He said it to you *when*? I just can't believe it."

"Cindi, you're going to hit the curb."

"Yes, yes, I know. No, not to you. To my IV," and again she corrected as I buckled my seatbelt.

The remaining twenty minutes of the ride was taken up with references to Roberto's mysterious speech, her disbeliefs ranging from the simple 'I simply don't believe it' to the absolute 'I absolutely refuse to believe it' while we drifted to the curb only to be corrected in response to my increasingly frantic warnings, going from the simple 'Cindi, you're drifting' to the absolute, terrified scream, 'We're going to crash!' accompanied by two frantic attempts to grab the wheel.

Finally we drifted into the eatery's parking lot and only then did Cindi hang up with a last comment, "I really, truly, absolutely can't believe Roberto said that."

In the end, damn it if I wasn't getting curious about this mysterious Roberto and all the terrible things he'd said.

The maitre'de, peering at a computer monitor, asked for our names. Upon receipt of same, he solemnly announced they weren't on the screen. Then, looking up, he said to no one behind us, "Robert Pastry, your table is ready."

My hunger pushed Cindi aside and I demanded a table with the ugly nastiness used by people who are used to three meals a day when deprived of at least two.

"An hour's wait," he said, studying his screen. "All our tables are filled. If you wait at the bar you'll hear your name announced."

Peering into the dining room I saw nothing but empty seats and tables and waiters idly scratching themselves.

I tried to point this obvious fact out to him, but pointing to the computer he told me that there were ninety-six people currently eating in the dining room.

Drinking on an empty stomach and anger over a sense of being put upon is a dangerous combo, but we went to the bar and gave our orders to a man who entered them on a computer monitor.

Cindi got a text message to call someone urgently and she left to stand in the parking lot to talk privately on her cell phone.

There were several TV monitors, one in each corner, so as I looked at one, an adjacent drinker looked at an opposite one; we faced each other as if we were talking together. I watched a woman's boxing match where two pudgy, mean-looking broads were pathetically flaying away at each other. The fight was stopped when blood erupted from a nose. On another monitor, a meaningless baseball game between teams from remote towns was slowly, very slowly progressing, so slow there was time to show numerous reruns of a particular hit or some individual striking out, urgent updating scores between teams thirty games out of third place, and even scores from completed games from yesterday and the past weekend. A third monitor was located over a table where a couple was conversing. Between sips and nods the woman stole peeks at the monitor's meaningless game show, showing contestants of a politically correct mixture of ethnicity and gender going into dervish ecstasy at the suggestion they could possibly win a couple of thousand. The last corner TV showed news with running expert commentaries on pictures of people running around with guns, riding around with guns, standing around with guns, or shouting at each other with guns, indicating that a war, a revolution, or excited terrorists on a tear (Are there really differences?) was in progress somewhere. A somber, frowning blond babe of thirty, out of red glossy lips, looking hard and profound at me, told me the killing would go on until all sides agreed to put down their arms and negotiate. If this didn't happen, well, she sadly pronounced her considered prediction: "The fighting will continue until one side wins or both sides become exhausted."

The blond had cleavage, definite cleavage, so much cleavage I counted undone buttons while wondering what sights would appear if another button—

Suddenly a batch of black children, sitting in dirt and waving empty tin bowls at flies, popped up on the screen and immediately deep sorrow and enormous concern popped up on the blond's coiffure lacquered head. Apparently children and their mothers were starving in some third world country, as if this was news. The only news, if you could call it news, was which particular country was it now. Starvation news shuffles between Bangladesh, Central America, all of Africa, and some American urban areas, especially on the holidays.

Grabbing some bar peanuts, salted and free (ah, the subtlety) I watched as the well-stacked blond asked the expensively dressed, well-fed intellectual expert on hunger, standing in the midst of famished children, what could be done. Dressed in an Abercrombie and Finch safari outfit he told the entire well-fed camera crew with him that I should send a buck to Save the Children.

The studio blond exuded concern and womanly caring from every square millimeter of her expensively made up face. She looked as if she was ready to forgo buying those expensive six hundred-dollar shoes, send the money to feed a hungry child and, in saving a child's life, suffer with only her fifty remaining pairs of shoes until spring. I doubted if she had time to send the buck, she was so busy telling other people to save the children.

In the studio next to her, an equally concerned, equally well-fed expert on hunger, looked for all the world as if he was going to jump from that several thousand dollar studio chair to fly to the hungry children's side and fight with all his might for the lives of the starving children. He told the blond and everyone chewing peanuts and sucking liquor in the bar, the cause of their hunger was the lack of food.

Looking startled at this thoughtful pronouncement, the blond asked the hunger expert what could 'we' do.

"Well," he said, "we (the 'we' refers to the government) must send food before it's too late. But not only food, but more aid workers. But not just more aid workers, but more money. But not just money, but technological tools to fight hunger. But not just_"

Sipping my drink I felt it slam my empty stomach and start playing elevator music with my brain's neurons. The subtle work of the peanuts succeeded and another drink followed. The tension slow-danced out of my body in step with the slow neuron music. Things weren't that bad. Screw it. Mentally I was strolling in mellow meadows. Three men standing next to me began to argue, not in a mean way but in a friendly way, and suddenly interrupted my pleasant perambulation among mental sunflowers. The eldest, handsome, gray at the sides, the rest salt and pepper, was stating with the emphasis and volume one acquires with the fourth or fifth double, "Damn it. I make the news. You guys think I just read off the teleprompter what Bill has written, but that's a gross oversimplification. The words are one dimensional, flat and linear, running in a straight line, but my face is the impact. It makes the news multidimensional. With an uplift of an eyebrow, a twinkle of my eye, a compression of my lips, or a flair of a nostril, I give a news story my approval or disapproval. The timbre of my voice says believe or disbelieve. The slight tilt of my head or a casual hand gesture tells people this is important or it's unimportant. The stare of my eyes tells volumes. I can make my eyes warm with love, moist with caring concern, or hard with outrage, all of which tells the viewer what to feel and whether the world is good or bad. Remember, you two, they listen to me, they watch me, they believe in me, they respect me, and they honor me as wise. In fact, they trust me more than themselves and accept me as all-knowing."

Noticing his and his friends' glasses were dry, he ordered another round with the flair of a face and hand that only a trusted, respected, beloved news anchor can achieve.

Since the tender of the bar was nearby, I also signaled for another.

One of his companions, a bald man with an ugly beard said, "You big bag of wind, you're just a pancake face with vocal chords. It's I who controls the news."

This was said in the joking spirit a new round usually elicits.

He continued. "You just read the words I write. If I approve of something, I write it using words that say, 'Viewer, you must approve.' If I hate something I pick words saying to the viewer, 'hate this.' If I approve of this man, my words make the viewer like him. If I disapprove of that man, my choice of words makes people hate him. The words I write, which you merely mouth, are the real power. In my chosen words lies all the control, and all your eyebrow twisting, nose flaring, lip action merely serve to buttress my words."

"Buttress your butt," the anchorman said. "It is my expressions that give total meaning to your arid words."

"Without my words you'd just be an empty face mouthing nothing."

"Hey you guys, let's not forget I'm buying the next round and as the news producer I'm the guy in charge of what people think."

They and I reordered and listened to the news producer who, with a leg on the rail and his elbow propped on the bar, pumped his ego. "Who makes the news? I do. I am the information gatekeeper. I determine the people will know this and be ignorant of that, and so I control what goes into their mind. In fact, I not only determine what goes into their mind but what goes into their guts. A cow dies of madness in a field a thousand miles from nowhere and if I give it exciting, big-time horror coverage and lots of video news minutes showing a cow staggering and slobbering about, what happens? Beef disappears from the plate. Some crackpot group decides artichokes are healthy, that they cure who-knows-what disease, and I, if I allow them three point five minutes of air time, presto, the public herd is head-deep into artichokes."

"Screw you," was the anchor's retort, while the writer gave a finger with one hand, and with the other poured liquid gold into his mouth.

Despite this negativity, the smiling news producer continued. "I tell them sad stories about little children in misfortune and generate money for the tots. I scare them with storms, earthquakes, and hurricanes, even if they are half a world away. Even if they haven't happened, I tell them they might happen and scare them shitless. I pull at their heartstrings talking about the death and destruction of people just like them. I tell them they are good people because they send some unwanted canned goods to people who don't want them. Damn it, the power! It's fantastic~" He was now inside his mind talking to it, repeating stories he often told himself every morning before work and every evening before bed. "Just imagine, how I present a subject can make it righteous and holy or ugly, small, and unworthy of good people. I tell them to eat this and forbid them another food. I tell them what is moral and what is immoral. Damn it, I'm the real pope of Communication Land.

"Remember, the difference between important news, unimportant news and no news is the time I give it, whether it's three minutes, thirty seconds, or no airtime. In fact, where I put it in the news program affects its weight and importance too. The lead story goes into their minds first, but the last story is the one they remember.

"Listen you two, it's my view that determines their view. My concerns determine theirs. My interests become theirs. My beliefs become theirs.

"We," and he spread his hands to include his drinking friends, "create issues or negate them. We can make men great, dwarf them, or make them disappear. We elect leaders we like, and we destroy the ones we don't like."

Exhilarated he said, "Tell me, isn't the news business the greatest? It's a hell of a power trip!" Evidently, exhausting his word armory somewhere between the fifth and sixth drink, the producer repeated, "Do you realize we're the gatekeepers to the mind of America?"

"Yeah, the gatekeeper," the news face repeated as the wordsmith signaled for another round.

The producer continued. "More than gatekeepers, much more than that. I make up the rules for entering. Not only do I enforce the requirements necessary to enter the American mind, but I decide what those requirements are. Can you imagine that? I'm a Moses, a modern law giver, damn it. In fact, shit on Moses. I'm greater because I don't just pass on God's laws to the people, I give my people my laws, and even better, I can change my laws according to the dictates of my digestion. I'm greater than any god.

"Today, with an unhappy stomach, this or that is wrong. Tomorrow a happy stomach and what was wrong yesterday is right today. Man, it's a hell of a high."

The three were feeling no pain. On the contrary, they were feeling very good, very high, so high they had trouble with their legs as they got up in answer to a signal from the obsequious headwaiter and were shown to their table.

Since they came in after me I deduced, in the land of communication, the communicators were privileged people. With my table at least two drinks away, my attitude was now ambivalent toward food. I ordered another drink to go with the merry group of spirits currently having a party in my previously empty stomach.

I'd barely taken a sip when Cindi came back excited, announcing Roberto had told Billy something. Then she asked if I believed it.

Another sip, "Really?" Sip, drink down, spilling just a little as I misjudged the bar's distance for some silly reason.

Pointing to a monitor, Cindi cried, "Oh look. It's Sean Peeon, my favorite actor. Did you see him in *The Avenger*?"

I confessed, without a social mea culpa, that I had missed it.

Glancing at the monitor, the movie idol dressed as a farm worker—er, correction, a *poor* farm worker—was sitting and speaking to a chic dressed beautiful woman leaning forward, inches from jumping his bones.

"Turn it up," Cindi said to the bartender. "I'm such a fan of his. Did you know he was living with Paula Abalas, who is pregnant with rapper Stinger's child? It's Stinger's sixth or seventh, her first. I hope she has a boy. You know she's been trying to get pregnant ever since she left Charlie Sheeney before living with the drummer of the Grateful Corpses. Oh, quiet... he's speaking."

"Yes, Courtni, I'm against this war. I was there at the battlefront for the weekend and saw everything and talked to everyone and I'm telling everyone, I'm against war."

"Really?" the twenty or so, plastic enhanced, hair lacquered, gushed as she leaned forward a little more. "And what is the state of your relationship with Paula Abalas?"

"I'm helping her through her pregnancy, which reminds me, AIDS research is underfunded, and tens of millions of black children are dying. When I speak at the grand banquet honoring my reception of the Academy's humanitarian award, I plan to courageously, forcefully demand the world stop killing children in war and stop letting children die from AIDS."

"Oh, that's so wonderful and great."

The station broke for a commercial about a feminine hygiene product, in which a diverse group of women in regards to race but homogeneous in regards to age, weight, and beauty passed the product among themselves, experiencing uninhibited orgasms when it reached their hands.

Turning to me Cindi said, "Not only is he a great actor, but a great thinker, chairman of so many charities, so interested in politics, the subject of so many articles and books."

"What has he done?" I asked, while watching the hygiene product reach a black broad who could pass for a suntanned white go ballistic in erotic excitement as she turned the product around in her hands.

"He's appeared on the cover of so many magazines. He's made over ten movies, had a child by Britney, received an Academy Award and is a UN ambassador at large."

He came on again, talking about how world peace is important to him and how curing hunger as well as AIDS and stamping out poverty were his goals.

"Is it true you've had difficulties with your co-star, Madonna, on the set of your new movie?"

Leaning back, relaxed, Sean answered, "Madonna is a great artist, a great intellectual, and a concerned feminist working to better the condition of women the world over. She's also co-chairman of our tax-exempt foundation to educate poor children. That gives you an idea of how much we care."

Liza said "Really?" and then added that Madonna also writes children's books.

Sean Peeon simply shrugged. "Ah, well, don't we all?"

"Was there tension between you two?" Liza asked.

Everyone knew what tension she was referencing.

"Well, I must confess there was a lot of tension between us on the set. Sparks flew between us and I believe that sexual excitement came through and is caught on our film, *The Loves of Martin Luther*, a sensitive treatment of Martin Luther's sex life. It's being released during Christmas."

Cindi said, "I've just got to see it," with the earnestness of taking religious vows.

"Now, about world health," Sean continued, "in my opinion—"

Cindi turned to me, uninterested in world health but keeping an ear to the TV in case anything really important was discussed on subjects dealing with exciting sexual gossip and tension.

"He's so knowledgeable," she told me.

Irritated, I told her, "Shit. He's just an actor, pumping himself up because he suspects he's an empty gas bag."

That opened both her eyes and her mouth in disbelief. "Don't you realize he's Sean Peeon? I really believe you don't understand the many facets of his personality, his caring, his political insight, his fight for so many worthwhile causes."

I put up a stop hand that didn't stop her, and she summarized the foolish panegyric to a PR agent's popularized film celebrity. Obviously, in the Land of Communication, being important has little to do with real accomplishment but rests with those who have the best public relations working to get them exposure. It's not what you do that defines you, it's only that 'they' talk about you endlessly. To be great in this land rests on words spoken and written and in fictional images communicated on news and entertainment programs.

"He's a nothing," I said in disgust.

"A nothing?" she exclaimed in real shock. "How can you say that? He's a great artist, a great humanitarian, a great thinker!"

Kindly, tinged with condescension, I said, "Look at the pathetic emptiness an actor embodies. Only politicians can imitate it. After all, to be a successful politician, you must be an actor, speaking your lines with believable sincerity, so it's no surprise that actors see themselves as politicians. What actually is an actor? Does he speak his own words or just repeats the words written by another? Does he speak these words as he wishes? Does he move, smile, cry, or laugh according to his own desire or does the director demand he speak in such a manner, walk now, sit there, laugh, cry on cue. Wardrobe people dress him how they feel he should be dressed. Make up people hide his real face as much as their arts will admit. Camera angles make him thinner, taller. As he speaks other's words as the director tells him and is dressed by others and shows a face only tangentially resembling his own, he must also empty himself and take on the personality of a fictitious someone created in another's mind. He is a puppet, and he's built and moved by others more intelligent, to dance to their purposes."

"Certainly not Sean Peon," Cindi protested.

Riding on a fifth drink's high, I continued. "In his everyday life he's an impotent queen bee surrounded by drones. Physical trainers pump him up, publicity agents tell him where to go, how to act and arrange for flattery and fictitious news items and magazine articles about him. Talent agents find him employment, financial agents handle his money, secretaries handle all the items in his everyday life, and of course numerous drones clean, drive, speak to him, speak for him, and listen to him, but never disagree with him. With such an army, all obsequiously shouting, "You are a great talent, a man above other men, a special man" no wonder actors drift to political activity, for there's no real difference. Politicians speak what their writers write, are slaves to PR people, consultants, and advisors as to where to go, how to say what has been written, how to dress, wear makeup, and in general play a role for the public, serious here, confident there, concern for them, helpful for those. Like actors they are surrounded by aids, arrangers, secretaries, drivers and go-fors, and like actors they are mundane personalities, trivial minds desperately trying to support grand egos."

"You know what you are?" Cindi said while I finished my drink. "You're a cynic." She said 'cynic' like you'd say 'pedophile.' I don't like you. I really don't. I don't think—" and her pager sounded.

After a glance down, she said, "Oh it's Roberto" and made a mad rush outside to find out what new outrage Roberto was going to utter.

She had barely disappeared through the door when our table was announced and so I went out to find Cindi. She was outside in the midst of a crowd, some who were smoking, some busily talking on their cell phones, some doing both.

I patted Cindi on the shoulder, and she glared back at me, telling me she was speaking. Then she said to Roberto, "It's only him. ... Yeah, I know. I can't believe it either. He doesn't even like Sean Peeon. Yes, he doesn't know the real Sean."

I shouted that our table was ready, but she only nodded and turned away. She told Roberto, "You didn't say that to her. I can't believe you did that."

I walked with dignity into the restaurant to dine alone. The waiter presented me with a cell phone, telling me I had a message from Cindi. Taking the phone I heard an angry Cindi berating me. "I absolutely cannot continue as your guide for reasons well known to you. A guide and her IV visitor must be compatible to be successful. The negative attitudes you expressed, especially about such a great intellectual and humanitarian as Peeon... well, it was hurtful to me and I've reached the painful conclusion we're absolutely incompatible. As Roberto told me, I must be true to—"

Cindy was interrupted by the head waiter who begrudgingly announced my table was ready.

The restaurant tables were still a desert of white, save for a few eaters whose tables formed an oasis. The headwaiter seated me at a stranger's table announcing, "Mr. Billings, your son Robert Billings has arrived."

The stranger complained his name was Rogers, but was told it was impossible as the computer printout confirmed this was Mr. Billings' table. Further expostulations from Rogers were answered with a "Bon Appetite."

Billings, or Rogers, was on the videophone sending pictures of his salad to someone called Merci. Ignoring me he told Merci, "See how fresh the lettuce is and the profusion of olives? And notice the little anchovies. Do you see them? Let me get you a close-up." And he moved the phone closer to the salad, then suddenly looking up, aimed the phone at me. "Merci, is this man my son?"

"I'm not your son, Mr. Billings or Rogers or whoever," I said.

"The head waiter had it on his printout. Hard to argue with his computer printout copy," he said.

"Don't tell me you can't recognize your own son!"

"What, Merci? You say you see a resemblance. But his name is Robert Billings. My son's name is William."

He moved the phone lens closer to me. "Merci wants you to smile."

Again I asked him, "Don't you recognize your son?"

"You could be him. I haven't seen him since my divorce. That was when Merci and I ran off together. You were only two, or was it three? Wife wanted child support, so Merci and I said screw her and just— Okay Merci, I'll shut up about it. Yes, Merci, I know, the back alimony. Yes, yes, I know I promised we'd get married as soon as my son grew up. We agreed it would be traumatic for him if he saw his father marrying another woman. Everyone agrees children must be protected. Now I want you to check out the table's beautiful centerpiece while I talk with William or Robert and determine whether he's my or Billings' son."

He placed the phone next to the table's centerpiece, a tea candle surrounded by a few plastic flowers. "Son—"

"Look, you're what, forty? I'm in my thirties. How can I be—"

"Certainly you don't look eighteen, but Billings' son could be your age. In fact, he could be you. Waiters, especially head ones, seldom make mistakes. Could you be an electronic identity thief, stealing my son's identity and planning to run up an expensive meal on his or my credit? Let me tell— Excuse me," and he grabbed the camera phone and pointed it at a waiter. "Merci, here comes the cravat of wine I ordered. I ordered port to go with our rack of lamb. Yes, Merci, the stranger is cute but he may be my son and saying things like that sounds sort of sick. Never mind him, here comes the rack, and its presentation is just gorgeous. Can you see it? Are you getting all this on disc so we can enjoy the meal together later tonight?"

I got up and moved to an empty table as Billings or Rogers, waving goodbye and pointing the camera at me, asked Merci if she could see me going.

At an adjacent table a man was flirting with a woman at the next table, blowing her kisses between smiles and soundless mouthings of 'I love you,' to which she responded in kind. On top of his table instead of a place setting were open ledgers, papers fanned about, pens, laptops, and pocket calculators, all of which he was busily using as he took video pictures. Her table had two meals on it. He was saying to the phone, "Mildred, I won't be home until ten. You can see all the work I've got on my desk," and he slowly panned his cell phone over the table. The other table, waving at him, held up a menu with twelve scrawled in lipstick on it.

Nodding, smiling, the man told Mildred the boss just said they might have to work until twelve. What, honey? It doesn't look like my desk? It's not. The entire office staff has moved to the cafeteria and let me tell you, it's chaos here."

The adjacent girl laughed and hit him with an olive.

Picking it up and tossing it back he told Mildred that the background laughter was the office staff releasing tension. Picking up a highball and taking a sip he inadvertently moved the camera, "What, honey? A waiter pushing a desert tray? Of course, the boss sent out for food for the staff. It's one of the catering people."

Getting up the woman came over and playfully blew in his ear. "Look Mildred, the boss just got my attention and I've got to get back to work. Yes, twelve is the earliest. You can see by all the papers on my desk—er, table—I'm swamped with work. What? You want me to pan the cafeteria? Sure, honey. I don't mind. Oh damn it, my batteries are going. I'll see you at twelve, maybe a little later."

He rejoined the woman at her table and they ate, laughed, and took pictures of each other eating and laughing. Suddenly his phone rang. Jumping up and running to his worktable he answered and turned pale. "Mildred, I— What? I sent a picture of a cheap slut laughing with pasta hanging out of her mouth and tomato sauce dripping from her lips? It's a joke. The work here is getting frantic and we're all just acting silly. Thought you'd get a kick out of it. What? She's Vice President of Development."

The woman laughed, they exchanged blow kisses, and I turned to the vegetable soup I hadn't ordered. I told Martin, my server, I'd like a beer, and he nodded, pushed some buttons on a hand-held computer and left.

Spooning my cold vegetable soup, I heard a middle-aged woman at a nearby table saying, "Oh Johnny, the omelet was delicious. How's yours?"

Curious I stared. There was no Johnny. She was eating alone.

"I'm sipping my Martini now. It's very dry, just the way I like it. A toast, how sweet Johnny. You always say the right thing." She raised her glass and touched a tiny tablet screen placing her where the second place setting should have been. She gave a water glass a nail flip for sound effects. "What Johnny? You're ordering another Manhattan? You haven't even finished your appetizer. I don't want you to get inebriated. Oh damn it, tell your waiter he's blocking you from your camera. All I can see is his back. My server is Quincy, a very handsome college student. Do you want me to send you a picture of him? Don't be jealous.

Say, your waiter is wearing flats. He's a waitress. Johnny, if we're to dine together I'd like it if you didn't ogle the waitresses. You're with me and it's insulting. You should be attentive to the person you are dining with, and— Did I hear a second dish being served and a female voice saying thank you to that waitress?"

"That was only the waitress thanking me for a tip."

"Listen, you don't tip every time she brings something to the table. Are you with someone else? Are there three of us eating together? How could you? This was to be our special romantic evening out and you're cheating on me. I don't believe you and I've half a mind to get up, walk across the street, and see for myself. If you're so innocent, send pictures of your table. Isn't that chateaubriand for two? Just for you? Ridiculous, you'll get sick and—"

While sipping white wine, which arrived instead of beer, I noticed a couple intensely watching a tablet videophone while eating. "Look," the woman said, "Francis is trying to get up."

"I'm sure he'll make it," observed the man.

"Oh Harold, I'm so excited. Little Francis is going to take his first step."

"Look, he just did," Harold observed.

"He fell, but he did take two... or was it three steps?" the mother said.

Harold added, "And we were there. We saw him take his first steps and now we have it on video. We'll be able to replay it on our vacation trip. Now pass the butter. My biscuit is getting cold."

The waiter brought me a platter of spare ribs, New Orleans style, and a phone the size of a credit card. It was an irate Cindi demanding to know if I had put her on Off.

Telling her I'd never put her on Off, I put the phone down and told the waiter I hadn't ordered spare ribs, don't like them, and had never picked clean a rib, spare or not.

In a huff the waiter put the ribs down and marched over to the kitchen computer. While waiting for my ordered steak, I put Cindi back to my ear and heard, "Are you there? You're fading out. Can you hear me?"

"Yes, Cindi. It's my curse. I can still hear you."

Suddenly Cindi cried, "Who's this? I'm talking to Vi. Look, I've got call waiting. Let me put you on hold 'til I tell Vi all about the absolutely beastly man I've had the misfortune to have been stuck with as a guide."

"Cindi, I can hear you."

Just then the waiter returned, unceremoniously grabbing the ribs, which I was now hungrily eyeing, and put them down at the late-night workers' paper-strewn table. Much to the man's horror, in a loud voice the waiter announced, "Mr. Billings, your ribs."

After telling the waiter he wasn't Billings, he then told him to put the ribs at the next table. Then into his phone, he said, "Mildred, my dearest, I'm certainly not using an alias 'cause I'm ashamed of what I'm doing. Let me explain and— Oh, we're breaking up," and he vigorously ran a fork over the mouthpiece.

Returning to my table, the waiter presented me with a bill for two pork chops and rice pilaf. My outrage for receiving a bill for nothing brought the headwaiter over.

Spreading out a long detailed printout he patiently went over it item by item showing I'd had the pork, the beer, the sauerkraut and the chocolate mousse. When I pointed out the printout showed no rice, magnanimously they subtracted it from the bill, then added the mousse, increasing the damn bill.

My stubborn refusal to bow to their printout brought the manager with a laptop, who patiently went over each pixel showing video pictures not only of two pork chops garnished with an apple ring surrounded by sauerkraut in the Bavarian style and pie a la mode that were sent to Table 8. After this polite but firm lecture he stood up and pointing to a discrete card next to my flickering tea light that identified this table as Table 23 I suggested just as firmly, but not politely, they had the wrong table.

Waiter, headwaiter, manager, all open mouthed, looked at the card and then the computer monitor. The manager sat down and feverishly typed at the keyboard, then smiling leaned back and announced, "The computer now has table 8 empty and table 23 had eaten pork."

Meekly I simply handed them my credit card and picked up the cell phone which, being on, continually vibrated during my bill controversy. For some mysterious and absurd reason I asked, "Cindi, is that you? It's me, the IV visitor."

She whispered, "Have you heard of someone whose text name is Pork 23?"

"What? It's me Cindi. I'm still in the restaurant paying for pork I never received or ate."

"Mr. Visitor, you have to be very careful. The government may be illegally listening in on my cell phone," Cindi said.

"Wait, Roberto is texting me. He's convinced his text messages have been targeted by the FBI. Everyone is worried over confidentiality issues which— Wait, I've got to text Roberto about the mysterious government agent Pork 23."

Suddenly Cindi demanded Roberto tell her who was someone called Sexy Beasty and how did those intimate pictures of her for Roberto's eyes only get on Facebook and now someone called Sexy Beasty is texting her.

"Roberto, he's asking for more pictures and wants me to come to his apartment. Of course I won't go. Certainly if you don't want me to go, I won't. You know we have something very special, and there definitely would be more pictures if you promise to keep them just between us."

Between her wonder over who Sexy Beasty could be and anger over Roberto sharing her most intimate pictures on Facebook, Cindi told me my new guide would meet me at the hotel for a late-night snack.

The credit card came back and I signed the receipt that listed veal parmigiana and mineral water. Picking up the restaurant phone to return it to the waiter, I was able to hear Cindi informing my new guide, "He's so very very absolutely negative."

Simultaneously at the midnight hour my two new designated guides deigned to arrive at the lobby. One was a gentleman of many years whose bulbous rose-red nose, protruding from beneath two red-veined eyes, spoke of many drinks over many years. He introduced himself as Kaycee Jones, feature reporter at *The Times*. He said 'feature reporter' as if he'd said St. Peter, and *The Times* as if it was the gate to heaven.

The secondary, less-pretentious guide was Briteness Bernard, an intern studying journalism at Princess U. She said 'Princess U' as if saying the name elevated her to a very special height. Relatively attractive, having an intense look behind large, black-framed glasses, Briteness eyed me like a barn owl checking out a mouse.

"Isn't it rather late to continue my visitational investigation?" I said.

Jones brushed this aside telling me he was used to covering important fast-breaking news stories at all times of day and night, and for him the night was still young.

Suggesting a late-night snack, he went into the dining room with vote-less Briteness the Owl and me, still hungry from Pork 23 following. Walking behind Kaycee I noticed his behind was rounder, softer, and had more jiggly than Briteness'.

Mentioning being after midnight it was now morning allowed him to order a Bloody Mary as an appetizer, and being uncomfortable after my liquor indulgence, I joined him. Looking virtuous, the Owl had low-fat cottage cheese on lettuce.

Kaycee began. "Well, where do you want to go first? Newspaper offices, TV studios, journalism schools, movie studios, radio stations, all the important places? Being a reporter—er, did I mention I'm from *The Times?*—say the word and we're there," and Kaycee said the word and two more Bloody Marys arrived along with the Owl's white lumpy cottage cheese salad. Keeping my eyes averted from the gross salad, I commented again on how late it was.

"Ah, *The Times, The Times*," and Kaycee sucked the celery stick clean. "Of course *The Times* . Where else but that pinnacle of information. All the news fit to print. Now, what you, as an IV, need to know is *The Times* talks only to people who matter, who know what time it really is.

"I know TV news idiots think they're hot shit because they speak to average dopes, scaring, worrying the public at the beginning of the half-hour, then making them feel good at the end. It's just cheap entertainment and shameless manipulation of the mindless masses.

"Now who do we frighten, mold and inform? Not the average slob but people who count, important people who can do things, who can determine policies. We are the fountainhead from which all wisdom proceeds, telling those who in their turn will tell the dumb what is good or bad, what should be done, what should be undone, who is great, who is evil."

Leaning back, taking a long healthy sip of blood, he concluded. "Ah, the beauty of it, the power of it." Looking at me he said, "You're not drinking? Had a bad night? I've been there, did that, felt that. Come, let's have one for the road," and he signaled the waiter who brought three glasses, two bloodies and one looking suspiciously like carrot juice. We continued to avert our eyes from Briteness as she sipped

"Don't want to appear to be a braggart, but I've been the recipient of several Pulitzers. Of course, only proper people writing in the right papers saying the correct things are worthy of being awarded.

"There was my article attacking corporate greed causing oil shortages wherein I brilliantly, ruthlessly exposed the corruption within big, greedy oil businesses hurting the poor working man. Let's toast the poor working stiff."

We tapped glasses and he laughed. "Then possibly you've read my series about big corporations polluting the environment. Ah, was I elegant or was I elegant?" he asked the celery stick he was holding above the glass. He was dunking and sucking it. The celery stick evidently said he was eloquent because he smiled; again baptizing it, he sucked it dry and continued. "Let me see, I was just out of the Harvey School of Journalism when I won my first Pulitzer. It was an investigative piece on the homeless problem. Poor people living in abandoned cars and eating out of dumpsters, poor honest, hardworking families who couldn't find work because of the—"

"Greedy corporations."

"Exactly, big corporations who put profits before people. Did all my work in my parents' home in Beverly Hills. I'm not ashamed to tell you

I cried. Floating in the pool I wept as I dictated to dad's secretary all the pain I imagined these people must suffer. Parenthetically, to be a *Times* reporter you need imagination, feelings and most of all a strong sense for the poor's pain. Let's toast the poor's pain."

I didn't tingle his glass but he didn't notice.

The Owl, looking wise, looking sad, looking as if she could still see all the intense undeserved pain populating his articles, said in awe, "Mr. Kaycee Jones is now working on another exposé."

"My fourth Pulitzer—*The Times* think it's time we won another. *The Washington Post has* won more than their share over the last two years."

Taking a wild guess I said, "Your article, an exposé of big greedy corporations hurting poor people."

"Do Pulitzer awards bloom on any other bush?" Kaycee said, then observed, "These Bloody Marys do pack a punch. Only had a couple and I feel them."

"That's your fourth," the Owl said and received the curt "Thanks" that heavy drinkers bestow on carrot juice counters.

"Whatever, I feel good. So what does it matter? Two, four... it's all the same." Looking at his watch he said, "Briteness, get your laptop going. I feel a key informant is going to call me at any moment."

Laptop at the ready, Briteness waited expectantly.

Finishing his fourth and deciding not to overdo the celery, he ordered a bloody minus celery or any other vegetable whose volume subtracted from the main course.

A sip, a smile, twirling around a previous drink's celery stalk, Kaycee made ringing noises followed by a startled look, a smile, a wink. He placed the stalk next to his ear. "Who's this? Ah, it's you, my important, reliable, high-up, unknown, anonymous source known worldwide as Deep Voice."

Leaning over to me Briteness whispered, "It's the latest in cell phone communicational technology. Cell phones in the shape of vegetables. Doesn't it look just like celery? And you can eat it."

I looked at her, thinking she must be putting me on, then thinking *Princess U graduate*, I concluded she may not be pulling my leg.

Kaycee repeated for our benefit what the celery was telling him. "What, the big greedy drug companies are not only doing nothing to stop AIDS but are working with CIA agents to spread the AIDS virus to Africa?" He turned to Briteness. "You getting this down, you fascinating intern? Damn it, Briteness, you're getting better looking as the morning wears on."

She blossomed with pleasure.

I suspected the Bloody Marys were the fertilizer.

"Mr. Deep Voice, I've got it all down. What is my confidential informant, high up in the know, whispering to me?

"Yeah, let's see. What am I hearing through this phone?" Waving the stalk, he gave me several winks. "Several important civil rights leaders have expressed outrage at the heartless, greedy, racist drug companies and are demanding a congressional investigation headed by right thinking politicians. Important sources high in drug enforcement as well as AIDS activists suggest criminal charges will soon be brought against corporate officials." Then, with profound Solomon-like emphasis, Kaycee added, "At the highest level."

Looking up, Owl noticed the celery was resting on the table and not against Kaycee's ear. "Your phone," she said pointing to the celery.

"My dear child, my very attractive child, there's so much I've got to teach you." Picking up the celery and holding it in the proximity of his ear, he continued. "Where was I? Oh yes, on my way to another Pulitzer. What is my confidential Deep Voice whispering to me? Oh, sources close to the Attorney General acknowledge tremendous pressure on him is building up to bring indictments against the highest drug CEOs."

"Another!" Kaycee yelled to a passing waiter. "And this time light on the blood. You're giving me plasma with no vodka."

"You dropped the phone," the Owl said.

"Oh, oh yes," and with a laugh, balancing the phone on his rotund stomach, asked it, "Deep Voice, my unnamed, important, high-up administrative justice-loving informant, are you still there? Good,

good. What's that? There's more exciting stuff besides AIDS? Did I hear you right? Lack of children's vaccines? Lack of proper nourishment for children and an epidemic of obesity, and bullying at schools? And these horrors were actually laughed at in highly secret meetings by greedy corporations as they devise nefarious plans to get corporate tax breaks at the cost of millions and millions of children's lives, while planning to raise drug prices to attain obscene profits at the expense of these poor children?"

An anemic looking bloodless Mary arrived; a sip brought a satisfied smile.

Pointing to Briteness' laptop Kaycee said, "Brightness, my drink of nectar, a Pulitzer is hiding in there. Soon those TV newscaster pigs will be pimping my story to the general public. TV always eats our slop.

"Well now, what's left? Ah yes, my informed, unnamed source tells me the Pan African Congress is calling an emergency summit to deal with the starvation crisis in southern Sudan. That the World Health Organization expects a million—er, no Briteness, make that *ten* million—will die in the next six months and— no, let's go with three months—unless the big greedy corporations agree to help the suffering multitude."

After taking a sip, he turned to me and pointed to Briteness' laptop. "Take a deep breath; what do you smell? I'll tell you what you smell. Millions in book sales, talk show interviews, awards, guest shots, lucrative lectures and munificent visiting professorships."

Turning to Briteness, he smiled. "My cute intern, you know at my place I have some really great news awards and Pulitzers. Maybe we could have an informal discussion on the importance of journalism in the Land of Communication. What say tonight?"

He looked at her as a cat about to catch an owl. She looked back, an owl, minutes away from having a plump mouse gripped firmly in its claws.

Putting away the phone, he ordered us roast beef sandwiches and beers, saying he didn't want to get light headed.

Given the amount of vodka he had consumed, I was surprised he didn't float above us and start speaking Russian.

Pointing to the celery I said, "But there's no real source."

"Of course not, but there could be, and if I, a newspaper reporter, say there is, who can dare impugn my honesty?"

"Can't they demand you name him?"

"Ah, ha ha, you can't demand. You can ask, plead, or beg for the name but I'm a newspaper reporter. You must trust that what I say I heard, I did hear, and when I say I saw it, you must believe I've seen it."

"On what basis?"

"Sir, can you possibly believe we reporters, sacred priests in the service of communicating information, would or could ever lie?"

"Never," Owl answered for me, fearing I might go negative.

Kaycee amplified. "Sir, when you enter the news profession, you enter a sacred brotherhood dedicated to getting at the truth, letting the chips fall where they may: we're the lifeblood of democracy. Where would people be without us? I tell you where: uninformed, that's where.

"Mr. IV, as a Pulitzer news man, as a *Times* news man, you can implicitly trust me and my words and believe in what I tell you. If you doubt, if you suspect my veracity, what will you have to fall back on? Only your own pathetic common sense. The common sense of a celery stick.

"Mr. IV, without me people would be forced to think, and let me tell you, a well-fed, comfortable person does not wish to think, nay, will do anything to escape thinking."

I said, "But no one was on your celery. There was no unidentified highly placed source." *Am I talking about celery? Shit, I'm drunk.*

"Sir, I'm getting annoyed, and let me tell you, you don't want to get on the bad side of the news media. If I say I've heard from an unimpeachable, unidentified high-up information source that you're under investigation for financial malfeasance, and illegally in the pay of greedy corporations, then sir, you are, no matter how you try to weasel out of it. If you try to pry my unidentified source's name from my lips,

I can tell you, extracting my fingernails will not evoke even an initial and the full force of law is my defender."

Turning to Briteness, Kaycee said, "My dear, delectable intern, pay close attention and you will see a man who knows how you too can make news in the news business.

"Briteness, call Mohamed Ali, the secretary of the Pan African Congress. Use your cell phone. Mine must remain pure in case important unnamed sources want to get in urgent contact with me; in fact it's looking a little wilted."

When Briteness made contact, Kaycee took the cell phone from her and spoke into it. "Hello, Ali. This is Kaycee. Look, I just received definite information from the unimpeachable Deep Voice that greedy drug companies have asked the World Health Organization to downplay the horrendous spread of AIDS in Africa in order to continue getting their obscene profits.

"What? You're not surprised? Heard the same rumors from some high-up deep-voiced friends you can't name? So you believe it's true?

"Good, I'm going to break the whole sordid scandal. Can I drop your name as being horrified and demanding a thorough investigation of this new outrageous scandal?

"Good, Ali. See you at the banquet for achievements of black educators. What? An award for me? Well, I'm touched. No, honored. No. both, and I certainly will devote a lot of newspaper space to pumping up the banquet."

Hanging up he told me, "Ali is calling his newspaper friends, telling them my story, and demanding they write opinion columns about it, how outrageous it all is. Another example of American racism.

"Now Briteness, my favorite intern, get me Bill.

She did, and handed him the phone again.

"Bill, Kaycee Jones. Yes, yes, we certainly had great times at the NOW Awards Banquet for Hillary. Ha ha, stop it, Bill. No more dike jokes. Look, I've got some hot news from the highest source telling me they are planning to raise tenfold the price of AIDS drugs sold to poor

African nations. What Bill? You're sure a hundred million will die? Children? Mothers?

"Certainly I'm using the Holocaust word. I'll leave the ethnic cleansing phrase to you.

"Am I sure? Well, Ali from the Black Caucus believes it has legs strong enough to run six months without stopping and he will soon be demanding an investigation.

"Yeah, if anyone should know, Ali would.

"Yeah, what? Throw mud? Hell, let's give them a mud bath. Tomorrow for the evening news? Great. And before I forget, thanks again for that award for fairness in political reporting. Got it spotlighted in my living room. See you at the premier of that documentary exposing how the FBI, the CIA and Nixon had Kennedy shot and then covered it up."

Putting the phone down, he asked me, "Well sir, are you getting a sniff, an inkling, of how real news is gathered in Communication Land?

"There's only one more thing remaining. Owl, get me Gladys at Assimilated Press, the AP, the first source of news for all newspapers, radio and TV."

Again, she did and handed the phone back to hm.

"Gladys, my love, I've got something big and I want to pass it on to you so you can run with it. I just received unimpeachable information from a highly placed, confidential government source, drug companies have hatched plans to raise the cost of AIDS medicine to African nations in the expectation of billions in obscene profits.

"What? My source? You know better than to ask, but it is unimpeachable, has the deepest voice. In fact, all his confidential information comes from his diaphragm.

"Let me add, the Pan African Congress, the Black Caucus, and Bill are so convinced they're demanding an immediate investigation. Certainly, call them. I know you always double check.

"What? Oh certainly you can say a hundred million dead.

"What? Not enough. Okay, make it a couple of hundred million. The hundred million refers only to babies.

"Stop trying to pump me for my source. My lips are sealed with Super Glue, but now I'm going to refer my secret source as Hot Sauce.

"Ha ha, Gladys. Don't be so cynical.

"'Bye. Oh, remember, on Tuesday, the fantastic party I'm having at my house for Feed the Hungry Organization. Casual dress, but be prepared to eat and drink. The catering firm I'm using is fantastic, and remember, this band I've hired plays a lot of rap music, so I want to see a lot of action from you. What? Of course I mean dancing! Gladys, you're too much, though, if you're willing I'm willing and the bedroom is right upstairs."

Kaycee hung up, patted Owl's knees and spread a contented smile at the now-empty hotel restaurant. "Well, I guess Briteness and I will be going.

"Say, do you mind if I throw your name into the mix? Peoples, an important foreign visitor, is horrified at the doings of greedy corporations in Communication Land."

"I absolutely forbid you to refer to me in any way in your article," I told him.

"You really don't want me to mention you? Don't you realize when I mention your name you'll be pumped up to such an extent, readers will swear you're the shadow behind your country's president, whispering directly into his ears and what he hears he swallows?"

"Look, leave me out of your fabrications. I—"

"Fabrications! Me, a *Times* man? Look my innocent visitor. *Could* my story be true? Do you definitely know the drug companies *aren't* depriving black children of medicine?"

"I suppose anything could be true if it's not proven to be false."

"My point, because you've never seen a pig fly doesn't mean at midnight when you're dead to the world the porkers don't soar.

"Note this—the black caucus believes, people who read the *Times* believe, at this very moment AP is reporting it as certain and certainly Hollywood zealots already believe without even being told what to believe."

"But it's still not true, and don't dare use my name," I retorted.

"Don't dare! Damn it, I'll mention your name and write some quotes about your disgust over corporate corruption and heartlessness."

"I'll deny it."

"Do, and I'll hint you're either cowardly and caving in from corporate pressure or have been bought off by drug CEOs. Either you're weak or you're corrupt, but one thing will be true, you will have said what I said you said.

"As for not being true, you shouldn't be so hung up on that truth stuff. Everyone knows that truth stuff is passé. My dear lord, if you speak only truth you'll remain everlastingly dumb. You've got to open your mind to be receptive to all sorts of communication, from all sorts of sources, about all sorts of things, even nonsense. Realize, to have an open mind is to embrace new ideas, and to view your truths as being not true and others' untruths may be true. Or both your truth and its contradiction are equally true or both are equally false."

"How can you live in such a world of shifting sand?" I asked.

"It's not easy. You must fight your inner self and embrace your social self. You must be a boxer, dodging, weaving in the ring, fighting against your self's hard core principals. Your self throws a hard right with all the muscle of basic bedrock principles at the social you, and in dodging, the social you keeps the inner self from hitting you in the head. Then social you counters with a left jab of 'there are no absolutes.' This backs up your inner self, who unsuccessfully wards off social you's 'different strokes for different folks' jab to the jaw, quickly followed by a one-two: 'diversity is wonderful' quickly followed by 'there's no truth except the one absolute truth that there is no truth.'

"Your inner self weakly counter-punches with 'that's an absurd contradiction.' Social you delivers to your inner self a series of rapid blows to the heart, listing all the names of all the Hollywood idiots, all the news writers, all the TV pundits, and all the college professors who believe there are no absolutes and your inner self goes down, and the social you raises its hands in victory over your self. Relativity is the champion.

"Wait, the inner self is getting off the canvas, telling you 'I can stand alone.' Seeing your inner self staggering up from the canvas, the social self goes in for the knockout with a quick flurry of words in print, in speech, in phony video images, in movies and on TV, and down inner self goes, crying out 'I can't stand alone against all this communicational crap being thrown at me.'"

The bill arrived and the dismayed Kaycee discovered he had inexplicably left his credit card in his apartment.

Knowing his forgetfulness was fake, I paid the bill, but again, it's all on your dime.

Briteness' cell phone suddenly rang. She told Kaycee it was for him, and he picked up the phone. "What? The South African Prime Minister has just accused the multinational drug companies of conspiring to kill two hundred million black babies and is demanding the UN investigate this genocide?"

Turning to me, Kaycee cried, "You see, the story has not only legs but those muscular legs are up and running on their way to picking up my Pulitzer."

"I've seen enough," I said and I started to get up.

Kaycee told Owl, "I don't want to brag, but I happen to know Dan Rather personally."

"Do you really?" gasped an impressed Owl.

"Intimately, my pliable intern. In fact, if you come to my apartment he may just drop in."

"He's my absolute hero," she commented.

Not liking that, Kaycee retorted, "My dear, he just reads the news to the people, sort of like a reader to the blind.

"Now I—" His actual phone rang. Raising a shushing finger, he uttered a series of 'no's. The first, a disbelief no. The second a shocked no. A third was a stern no and then a series of yesses, all culminating in a broad smile at his conversation's end.

"Briteness my love, put in my diary at six o'clock tonight a round table discussion will be held at PBS on this latest drug scandal. I'll be moderator as several of my friends disguised as news analysts will debate the—"

Foolishly interrupting, I asked what would be discussed.

"Discussed? My dear visitor, it's been choreographed a thousand times... my questions, their answers. We know our roles in the drama called analysis of the news. Having performed so often, there is no need for scripts and rehearsals. The only difference between hard-hitting journalism and the theatrical stage is in one a curtain falls, in the other, one play's last act melds into another show's beginning."

Curious I asked, "Who was on the phone?"

"Sol, my agent. He's also Tom Brokow's, Gladys' and Peeon's agent as well as the campaign manager for Senator.... well, better not say. Let me tell you, there's no one better than Sol at arranging impromptu, no holds barred, hard-hitting, mean, tough news discussions with my friends and his clients at a non-partisan roundtable forum on PBS."

Kaycee didn't mind my bailing out as he gathered up Owl, saying they had a couple of hours before his in-depth TV analysis of his fast-breaking story on CNN so they could stop off at his apartment.

Giving me a wink he suggested possibly Diana Sawyer would drop in for a drink. He walked away, Owl's arms around him, supporting his flagging, stuttering steps, as he excitedly talked into a celery stick.

AFTER COMMUNICATION LAND

There are many reasons to find that bar and seek that drink: exhaustion, desperately needing a pick me up; depression, deep into the mind's dark alleys, needing to achieve if not a high at least get to a normal level; jubilation, needing to toast the mood or the event; anger, needing to fuel the inner fury; boredom, needing stimulation; disappointment, needing to mend dying hopes; sinfulness in life, needing self-forgiveness; uncertainty as to one's future course, needing to achieve certitude; unloved, needing an infusion of self-pity; in love, needing to enjoy the affection; lonely, needing the drinks' companionship; aimless in the night, needing a place to go; in need of a family, the caring bartender, the father, and around you cousins, brothers, all motherless;

in need of men's respect and attention, searching where the disrespected congregate; in need to mark a holiday, the bar is always festively dressed for all occasions; in need of a friend, find it in the place where the friendless go; in need of an anchor in a chaotic life, the bar and its inhabitants never change; in need to escape your reality, the bar is filled with fellow fugitives; in need of a home, a place for comfort, the bar is an accepting, never-judgmental home to the homeless; in need of a new persona, the bar is where you can be a hero and the illusion is your new reality; in need to excuse yourself, explain yourself, the bar thrives by excusing all, of all; in need to feel strong, to feel brilliant, the bar holds your audience if you buy; in need of light and gaiety, the bar is always colorfully lit; in need of quiet, repose, to reflect, it's to the bar to study your beer. The bar is the place to go for those having no place and desperately need a place.

Finally, in my case after the ordeal of Communication Land, I needed a stiff drink to regain my focus and get my life regrounded. Communication Land is not real. It thrives on misinformation, misinterpretation and distortion of the report. It distorts what is real, and if carried to excess creates a fantasy reality more real, 'til reality comes up and bitch slaps you.

So in the hotel bar with a double whiskey and beer chaser, I sat trying to rediscover my beliefs, trying to overcome the horror of being the only rational man in an irrational world.

Only when the double was gone and the beer halved did I open my mail. Pru was stingy and mean in both the length of her protestations of love and in the portrayal of that love. I ordered another double to assuage sudden feelings of being unloved and alone in this cold world. The letter with scant mention of her love for me contained abundant words about herself.

Out of love for me she had dinner with Hoar. Two lengthy paragraphs were devoted to her reaction to the dinner: it was expensive; she had a flute of champagne. (A flute? Where did that come from, if not out of Hoar's mouth?) Her baby lamb chops were like no other, the service was impeccable, the flaming brandy soaked desert was beautiful, there was a trio playing music and Hoar had them play *Be My Love* just for her. She did tell him it was inappropriate, but still it was very nice of him. After dinner, like a gentleman, he wanted to escort her home but somehow with her mind befuddled with after dinner drinks (plural!) Rudy somehow arrived in a cab and took her to her apartment. Apparently he gallantly assisted her inside and made them coffee. She was so ashamed at not having anything in the way of cake to offer.

Description of coffee with Rudy in her apartment abruptly ended before the cups were put down as she gave a synopsis of Hoar's view on my visitation reports. Did I realize I was being too negative, too cynical, too sarcastic and was becoming an embarrassment to the department? Hoar felt betrayed after his good offices in getting me the appointment, and I was now making him look bad.

Rudy's letter, a confirmation of my suspicions of Hoar's intentions toward Pru stressed how he rescued Pru, being much more inebriated (don't use drunk in describing nubile girls) than the last time. (The last time?) Being suspicious of Hoar, he had a cab waiting outside the restaurant and was able to take Pru home and see her safely into her apartment. He wrote nothing after 'into her apartment' but gave his usual, you're doing great, everyone's cheering your reports.

Putting the two different evaluations aside, putting aside my anger at dirty old man Hoar, putting aside my suspicion of Rudy's coffee in Pru's apartment, I ordered only a single whiskey to take the suspicion away. The liquor, rather than focusing the mind and elevating the spirit, only added to my confusion. There being so much in contradictions and suspicions I couldn't focus, I couldn't decide which mood to wear.

In such an irresolute attitude, I didn't bother to escape when Sunni sat down next to me and ordered a Vodka Martini with onion. Her face was that of a mastiff robbed of a slab of raw meat it was about to swallow. She tossed the onion over the bar and cut in half the Martini. Being neither here nor there but certainly not up, I asked where Hinki was and said, "I thought you two were close."

The Martini was quickly put out of its misery. His brother was immediately ordered before she turned and spat out, "Hinki's a bastard."

Since that was my estimation the first time I had met him, my only surprise was in her realizing the fact. I didn't need to probe for more information as she poured forth. "Do you know he has a girlfriend back at the sociology department?"

"No. I'm truly surprised." My surprise was in how any woman with eyes could see any advantages in Hinki.

"Can you imagine how surprised I was when I found his whore on his Facebook page, listed on his IPod, and in disgusting obscene photos on MySpace. He lied to me, told me—no, *swore*—there was no one in his life but me. I feel so betrayed I could scream."

With two Martinis inside her I feared what would come out would be very loud and embarrassingly nasty. To interfere with what she might do I ordered a third Martini for her, and a beer for me.

She glared at the bartender who, after slipping on the onion, glared back. With our drinks came Hinki—not an apologetic Hinki for cheating, not a shame faced Hinki caught in lies, but an outraged Hinki—greeting Sunni with a loud, "So there you are." The situation suggested entertainment and I looked forward to their conflict.

Sunni, busy with her Martini, allowed Hinki to get in the first salvo. "How could you invade my privacy? How did you get my password? How dare—"

Slamming her Martini down sufficiently hard to bounce the onion onto the bar, Sunni countered his outrage with the ploy of disabused innocence, "I trusted you! You said there was no one else in your life but me! You lied!"

The lie was said as if it was the first lie in creation, the Garden of Eden snake's lie to Eve.

Knowing better than to try to defend against the lie charge, Hinki continued with his privacy issues. Sunni had no right to steal his password and read all his personal stuff. This was said with the vehemence of a person whose personal stuff was really interesting and sexually inflammatory.

Not a person to retreat, to explain, to even remotely admit wrongdoing, Sunni aggressively said, "It's a damn good thing I *did* read your stuff. If I hadn't you'd still be lying to me. You're a despicable cheater!"

Hinki complained, "Shit, did you have to write to Pokey about us? That was outrageous and very vulgar."

"She had the right to know what a bastard she's sleeping with."

I said, "Pokey?"

Wiping the bar, the bartender smiled at Pokey, picked up the onion, and told the two to keep it down.

An indecisive Hinki looked at the bartender, who asked if he wanted anything, tried to look at me who was hiding behind a beer head, looked at Sunni, Martini in hand and the hand was cocked, decided there was nothing to be gained by staying, so he left. His farewell salvo at Sunni was a weak, "I don't want to see you again."

Sunni responded with, "Stay out of my room and get all your shit out or it's going into the hallway." That last 'shit' purged some of Sunni's anger. Turning to me she asked if I could believe what he did.

"Never—it's absolutely shocking," I said.

"I shouldn't have trusted him but I'm too trusting. I believe we should trust people 'til they're proven shitheads."

Well, I thought, *we're entering the poor innocent me drunkard's stage.*

"Let's have another," she suggested, and having no other place to go nor anything to do in that other place, I ordered a whiskey and a Martini; the Martini came onionless.

Without giving an inch of movement, Sunni said, "We should eat." I agreed and stayed put.

"Hinki's a bastard. You know he said he loved me. You know I really loved him. Oh, I feel so used."

Seeing I was only an audience for the monologue she was delivering to herself, I remained noncommittal, which suited her. She proceeded to contrast herself with Hinki and no surprise she was trusting, loving, caring, giving, and Hinki was a manipulator, a user, a liar, and an all-around bastard. After confining Hinki to a well-deserved hell she looked out at mankind, and after a brief deliberation with her Martini sent all men to join Hinki in hell. Noticing one of the villains was before her, sympathetically listening to her, I received exoneration. "Hey Edmund, you're all right. You're not like Hinki. Do you have a girlfriend back home?"

Sinning, I confessed to myself to be a member of the lying mankind. "No Sunni, there's no one."

"Neither do I. Look, do you want to come upstairs? We could order room service."

Thinking *Thank goodness for the dime*, I was about to join Hinki in the world of lying bastards, and knowing her state of inebriation was counting on it.

My innocence was saved when she suddenly confessed to being drunk and angrily declared she needed to get upstairs before Hinki stole any of her stuff from her bedroom.

Leaving half a Martini, moving her round bottom off the stool and almost falling, she had to grab on to my arm, telling me she feared Hinki might steal the souvenir picture of her kissing a marble replica of Michael Jackson's glove in front of his mausoleum before I could selflessly volunteer to walk her to her room and order us room service dinner, she left and left me profitless for my manly lie. After the whiskey I just didn't care about anything. It was all shit, the hell with it all. In this mood, dinnerless, I went to my room to sleep.

PART III

LANDS OF JUSTICE

1

Legal Land

Holding the law as a beacon of justice, Legal Land was held in great esteem in my land. Legal Land was described as loving the law, as if married. Lawlessness was simply not tolerated in Legal Land. To place a toe, even the little one, outside the law was treated as a social outrage. Disrespect for the law was sacrilege. Ignorance of the law was inexcusable.

In Legal Land my two official guides, Kurt Kunster and Alan Durch, greeted me with formal speech. Kunster pulled out a legal-looking paper in preparation for reading my official greeting. He wore half-granny glasses and had his long gray-brown hair tied in a foot long pony tail. Solemnly he nodded to his companion Alan Durch, who, I'm sure, had a face hiding behind the thick, curly hair growing out of his ears, falling down his cheeks, wiping his nose and obscuring his mouth 'til gravity pulled it deep into his shirt front. One could only estimate his facial features. Even his eyes were a deep mystery, hidden behind dark glasses.

From behind and beneath his hair, Durch asked if I minded his recording their welcoming speech.

Telling Durch he could record, I couldn't help wonder what he was hiding behind so much thick, ugly hair: perhaps a threatening, malicious mien that, if revealed, would put women to flight; or perhaps the aspect of his face was of such irregularity and distortion as to warrant camouflage and revealing it would repel all but the strongest of stomachs; or perhaps the mouth was insignificantly small, or the lips thin, or the cheeks girlishly plump and round; or perhaps all of the above, combining to suggest a weak, vacuous personality. Was it a pathetic effort to stand outside the crowd to be individualized in everyone's mind as "'the guy with the beard'?' Why was it there? Why did I bother about its presence? Or perhaps that was' the reason for wearing all that hair?

As I nodded, the tape recorder was turned on and Ponytail Kunster read, "By authority of the Absolute Bar Committee, otherwise denoted within this document as the ABC, I am empowered to issue this welcoming oration to you with the provision it may be withdrawn if there is any misrepresentation on the part of the Investigating Visitor, known as the IV, as to the purposes of his visit, or if the ABC in its official capacity, possessing an official quorum, finds sufficient justification by majority vote to determine the IV visit by Edmund Peoples to be detrimental to Legal Land, to be identified in all other places in this document as LL. The ABC of LL is sole determinator of any cause for the withdrawal of this welcoming proclamation to the IV." He glanced up at me. "Do you understand the above?"

Not having the slightest idea, to move things along I said, "Yes, I guess I do."

"Please sign here and initial there."

Thinking *They certainly take their greetings seriously*, I did so.

Ponytail, turning to Bushy and getting a nod, said into the recorder, "Attorney Alan Durch has given visual affirmation that I, attorney Kurt Kunster may proceed."

Not liking his nod to be put on the record, Bushy told the tape his visual affirmation, by way of a nodding ascent, was restricted to the reading of the greeting and in no way was to be interpreted as his assent to any errors in the request to read the greetings nor voice inflections employed by the reader, Kurt Kunster.

Ponytail flashed an annoyed look at his beard hidden co-counsel before announcing to the recorder, "I am about to read to the purported IV visitor, Edmund Peoples, but before I do let it be noted the recipient of this welcoming proclamation has sat down on the grass."

Leaning over, Ponytail asked if I objected to his describing my posture while hearing the proclamation.

I told him no, and if he didn't get on with reading it, I'd be reclining, going to the prone, even sleeping.

Ponytail straightened up and whispered to Bushy, "Did you get that on tape?"

"Yes, Kurt," Bushy whispered back.

Satisfied, Ponytail announced into the tape recorder, "I will proceed reading the welcoming text as prepared by and authorized by the ABC Executive Committee."

Here he paused looking to make sure the recorder and I were listening. Satisfied everyone was still there, he cleared his voice and read in a phony deep bass, "Welcome." Leaning into the recorder, Ponytail stated, "The clearing of my throat is not to be interpreted as part of the corpus of the proclamation."

We were silent. I was waiting for more, and they waiting for my reaction, so I prodded them. "And...?"

He asked if I understood ABC's greeting proclamation.

Puzzled I repeated, "And? Is that it? Welcome?"

Bushy carefully folded the proclamation and, putting it into his leather briefcase, said they could add no more to the text of the proclamation. It would be outside their authorized powers.

In genuine confusion I asked, "What was all this nonsense about?"

They informed me all questions should be put in writing and submitted to the ABC Steering Committee, who would direct them to the appropriate committees for consideration. If replies were deemed necessary, responses to the query would, after due consideration, be efficaciously sent to the questioner.

With pride Ponytail said, "We try to get a definitive response within three months of the time of the question's submission to the appropriate committee."

Bushy whispered into the tape recorder, "We say this with the caveat that what we say is not binding on the ABC or on any of its members, singularly or in association.

Ponytail said, "There is now an affidavit I have to read to you in the presence of a third party," then, nodding to Bushy, asked if he consented to being the third party for the affidavit.

Solemnly as if saying his wedding' 'I do', Bushy said, "Let my name be the third party of record."

"Let it be noted for the record, Alan Durch has agreed to be the witness to Mr. Peoples' responses to the ABCs official affidavit necessary for entry into Legal Land.

"Now Mr. Peoples, before being allowed to enter Legal Land, you must affirm all of the following with a loud distinct affirmation into the recorder, in the form of just 'yes'."

"Yes, or just yes?" I impishly asked.

"Yes, just yes, but not the 'just' and if not yes, a no, but omit the 'a'—just a simple no."

Bushy interjected to advise me of my option of remaining mute, but if I availed myself of that option, a 'no' would be automatically recorded. In giving no response without the 'a' my visa would be denied.

Pulling out another legal paper from his briefcase, Ponytail, through his half-granny glasses, read the questions in weighty tones, with ponderous silences between each question. The silence between each question and my answer allowed the two lawyers the opportunity to stare hard at me, as if I were an antagonistic witness. The unnecessary elongated silent punctuation and the accusatory stares made concentration difficult; I had to drag my attention over, through, around and under the many pregnant pauses to mumble the expectant 'yes' at the appropriate places.

"Do you respect the legal profession?"

"Yes."

"Do you respect the courts?"

"Yes."

"Do you obey the courts?"

"Yes."

"Do you listen to and follow the advice of all legal professionals?"

"Yes."

"Will you always act in a legal manner?"

"Yes."

"Do you abhor and detest vigilante law, believing it's never justified?"

"Yes."

"Do you affirm everything inside the law is legal?"

"Yes."

"Do you affirm that outside the law, everything is illegal?"

"Yes."

"Do you believe that outside the law there's darkness, chaos, ruin and death?"

"Yes."

"Do you believe the law is always good and no law can ever be evil?"

"Yes."

"Do you believe the law protects people and never hurts people?"

"Yes."

"Do you recognize the only people who can lawfully interpret the law are judges?"

"Yes."

"And what they say the law is, is the law?"

"Yes."

"Do you believe only lawyers can understand, discuss and argue the law?"

"Yes."

It would be redundant and tedious to list all the numerous statements I had to answer yes, but the last one was something about dying for the law followed by worshipping the law. By that time I was so dazed, bored, and stupefied I'd have said yes to loving both Bushy and Ponytail in the biblical manner.

Ponytail gave me the ten-page document, asking if I'd initial each page and sign the last.

Bushy then asked for identification before he notarized my signature.

Being past noon when all this absurdity was completed, I suggest lunch before visiting Legal Land's major institutions, schools, hospitals and certainly the courts of law.

"You can't eat at my house," Ponytail hurriedly said, as if I had asked, adding, "I won't be held legally liable for any unforeseen mishaps occurring under my roof."

"Don't think you're coming to my house," Bushy said, adding he wouldn't be held legally liable for any mishaps either.

"No, no," I explained. "I was thinking of a restaurant. Is there one nearby you'd recommend?"

"Recommend? Recommend?" Bushy cried out. "You'd just love us to recommend one to you and then if you got sick from food poisoning we'd be held liable!"

"Or eating there, become fat and die a horrible obese death," Pony growled.

Bushy continued. "Then what would you do?"

Being totally empty of any answer, Pony Tail answered for me. "You'd sue us."

Raising his hand in horror, Bushy added, "You'd try to get damages for any mishap. There is the specter of tort. Tort could strip you naked. Do you think you're in an uncivilized, unsophisticated county where you can pour hot coffee on your crotch and not get a million in damages? Well, guess again."

Finally Bushy confided, "Besides, there are no public restaurants. Kurt and I sued the last one, some pathetic, unsafe, unsanitary mom and pop hotdog stand."

"Food poisoning?" I asked.

"Nah, irresponsibility—with total disregard for public safety, they put too much sauerkraut on a hotdog. An innocent, unsuspecting consumer, while eating the unsafe sauerkraut-loaded hotdog, innocently spilled some of the dangerously overabundant sauerkraut on the floor. Then innocently he slipped on the slippery strings of the kraut. "It was an open and shut case and our jury awarded a couple million in damages, driving that dangerous hotdog stand out of business."

I asked, "Could the hotdog stand pay a million?"

"'No, they couldn't, so the court paid our fees and the plaintiff got all the defendants' supply of hotdogs, kraut, mustard and ketchup."

"So no restaurants."

"None."

"Is there a deli where I could purchase some cold cuts."

"None. The last went out because of a dropped baloney slice and—"

"Gone with the hotdog stand," Ponytail said. "You've got to protect the public from money-hungry, cut-corner food merchants."

"What about grocery stores, supermarkets?"

"None. The last one went when an unsuspecting pedestrian walked into window glass that was too clean."

"How do you get food? Where do you two eat?"

"Imported from other Lands on an individual basis," Bushy said. "Though of course we've got numerous law suits against the companies in other Lands, and if they ever step over our boundary line, their ass is ours."

Ponytail said, "Though some Lands are refusing to send food to our people after we sued a Land over a consumer's order of Swiss Cheese with one too many holes and came up short by almost 100th of an ounce. You short one person a 100th of an ounce here, another there, and before you know it you've robbed the public of a couple pounds of cheese. Answer me—without lawyers, where would it all end?"

Thinking *I'm going to starve*, I suggested a quick visit to a school and its cafeteria.

The grammar school was a decrepit building reminiscent of Education 'Land's school. It was in sore need of major repairs, if not demolition. When I commented on that fact, Bushy lamented the schools were underfunded.

A ring of proud parents with cameras were standing around the children's playground watching the young children frolicking about seesaws, swings, and sandboxes when suddenly a child fell from a swing and scraped his knee.

Screams of horror and anguish were emitted immediately by the mother as a man and the mother ran to the child. The man taking pictures demanded the child cry louder into a recorder, and move his scraped knee into the light for a clearer video. He had the child squeeze it for more blood. Smiling, my guides explained the mother was fortunate to have a personal injury lawyer standing next to her.

A smiling Ponytail pointed out a well-dressed gentleman warmly greeting the other picture taking gentleman. "Ah, here comes the school liability insurance carrier's lawyer, and I'm afraid he's a little late."

After the pleasantries they pulled out tape measures, tape recorders, more video cameras and still cameras, and fell to measuring, recording everything that could be subjected to the above instruments.

"Law suit?" I asked.

"Certainly. See all the women observing the children playing?"

"Mothers concerned for their children?" Then I noticed the men. "And are all the men fathers?"

"They're lawyers concerned about protecting the parents' and children's legal rights if any child gets hurt. It's the legal way.

"If you want to go inside the school, you'll have to sign a liability waiver excusing the school from any responsibility for any and all injuries sustained on school property," Bushy said.

"But don't worry," Pony said with a sly smile. "Those waivers won't hold up in court."

"Then why sign it?"

"Simple," Bushy said. "To argue for and against the signed waiver's' validity adds a good month to the trial and is the basis for lengthy appeals."

Pony added, "And"" a good month to legal fees... heh, heh."

"I see."

As we went in, Pony with another "'Heh heh'" and a sly, knowing wink suggested I notice how the carpet on the third step was dangerously loose and frayed.

Explaining I hadn't time to sue anyone, I said, "Forget this school. Let's go to the university."

"No problem in suing," Bushy told me. "Give us the power of attorney and we'll handle all the legalities. You don't even have to be here. It will cost you nothing and at the end, you'll get a settlement check in the mail."

"I see. Still, let's take a look at the university. I'm hungry and I have to visit the next Land pronto."

We had to walk to the university and when I commented about the lack of taxis, Bushy explained in one word: "Sued."

"And the lack of cars?" I asked.

With pride Ponytail explained, "First we sued the auto insurance companies out of existence, then sued the manufacturers for unsafe cars, and then sued the drivers 'til now we're a healthier land. Walking everywhere, we have no auto pollution and Legal Land has the safest motor accident record, second only to Health Land."

"Public transportation?" I ventured, then I quickly answered myself. "Sued", right?"

"I'm glad to see you understand where we're coming from," Pony said.

As we approached the university, which was in greater disrepair then the grammar school, I suggested the lack of school funding as the possible cause.

"Lack of contractors," was Ponytail's laconic response.

"Lack of confidence in their skills," Bushy added, which added to my puzzlement.

Ponytail, interrupting with such enthusiasm that it suggested a personal connection, said, "An innocent university arts student, unaware that putting a roll of toilet paper down the toilet and flushing it would back the water up, was traumatized when this huge polluted back spill came rushing out at him. Fearing for his life and with understandable thoughts of drowning in the stall, he incurred a gash on his thumb trying to open the stall door—a gash that required two whole staples and possibly will leave a lifelong scar and potential future thumb trauma that could interfere with a future of a lucrative oil painting career.

"Well, barely escaping with his life, he is still under a doctor's care for possible future infections contracted by standing in fetid waters, and of course he needs life-long psychological counseling for all the submerged damage lurking just below the poor boy's consciousness, ready at any moment to surface and inflict permanent mental disability."

Rubbing his hands together, Bushy amplified. "We sued the contractor and the subcontractor for installing toilets incapable of handling a roll of paper, which could accidentally drop into the place that everything eventually drops into. Besides the substandard toilet, there were no posted warnings concerning the danger of trying to flush a roll of paper. Then of course, there was the mortally dangerous stall lock, almost taking off the poor boy's thumb.

"The school was also made to pay for their responsibility in this horrific tragedy due to the lack of posted instruction for the students to follow in case of toilet stoppage and the ensuing flood. Not only that, there was the unacceptable disregard for the health and welfare of students in their charge, given they didn't post faculty or administrative person along with a nurse and plumber in the lavatory to help students in case of just such an emergency."

"And," Ponytail added, "we sued the county over the inexcusable EMT delay in response time and for not sending a helicopter to the horrific scene of carnage where the poor boy, our client, was profusely bleeding from his almost severed thumb and grew faint from the loss of blood. Did we mention the two staples and the scar and the future career-ending trauma? In just the right light and pointed out to you, it's readily visible. Can you imagine the social difficulties in obtaining dates and artistic employment with such a grotesque disfiguring scar?"

Bushy was starting to get a glazed look as his mind walked backwards into a happier time as Ponytail concluded. "Won ten million, ten bucks in actual physical damage, the rest for punitive and psychological damage."

Bushy continued his reminiscence aloud. "You should have seen his mother." "I have it on video for future instructional purposes. In court, she was flushing Monsoon tears, rolling on the floor, throwing her hands to Heaven, screaming, and tearing at her clothes, all at the memory of her horror seeing her son's blood. She fought the court guards who tried to restrain her from running up and hugging her son when he was brought into court on a stretcher. It took a shot from a stun gun to keep her from attacking the university' president when he took the stand for placing her child's life in jeopardy."

"Great video... simply the greatest," Ponytail had to admit. "In fact, it's copyrighted and used in advance classes on product liability at all law schools."

"There's the very student now!" exclaimed Bushy, pointing to a scrounge, slouchy youth walking across the campus kicking a beer can.

I observed that he certainly didn't look like a guy who had gotten ten million.

"Well, the case is only two years old and there's the appeal process, and the contractor and subcontractor have declared bankruptcy and moved out of Legal Land."

"And the insurance company?"

"In Legal Land there are none, even after passing laws stating it was illegal for them to move, demanding they must remain to insure people, institutions and products so we can sue them and get awards. Can you imagine? They still left Legal Land and they refuse to insure so much as a blade of grass."

Bushy said, "Especially after we sued that company for the internal injuries an infant suffered from eating a blade of grass."

Ponytail said, "We only got half a million. It was one of those rare, tough, hard-hearted juries you unfortunately get sometimes."

"Yeah, we were all surprised at the miniscule award," Bushy said. "We sued the insurance carriers for illegally moving from Legal Land and if they ever come back... well, it'll be Rolls Royce and Rolex time at the ABC."

Suddenly the youth with the scarred thumb saw his lawyers and came over. "Hey, man, I've got a new suit for you."

"Yes!" both of my guides enthusiastically shouted, then quickly turning to each other, hurriedly whispered, "Joint counsels, fifty fifty," in unison.

"My stupid English professor is threatening to give me a B just because I failed his stupid exam and for reasons of conscience I refused to hand in a term paper. Man, talk about your hard-ass bastards."

"Say no more!" Ponytail shouted. "I see a discrimination suit against the professor who discriminates against youths with scarred thumbs and who unfairly bases grades on arbitrary onerous assigned papers and randomly chosen unfair test questions.

"With a functional disability in writing due to your thumb injury you shouldn't be unfairly penalized."

"Huh! Yeah man, I think I know where you're at. I think I know where you're going. I even think I know your deeper meaning: you mean I'm gonna get what I deserve."

Bushy continued the discourse. "Tell me, my disabled student, did that bigoted professor ask you questions in class?"

"Well, I missed a few classes. It's an eight o'clock class... you know what I mean."

"We know your meaning and we know you miss classes because the university, despite your disability, assigned you to that unseemly early class, knowing you'd have preferred a later class due to putting in long hours well into the night studying hard for all your classes, much harder than other students, due to your thumb disability."

"It's the only class I've got."

"And with a damaged thumb, with a writing disability, it's an awesome, heavy load to put on the shoulders of a first year student. Did they supply you with tutors?"

"Er, I've been here three years."

Bushy, taken back, said, "My, how time flies."

Ponytail, pushing aside his co-counsel, raised his client to the level of multi-disabled. "Your inability to get an A in this class is a direct result of the poor education you received in high school."

"Huh!"

An excited Bushy said, "Your failure to achieve your true grade potential is a result of poor study habits instilled, encouraged, and inculcated by an uncaring elementary and secondary educational system totally disinterested in their students' education and wellbeing."

"Huh!" the student said.

"And suffering from acute self-esteem depravation due to the traumatic experiences in prior educational systems, which also issued you poor or failing grades, you now feel incapable of succeeding in your studies and don't believe you can achieve the academic heights your fantastic intellectual potential warrants," Ponytail added.

Bushy concluded. "Multiple lawsuits against preschool, elementary, junior and senior high school and the university."

Quickly each whispered to the other, "Joint counsels, fifty, fifty?"

"Huh! Hey, just a damn moment. I got all A's in high school, junior high, and elementary school. In fact, I skipped a few grades. The stupid teachers loosened up their grading criteria after the successful class-action suit brought by the parents of all the D and F students. Before we won the suit, everyone was uptight; you know what I'm saying. Shit, now the damn schools are really successful: everyone graduates with all A's. You should see all the happy pusses on parents and administrators on graduation day. Man, every student is a brilliant student. I graduated summa cum laude along with everyone else. There were sixty class valedictorians out of a class of fifty."

Bushy and Ponytail thought for a moment before Ponytail said, "No problem. If the obverse of a suit is no-go, just go into reverse, social promotion, passing on students who are educationally deprived, making them suffer the pain of rejection at the college level. Oh the hideous inhumanity of this pernicious system of social promotion! They must be made to pay for the irreparable damage they do to innocent, parched minds thirsting for knowledge!" He turned to Bushy. "What say, Kurt? A couple of mil?"

Kurt was deep in his briefcase, looking for contingency forms for the youth to sign, a youth of twenty-three, if a day, and an ugly twenty-three at that, and I didn't look at his thumb though he stuck it out for me to see.

After signing the forms and after prodding, the youth mentioned the unbearable pain in his thumb, to which Ponytail replied, "Great! You've reinjured your thumb due to the inordinate amount of writing your professor has unnecessarily inflicted on you. Wear an elastic bandage on that thumb when in class and don't be ashamed to jump up yelling and run out of the classroom if your thumb pain gets to be too much. Go to the university nurse—and remember, always document each visit."

"Huh? Man, you mean you want me to go to classes? It's eight o'clock. You know what I mean. I got a social life. Let's get our priorities straight."

Bushy interjected. "Sleep disorder! The sadistic university requiring eight o'clock class is creating a severe sleep disorder leading to mental and physical fatigue, not only resulting in the poor grade of a B, but by your class writing assignment, renewing the excruciating pain in your injured thumb. You must put a cast on your thumb."

Ponytail gleefully shouted, "And possibly put your arm in a sling," then added, "Now, this is the first B you received in all your years of schooling?"

"Hell, yes," the youth said with a certain amount of pride. "You think I'm a dummy?"

"Of course not. Your prior grades prove you possess great intellectual prowess and this threatened B is obviously an attack by a bigoted professor on a poor, disabled student."

"Yeah, I almost got a B in Advanced Physics in high school but Mom saw the principal, got in his face and did some yelling about lawsuits and I got the A I deserved."

Surprised I said, "You took Advanced Physics!"

"Huh, sure man, why not? I took all those advanced courses—Chemistry, English—all that advanced shit. They tried to keep me out, but Mom, with a whole bunch of other parents of deprived guys like me, threatened class-action lawsuits and well, I and all my friends not only took all that advanced crap but we had our own separate classes and everyone aced the courses."

"I see" I said, and I did.

Bushy demanded the student put his entire arm in a cast and said a neck brace wouldn't be amiss.

By the time all their legal paper work was signed, initialed, notarized, folded and deposited in the leather briefcases, I wished to leave Legal

Land as quickly as possible. I suggested a quick visit to view Legal Land's hospital. Being hungry, I hoped to grab some food in the hospital cafeteria. After all, they had to feed the patients, and I was sufficiently desperate to be happy to devour hospital food.

When Bushy said it was about a mile walk, I inquired about bike rentals.

"None. The manufacturers of unsafe, life-threatening bikes went bankrupt after that senior citizen was run over by a tricycle and suffered permanent knee injury."

"There are no sidewalks," I said.

"There are no cement contractors after that horrendous multi-person catastrophe," Bushy said. "Can you picture it? A group of joggers tripped over a crack in the concrete and fell over each other. They were stacked six high, all screaming in pain. Some women joggers, seeing the mayhem, were so traumatized they might never have children."

We finally reached the hospital just as my stomach was flashing its On Empty red light.

The building was in even worse condition than the educational ones: windows were broken, litter was strewn all over the weed-covered land, and people were hanging from windows screaming for pain relief. Through the door-less entrance I could see patients crawling through a dirt-filled corridor, tearfully pleading to be put out of their misery.

Shocked, I cried, "This is terrible! It looks like a Japanese prison camp! Where are the doctors?"

"Malpractice," Bushy sighed. "The quacks left for other countries."

"And the nurses?"

"Ditto," Ponytail answered. "The damn broads got scared and, taking their starched whites, left."

Looking at the pathetic, suffering individuals, I asked my guides if someone could give these poor souls some medical relief. The suffering was so heart wrenching, I suggested possibly the patients could administer to themselves.

Horrified Bushy said, "Not allowed. That would be illegal. Only doctors can legally prescribe."

"Besides," added Ponytail, "There aren't any medicines since we won the unlawful death suit of that alcoholic who OD'd on cough medicine, and there was the class-action suit of all those people addicted to prescription and non-prescription drugs.

"We, in the legal profession hard kicked drug company asses until they were soft putty."

Bushy, looking skyward, pontificated. "Yeah, that's what we're here for. It's not about the money; it's to protect the little guy from the nasty, mean, money hungry drug manufacturers. It's definitely never about the money. It's always our commitment to and love of justice for the little guy that keeps us going."

Ponytail piously added, "We just care for people. We do it all out of love for the little people."

"So that results in unsanitary hospitals with no doctors, nurses and drugs?"

"But there's no chance of medical malpractice thanks to the legal profession. If you're admitted, the treatment you'll receive will be the right treatment."

"But there's *no* treatment."

"From an outsider's restricted pedestrian view, from the uneducated man in the street perspective, from those uneducated in the nuances of the law, they would say that, but from the legal overview it's a perfect hospital. Nothing goes wrong here. If a patient gets treatment, it's the right treatment. No one in Legal Land dies from medical malpractice. We take pride in that record of good health."

Exasperated I repeated my challenge. "But there *are* no treatments!"

And they said, "You can't deny the results. There are no medical mistakes in the treatment patients receive."

"Why do people go here?" I asked.

"Out of habit. You feel sick, it's only natural to want to go somewhere where you hope to receive care," Ponytail commented, then suggested we go see Legal Land's justice complex, only a walk of a mile.

Hungry, fatigued, haggard, and depressed, I debated, then decided after all I was here in Legal Land. To leave without observing the main reason for visiting would be dereliction of duty and possibly be subject to action by some lawyer somewhere. Of course the suit would be for some higher nobler purpose other than money.

We arrived at a magnificent complex of marble, glass, and steel spread over fifty landscaped acres and climbing twice the acres' length in its height.

"This is magnificent!" I exclaimed in awe.

"The majesty of the law, the dignity of the courts, and the legal profession deserves nothing less."

"What about lawsuits?" I asked, remembering the desolation they had wrought over the land.

"Oh, well there's the unwritten 'above the law' law," Bushy said.

Ponytail amplified, "The courts, the judges, and the lawyers must be free from any intimidating threats of lawsuits if they are to serve the best interests of the law. After all, the law is above everything, and nothing is above the law."

"What about the citizens?" I challenged.

"The law says who are and who are not citizens. Today, if the law says you are, then you are, and tomorrow if the law says you're an alien, then you become one. You have nothing to do with the matter, the law has all to do with the matter."

"Is not the law's purpose to serve and protect human life?"

They both laughed. "How endearingly naive you are!" Ponytail said.

"How judiciously innocent you are!" Bushy observed, then added, "Doesn't the law say who's alive and who's dead or comatose? And when a human embryo is a human being? And if the law can state that, are there any restrictions on who else the law may declare alive or dead?"

Ponytail expanded the argument, "The law says this is right and that is wrong, and who embodies the law if not lawyers and judges?"

"Are the judges subject to the law?" I asked.

"Certainly they are," Bushy said.

"But," Ponytail said, "as the voice of the law, judges interpret what the law says and doesn't say, so only they can pass judgment on themselves. Judges are both above the law and subject to it. Judges are the sole judges of judges. Is that clear?"

"Whatever," I said, feeling an insipid headache, whether legal or not, growing just behind my eyes. It was not a hunger headache; that one had long ago matured, grown old and was buried somewhere in the back of my head.

"Do you want to see an actual trial?" Pony asked.

"Well, just a quick look-see because I'm not feeling all that well," I said.

"Really? Not well?" Ponytail said in mock empathy. "Who's responsible for your pain? Someone must be responsible. Name a name and I'll name the suit and its dollar amount."

"Terrible!" Bushy exclaimed in mock horror. "Certainly out of care and concern we'll represent you on a contingency basis."

With a mental tension headache just behind my eyes, now walking backwards to meet the resurrected hunger headache that was strolling forward, I made my excuses preparatory to leaving. However, I first asked for an aspirin, two or three if they had them.

"Aspirin?" Bushy cried. "That's a dangerous drug, deadly if abused. You want me, an officer of the courts, to break the law and dispense medicine? Do you want to sue me, see me in jail?"

Ponytail said, "Only doctors can prescribe such powerful drugs. Unfortunately after we sued the doctors and druggists, they no longer exist in Legal Land."

"So there are no drugs, no construction, and no businesses, and all the public buildings are decrepit, and in the schools, nothing is taught and everyone learns perfectly everything that is taught, in the hospitals there is no treatment but everyone receives faultless treatment, and on the road there are no cars but there's never been an accident, and there's no food but it's all healthy food."

Mantra-like, Ponytail kept repeating, "You see? Lawyers solve problems and create a wonderful world for their clients."

"Look, my head aches and my stomach hurts. I'd just like to leave."

Bushy said, "You can't leave us so soon."

"Yes," Ponytail said. "Absolutely, what you need is rest and I know the very place. The lawyers' ABC Executive Lounge. It's an annex to the court complex."

In my weakened state, and with their assurances of soft leather and strong drinks, I found myself in an opulent club room filled with pompous, plump men talking to each other under clouds of cigar smoke and sipping from brandy glasses between making casual swipes at passing finger food.

"There's tobacco, liquor, food!" I cried in surprise.

"As lawyers, it's understood we don't sue each other, and so we are protected from the law," Bushy said.

Ponytail added, "It's a matter of honor among honorable men."

Seated in a chair so pliant my ass kept going down until it was level with my ankles, I refused a brandy and cigar, but with two hands dug into the finger food passing by. Then I carelessly inquired about the truth in Legal Land.

An elderly lawyer nearby shouted in mock horror, "Truth? You dare mention truth in the presence of lawyers? Is it out of ignorance or are you just trying to be insulting? The next thing you'll be talking about is justice," and he and the other lawyers sitting near him all heartedly laughed.

"We, the advocates defending the poor and downtrodden, the innocent wrongly accused, and the weak from the powerful, mendacious forces, can't be overly concerned with truth or justice." He paused for my reaction, and when I gave him a lukewarm nod to his bombastic self-serving assertions, he and the others burst out with uncontrolled laughter. With tears of mirth he shouted, "Gotcha! I got you big time! That twaddle is what we lawyers put out on TV programs for the edification of the general public. Everyone knows the poor souls need clouds of idealistic hot air floating over their daily lives to feel their society is a just society and by devolution they become just."

Between gasps for breath from excessive laughing, the elderly gentleman leaned forward and said, "I wouldn't be surprised if he believed MDs aren't in medicine for the money." This generated more generous laughter.

Another gentleman asked if I really believed people deeply care about the poor, homeless, the starving, and not about number one.

This brought on a renewed round of laughter from the cynical lawyers. After the irritating mirth died a slow death, my guides said it's a shame I couldn't see a case of murder defended by Mr. Sire.

Bushy told the group, in his opinion the creative lawyer Sire is the greatest. He said, "Hell, if you slit your wife's throat at noon in a busy mall, if you can afford Sire, you'll be as safe as a baby in his mother's arms at two p.m."

"Talk about mothers and babies, remember how Sire got the mother who killed her four children by drowning them acquitted with all that post-partum depression crap?" another lawyer said.

Bushy said, "Look, let's keep focused here. I think our Visitor should see our courts in action."

I demurred about going into a courtroom, maintaining that I was pressed for time, but Bushy said, "One peek into a courtroom to obtain a more complete idea of our legal system."

Walking in, given the room's cathedral's opulence, I understood why courtrooms are called temples of law: the rows of pews, the railing separating spectators from participants, the height of the dais behind which sat religiously robed judge.

Under the stern eyes of the temple's uniformed guards we silently walked down the marble center aisle, heads down passing the pews. Obviously only solemn, reverential attitudes were permitted in courts.

Nearing the railing separating the worshippers from the anointed priests—a.k.a. lawyers who, inside the railing were the only personages to participate in the ceremonies—I was surprised at how high the judge were sitting. I had to tilt my head up to view the altar and the high priest dressed in a somber medieval black robe. Near at were beautifully bound books with gilt-edged pages, the law books, the holy books of this temple. The high temple priest was telling the ordinary priests, standing respectfully below, what the books said. On either side of the judge sat busy temple functionaries, their heads bent low as they recorded all the wondrous words uttered by the high priest, so sacred they must be preserved. Standing respectively before the altar, ordinary priests would address the judge from the court well with reverential words such as "your honor."

Observing the proceedings, I felt no high priest in ancient Egypt had commanded such authority, respect, or occupied such a magnificent temple in which to hear the peasants' abject supplications made through anointed temple priests.

"It's almost a religious ceremony," I whispered as we sat on hard wooden spectator pews as opposed to the upholstered ones on the other side of the railing where priests of law with their assistant acolytes sat at polished mahogany tables.

A stern look from a temple guard quieted me as I listened to the pleadings of an anointed one, blessed to be allowed to speak in the temple. "With all due respect to your honor, the case rests on the interpretation of one word, and the word is 'served.' My client, the proprietor of The South of the Border, Under the Table, Out of the Truck, Ecologically Green, Slow Cooked by the Sun Pork, All You Can Eat for Under a Dollar Buffet Restaurant is not responsible for the hundred who suffered food poisoning and the more than twenty who died because the law states clearly that anyone *serving* tainted food is liable. But your honor, I humbly wish to point out that my client *served* no one. The customers served themselves; thus the law is not applicable in this case."

Immediately an excited, heated debate ensued over the meaning of "served" and the defense tossed into the arena another legal challenge. "Your honor, my client is an illegal immigrant, and since he's broken a prior law by entering the country illegally, certainly that law takes precedence over any alleged food poisoning illegality. He is willing right now to plead guilty to being here illegally and accept his punishment, to be deported by air-conditioned bus. Now, once he's been deported any legal action connected to the alleged crime of serving tainted food can only take place after the legal due process of obtaining his extradition are followed. There's also the matter of compensation for all the pork the government seized."

My attention was on the group of lawyers, secretaries, stenographers all gathered about the bench and its one high occupant as they all argued which crime took precedence and the precise meaning of "serve" when a smiling, unctuous gentleman slipped between Ponytail and Bushy and sat down, breaking my concentration. Both lawyers turned pasty pale.

"Simon?" Bushy said in an inquiring tone from his hairy sheepdog face.

"Simon!" Ponytail whispered in fear, his tail tight against his backside. Both nervously asked him whom he wanted to see.

Turning to Bushy he said, "You, and here you are," and handed him a sheaf of legal papers. With hand over heart, Bushy groaned mightily.

With hand over heart Ponytail joyfully exclaimed, "Hah, you're the one being sued! I warned you not to go against the solemn sacred unwritten law of, 'Thou shall not sue other lawyers,' and now the almighty's retribution has struck you down!"

Looking through the papers, Bushy cried, "I'm being sued for malpractice by six different lawyers for my suing them! In addition, another four lawyers are bringing me before the ethics committee for conduct unbecoming the profession! Finally, all ten lawyers are suing me for defamation! Heavens, I may be disbarred and become one of *them*!" He indicated the worshipping visitors sitting reverently in their assigned pews.

Turning to Ponytail he begged, "Can you help me? Act as my counsel! I'll even pay you!"

Ponytail emphatically said, "I'm wanting to. In fact, I'd love to. I'm excited to take on a challenge so formidable, but in fact it's so formidable that in all modesty I must decline. I humbly submit I'm unworthy to undertake your case. You must find a better legal mind than mine. Failing that, knowing no one who is your peer in arguing, parsing and creating obfuscations, you'd best be your own attorney."

Bushy's nose started leaking into his beard as he sobbed, "Oh, by the blessed and most holy Supreme Court, I'm lost!"

Ponytail, smiling at his friend's sudden misery, led us out of the court as I heard defense accusing the state of dereliction of duty for not inspecting The South of the Border, Under the Table, Out of the Truck, Ecologically Green, Slow Cooked by the Sun Pork, All You Can Eat for Under a Dollar Buffet, and so it was the state's fault people died. After all, how was the proprietor to know his food was bad? The last thing I heard was the judge exclaiming his shock over the state's manifestation of bigotry, intolerance and racism, of trying to keep an illegal Mexican from obtaining the Legal Land's dream. Hearing of such atrocious government conduct brought cries of outrage from the temple pews until, when it reached a crescendo, several women started to weep uncontrollably and one man in a seashell-pink shirt fainted.

"The man will get off even after poisoning hundreds," I said as we exited to the corridor.

"Don't worry," Ponytail replied, "on the civil lawsuits for damages he'll be convicted and have to pay millions."

"But he doesn't have any money."

"Don't worry. The dead's relation's lawyers won't be on a contingency basis but straight fee, so the sick and dead's relatives will pay. Remember the second great unwritten holy law: lawyers always get paid."

Suddenly Bushy ran up to us shouting incoherently, "Kurt Kunster, my best friend, my law partner, my fraternal brother, I can't believe you're one of the ten contemptible shysters suing one of their own, namely me!"

Ponytail, pulling himself up to his full height, replied, "Bushy, you know my motto, there never was a bad suit—yes, there are cheap suits, poorly constructed suits, ugly suits, thin suits, garish suits, frivolous suits, annoying suits, and funny suits—but there is never a suit that doesn't fit me if that suit can be worn with profit."

Nearing the exit, a sinister-looking character sending dark sliding glances through half-closed eyelids slid up to us and said to Bushy, "Hi counselor. You did a good job. They just released me."

Both Bushy and Ponytail looked uncomfortable as they greeted the gentleman they referred to as Snake.

Snake alternately mumbled out one corner of his mouth, then the other, as if he had bad fitting dentures "Bushy, as I told you in our first conference, I did rape and kill those six grammar school girls, and the coppers thought they had me dead to rights, what with DNA and the eyewitnesses to my last foray into exercising my right to my sexual expression of free love. You were my only hope to escape jail time and even the death penalty."

Bushy, a little uncomfortable, explained to me, priest to a novice, "If we are not to become savage barbarians and descend into lawless vigilantism we must insure that every person, no matter their despicable crimes, no matter how sure their guilt, has the best legal representation at his trial. Am I right, Kurt?"

"Absolutely."

"Yeah," Snake agreed, "but it was your pointing out the DNA samples taken from the victim weren't properly labeled 'til two days after my crimes. Being contaminated and with the chain of possession in question, you got them thrown out. Hell, I had to laugh at the victim's relatives screaming in outrage. Guess those ignoramuses have a lot to learn about the law."

Bushy explained to me. "Er, some may say it was just a technicality, but I say, with a man's life at stake, every small and insignificant technicality, no matter how miniscule, becomes an Everest, impossible to ignore. Am I right, Kurt?"

"Absolutely."

Turning to me, Snake amplified. "There I was, fresh from raping and killing this eight year old girl, and the cops breaking in, catching me dead on, naked, standing over her body, confused, so I confessed. Well, Bushy here pointed out the naturally traumatic state I was in, being confronted by the police in such a horrific situation—naked, being yelled at, being called all sorts of nasty names, as well as being horrified myself at the beastly crime I had just committed—I couldn't rationally process my rights as a defendant."

As if it were all a great joke, Snake continued. "Bushy pointed out, being that psychologically damaged and suffering such great humiliation that any normal person would feel in being discovered doing such obscene things to a little girl, it was impossible for me to understand my rights and appreciate the importance of what I was saying."

Bushy, face masked by hair, shuffled his feet and repeated the lawyer's mantra. "Every person charged and tried for a crime deserves the best defense his counsel can muster."

"Look, with double jeopardy protection I can tell you I did it. I'm not proud of it, but hey, different strokes for different folks, know what I'm saying?"

Disgusted, I said, "Different strokes, but only if you don't hurt another person."

Snake looked at me. "I recognize you. You're a foreigner." Then peering at me intently, said, "Now look man, you taking a breath robs me of my air, right?"

I didn't answer.

"Well, anyway you should have seen my counsel here destroy that eyewitness. Anyway, first, he destroyed the ID lineup, pointing out I was the only depraved sex deviant in the lineup. The rest were cops, and everyone knows they stand different, more upright, with more authority in their body language. I was thinking I was dead meat, so I was slouched, looking defeated. In other words, I looked like the guilty murderer of little girls that I was. Bushy was able to show the lineup wasn't fair."

He turned to the lawyer. "Bushy, you had everyone scratching his head with that one. Hey, wasn't it after that bullshit defense of yours when the father of victim jumped over the railing and came at us? I really believed it was you he wanted to beat to a pulp."

Bushy nodded. "Yes, and he got a good punch in before the court guards got him under control. Of course, I'm suing him. Got a permanent limp." Bushy limped in a circle to show us. "Also I suffered psychological damage. I now dread appearing at other trials, in other courts, because I'm fearful of other attacks. I'm representing myself."

Full of pride at Bushy's legal legerdemain, Snake continued. "This great man, this defender of the guilty, showed he was worthy of every penny Legal Land's Public Defender's Fund was paying him to defend me. When he went into my childhood, I looked woe begotten at the jury. When talking about my trauma when my parents' divorced, I cried out, 'Daddy, I needed you! Mommy, I love you!' When he talked about me being bullied at school and being treated differently, I expressed my devastation by wiping away a few tears. When this lawyer of mine went into graphic, heart-rendering details of all the childhood sexual abuse I suffered, I had to cry uncontrollably. Being psychologically scarred I couldn't relate to people. I tell you, given his graphic, heart-ripping descriptions, I almost believed the sexual abuse actually happened. Hell, the members of the jury, empathizing at my supposed beaten, sexually abused, unloved, parentless childhood, were crying harder than I was, and I was on trial for my life. After the trial a matronly woman invited me to stay at her house 'til I could psychologically recover from the trauma of the trial. I might take her up on it, especially if she has any daughters or nieces staying with her."

He turned to his lawyer again and held out a card. "Now Bushy, here's something you may be interested in: the address and number of juror number 7, that gorgeous twenty year old blond who kept smiling at me? She's a little old for my tastes, but you might be interested in—"

Quickly Bushy said, "I don't think we need to go any further," as he palmed the card.

Smiling, Snake continued. "Anyway, Bushy, I can't thank you enough. I was almost put out of action, but now I'm moving into a new neighborhood near the Kinsey Elementary School. If I get into trouble, I definitely feel insanity is still on the table as an unused option."

"Snake, I feel it may be inappropriate to represent you a second time, as I have to defend myself," Bushy said.

"Shit," Snake asked, "what will I do?"

Presenting with a flourish his embossed card, Kurt Kunster said, "My card."

Taking it, Snake mentioned he might need it, saying he had to leave now as he wanted to stock up on chocolate candy and Barbie Dolls.

Outraged, I exclaimed, "You're going to rape and kill more innocent girls?"

"What did you say?" Snake growled. "And who the hell are you again?"

Trying to elevate myself with my official title, I replied with false superiority, "Investigating Visitor Ambassador Extraordinary."

Telling me he wasn't impressed, menacingly Snake said, "Not only an investigator but an extraordinary one. Well Mr. Extraordinary, I take exception to your judgment about me. You know what I think? I think you think too much of yourself, and I think you think you're better than me. Do you think that?"

I was thinking that hidden within all the thinking there was a definite threat, so I cowardly confessed of having no such thoughts.

"You need to be taken down, sliced in half." And he produced a knife of enormous length and started for me, aiming his hard, sharp blade for my very soft important intestines.

There was no defensive reflexive action. Shocked, I gaped, eyeing my oncoming death. After all, who could expect such danger in front of a court of law surrounded by lawyers? I was an inch away from seeing up close and personal my intestines, when suddenly shots were fired. The knife stopped and Snake dropped dead, shot by a raped girl's father.

I was shocked with gratitude and thinking of hugging and kissing the girl's father, but both lawyers were aghast. "Oh heavens! Vigilante justice! Can you imagine such a terrible thing?"

Bushy cried, "This is what happens when people don't listen to the law, don't obey the law, don't respect the law. They take the law into their own hands and out of our capable hands. Hopefully they'll hang the vigilante who dared go outside the law. Vigilantism, the greatest crime of all crimes, leads to lawless chaos."

With prestidigitation worthy of street magicians, they had business cards in hand as they ran to the vigilante. He threw their cards back into their faces, shook his fists at their faces, and cursed to their faces. They simply smiled back at him, magically producing more cards.

My body involuntarily shaking, I had started walking away, too excited to feel tired, hungry or discouraged when Bushy yelled, "Where are you visiting next?"

"The Rights Land, " I said.

"Fantastic! Can I accompany you there? It's a wonderful land. Lawyers being sued often migrate to Rights Land. They do things the right way there and I need to get away from the distractions caused by these ridiculous, trivial, incestuous lawsuits against me."

As Bushy and I hastily made our way to Legal Land's boundary, we approached a group of five people deep in conversation. They were so engrossed in their discussion, they seemed oblivious of our approach and, blocking our way, forced us to step down to the gutter.

As we passed them, a woman of mature years and a mature figure screamed a sound reminiscent of nails on blackboards, while teetering, arms flaying, and doing a couple of exotic half-turns before falling gracefully on a patch of grass ten feet away.

After everyone finished observing and appreciating the performance, I became the center of attention. Between sobs of pain and howls of agony the mature woman with shaking hand pointed at me shouted, "He pushed me! In his hurry he pushed me, and I'm suffering back injuries! Permanent, paralyzing back injuries!" She magically produced a neck brace.

Seeing her sitting on an ample rump, hearing her lusty continuous screams of pain and shouts of accusation, I doubted the seriousness of her injuries. Besides, I never touched her, and the theatrical dance of injury was so pathetically false, no one could or would believe her. I accused her of acting. I excused myself from any fault, stating that I had never touched her, never mind push her to the ground.

The remaining group of four split into two groups. The two women ran to the screeching mature-figured invalid, adding their cries of alarm to hers.

The two men of the group approached me, shouting their outrage over my reckless, careless disregard for an elderly, overweight, frail Dagmar and saying that it would cost me dearly. One told me he was a lawyer, and not surprisingly, his companion, in threatening tones, acknowledged he was also one, and suddenly two embossed business cards found their way between my fingers.

"We saw what you did," one said.

"Total disregard for poor Dagmar's safety," the other said, while both stated only a civil trial for damages could teach me the important lesson of respecting women of mature age suffering weight challenges.

I turned to Bushy for reaffirmation of my total innocence.

Being embroiled in frivolous lawsuits himself, he said he couldn't personally stay and defend me, but asking if my country would pay for my defense. "If so, I can administer your defense from Rights Land through a surrogate legal team."

One of the ministering women, wiping her tears, explained she was Venus, the victim's best friend and a court bailiff, and being an officer of the court she placed me under arrest.

"This is a scam!" I gasped as I grasped the situation.

"Scam! Scam!" they all repeated in horror and disbelief.

Bushy said, "It can only be a scam if, after your trial, your innocence has been determined, and then after the trial of those you accuse of scamming you is over, and they're found guilty of scamming you. Of course, if they are found innocent, they can sue you for accusing them of scamming you, and if found guilty, you would be fined treble damages. Of course you could appeal the verdict, and if you're lucky and the verdict is overturned, you could have a retrial and then—"

One of the men smiled at Bushy, "Sir, you show a deep grasp of the law. Could you possibly be a lawyer, a member of the bar, a fellow of our sacred fraternity?"

"My card," Bushy said, and miraculously each of the lawyers were holding the others' cards.

Venus, the court bailiff, grabbed me by my arm with the strength of one grabbing hold of a fortune, and more in surprise than actual pain I cried out.

Like a war-horse hearing the bugle sounding charge, Bushy turned to me stating, "Do I hear pain? Do my ears reverberate with sounds of distress?" and with reflexive action I had his card as well as all the other lawyers' cards.

Knowing enough of Legal Land to realize I was caught up in legal ensnarement and could easily spend the rest of my life in perpetual motion traveling between lawyers' offices to courtrooms and back again and dropping a fortune on each ride on Legal Land's merry-go-round, I decided to act and how to act. Vibrating from toe to hair, I landed on the ground, rolled about and cried out, "I've lost all feeling in my arm!" I let it dangle to my side, then pointed with my good hand at Venus and accused her of using excessive brutal force resulting in serious nerve damage, causing my hand to be permanently paralyzed.

Standing up I suddenly felt the nerves in my neck go numb and my head uselessly drop off to my shoulder. As they stared open-eyed at me, I dropped my other arm and letting it wave jerkily at my side and cried out, "There goes my right hand! Oh my gosh! I feel my left leg is starting to go, as well as control of my bladder." Again I fell to the ground and, if I do say so myself, with much more conviction than stupid Dagmar. On the ground twitching as if possessed by a thousand demons, I shouted at Venus, "I'll sue you!" and to her horror she miraculously found three legal business cards in her hand.

Dagmar was now sitting up with open-mouth appreciation at my performance.

I yelled at her too. "And I'll sue *you* for being the proximate cause of my condition." Just like that, she had three cards in her lap. Finally, I turned to the lawyers. "I'm going to call all of you as witnesses in my lawsuit, and being my witnesses it would be a conflict of interest if you represented Dagmar in her suit against me." With sudden inspiration, I continued. "And of course, I'll sue Legal Land for hundreds of millions."

Dagmar, the sudden recipient of a miraculous cure worthy of earning someone sainthood, her neck brace gone, was jogging away. When I asked Venus for her last name, badge number, and address, she averred: she had no name, no badge number, and didn't live anywhere. In fact, she wasn't there. And she quickly ran after Dagmar.

The lawyers, with bad grace, mumbling to themselves as they debated whether they could sue me for their loss of a profitable lawsuit before acknowledging defeat, departed as well, leaving Bushy and me to continue our journey.

Angrily I observed to Bushy, "There's no system of justice, it's only a legal system, and the two systems are poles apart. Justice is inversely proportional to the size of the legal system. The more laws, the less justice; the more legal precedent, the less truth; the more erudite the lawyers, the less common sense; the more numerous the lawyers, the less rational the discourse."

Bushy sighed. "Obviously you don't have a legal mind."

AFTER LEGAL LAND

Returning to my two-room suite (still thanks to your dime), I was shocked to find no letter or text messages from Pru or Rudy. Accustomed to their interest in me, and after my experiences in Legal Land, I needed that interest. Showering to cleanse the law from every pore and hair follicle, I was numb with shock at what they hadn't sent. Dressing, stepping out of numbness, I rediscovered my deep disappointment and personal aggrievement from receiving no communicational support.

After the hurt of being let down by my love and my best friend, I analyzed the messages conveyed by no messages. The absence of Pru's letter was the one I intently read and reread the most; the letter not sent carries more meaning than a dozen letters sent. (Ah, the world of metacommunication.) Feeling alone in foreign lands, I tried to find excuses for her to keep her needed structural support. Being 'too busy' was the excuse I resurrected, only to be ruthlessly buried by my ego's questions: if I was so important to her, shouldn't she find the time to write? If she really wanted me to succeed, shouldn't the demands of her everyday life take on secondary importance to supporting me in my work? If my plans for our future together were hers, shouldn't they bind her tight to me and cause her to want to minister to my needs? If I'm here in a room alone, discouraged from my visits, shouldn't she expend a little effort to write and raise my spirits? If we're connected by true love, shouldn't she understand my needs without having them expressed? If in her heart our love is supreme, shouldn't everything else be unessential? If she loves me, shouldn't she realize, even at an intuitive level, that a letter from her is critical for my well-being? Her conscious or unconscious lack of consideration was undermining my work, our love, and our future together and forcing me to doubt, fear, be isolated, and mistrust. All these thoughts forced me into a mental black room with only loneliness for company.

Self-pity struggled with justified anger. The conflict continued without resolution. Each, in turn, won a round, but neither could win the fight, possibly because each supported the other. I was becoming mentally exhausted with entertaining the draining mental conflicts of why, being innocent, I should experience hurt so severe. Becoming temporarily bored with constantly traveling between now-familiar reasons to be disappointed and angry with Pru, I turned to Rudy.

Feeling justified in feeling betrayed by his lack of a letter, my disappointment and anger was dampened and difficult to keep ignited. In a wet cloud of honesty, my difficult self-admission was that if our positions were reversed, my commitment to him would probably be less rather than more. Still the overall message I took from his no message was a deep sense of betrayal accompanied by additional heavy feelings of loneliness. The world and everyone in it were separated from me; a chasm had opened between me and all those out there. A sense of me against them took hold, reinforcing the belief that the only one I could count on is myself. I must say such thoughts did contain sweetness for the ego.

Fearful of going too far in severing the threads of my connection with Pru and Rudy, I had to entertain recurring thoughts: my outrage was an overreaction; enjoying my outrage injected into my hurt feelings a sense of hypocrisy.

With food so far from my mind, I went directly to the hotel bar for a needed pick me up, or a sorry-for-me or damn-everyone-and-everything drink. Staring at the just-arrived second drink, I was bursting with newfound magnanimity; even though my anger was justified, I forgave their betrayal. Midway into the second drink, I suspected I was making too much of the non-messages; being too sensitive, my reaction was unjustified, and everything between the three of us was as it was.

Staring at the third drink I was angry—so angry I was ready to tell Pru the marriage was off but I hadn't actually proposed yet. The snake in the grass Rudy could go to hell for all I cared and I'd tell him off when I see him. At the fourth drink inexplicably I formed a deep friendship with an understanding gentleman who had been imbibing next to me. He completely understood my situation, sympathized with my hurt feelings, supported my anger, and, though not really grasping his personal problems, I returned appreciation for all of his difficulties. While we were in good companionship and vigorously arguing over who should buy the next round, he was called away by a friend. We parted with a firm handshakes and a feeling of strong brotherhood.

Ordering my... er, whatever the number, I began to ruminate over Sunni and her fight with Hinki. With their separation I had hopes to supplant him. Then they came in, excited over something. Noting Sunni holding Hinki's arm, I felt alone again. I also noted Hinki was surreptitiously carrying something covered with a napkin. It took a few minutes of concentrating on their excited ramblings before I realized they were vibrating over food. The Limbo bar measuring my opinion of the two reached a new low when Hinki removed the napkin with a flourish to reveal a fork they had stealthy pilfered from the dining room. With one hand—all feeling had left it at the third drink—I tried to reach for the fork only to be denied by Sunni. As if protecting her first born, she yelled for me not to touch the fork. Hinki asked me if I knew what he was holding.

"A fork wrapped in a napkin," was my literal answer. "Look, let me buy you two a drink (your dime), and we can talk, or more accurately talk about the bad no news I just received." I had to admit that last didn't sound right.

They were so socially inept, so wrapped up in themselves; I didn't get into my bad no news. Hinki waved the fork in front of my face and Sunni's purple fingernail pointed to something green between the tines.

"What in the hell?" was my natural response.

Sunni announced, "A million dollars, right Hinki?"

"Could be ten million."

After staring at it, I told them it was a piece of lettuce. Satisfied at my observation, I took a sip of my drink, which surprisingly I found already in my hand.

Sunni said, "Let's take another picture with Peoples holding it. He can be our witness."

"Witness for what?" I said.

Hinki added, "Peoples, would you be willing to sign an affidavit as to what you see on this fork?" Then he glanced at his partner in upcoming crime. "Shit Sunni, where can we find a notary at this hour?"

"The hotel clerk should know," Sunni said.

"Say Peoples, put your drink down. It's in the camera frame. Your affidavit would be meaningless if it was shown you were drunk when signing it," Hinki said.

Putting the drink down, I said, "I'm not drunk and it's only a little piece of lettuce."

Sunni took a picture of Hinki holding the fork close against my face.

Turning to retrieve my drink, I was surprised to see the glass empty. I knew I must have finished the drink, but when? It was a mystery. As the bartender was putting my fifth... sixth?—er, never mind, the number doesn't matter—Sunni asked the bartender if he could notarize my signature on the fork's picture.

Looking at her as if she was on her tenth, he declined and quickly found business farther down the bar. Hinki took more pictures of the fork with a front view, a side view, a back view, a close-up view, and an enlarged view of a piece of lettuce the size of which an ant could carry away.

Having come from Legal Land I had an idea of where they were going with this lettuce piece.

With an eye to future rewards for damages, Sunni said the fork was her utensil. To justify his claim, Hinki said he was the first to spot the errant lettuce on the fork. "We're going to go fifty-fifty, right Sunni?"

Fearful of committing herself to a verbal contract before a third party, Sunni ignored the fifty-fifty by asking me how much they should sue the hotel for such a dangerous health violation.

With my squinting at it and sensing my confusion, she explained how big the lettuce was, how old it was, how diseased it was. Hinki explained the health danger the lettuce posed, maintaining it could have easily fatally poisoned unsuspecting Sunni if he hadn't discovered it.

"I was so shocked at finding the dirty utensil that I couldn't eat," Sunni added.

Hinki added, "Neither could I. Who knows how many putrid poisons we'd consume while eating our dinner if I hadn't spotted the lettuce?"

An excited Sunni said, "We could have already been poisoned from unwashed utensils."

Hinki interrupted to recount how the waiter had tried to forcibly take the fork from them and substitute a clean one. "And Peoples, his apology wasn't very convincing. Probably filthy utensils and dishes occur often, poisoning customers. There might already be a class-action suit. It's an outrage."

Carefully raising my new drink I said, "It certainly is; it's all outrageous."

Making sure the fork and the residing lettuce was never in reach of Hinki, Sunni exclaimed, "If the dinnerware is so filthy, can you imagine the horror residing in the kitchen? I'm sure they spit into the soup."

Hinki emphatically declared how lucky they were to have several cards from lawyers living in Legal Land.

As they were walking to the hotel office, they were busy arguing over which lawyer was best and how much could they expect to get, and a worried Hinki, still making fifty-fifty talk, received no confirmation. Being so close to each other I suspected they would share a bed, if not tonight, certainly before our visitations ended.

Finishing my drink, I noted the empty glasses reflected my emptiness, and I went to the elevator with a body as unsteady as my undernourished body and emotions allowed.

2

Rights Land

My initial naïve idea of this Land was gleamed from their country's name, that here things were right, and being such, after my previous visit fiascoes, I would finally learn valuable positive information to report to my country.

So far all my visits had given me was a list of things not to do, because if done, they would lead to chaos, misery, poverty, injustice, and bigotry, the exact opposite of what they were trying to achieve. And the amazing thing was the believers' stubborn blindness to their disasters. Like socialists, after years of socialism and in the midst of one's destitute country reduced to begging for money from capitalists, they stubbornly maintain that despite the evidence, they have the better economic system and capitalism is a failure.

And they say people are rational.

"Hi sweetie," someone yelled at me, interrupting my reverie as I viewed a man coming toward me, or more correctly, bouncing toward me, hand waving, wearing a generous, brilliant smile and absolutely nothing else, with you know what bouncing up and down out of sync with his feet.

Looking down in shock, then quickly looking up, looking down in disbelief, then quickly looking up, then looking down in disgust, then quickly looking up, and with his lower hair coming closer, he forced me to back up and talk to the space over and to the right of his shoulder.

"I'm Butterfly, your guide to Rights Land."

"You're naked!" was my reflexive response.

"Well, yeah, but you shouldn't notice. Your noticing makes me feel uncomfortable."

"You're privates are painted silver."

"Well, yeah, like hi ho silver and away we go. Does it disturb you?"

Politeness be damned. I said, "It's revolting! It's disgusting!"

"Well, it's out of the closet; deal with it," he said, giggling.

"Is your name really Butterfly?"

"Why not? I have the Right to call myself anything I wish, and I wish Butterfly. If it bothers you, tough."

"Look, you're obviously in your sixties and grossly overweight, should you be going around naked, painting your privates, calling yourself Butterfly?"

"I'm a nudist. The human body is a thing of beauty and we shouldn't be ashamed of it. Listen young man, you should be strong enough in your own sexuality to shed your own hateful sexual phobias and be exalted in the right to being sexually free."

"You're so fat you've got breasts. You lost your ass, got fat hanging from your arms and skinny, varicose-vein legs. To be honest, your body is ugly."

"To you it might seem so, but to me, I'm beautiful," and with that he twirled around so I could better appreciate his backside.

"Look, I really don't see how you and I can function together. Could you see about arranging a guide who wears clothes and is less... er, flamboyant?"

"Look, your negativity is hurting my feelings and that's just not right. In Rights Land the only rule we have is you're always right. You can't be not right. Everything is right in Rights Land."

"What the hell are you saying?"

"In Rights Land it's wrong to say something is not right or even imply something may not be right."

Getting used to talking to the air above and to the right of his ear, I said, "Look, let's get started. Maybe after seeing your institutions and learning about your social mores I'll be better able to grasp your meaning."

"Fair enough," he agreed, then suggested we hold hands while walking.

"No! Good heavens, no," I emphatically staid to his shoulder, taking three giant backward steps.

He sighed. "Visitors are always uptight." He added, "I have a right to hold hands with whomever I wish, and you have the right to refuse, unless, by refusing you're implying you think it wouldn't be right to hold my hand, and in Rights Land that kind of thinking is wrong and hurtful. So do you want to hurt me?"

"No, certainly not."

"Good. Let's hold hands, and besides making me feel better, you'll experience a wonderful sense of freedom."

"Forget holding hands," I forcibly told him.

"Possibly you don't realize it, but you're being judgmental as well as being hurtful. You had better realize in Rights Land no one has the right to make negative judgments or comments about others. Negative judgments are hurtful to others and therefore not right, therefore not allowed in Rights Land. In addition, Mr. IV Peoples, there isn't a more grievous sin than making judgments about another. Your 'I'm right in judging your wrong' implies the existence of inequality among people, which is just wrong, hurtful and elitist."

"Look, your ugly nude body disgusts me, your silver-painted accoutrements and our holding hands are perversions, and your justifications are ridiculous."

Aghast, with tears flowing, Butterfly shouted, "In Rights Land there are no perversions and nothing is ridiculous, and now you're making me cry and I'm going! I've got to get back to the synagogue and conduct services. Although I'm not Jewish, I'm the head rabbi."

As he bounced off, turning he yelled back he had the right to show me his hairy backside.

Thinking it would take several whiskeys to wash his image in all its disgusting shapes from my mind, I decided to wait only an hour for a new guide. If one was not forthcoming, I would simply leave, go back and see how Sunni and Hinki were making out.

Forty minutes passed before a new guide came forth. With a welcoming smile and his hand extended, a strange stranger came up to me dressed in a black leather, sleeveless, unbuttoned vest and matching tight leather pants and combat boots. His colored blond curly hair chest escaped out the sides of the vest and atop his head was a sweat-stained cowboy hat. His face was adorned with lip rings, nose rings, eyebrow rings, and earrings, and hanging from his nipples were more rings.

He said, "Hey man, you da man I show?"

For a fearful moment I thought he was talking about showing himself.

Angrily he observed, "You're staring at my tattoos! They bother you?"

His arms, neck, chest were ablaze with undecipherable pictures, names, sayings that had as their motif death, hate, devil worship and his undying love for Mother and someone named Daisy.

He noticed my distaste for such a pitiful display. It was as if he were advertising that beneath the vulgar skin canvas lived a great loser who unconsciously advertises his empty self with a loser's pride: "I'm a nothing and proud of it."

He continued. "My dress bothers you, my tattoos disturb you, my rings and jewelry distress you?"

Suffering hunger pains, I was in no mood for politeness. I said, "Yes."

Taken back, expecting politeness, which would enable him to be able to attack me as being hypocritical, now he was forced to defend himself. "I've got a right to dress anyway I like and if you don't like it tough."

Despite my hunger I felt combatant. "Certainly in Rights Land I have the right to object to the way you dress."

"No way, man. You can't object either by word, deed, look or thought because by objecting to my appearance you're committing mortal offenses in Rights Land. "One," and he held up his right middle finger, "by objecting you are denying my right to dress as I please, which is not doing the right thing in Rights Land. Objecting to someone else doing what he or she wants is not permitted if it doesn't hurt anyone. Second," and the middle left finger came vertical, "by objecting you reveal yourself to be a judgmental, closed-minded up-tight clothes bigot, and that type of person is always in the wrong. Finally," he shouted while vigorously waving both middle fingers at me, "you hurt my feelings! You've made me feel bad, and even worse, different. You can't imply there are right or wrong ways to dress and act because there isn't any wrong way to dress.

"Now, I'm leaving. No way am I going to guide such a clothes prejudiced bigot. Wait about another hour and maybe another guide will be sent. For your information, I've got to get back to my students. I'm the Contemporary Morals and Ethics professor at Rights University."

It was either I turn back to the Legal Land and try to purchase food and aspirin from an uninsured, uninspected, illegal, under the table purveyor or hope for a normal guide. *Certainly people other than freaks must inhabit Rights Land.*

While I was sitting on a stone, one hand holding my throbbing head and the other rubbing a stomach bloated by hunger, who should stroll up but Bushy, briefcase in hand, complaining. "Damn those cannibal lawyers! In Legal Land they're running out of people to sue and now they're turning on their own. I decided it was best to leave. Screw their summonses, liens, dispositions, and orders to appear. Here they can't find me and in the Rights Land, you have the right to ignore other countries' legal papers. Bless Rights Land," he said and looked at the ground as if debating whether it was worth a kiss. Deciding it wasn't he suggested we walk together to the city. He pulled a couple of apples from his briefcase and offered me one, explaining that while escaping from Legal Land he purchased them from an illegal fruit vendor hiding behind a bush. "The legal stuff is damn expensive." Then he said that after he'd made the purchase, he'd served the seller with legal papers notifying him he was suing him for selling food without a license, without inspection, without refrigeration, without insurance, without—well, I suspect all these subtle legal matters can seem complicated to the lay person." In the end he suggested after eating the apple I should complain of an upset stomach, fever, nausea, and loss of sex drive on a notarized affidavit he'd provide. "Food poisoning is a fantastic moneymaker for all concerned."

In the disadvantaged (not right to say slum, so the inhabitants wouldn't feel bad realizing they lived in a slum) section of the city in Rights Land we saw a policeman stopping a transaction of the oldest profession progressing in an alley.

"Look!" Bushy cried with joy. "Business before our very eyes!" He ran to the three—the policeman in uniform, the other two partially dressed, all loudly arguing points of rights—and pushed them aside.

Between them he yelled at the policeman, "You can't stop her from selling her body, she's got a right to do with her body whatever she wishes, and she's decided to rent it by the hour."

"By the minute," she said.

Bushy continued. "And this gentleman has the right of purchase. This is a marketplace transaction, which is the basic right of business."

To the woman, Bushy said, "My dear, my card. On a contingency basis I'll be glad to defend you, to champion your right to your body against the horrendous assaults by the Gestapo State. We'll sue for millions." Turning to the seedy looking man who was lighting up a crack pipe, Bushy extended his card as well. "The state had no right to interrupt you before the climax of your business, leaving you so shattered, unfulfilled, and frustrated that you're turning to drugs for relief. Certainly you deserve a substantial monetary recompense."

"I'm out ten bucks," he said.

"Oh yes, but even more for the mental and physical anguish you're currently suffering. I'm thinking millions. You have your rights, and I for one will not tolerate any right being abrogated."

Turning to the policeman, who was busily writing out a citation, Bushy offered to defend him against these two frivolous lawsuits by countersuing the woman and her client for millions.

When the cop explained that neither he nor they had any money, Bushy patiently explained, "The City will pay for your defense, and you'll sit on your ass at full pay for years while the trial goes through the courts. After all, you've got rights. And," Bushy said as the policeman was looking hard at the crack pipe being passed between the two business associates, "don't interfere with people enjoying recreational drugs. They have a right to do what they deem is right unless they're hurting another person. Am I right or am I right?"

"You're right," they echoed, and we left the buyer and seller arguing over the business ethics of refunds as the policeman angrily tore up his citation.

Smiling, Bushy crowed, "Hah! In Rights Land, who protects those rights?"

"Lawyers," I said.

"And who extends those rights?"

"Lawyers and the judges who are lawyers."

"Breathe the air. It's lawyers' air. You have a right to it," Bushy cried.

He expanded on the right to use drugs and share drugs, as they hurt no one. The right for people to have the state provide a safe place for drug use, a convenient marketplace to buy and sell safe drugs, but only sell in small quantities for personal use. Small amounts are okay, especially for medical use.

A drunk staggered up to us and, sticking out a dirty hand, demanded money.

"Get a job," I said, trying to go past him.

Grabbing my arm standing inches from me breathing into my nose bad liquor and vomit through toothless gums he argued, "Hey, I've got a right to live, I've got a right to food, I've got a right to the money I need for food. I'm a citizen of Rights Land."

Standing well to the side, Bushy explained to me, "Certainly you'll agree he has a right to life, liberty and happiness. If you deprive him of needed money he hasn't the liberty to purchase happiness and without the wherewithal he can't eat and will die and therefore lose the right to life."

I backed away from the bum's fumes, fanning the air with my hands.

"Hey," the drunk cried, eyeing my hand motion, "are you trying to dis me, saying my breath is bad? You have no right to do that."

"You have bad breath and I don't want to breathe it."

"Woo!" Bushy cried out in horror. "You can't do that, offend another person with your own prejudices. He's got the right to exhale bad breath, and can you absolutely prove it's bad breath or is it just your snotty nose experiencing prejudice against the man's fragrant odor?"

"Yeah, but don't I have the right not to smell it?"

"Certainly, but if in exercising your right by stepping back and fanning the air you disrespect him and hurt his feelings, you implicitly deny his right to bad breath. My dear innocent, you must tread with care in Rights Land. By visibly indicating your judgmental attitude, you indicated not only was his breath bad but that you were too good to breathe it, saying in effect you're better than him. In Rights Land, all having the same rights, all being equal. No one is better, no one is worse, and you can't imply by word or action, that you're better than anyone else."

"Yeah, Mr. Bigshot. Give me some money. I'm hungry," bad breath said.

Adamantly I told him, "I'm not giving you a damn thing."

The bum became outraged at my refusal. "I'm hungry! You've got to give me some money! It's only right. It's my right living in Rights Land."

I was thinking, Hell, *I've only had that illegal apple and could use a meal myself,* so I told both Bushy and the bum to drop dead. Bushy and the bum got excited at that with the bum pulling a screwdriver out of his sock to threaten me. Holding it by the metal end and pointing the handle at me, he diluted much of his threat.

Like a prize fighter, he was trying to bounce from foot to foot but with each shift of the weight, the bounce turned into several staggering steps in one direction. Intellectual people of higher sophistication and better judgment would describe the stagger as a dance. Unsuccessfully trying to stay in my immediate vicinity, he screamed, "He pushed me, trying to make me fall! He's not standing still, so he's cheating, and that's not right!"

Bushy, now standing like any good lawyer right behind me, said, "Damn it, give him some money."

"Why the hell should I?"

"Though you do have a right to your money, there are restrictions. In Rights Land, the right to your money is not solely your right. In this instance he has a right to live, you have a right to your money. Now which is the superseding right? Your money or his life? Can you morally deny that his right predominates? So social justice and human rights demand you must give him some money. Hopefully you're not so morally callous as to see a fellow human dying of starvation and not extend a helping hand. That wouldn't be right."

"He'll just spend it on booze."

"That's his right. You have no right to say how he should spend his money."

"But it's my money."

"Not after you give it to him; then it's his money, and he has the right to spend it as he sees fit."

"But to give him money is enabling him to destroy himself."

"Look, he has the right to live his life as he sees fit, and I think it's presumptuous of you to think you know better how he should live his life. You don't know what his personal needs are. Now Mr. IV Peoples, I'm sorry to have to say you are not only very judgmental and selfishly materialistic but also suffer from a 'know it all' self-conceit."

"Screw you," I told Bushy, and told the bum again to drop dead. I gave him a push in mid-bounce (stagger), sending him into a wall, which he tried hugging before sliding down.

Walking away I turned to see Bushy whispering to him and putting his card in the bum's hand.

When Bushy reached me I accused him of trying to get the bum to sue me.

"Heh, heh, nothing personal, but in refusing him money you did contribute to his hunger, causing him physical pain. You did show bad breath prejudice causing him mental anguish, and in pushing him into that wall caused him grievous bodily harm, probably leading to permanent physical disabilities that will interfere with the possibility of his pursuing a career in astrophysics, and remember, I have a witness."

"Who?"

"Me."

We had traversed barely a block when a woman of full of figure and full of makeup came up to us dragging six children ages two to twenty.

"I need money," she said. "I know you have it and I have a right to it."

Startled, begging her pardon I asked, "Who the hell are you?"

"A single mother!" she shouted, and shouted the 'single' as if it was worth a Nobel Prize and the word explained everything. She continued. "A single mother fighting for the rights her children have."

With the previous encounters in mind I pointed out they all looked well fed, thinking *Over fed would be more accurate.* I left it at just well fed.

"It's not food, but clothes. They have a right to be clothed."

Again I pointed out that all six looked well dressed, thinking *Possibly overdressed, especially the mother.*

"Certainly they are clothed, but how are they dressed?" Grabbing the twelve year old she pointed at his sneakers. "Look! Just look! Those sneakers aren't Michael Jordan's! They're cheap no-name sneakers!"

I foolishly said, "And...?"

"He's ashamed, and I'm ashamed. Certainly we have a right to be dressed as well as everyone else. We have a right to self-respect, and how can we exercise our clothes rights if everyone has two hundred dollar sneakers, and my poor boy is embarrassed to wear Wal-Mart twenty dollar ones? He cries at night, I cry at night, we all cry over the denial of our rights. How can he play basketball with cheap sneakers? Oh, the psychological damage done, as well as ruining his chances of playing in the NBA!"

Grabbing her sixteen year old daughter she pointed at the her brief skirt, near bikini in material, and covering just as much. The mother said, "That skirt is not a Britney Spears skirt. It's- it's- it's Wal-Mart cheap! It's a knock off!" Then she moaned, "Oh, the psychological damage done!"

Agreeing with the cheap word if not with her meaning, I said, "It's certainly cheap."

"She's ashamed to go to school because all the girls say she's cheap because she dresses cheap. She cries at night, I cry at night, we all cry at night. How can she go to school and become an honor roll student dressed in Wal-Mart clothes? She has a right to be dressed like everyone else, lest we suffer serious psychological damage and blighted futures, so give me some clothes money."

"Certainly not," I said. This was getting ridiculous.

"Look," she said. "I'll let you off the hook for the sneakers and the skirt." She grabbed a surly youth smoking something that affects the mind, but thank goodness not evil tobacco that affected the lungs. Dragging him to the fore she said, "He has a right to an education. You have a duty to give him the money for college."

Looking at the sleepy eyes, the slouchy posture, and the funny looking butt he was holding with a toothpick, sucking at it as if it contained the world's only air, I hazarded a guess. "Does he have the grades to get into college?"

"Bah," she brushed that aside. "The college recognizes how unjust it is that because of his lack of money he didn't receive the personal tutoring he needed in high school, tutoring he had every right to receive. So the college, to rectify this injustice, waived admission standards as well as his tuition, and they will supply tutors."

"If that's so, why are you begging me for money?"

"Living expenses. He has a right to live just like all those rich paying students, doesn't he? And don't be mistaken, I'm not begging. I'm not a beggar; I'm demanding my rights. Remember, he has the right not to be embarrassed, the right not to feel inferior. He needs beer and pizza money so when all his friends go out partying, he can go with them, buy his fair share, and hold his head up high. So give me some money for my son's education."

"I certainly will not and I suggest your son seek part-time employment if he wants beer and pizza money."

I walked away quickly, with her shouting at my back, "You reactionary bastard, for the sake of mere money you deny my son his basic right to a complete education!"

After giving her his card, Bushy caught up to me. "She should sue the university. Imagine short-changing that poor boy. Besides supplying free tuition, room and board, books, special tutors, certainly, pocket money is needed so he can participate in and experience the full college experience.

"What rights have the poor if not the rights to live like the rich? If you can't live like the rich, your rights are empty, just vacuous phantoms. We'll—er, *she'll*—win millions in her suit." Bushy orated with the pompous smile of one who's fighting against injustice done to the poor and for the rights of the downtrodden and who expects to win big money for everyone, especially the main one.

We had not gone more than two blocks when a bizarre, middle-aged man wearing only shorts approached us demanding money.

"Drop dead," I said, seeing that he seemed healthy and able bodied.

"I need money for tattoos," was his reply and certainly he had them, from neck to toes. On each cheek he had bleeding daggers, and across his forehead was the word *chaos*.

"You have tattoos," I said.

"Yeah stupid, I want money to get rid of them. You know, laser treatments. They're damn expensive, so give me some money."

"Look, you're healthy. Work, save some money and pay for the treatments yourself."

"Can't. I want to be a Wall Street financial advisor. It's a matter of social justice that I have the right to practice the profession of my choice. I'm denied my rights because of these tattoos. Apparently people lose interest in having me handle their money because of these hands," and he showed the top of his hands. One displayed the word *kill* and the other, *riot*. Miniature assault rifles covered his thumbs.

"Can you grasp the prejudice, the ugly bigotry against tattooed people who have both the right to their tattoos as well as the right to work at jobs they like and the right to have people not see tattoos in a negative way? It's a matter of social justice. Beneath my tattoos I'm one hell of a financially responsible family type guy.

"Hey, just because I have no experience, no education, and some minor felony drug convictions is no reason for me to be denied my rights to my chosen career. Out of social justice give me, say, a thousand. That will help me laser erase the daggers."

"Look, you can drop dead for all I care," and I walked away only to be stopped a few hundred yards later by another strange person. Guessing from experience I said, "No money."

"I need tattoos," he said. "Do I or do I not have a right to tattoos?"

"I suppose you have that right if you're too stupid not to realize you're a loser and sufficiently stupid to want to announce the fact you're a loser and obtain indelible marks announcing the fact."

He ignored my brief editorial. "What good is having the right if you lack the financial means to act on your right? If the lack of money prohibits you acting on your right, you're basically denied your rights and in fact you don't have rights, which isn't right."

Amused, I agreed.

"So," he said, "if from social justice I have a right to a tattoo, that right implies the right to *get* a tattoo, which leads to the right of having the money to get the tattoo. Now lightly skipping over those solid logical stepping stones of rights leads us to my right to get money from you for tattoos, so give me some money."

Before I could tell him and his social justice theory to get lost, the tattooed man came up repeating his demand for laser money, calling me a tattoo bigot and mentioning one of his felony convictions was for beating the shit out of a cheap tattoo hater.

A crowd was gathering, all yelling curses that I wouldn't support the rights of people, that I was bigoted, didn't believe in social justice, and suffered from numerous phobias and that I should give everyone all my money as they all had the social right to satisfy their needs, and that was only social justice.

Especially annoying was a midget who, constantly banging on my knees, demanded my money for basketball lessons, saying he had a right to be a professional basketball player. There were several women demanding money for breast implants, as well as some demanding nose jobs or wanting liposuction or sandpapering their skin or get pouty lips as they all had the social right to look MTV sexy. In addition the group needing to exercise their rights to wear makeup demanded lipstick money, and when they finally look hot, they would need birth control money..

Bushy, pushing his way into the center of the angry rights people and while passing out his business cards faster than a Vegas Twenty One dealer shouted, "Law suits!"

In chorus they gleefully yelled, "Sue! Sue!" as if at a rap concert. While the crowd was distracted in grabbing for Bushy's cards and visions of free money, I was able to escape. I ran down the street 'til the lack of breath, and my head and stomach aches brought me to a halt. Leaning against the wall, a few paces from me was a seedy looking black who, glancing sideways, said, "Money" and put his palm out.

"Why?" I panted.

"I'm black," he said, shaking his hand impatiently.

"So?"

"You're white."

"Yes."

"Social justice. Give me some money."

Returning to my starting point, I again asked, "Why?"

Pushing off the wall he angrily turned to face me. "Reparation rights."

"What reparations?"

"Slavery reparations."

I said, "Yeah? Well only after you pay death benefits for my ancestors who died fighting to free your ancestor's sorry butts."

"Hey, you can't say that to a proud African American. That's not right. You better watch out, and just give me money."

"I have no intention of giving you any of my money, and screw your reparations."

"Hey man, you say that again and I'll have to do it to you. I'll have no choice because you asked for it."

"Asked for what?"

"To be branded with the hateful stigma, to be labeled an inhuman beast, to be placed in the land of the eternally despised."

"What the hell are you talking about?"

"About? About? I'm talking about racism. Don't you realize if you don't give me, a black man, money, out of social justice I'll have to label you a racist? Now give me some money. I'm getting angry and very close to throwing racist at you."

From his strange world somehow he expected a fearful response from me to his name calling threat, accompanied by my fulsome responses of denials, apologizes and certainly immediate offers of money. All I gave him was, "Drop dead."

"You asked for it," and backing away to give greater space to his words, pointing at me he cried out, "You're a racist! You won't give money to a black man and you told a proud black man to drop dead!" Looking about he yelled, "Oh where are the civil rights lawyers? Where's the NAACP when you need them."

Smelling a fearful lawsuit, I said, "Why should I give you money?"

"Because my great, great, great grandfather was a slave and we've been deprived of my rights and therefore, in Rights Land I have special super rights, so give me all your money and I won't call you a racist. In fact I'll call you a friend of blacks and, if you give me a *lot* of money I'll call you a Clinton black. Can't be fairer than that."

Exasperated, I said, "Look for all I care you can call me racist, bigot and whatever, but screw you, I'm not giving you any of my money."

Puffing mightily, Bushy, coming up in time to hear the last of our dialogue, wordlessly gave the black guy his card. He gasped, "Sue... discrimination... millions." Then he pulled me away with a face as white as death, and in horrific tones, said, "A black called you a racist! You realize how dangerous that is? If that got around you'd be socially shunned, financially ruined, possibly jailed, and certainly sued."

In response I told him I wanted to get out of Rights Land as soon as possible.

Disagreeing, he said, "Personally I'm setting up my practice here. Lots of good legal work needs to be done in defending people's God given rights and defending the cause of social justice in the name of equality."

"Screw social justice, whatever that is. What say we get something to eat?"

My stomach was gaily frolicking with anticipation as we entered a restaurant and sat in a booth.

The waitress carelessly slid the menu at me. Scanning it again as in Health Land I saw no meat. "There're no meat items," I said both to her and to a very disappointed stomach that stopped its anticipatory frolicking and was now angrily staring at its lining in disappointment.

"Hey," she said, "animal rights. They have the right to life just the same as you. They feel, they love, they breathe free air and they have rights just like you and me."

"Ah, but they don't vote," I maliciously said.

Somberly she said, "It will come. The right people are working on it and believe me, it will be a better country when horses and cows finally have the right to vote."

"No fish dishes?" I noted aloud.

"Right to life," she said.

"The vegetable items... the pasta entrees are all very expensive. In fact they're exorbitant."

"They're organic."

"Organic?"

"Sure. My children, all children, have a right to natural foods not poisoned with pesticides. You've got a problem with that?"

"Er, no, but who could afford such extravagant prices? Twenty dollars for a carrot? That's got to be a misprint."

She looked and said, "Yeah," and changed the two to a three.

"Why? Certainly being organic couldn't add so much to the price."

"People and their children have the social right to a natural uncontaminated environment—you know woods, streams, butterflies, squirrels, cute chipmunks—so with lots of farms now natural parks or natural forests, less land is available for the cultivation of organic carrots. Now what do you want. I suggest the eighty dollar cauliflower salad or the hundred dollar uncooked asparagus surprise."

"Why uncooked? Certainly you could at least cook it. In fact, there's nothing cooked on your menu. It's all raw, uncooked stuff."

She leaned over and in a low growl asked, "Are you a secret smoker? I mean tobacco, not marijuana. Marijuana's okay. You have a right to it, if you say it's for medical reasons or for recreational use."

Nonplussed, I shook my head.

Still inches from my face she demanded, "Smell that air."

Now confused and bewildered I sniffed.

"What are you breathing in?" she asked, as if it was the only question on a life or death exam.

"Air," I hazarded, totally lost as to where we were going.

"Pure air, God's air, clean air, great air, and why is it pure, clean, great?"

I needn't bother thinking of an answer.

She said, "We don't cook, we don't use wood, we don't use oil, we don't use gas, we don't use coal and we don't use electricity because it's made from one of the above. We just don't cook and so the air is unpolluted. People have a right to clean air."

"What about heat?"

"Don't have it."

"What about winter?"

"Put on lots of clothing."

Suddenly I realized I had seen neither cars nor buses as we were running from one angry person demanding his rights, to another angry person insistent on his rights, and all their rights eventually demanding my money.

"No cars?"

"Certainly we have no cars. Breathe that air again."

I did and smelled carrots.

Bushy, finishing his perusal of the menu, gave a low whistle. "Man it certainly is expensive living in Rights Land."

Deciding to forgo the thirty-dollar organic carrot I asked if I could have a glass of milk.

"No milk. We've forbidden robbing of cows of their milk. Cows have the right to their milk and until cows waiver that right, no milk."

"How can a cow waiver—"

"It's being worked on along with the voting problem."

"Some water?" I begged as my rioting stomach was burning its lining in protest.

"Ten dollars for the twelve ounce size, five dollars for five ounces."

"For water?" I cried. "Don't tell me it's got to give its permission."

"Streams, lakes, wooded brooks, the habitat of fishes, frogs, microscopic bio. Can't deplete them. The water inhabitants have rights and our children's children have the right to see and enjoy our water heritage, to see fish swim, frogs frolic, to see water lilies and algae grow, so water use is severely restricted and therefore it's got to cost. Now, what do you want, the twelve or five ounce?"

"This is ridiculous!" I was trying to get up when suddenly an ugly bag lady pushed me back down. "Hey, give me some money. I'm hungry."

"Who isn't?" I asked the waitress why they allowed beggars to annoy their customers with impunity.

"Beggars?" the bag lady cried out in indignation.

"Beggars?" the waitress cried out in horror, then chastised me. "That's a demeaning word. It's not the right word to say in Rights Land."

"I'm insulted and only money will make it right," the bag lady said, shoving her dirty hand in my face.

While the bag lady's hand was an inch from poking out my eyeball, Bushy explained, "People have a right to request money in public places. It's called a right to free speech."

"I'm leaving," I said, and brushing aside the dirty, threatening hand, I got up.

The bag lady cried out, "He struck me!" She staggered back a good ten feet and cast about for a soft landing place.

Walking out, I noticed Bushy excitedly talking to the bag lady and passing her a card.

He joined me as I, filled with outrage, a headache and a stomach ache quickly walked to Rights Land's borders.

Bushy said, "You shouldn't have struck her with your fist, maybe permanently wounding her. Never mind the psychological damage. She's so traumatized she may not be able to beg again, which could lead to her death and would be life threatening, and you might have damaged her reproductive rights. She should be living in Legal Land. Then she'd be protected."

"Reproductive rights? She's at least sixty!"

"She could carry someone else's frozen embryos. I'll have to sue you but we still can be friends. After all, I don't want to, but she does have the right to seek financial redress for the enormous injury to her reproductive self, to her self-esteem and for hitting her just because she's a woman. Do you realize you committed a hate crime against a woman on top of your recent hate crime against a black? At such an egregious insult I had to offer my services at no charge to her." He struck a noble pose on the last tidbit as if neither of us heard of contingency.

"Look, you'll have a hard time getting any real money from me."

"True, so true, but you're only the key that opens the door to where the real money lives. Being the representative of your country, if you misbehave by nearly killing a poor elderly woman, by logical extension your country is just as legally guilty, and it's raining money."

Disgusted I said, "Have you no shame?"

"Shame? You talk shame to a lawyer? Sir, fighting for the rights of the little guy, lawyers certainly can't afford feelings of shame or try to be fair in our dealings or honest in speech or show integrity in our conduct. Hell, such principals would be serious handicaps to representing our clients and their right to the best, most vigorous legal representation. Er, with all that said, Peoples, out of a sense of social justice, could you give me fifty? I saw an organic grown worm-free apple and I'm hungry."

"After you've threatened to sue me and my country over a fabricated BS assault, you now have the temerity to ask for a handout? You certainly have no morality."

"Hey, just because I'm bringing you to court is no reason we can't be good friends. In court, calling you every name, accusing you of every unutterable perversion is no reason out of court we shouldn't share lunch, laugh and joke as good friends."

"Drop dead," was my reply. My anger refused to afford me a better rebuttal, but I felt he deserved a great one.

"Too serious, my friend... you take everything too serious," and laughing he went to slap my back.

Moving from his touch, with anger still damning the free flow of my thoughts, I simply told him to bug off and resolutely walked forward. I was so intent on not seeing or hearing Bushy that I walked into another bum, early twenties, wearing a long silly goatee. His beard's name described his person very nicely.

"Hey," he cried, "you've got a nice coat. I like it. Social justice demands you give it to me," and he started to take off his patched-up rag.

"This Rights Land is more the land of thieves' rights. Certainly I won't give you my coat. What right have you to it?"

"Rights?" he cried out in shock. "You speak of rights and you're wearing a better coat than I? What right have you to that coat while I have only a rag for a coat? It's only social justice that you share your good fortune with the less fortunate. Not to do so would be unjust, cruel, selfish and just plain not the right thing to do, denying a fellow citizen his right to dress as well as anyone else, especially as well as you."

"You're nuts if you think for one moment I'm giving you my coat."

"You don't like my looks. My beard offends you."

"Honestly, yes, it does. It's ridiculous. You look like a pathetic comic character in a 19th century French farce."

Bushy, now next to me, and the stranger were aghast at my honest answer. Bushy surreptitiously slipped him a card that was quickly palmed.

"I have a right to your coat and I have a right to be insulted and angry at your refusal."

"Why in the world do you have a right to my coat?"

"I appeal to the universal right of those who have less to demand more from those who have more until we are equal. In the name of my birthright, in the name of social justice, in the name of democratic equality, I'm asserting my rights: I need it, I want it, I demand it and I have lots of rights. After enumerating my rights, what else is there to be said? Now give me your coat."

"No. Just because you need it gives you no justification for you to demand it. All you're looking for is charity."

"Charity? Charity? Now you really *are* insulting me! Saying charity to me suggests I'm an object of charity, and I am certainly not that. Are we not citizens? Are we not equal? Do we not have the same rights? Give me your coat. I'm getting annoyed with you."

Heatedly I said, "Since when does sharing citizenship give you the right to demand another's possessions? Certainly citizenship should, if nothing else, give everyone the right to their coat and protect themselves from thieves."

The bum said, "Are we not fellow human beings sharing common beliefs in equality? And humanitarian beliefs, common decency and social justice all support my right to your coat and it's your moral duty to give it to me. Take it off. I'm getting mad. You know I have the right not only to your coat but your pants as well, but I'm only demanding your coat out of my deep sense of humanitarianism. Give me your coat. Keep your pants. Now how fair is that?"

"Screw your humanitarianism! To be human confers no rights, and it doesn't baptize you into either my coat or my pants. Now take yourself and your ridiculous goat's beard away."

My beard crack was nasty but justified when faced with daylight robbery where adding insult to injury, the thief tries to make *you* the dishonest thief and morally wanting and himself the honest victim, all out of some vacuous cliché about a nebulous social justice concept.

The goatee didn't give up but went holy in his holdup. "Remember what Jesus said about it being right for you to give your coat to someone in need and help the poor. Now for the last time, give me your coat and save yourself from going to hell for denying me my moral rights. If not,

I'll punch you in the face and take it off you. Remember, I just want your coat. I don't need your pants. We'll leave that 'til tomorrow. Then we'll see."

I said, "The Christian command to give does not confer on you a right to demand. Whether I give or not is my choice and you have no rights regarding it. More to the point, Jesus' message was not about helping the poor but for righteous people to disregard and shun material goods. He preached the moral goodness of poverty and freeing one's self from the ensnarement of material concerns."

Balling up his fist and shifting his weight he was about to extract by force what his pseudo rights and moral arguments couldn't coerce. By simple expedient of grabbing his goatee and pulling hard I had total control as he screamed in pain. I pulled down, he bent down. I pulled to the left, then to the right and he followed crying to be released, begging for release. I decided to stroll about with his goatee and with tears in his eyes he meekly followed, bent over in a submissive attitude, loudly forsaking any claim on my coat.

Though stooped in an awkward position he was still able to accept Bushy's card while swearing aloud he would never think of suing me for assault.

With a final hard tug I let go of his hairy chin and, after backing away several feet, he yelled I had no right to do that to his beard.

Wiping some dirty greasy hair from my hand, wondering if more than ten dollars' worth of water was needed to wash it, I told him I did have the right to pull his goatee because I could, and if he doubted that I'd prove it by giving it another hard pull. "Remember, the one who possesses the greatest power is always the one with the greatest rights, and the one with the greatest rights is the one possessing the greater power."

As I walked away the bum cried to the back of my coat, "This ain't right! As a poor person I have a right to your coat and I'll get Rights Land's legal authorities to give me my rights and force you to give me your coat."

187

Bushy ran up to me telling me that I was a walking gold mine for him and did I think my Land would pay when I lost my lawsuits.

Having the one fixed idea of leaving Rights Land and get to Acceptance Land as soon as possible, I ignored him.

An exhilarated Bushy whispered, "I must have given out at least twenty cards. If everyone exercises their sacred right to sue, I'll have to open my own legal firm and incorporate. Look Ed, take it easy on the next group we meet. I'm down to my last twelve business cards."

"I'm leaving for Acceptance Land."

"Shit. Don't do that. I'll kick back some of the contingency fees to you. We've got a fortune in Rights Land. Look, here come some more clients."

And we both stared at three youths approaching with hip hop steps and giving passersby bizarre finger gestures and they shoved an obese woman to the curb.

At the potential lawsuit Bushy, giving an approximation of a shark's smile, quickly swam to the flaying woman in the street. "Don't say anything," Bushy advised her. "I'll handle it all."

From their boisterous behavior, from the laughter exchanged between them, from the conspiratorial whispering among them—I knew the signs, signs of failures in life about to prove what they suspected and trying to deny and what everyone else knew—they were losers.

Best cross the street, I thought, but with doubt. In nature to show the back is often a stimulant for an aggressive attack.

Smiling orthodontic even hygienically bleached white teeth from his hairy face, Bushy reassured me, here in Rights Land, as in Legal Land, the lawyer is supreme. Under his protection I could relax while watching the money fall from heaven.

Encircling us and meeting Bushy's show of teeth with their own they asked us for loose change so they could buy illicit drugs for severe medical reasons.

After mumbling that I had no change with all the bravado of a condemned man eyeing the needle, I listened to a smiling Bushy tell them he was a lawyer. After dropping the lawyer word he paused so it could evoke the awe and fear that holy word always achieves in normal circumstances. Unfortunately losers do not fear the law because they have nothing to lose, so Bushy's announcement fell anchor-like in shark infested waters.

Bushy, given his prosperous appearance as well as his preposterous facial hair and pompous attitude, should have attracted their attention. However, despite my trying to devolve into an insignificant bystander far distant from the group, they turned on me.

"Hey, you ain't from here," the one on my left accused.

"Er, no... I'm a visitor."

"From where?" the one on my right asked.

After telling them, hoping to put a period to their curiosity, I smiled, adding how impressed I was with their Land. As soon as I said it I felt the coward, and hearing my tone, seeing my nervousness, smelling my fear, the one facing me said, "Who said you could enter our Land? We didn't give you permission. You have no right to be here."

"Are you trying to disrespect us?" the one on my right asked, while the one on the left asked if I was looking for trouble and if I was, they would gladly oblige, and if I was not looking for trouble, money would be accepted as a token of my good will.

As I was debating an appeasement position versus an aggressive posture, Bushy, watching the situation develop from the sidelines as all good lawyers do, suddenly spoke up. "Peoples, if they beat you I'll sue them for you." Then to the menacing trio, he said, "If you beat him up I'll defend you, claiming you were incensed when he refused your right to his money."

Shit, I was dead. The one on my left said, "Well, Mr. visitor, it's time you got yours," and a chain appeared.

The one on my right suggested it was time for me to learn a lesson and a bat appeared. In front of me, a knife silently said hello.

Bushy yelled over their backs, "Don't worry, Peoples. I'll see that you get your rights in court even if on a posthumous basis."

It's miraculous how the mind can achieve supernatural inspiration once gassed up with adrenaline. Getting a full injection, I yelled at

Bushy, "Whatever you do, save those endorsed cashier checks and bearer bonds. Don't let these guys get all that easy money. Take my share of the million to my mother."

As if a film director had shouted "Cut!" all action ceased and the trio, like a page, turned to Bushy, changing the lawyer's shark smile into a defendant's minnow frown of distress.

"What money?" the one on my left asked no one.

"A million!" the one on my right exclaimed to no one.

"The hairy one's got it," the center one observed.

In absolute fear the hairy one first squeaked out denials, then, telling them he was a lawyer, implied they should be afraid. Finally turning his back to them, he ran faster than a lawyer running after a crashing city school bus.

All equally motivated, my three tormentors, waving a chain, a bat and a knife, took up the hunt, leaving me to cross myself, vowing novenas and hypocritically wishing Bushy good luck.

AFTER RIGHTS LAND

It was fitting that Rights Land was contiguous to Legal Land as there wasn't a lawyer's brief separation between them. My only observation on that score was that I should have visited Rights Land first as it depended on Legal Land for its existence. Leaving them, the most irrational lands, I was about to visit Acceptance Land.

Sitting in my suite, sipping a giant Starbucks Espresso, I opened Pru's letter first. In her first paragraph she expressed her apology for not writing sooner. Feeling her apology was appropriate was short lived, as in the subsequent paragraphs she went into the cause of her not writing. Apparently they were so busy at work that she and Hoar couldn't take their coffee breaks, but Hoar had indicted he had important information about my assignment, and suggested a quick after-work coffee.

She expressed her astonishment to find Hoar's idea of "after-work coffee" was cocktails at a very posh lounge providing live band music and dancing. Enjoying a Cosmopolitan (she'd never had one before) and seeing the upscale lounge, she confessed to being unsettled by the unexpected elegance. Unsaid, what was she unsettled about? Reading that sentence, I immediately became unsettled by her implication of what was unspoken but suggested. In her next sentence she expressed her undefined fear over Hoar's intentions (was she so innocent?) and was completely mitigated when, after refusing to dance with him, he wasn't in the least upset, and without asking ordered her a second Cosmopolitan

Shit. Upscale lounge... band... dancing... cocktails. Cosmopolitan. Each word was a letter opener stabbing my wellbeing. The next paragraph was gossipy girly talk about how her second drink went absolutely to her head. Being a gentleman Hoar suggested dinner as an anodyne to the drinks, but she refused. Feeling the effects of the drink she wanted to get back to her apartment. Despite the dinner refusal, Hoar, the gentleman, wouldn't think of her going home alone and volunteered to accompany her. She was leery of accepting his offer, confiding how difficult it would be to not invite him up for coffee. Fortunately, as they were leaving Rudy was passing by and deftly positioned himself between Hoar and the opened taxi door, and was able to escort her home. So concerned over her unsteady condition, he was kind enough to offer to go up with her and make her some coffee. Light headed, she refused his kind offer and just went to bed. Thus was the explanation why no letter, and the explanation gave no comfort; in fact, it gave more pain.

Throughout all the paragraphs, only one consisting of five brief sentences contained words of love, of yearning, her desolation in missing me, and of confidence in my abilities. The last sentence expressed her trust in my fidelity to our love, despite the many enticements I must be encountering, evoking the same nervousness felt when someone tells you they trust you not to steal from them. Nowhere in the letter was even a hint of Hoar's important information concerning my mission. That lack told me a lot.

Pru's letter didn't inflame love's passion, rather it initiated and energized flames of jealously and doubt. If Pru's letter was deeply troubling, Rudy's letter rained gasoline on Pru's letter. Following Pru and Hoar to the ultra-expensive 5 Seasons Lounge and waiting over two hours outside in surreptitious scrutiny, he had observed Hoar buying Pru at least three cocktails. Conclusion, Hoar was trying to get Pru drunk. She came out of the 5 Seasons very unsteady and vulnerable. Hoar had definite plans that Rudy fortunately was able to frustrate by getting Pru into a cab and taking her home. He had offered to make her coffee to sober her up, but she refused, but anyway given the time watching over Pru he didn't have an opportunity to write but he was sure I would understand.

Rereading both letters I could entertain suspicion of Hoar and also couldn't help feeling wary of Rudy's solicitude for Pru. Both letters contained nothing I could use to assess how my mission was being received. The letters were filled with soapy melodrama, unsatisfying and definitely unsettling.

Walking into the hotel dining room, preoccupied by the letters, I unconsciously responded to Hinki's and Sunni's waving me to join them. I marveled at the improbability, Sunni was finishing a Cosmopolitan. Coincidence, or was someone upstairs playing mind games with me?

Between sips of a Scotch and soda, still excited about the possibility of millions in awards, Hinki announced they had been extremely fortunate to obtain the services of a great lawyer, Alan Durch, for their lettuce lawsuit.

After taking a moment to make the connection to my saying "Bushy," Hinki said the beard was a well-known indicator, advertising that Durch was a staunch liberal defender of the little guy against big corporations.

Eyeing her empty Cosmopolitan glass, Sunni added, "He told us to sue the hotel for having an unsanitary kitchen for at least a hundred million, and he assured us at least ten million."

"And it's not costing us anything. He's not charging a fee," a smug Hinki said.

"It's on a contingency basis," Sunni said, correcting him.

Covering Sunni's hand, Hinki told me it's all 50-50 between them.

Sunni put her free hand over his, "We'll have to wait until we actually get the money."

With his last free hand on top of her two, completing the hand pyramid, Hinki said to me but to Sunni's ears, "There's going to be enough money for everybody."

Destroying the four hand pyramid by reclaiming her two, Sunni said to me but for Hinki's ears, "Durch says I have a right to the money. He even suggested I may develop a lettuce intolerance that would keep me from getting all those leafy lettuce vitamin benefits."

"And Durch explained that since I had the traumatic experience of seeing dirty forks, I was subject to a fork phobia and condemned to eat with my fingers, which could easily destroy my health through unsanitary finger eating," Hinki added.

Sunni said, "Besides, losing my right to eat lettuce, and by extension all green foods, will lead to serious health problems. I used to drink Grasshoppers. Now just the idea of a green drink, even green tea, brings on an anxiety attack."

Hinki, not to be topped, mentioned his right to eat at restaurants has been seriously curtailed by the sight of that filthy fork, which haunts him every time he enters a restaurant, and very few restaurants except for Arabs allow for finger eating. Ill nourishment, even death by slow starvation, could be his fate.

I noted the waiter bringing Hinki an order of thick prime ribs. They had cost some cow at least three ribs and was still bleeding red on the plate.

Having a cottage cheese salad, Sunni said, "We have to be very careful of what we eat and where. The hotel's insurance carrier might have investigators taking evidentiary pictures of our eating."

"Yeah, Peoples, keep an eye out for any suspicious characters," Hinki cautioned.

Staring with purpose at the two, I readily told them I had experience in recognizing suspicious and weird characters.

Putting down their forks, each pulled out papers in blue covers leaking legalese. After a preface of "Dear Edmund," Sunni expressed her firm belief that I would want, more than anything else, to sign an affidavit prepared by Durch indicating my observation of her traumatized state after the sight of lettuce leaf: how her stomach revolted, how she had to rush to the ladies room, how I was so fearful of her health I almost called 911, how two women had to hold her over the toilet.

Hinki's blue ribbon special was a Durch generated affidavit he passed to me over bleeding cow's prime ribs, how prior to noticing Sunni's lettuce I noticed their waiter dropping a fork, and after picking it up and after a quick napkin rub, gave it to Hinki, and how the waiter had to carry him to the men's room to administer first aid employing smelling salts and CPR.

Not to prolong the difficult situation my refusal generated, they promised that after I read over their papers I would gladly sign. That forestalled any further argument and I left them, ear to ear, earnestly talking to Bushy on a cell phone.

PART IV

HAPPY LANDS

1

Acceptance Land

Next on my itinerary was Acceptance Land, where tolerance is enforced and diversity is encouraged and applauded. It had been hailed by numerous political, intellectual and cultural thinkers back home as the par-excellent example of how prejudiced and bigoted attitudes are being erased, and how peace and harmony can be fostered by people living together in acceptance, respect and love for those not like themselves. Acceptance Land's fundamental premise is that all people are the same. There are no real significant differences in people, so one must respect and celebrate the differences as you ignore the differences. Our intellectuals told of great pragmatic advantages in achieving dynamic progress in social, cultural, intellectual and arts created by energetic interaction of diverse peoples who are not really basically different. A little confused, I suspected there was a contradiction in everyone being the same and the dictum to respect all differences.

Stepping across the border I was greeted by three guides: a black man with an unpronounceable string of Arabic names beginning with Ali and ending with Mohammed, an oriental woman obviously pregnant called Cherry Blossom, and an American Indian dressed in jeans, a sports shirt, and buckskin jacket with a feather stuck in a sweat hair band by a hairpin. His first words to me were, "Up yours."

I took immediate umbrage at this impolite greeting 'til he said it was his name. After Mohammed, Cherry Blossom, Up Yours and I exchanged greetings and obligatory hugs I expressed the hope that my itinerary would enable me to inspect their world-renown progress in melding diverse groups into a homogeneous whole, while simultaneously maintaining each group's individual cultural differences and fostering group pride in those differences.

As I said this I felt somewhere there were dozens of contradictions hidden in my words but I had neither the time nor the inclination to uncover them. The mention of an itinerary quickly led to an argument: Mohammed forcefully suggested a visit to the Black Arab Culture Center; Up Yours was vigorous in proposing we visit an Indian cultural artifact museum housed in a reservation casino; and Cherry Blossom, rubbing her extended stomach in a clockwise motion, whispered that the unwed mothers' facility located next to Acceptance Land's high school would be best. Mohammed's voice rose in defense of his Culture Center, Up Yours started to threaten physical combat in honor of the artifacts of the casino, and Cherry Blossom, ceasing her tummy rubs and her whispering, was quickly ratcheting up the decibels in maintaining her suggestion of visiting unwed mothers.

Fixing on a secondary school, I suggested we first visit the educational institution where I could study how the children learned the ways of tolerance and begin their travel on the road leading to the acceptance of diversity.

With bad grace the two men agreed, and a hopeful Cherry Blossom mentioned that while at the school we could easily visit the unwed teen mothers' facility housing in the school annex.

To soothe Up Yours' ruffled feather and Mohammed's wrinkled brow, I promised to visit their special interest places as well.

On our way, as my guides continued to bicker as to which of their places we should visit after leaving the high school, a group of women in various stages of undress, up to and including nudity, blocked our way and aggressively propositioned the men and Cherry Blossom. They sensed that I was an outsider so I received special attention.

Mohammed cursed them, Up Yours ridiculed them, and rubbing her tummy Cherry Blossom threw some nasty whispered words at them.

After continually yelling "No!" and forcibly brushing away intrusive hands groping for our private anatomical parts, we were finally able to escape their impertinent solicitations. When I commented to my guides that the prostitutes' shameless conduct was inopportune, completely disgusting and degenerate, I was quickly chastised.

"Don't be judgmental," Cherry Blossom said.

Up Yours told me being judgmental was the first step on the down escalator to bigotry's dark ugly basement.

Mohammed ended with the observation that one should always remember judging a person's observable conduct blinds you to their true inner worth. "And it puts you into a mental straightjacket called stereotyping."

"Well," I told them, trying to maintain my position, "it's a shame to see women prostituting themselves."

That comment stopped them in their tracks and they turned on me.

Cherry Blossom stoutly maintained their bodies are theirs and they should be free to employ them as they see fit and I had no right to make any judgments, especially moral judgments, as to what they can and cannot do with their bodies.

Mohammed maintained it really wasn't a crime because a crime is doing something that hurts someone else and surely in their business no one's hurt. Then winking at me he added, "Pleasure given for payment received."

Then Up Yours maintained the women were performing a great social service, for "without them the crime of rape would increase." He also reminded me, "Don't judge anyone until you've walked a mile in their moccasins and, after all, we all have needs." The latter was shared with a leer, suggesting he had deep dark needs and I shouldn't be frightened of my own dark needs.

Still I argued, "It's degrading to both the poor women and the men who engage in such morally corrosive, corrupting activities. After all, doesn't this activity say all a woman's worth is twenty or thirty dollars for twenty minutes in a parked car, and wouldn't a man's self-esteem be lowered by engaging in such degrading behavior?"

In unison they shouted, "Judgmental!" at me as if they'd caught me scratching my crotch in public.

"To cast the first stone, one should be free from sin," added Mohammed, ending that proviso with a wink, indicating he certainly wasn't in any position to cast stones and wasn't ashamed to be stone-less.

Cherry Blossom told me there was nothing wrong in what they did. With the ugliness residing in my mind, I should cleanse my thoughts and purify my mind before judging others. Apropos of nothing, rubbing her tummy counterclockwise she whispered, "Of course, I certainly would never engage in such employment."

Up Yours told me, "It's your closed uptight Victorian mind that's afraid of experiencing different free expressions of contractual sexual experiences." Looking pious, looking up to heaven, looking profound, and looking sad he laid his statement to bed, saying it was the white man who had foisted the practice of prostitution on poor Native Americans after raping, starving and killing them with smallpox. Before Columbus there was only health, peace, and abundance, never rapes in Native American Land.

Linking arms, all three gave a spirited version of "We Are the World," ending with the de rigueur group hug. To move us from the pre-Columbus nonsense, I said, "Yeah, whatever," which did move us to encounter a group of shaggy, listless men dressed in rags, some shuffling around, some standing, some sitting, some falling down, some lying on their backs wiggling hands and feet like beetles drunk on DDT. Those who possessed any degree of mobility, no matter how uncertain their steps, approached us offering pills of various colors and sizes, mumbling uppers, downers, and speed as well as suggesting the lowest prices for crack, weed, and heroin.

"Drugs!" I exclaimed. "They're selling drugs out in the open. How is that allowed?"

Mohammed told me to chill out or I'd hurt the purveyors' feelings.

Cherry Blossom told me to be cool. Certainly I didn't want to cast aspersions on their lifestyle.

Up Yours told me not to get up tight and not to turn my back on them. "After all, we all tried a little weed," he said, and his smile suggested more than a little.

"Yeah," Mohammed said. "Who hasn't done a line in their life? I'm sure your nose walked a couple of miles down the white line of life's road." He ended this with a wink, suggesting he had traveled the white line from New York to LA and back again.

Up Yours said, "Y'know, certain drugs are used in the Indian culture to get in contact with nature, you know, enlightened religious experience."

I honestly said, "No," to Mohammed, a curt "Bullshit" to Up Yours, while pointing to the zombie-like figures before us who were feeling nothing. If they were able to feel anything, it certainly wasn't a religious experience.

Whispering Cherry Blossom countered my observation with, "Hey, different strokes for different folks; you've got to go with the flow."

"Hey," Mohammed asked, "who are you to condemn what they ingest up their nose, in their lungs, veins, stomach? Maybe you don't need it to function, but these people are hurting so bad they need to travel over the bridge of drugs to get from the pain of the drug absence's to the pleasure of drugs and back again over the bridge to the pain." He proceeded to purchase a few small irregular white granules to show he was in pain. "Pain," he explained, "that's inflicted by white racists."

Up Yours, purchasing some ugly mushrooms, told me many people are searching for a higher level of existence and want to experience deeper insights into nature.

Finally they all reminded me it was a victimless crime. If they did harm to anyone it was only to themselves.

"And when they steal to support their addictions?"

Cherry Blossom said, "In Acceptance Land we have courageously dealt with the drug problem, which really isn't a problem but a life choice. If you can't afford your drugs there are numerous medical clinics dedicated to relieving pain that will give you some gratuitously."

Mohammed added, "And houses of counseling and rehab to help lead you from your addiction whenever you decide it is interfering with the quality of your life."

"Whatever." I sighed. If the visual evidence of having these pathetic creatures in front of them didn't convince them of the stupidity of their arguments, any words I could utter would be inadequate.

As we made our way to Acceptance Land's educational complex, my guides lectured me. After their gratuitously diagnosing that I was suffering from a closed mind, fearing to open itself to different ideas; a rigid mind, unable to think outside the box; a mind so small it was incapable of grasping new ideas; and a mind hiding within a tightly structured world because my repressed personality was incapable of adapting to challenging new life alternatives, they prescribed the remedy: strip away the rules and structure that my parents, education and society have placed upon me and dive into the exhilarating, liberating ocean of freedom to be diverse.

To my inquiring as to the existence of any solid earth boundaries to contain this ocean of freedom, Mohammed said, "Certainly. There is the paramount rule not to do anything that hurts another person."

"To respect everyone—their person, their culture, lifestyles, beliefs," Cherry Blossom added.

Up Yours told me, "You must love others' differences so much that you want to be like them. If you don't earnestly want to be an Indian or black, it shows you don't love but hate Indians and blacks."

Despite being an invited guest charged only with recording my observations about a culture celebrated for their openness to diverse ideas, the mendacious imp hidden in all of us, irritated by their pomposity, spoke in a soft, pseudo-inquiring voice. "And what of those who hold ideas that abhor your ideas?"

There was a strange silence within which, with difficulty, they tried to absorb and digest the existence of a thought counter to their own.

Finally Mohammed suspiciously asked me to explain myself.

A confused Cherry Blossom asked me what I meant.

Up Yours, vaguely grasping what I was implying, asked, "Do you doubt the righteousness of diversity, the high morality of being morally nonjudgmental, the progressiveness and freedom of being open to new, diverse ideas?"

I repeated my question. "Could a person who supported a position counter to your ideas of diversity be accepted under the umbrella of your openness to diversity?"

"To be against diversity," Mohammed sternly said, "would mean you maintain there are positions, ideas, cultures, and morality better than others."

Aghast, Cherry Blossom, holding her stomach with both hands, moaned, "That would mean that you're judgmental, saying this is right, that is wrong; this is better, that is worse; this is good, that is bad. Oh, you frighten me."

Up Yours, his brows knitted together over hard, staring eyes, told me in a threatening growl, "Watch it, man, you're just one word away from being an elitist, a sentence from being a bigot, and a conclusion from being a racist."

My internal malevolent imp refusing to be stilled made me ask, "Isn't there a contradiction here? How can you maintain yours is an open, diverse society and yet refuse to tolerate ideas that tend to deny your premises or argue against your conclusions? Are you not just as closed minded and judgmental as those you oppose? From all you say, you obviously feel your societal and philosophical positions are superior to other positions, allowing you to justify closing your mind to contradictory or alternative positions, and that makes you an elitist."

A pouting Cherry Blossom cried out that I was confusing her. A glaring Mohammed, with clenched fists, told me that kind of talk could get me five hard in the mouth. A snarling Up Yours taking a karate stance reminiscent of a surfer about to fall called me a name as if it was an insult: "You're white! You're a white man!"

Pushing that mischievous mental imp far back and bringing forward the reason I was here, to placate them, I tendered an apology followed by an innocent disclaimer that I was just being curious. I ended with a "Whatever."

Mollified to a partial extent, Mohammed still mumbled about someone needing his teeth cleaned. Cherry Blossom, shaking her pretty head and vigorously rubbing her tummy, asked her fellow guides, "He can't really believe diversity is wrong." A scowling, growling Up Yours announced shooting was too good for bigots, racists, elitists, and other bastards.

Cherry Blossom got agitated over "bastards," complaining that Up Yours was disrespecting all single mothers and he sounded sexist.

Mohammed sensed a racist comment about black mothers in the word.

A frightened Up Yours protested. "Shit no, I didn't mean to imply that bastard children are bastards, never mind illegitimate. They're wonderful love children, born to brave, courageous single mothers."

Mohammed, still not satisfied, threatened Up Yours with a serious dental rework. "You better watch your language in Acceptance Land."

Realizing this trio was militantly against counter ideas and could react violently if challenged, I decided it was best to carefully watch my own thoughts and guard my speech.

Passing several burning buildings with rioters running in and out through the smoking store windows carrying TV and armfuls of clothes, elicited condemnation from my guides. Mohamed condemned the businesses for charging the poor too much and now they're reaping the just rewards for owners who were too rapacious..

Up Yours mumbled, "Walk a mile in their shoes before you make any moral judgments about the rioters."

Sad-eyed Cherry Blossom whispered, "It's so distressing to see how society fails them."

Mohammed picked up 'them' as if it had a handle. "Yeah man, if you're poor, society made you poor, keeps you down, and doesn't make you feel loved, so who can blame people if they do a little looting and burning. You've got to do what you've got to do."

"Right on," Up Yours said. "If society discriminates against the people, keeps them outside the social tent, well it's only to be expected people will feel alienated and in striking back, try to sneak into the tent."

Giving way to a tear, Cherry Blossom whispered, "They're only seeking what they need to survive."

"Amen sister," and turning to me Mohammed said the riot started because someone reported hearing the N word, and he paused to allow me to take in the heavy import of this letter as if it explained and justified all. He continued. "Now you see the result of such a racist comment from a closed minded bigoted fascist. Can you blame people from reacting violently to such an egregious provocation?"

Surprised, I repeated, "Egregious?"

"Yeah, occasionally I use an educated word. It gets whitey all excited," Mohammed said.

Pointing to the burning buildings and the rioting crowds, Cherry Blossom cried, "See the hurt, the damage done to society by prejudice and hate speech? Hate speech is outlawed. Now only talk of love is permitted here."

"Whatever" was my reply as we skirted the rioters.

Finally passing through well-defined series of delineated black, Hispanic, Chinese, Haitian, Indian, (American and India), homosexual, homeless and drug neighborhoods we reached the school where open-mindedness is inculcated and diversity celebrated. We moved through the school's spacious lobby, which was decorated with African artifacts and signs celebrating Kwanza.

Passing through metal detectors held by security guards we entered the principal's office. The principal was a woman of color, but of such a light shade that you had to stare and wonder whether she was light black, dark Hispanic, or a white woman who fell asleep in a tanning bed. However, because she was wearing a turban, a sari and between the eyes a red dot, I guessed Indian. She was chastising a young girl for being insensitive to the beliefs of others by wearing under her blouse a cross. Apparently while the girl was changing for gym the cross was exposed to the eye of a girl who had the approved diverse views toward religion and so was understandably shocked and almost rendered senseless by the sight of someone visually pushing their beliefs on her in a tax-supported public school. Complaints were made, outrage was heard.

The miscreant was summoned, and after a stern dressing down for her gross insensitivity toward her fellow students' belief in non-belief, she was allowed to leave, but only after promising to apologize to the traumatized girl and vowing never to wear the cross to school again lest others be traumatized by the sight.

As the door closed behind the tearful student, the principal complained how she had to be ever vigilant if she wanted to inculcate a sensitive acceptance atmosphere in the educational system.

"Right on sister," said Mohammed, echoed by an "Amen" from Up Yours, a "So sensitive," from Cherry Blossom and a "Whatever" from me.

We were assigned a fifteen year old girl to show us around. She would have been attractive except for the brief tight T-shirt covering a few but not all of her ribs and a skirt starting three inches below her navel and reaching down to the top of her thighs. Supplementing numerous pieces of normally worn teen-age jewelry were nose and navel rings, six earrings per ear running up from the lobe like a golden ladder, gold safety pins keeping her eyebrows attached to her forehead, an ersatz diamond embedded in the side of her nose, and a large gold ball piercing her tongue. All in all she looked like a pathetic of copy of women who do it all, and do it quickly, cheaply, anywhere, with anyone, which, if there was any question, it was answered by what was printed on her T-shirt: *I do it all.*

Walking down the corridor to a History class, either expecting to shock us or show how liberated she was, she told us she smoked.

I said "Whatever," while my trio hoped she'd stop smoking and if she didn't stop, hoped she smoked only outside school, advising she should seek counseling and, finally, if she continued smoking after counseling it might be best for her and everyone else's health if she limited her smoking only to medical weed.

"Screw you," was her comment.

Between my surprise and shock, my guides whispered to me, "Be open, nonjudgmental, different strokes for different folks, be free to speak what you want to say and how you want to say it."

The History class was in progress. The teacher, an intense gentleman sitting cross legged atop his desk, dressed in a flowing robe with gold embroidered astrology signs and a ponytail reaching past his butt was stoutly stating, "America was discovered by Native Americans."

"Right on," murmured Up Yours, then frowned as the teacher went on to indicate that some say Polynesians from Hawaii were first and of course there's irrefutable evidence that the Chinese landed on the west coast before Columbus. He then pointed out that the Chinese, from a deep respect and love for the advanced culture of the indigenous Native Americans, left the land and people undisturbed.

"Oh, how sweet!" a glowing Cherry Blossom whispered.

Up Yours commented, "Screw the Chinese."

Mohammed mumbled, "Columbus and his crew were really blacks from Nigeria. History is so racist."

The teacher continued. "Of course ignorant people continue to maintain Columbus landed," and here he gave a condescending smirk, "and discovered America." Turning serious he asked the class, "What did Columbus really do in America?"

"Enslaved the Indians!" shouted a black student.

"Spread disease, destroyed the great Native cultures!" cried the Hispanics.

The girls, in horrified shrill screams shouted, "Raped all the women!"

Summarizing, the smiling teacher agreed with the class that indeed the white man stole, pillaged and killed people and destroyed the environment.

Then uncrossing his legs he firmly told the class they must respect the advanced culture of the indigenous Native Americans and admire and emulate the Indians' deep respect and love for the land, the animals, and the entire Eco system.

The students cheered with gusto while the teacher gleefully encouraged the students' loud responses with his cries of, "I hear what you're saying," and "Feel the pain of poor people."

It was only when, in a burst of enthusiastic joy the teacher, jumping down from his desk, disappeared under the front row desks that I realized he was a dwarf.

"He's a—"

"Don't say it man; words can hurt," came from Mohammed.

"Don't recognize it; looks can hurt," came from Cherry Blossom.

"Don't think it man; open and cleanse your mind of dirty thoughts," came from Up Yours.

"Whatever," I said and asked our fifteen year old jewelry bedecked, minimally dressed school guide who self-advertises *I'm cheap, I've done it, I am doing it, and I will do it*, whether we could see another class.

And so we did, an Anthropology Class filled with students hearing a lecture about the advanced culture of the Incas and a large number of cities with interconnecting trails they built. The Mayans were equally extolled with their temples and calendar, American Indians with their respect for nature, and African Zulu's, who—

I left; there was nothing for me there. In fact, there was little there and the little there was inflated into intellectual nonsense bordering on the comical.

As we walked down the corridor, sensing my irritation, Mohammed told me to remember every group must feel pride in their heritage. Cherry Blossom mentioned everyone should feel good about themselves, while Up Yours commented about different cultures finally getting their rightful place in History and Education.

My trio ushered me into a Health Class conducted by a teacher in a plaid dress. She had braided hair and a pronounced lisp. Given the five o'clock shadow showing through an inch of pancake and the breasts, one larger than the other, I whispered my suspicion, "She's a guy, right?"

"Don't notice, don't say, don't think," Cherry Blossom warned. "She's suffering an identity crisis."

"Don't label people," Mohammed said, chastising both of us. "He's very sensitive."

"Should he be teaching in drag?"

Shaking the tassels on his buckskin jacket, Up Yours said, "Don't judge people by their clothes; it's the inner person who is important."

While carefully adjusting his feather, I noticed the exposed label read *Made in China*, though I'm sure his Indian jacket was authentic, coming from India.

Noticing us, he, she, or whatever, in showing off his class of twelve year olds, asked them, "What is the main rule in having sex?"

"Use protection!" they shouted.

He added a smile as he said, "Of course you could practice abstinence." Then with his smile, he added a wink. "But everyone knows, with the power of sexual urges, that's impossible. Now is there any type of sex that is wrong?"

A girl of twelve, with a body of a fifteen year old, dressed as if she strolled the city streets after midnight, and indicating an attitude that suggested no suggestion would surprise, offend, or shock her, said, "Without protection."

"Other than that?" the man dressed in a dress asked.

Another girl, whose puberty had come, shouted, "Have it only when you feel you're ready to do it!"

"Yeah, baby!" a leering, pimpled youth cried out.

"And who determines when you're ready for sex?"

"We do," a girl wearing a push-up padded bra said, then turning to a sleepy looking youth, she smugly said, "Right Johnny?"

"Yeah, ho, whatever you say," was the uninterested response.

Proud of his students' responses, the teacher summed up the rules: have protected sex; have sex only when you feel ready; don't let anyone pressure you if you are not ready; and all types of sex are wonderful and there are no taboos.

"Now, are there any other rules?" he asked.

"Don't have it twenty times a day," the pimpled pupil cried out, receiving laughter from the class.

Smiling, the Two for One teacher jokingly said, "Robert, if you can, you can."

Once the class settled down, the teacher again asked, "Are there any other restrictions? For example, threesomes?"

"No!" the class yelled out, as a wit sitting in the back added, "If you haven't had it with three, you haven't had it."

"Is mano a mano wrong?" the teacher asked.

"No!" shouted the class, as a nasty someone yelled, "Willy, you should know all about that."

A flushed Willy stood up and angrily replied, "I'm gay. It's good to be gay. It's natural to be gay. I'm proud to be gay. Get used to it."

Sarcastically the class applauded.

"Is pornography wrong?"

"No!" the class roared.

"But only if you're over eighteen," The Two For One teacher said. His smiling at his caveat brought on hilarious laughter.

Looking toward a relatively isolated dark rear corner of the classroom I noticed two students, their desks piled high with books and coats, seriously conferring together. Thinking they shouldn't be wasting classroom time talking, my censorious thoughts were snapped right out of my mind. The boy was fondling the girl.

"Look at what those two are doing," I whispered to Mohammed.

He peered, he stared, then nodded, smiled and said, "Yeah, they shouldn't be doing that in class, but we shouldn't be judgmental."

Seeing where our attention was diverted, Cherry Blossom looked and sighed. "Oh, how sweet! I guess they're ready."

While Up Yours said he was getting excited.

Noticing the rear adults staring with various attitudes at the two now occupying one chair, the Two for One teacher called out, "You two, stop that immediately. Can't you wait till after school?"

"Why should we?" the girl said. "I'm ready. Billy is ready. What's wrong with us expressing our love wherever, whenever, and however we want?"

"But in my classroom?" the Two for One responded, a little taken back by the challenging response.

"There are no rules," the boy argued, tossing the sexually confused teacher's rule back at him.

"You're disturbing the class. How can they learn with you two acting up?"

The boy shouted to the teacher, "Hey, you queer, if it bothers them, then that's their problem, not our problem."

The girl said, "We're not telling them to watch, and why are you watching? You dirty old fag."

The teacher took the exchange as an occasion for a class learning experience. "Let's not use hurtful epithets. Being a transvestite is nothing to be ashamed of. How I dress is no one's business. I'm proud of my sexuality. Now you know there's a time and place for that conduct and the class is neither the right time nor the right place."

"Prove it," the girl said.

Like a fish sucking for air, the Two for One teacher moved his lips in and out but no words came forth. Defeated, he turned his back and started writing the homework assignment: find five different places other than from the school nurse where students under eighteen years of age can obtain birth control, condoms, pornography and sex toys.

Apparently the romantic 'It's the right time' had passed without conclusion for the two in the back. With bad grace they separated amid the banging of their books and angry mutterings about uptight queer perverts.

Leaving the classroom I was shaken, walking in a daze and was guided into the next classroom, a History class that was currently studying Black History. The black teacher, whose two-foot long dreadlocks kept continually bouncing off his bizarre-looking multi-colored flowing robes, excitedly asked the class, "Who fought the Civil War?"

"African Americans," the class of almost all black students answered.

"Yeah, man, and who won the Civil War?" he asked.

"African Americans."

"Who fought the Revolutionary War?", he asked.

"African Americans," was shouted back.

"Who won the Revolutionary War?"

"Us blacks."

"Who discovered America?"

"A black sailor was the first to step ashore," an intense student answered.

"Right on. And who fought in WWII?"

"Blacks."

"Who won the war?"

"Blacks."

"Who didn't get any credit?"

"Blacks."

"What did we get?"

"The shaft."

"Who built the railroads? Tamed the West? Built America with their blood and sweat?"

"Blacks."

"Who got the credit?"

"Whites."

"What did we get?"

"The racist shaft."

"Who are the greatest athletes?"

"Blacks."

"And musicians?"

"Blacks."

"And scientists?"

"Blacks."

"Writers?"

"Blacks."

"Who gets the credit?"

"Whites."

"What do the African Americans get?"

"The shaft."

Back in the corridor I turned to my guides. "It's all nonsense. How can such racist bullshit be taught?"

"Careful," Mohammed said. "To say it isn't true is to say blacks didn't fight in WWII, but some did, and if some did, can you prove the war would have been won without them? And if you can't prove absolutely that whites could have won the war without black help... well, then blacks won the war."

"Besides," Cherry Blossom put in, "it makes African Americans feel good about themselves and isn't that really the most important historical lesson to be taught?"

Irritated I said, "It's not the truth."

"Hey man, let's not get all out of joint over this obsession with truth," a pragmatic Up Yours responded, adding, "As the great Native American philosopher, Smoke In Your Face said, 'Not only is beauty in the eye of the beholder, but so is truth.' Hey, what's true to me is what works for me, and what's false to me is what doesn't work for me, and don't put your absolute truth and falsehood nonsense on my back."

"You've got to accept the other guy's truth as true, even if you think it's false. It's not easy to do. That's why education is important," Mohammed pompously added.

"Besides," Cherry Blossom said, "It's so very very wrong to hurt other people's feelings by saying they're wrong. As educated people we live our lives on the fundamental principal that no one is to be hurt physically or psychologically, and in addition everyone has the moral duty to make others feel good about themselves and be filled with high self-esteem."

Up Yours added, "Always remember the great truth: different strokes for different folks. If you keep that as your moral compass, you can never go wrong."

Ali suggested we should visit Dr. Bishop Percy, Acceptance Land's great spiritual counselor and religious thinker.

Walking the corridor to Dr. Percy's office we passed the offices of a marriage counselor, a student counselor, a parent counselor, a sex counselor, a drug counselor, a financial counselor, an eating disorder counselor, an exercise counselor, and a fashion and dress counselor among others. The sex counselor, apparently friendly with Up Yours, waving to him, asked, "It's still on for Friday?"

Dr. Bishop Percy, as befits a spiritual man, wearing a heavy hint of emaciation beneath a flowing white hair, looked like seventy but moved like forty; his age was undetermined. Not waiting for the introductions to be completed, Dr. Percy had me in a hug. I can only be thankful he didn't go for a cheek kiss as his trimmed and sculptured beard, a nice accouterment for the spiritual look, in rubbing my cheek would feel disgusting.

Taking his position behind a delicate white desk often seen in French boudoir movies, he gestured toward a pair of couches. We sat, rather sank, in velvet couches so plush and soft even Ali had difficulty raising his superiority above the paisley flowery cushions.

I hadn't expected a monastic austerity but with the plush red carpets and the soft pink lighting, his office was what I'd expect from a high-class madam operating in the age of Louis XIV.

Noticing my noticing, unasked, Bishop Percy explained, "Given I have to help troubled people resolve great spiritual problems, I've found the more-intimate, less-threatening atmospheres more conducive to relieving and resolving individuals' religious and spiritual pain."

Trying to keep my back straight while continually slipping into a semi-reclining position on the couch, I asked his religious affiliation.

Instead of an answer I got a laugh and a wink.

Confused and a little irritated, I repeated my question.

"I'm affiliated with all religions and belong to none. I believe in all Gods, and believe none."

With my confusion increasing and my irritation growing, I asked for an explanation and received ecumenism blow theory.

Picking up his white spindle-legged captain's chair with a pale-blue silk cushion, he placed it down so close to me that I couldn't cross my legs without making contact. With his hands on his knees, inches from my knees, I was fearful over what would be their next landing place.

He said, "In religious ecumenism thought, spiritual acceptance is the gospel message."

As I anticipated, he launched an assault on me with a forefinger tapping my left knee. "I see from your demeanor you don't understand." Leaning back, he smiled at me and winked at Cherry Blossom. Mohammed, sliding down the cushions, a moment from lying on the floor, was too busy struggling to regain control of his seat to give the haughty look he enjoyed bestowing.

"First," Bishop Percy explained, "strong religious beliefs generate feelings of superiority, and if you feel your religion superior, then you must feel the other religions are inferior, and it's a short step to believing their believers should be converted from their false beliefs while simultaneously they must be kept from trying to convert your true believers to their false beliefs. The result is intolerance, wars, persecution and prejudices. To stop such deplorable results we preach acceptance, tolerance—in a word, ecumenism. If no single belief system is true, then all beliefs can be true and no belief system can be false. The result, all are equal, all is love."

Leaning forward so close that I had to fight to keep from staring at the chin mole buried in his beard, he asked if he could play a "We are the World" CD.

I said, "Hell no."

Bishop Perry sighed and then continued. "Do you see the democratic spirit in ecumenism? Do you feel the excitement ecumenism brings to the human spirit?"

Watching his hands, which were showing signs of again invading my personal space, I told him I felt it was all stupid talk, a spiritual void, a walk into empty blackness.

Damn, he squeezed my knee, then withdrew his hand before I could swat it away.

He said, "No, no, it's freedom. It's democratic, it's acceptance, it's all so intellectually deep and exhilarating. All spiritual beliefs are equal, so you're free to take your choice, switch from one to another until you find the religion suited to your individual needs. If you like a lot of stupid rules, Jewish Orthodoxy is for you. If you like emotion, Southern Baptist might be right for you. If you like ceremony and tradition, Catholicism is for you. If you like animals, there's animism. If you like doing a little religious drugs, Rastafarianism is for you. If you like trees, sky and moon, you've got to look into Native American Spirituals. Say you're a laid back reflexive person, sort of into yourself, Yoga, Zen is where you go. Of course, if you hate to leave life, sort of want to live forever, I suggest Buddhism and reincarnation. Now, the best is Atheism. I advise all my spiritually troubled students, you can't go wrong with the Atheistic belief system."

"But it's a belief system without beliefs," I said.

"No. It's the religious belief system which, because of its lack of beliefs, it makes you free. You're a free spirit and will feel better about yourself no matter how exotic and esoteric other beliefs are. You can't do better than Atheism."

He lost me in the forest of beliefs. Unfortunately, he continued. "In the Land of Acceptance, religion is a magnificent varied buffet where you can always go back for a different dish. Your taste or needs at any moment in your life decides whether or not a particular religion is for you. With religious ecumenism you can see why education is so important. Children must be taught about diverse religions as opposed to their own so they can make informed choices depending upon their needs and likes at any given time." He pointed a forefinger somewhere between my navel and crotch. "You may be predisposed to be a Muslim of the Sunni persuasion and out of ignorance not know it. Hell, do you fancy having a couple of wives? Well, there's your chance. As for free love and drugs I, suggest… well anyway you get my point."

Eyeing his hands, I said, "Sort of like capitalism. The consumer is in charge. The buyer, not God, chooses his own path to salvation."

"Exactly. No belief system is better than any other. In the Land of Acceptance we constantly struggle against those who, maintaining their religion is better, commit the first spiritual sin, an intolerance to other's religious beliefs. The second spiritual sin, which comes from the first, is believing one's morality should be a guide to everyone else's social and political life. Religion and its various moralities should be kept locked inside a church to be visited once a week, if at all."

"If all are the same, why join any?" I asked.

"Well, it may feel good to join—"

We were interrupted by a loud crash. Dignified Native American Up Yours had slid off the couch and was sitting on the floor. Red faced, trying to maintain his superiority, struggling up, he finally achieved a standing position in a far corner, arms folded, glaring at the couch.

I repeated my question. "Why join any religion? In fact, why bother believing in any morality or any God?"

"Just the point—why join? I haven't. I'm totally ecumenical. To a Muslim I'm a Muslim. To a Mormon, I'm a Mormon. I love all religions, support all religions, tolerate all religions, but am free from all of them. It's an exciting but exhausting position. Being in so many religions I'm more religious than any religious believer."

"I don't know how you can say that."

He finger patted my knee. "If you're a Jew, you can only be holy in the Old Testament way. If a Muslim, then you can only be holy in the Koran way. But I'm holy in a way that transcends their parochial restricted ways. By believing in all religions you're free to be holy in a totally individualistic transcendental way."

Debating whether to spread my knees and risk worse touching, I decided to keep them in a closed defensive position. I asked about sin.

"There is no sin. In Acceptance Land there is no sin. One person's sin is another's tenet of faith. Believe in one wife or lots of wives or no wives. Fast or gorge yourself. Deny yourself or enjoy yourself. There's a religion to absolve all sins and if there isn't one, start your own."

"There is one sin," Up Yours thundered from the corner. "You can't interfere with anyone, can't hurt their feelings, can't criticize their beliefs, can't maintain any superiority. You must show respect to their activities, and they have the same valuation as your own."

"Excuse me, Mr. IV Visitor, we should be moving on to our next visit," Cherry Blossom quietly suggested.

Dr. Percy moved his chair back to his girly desk and as I struggled out of the couch, I asked him what question was most frequently posed to him as a spiritual advisor and religious counselor of young people.

"Easy. Troubled people, insecure people afraid of religious freedom, ask me what they should believe in. When I tell them they should believe in whatever suits their needs at the time, they become scared of the freedom my answer gives them and they ask, 'But what is the true belief?'

"Well you should see the astonished look when I say they're all true and none are true. True is what you say is true, false is what you say is false."

At the door, beckoning me to join him, Mohammed corrected Percy. "Percy, nothing is false except the belief that something is false. The opposite of a true belief is never a false belief but another true belief."

In Acceptance Land I confess I felt awash in if not idiocy, certainly in nonsense.

Hungry, turning to Cherry Blossom, I asked if we could get some sustenance.

Mishearing, a winking Mohammed said, "I can't tell you where you can go to buy the substances, but I can point you in the right direction."

Cherry Blossom said if I was going to get substances, she'd like a little weed.

Up Yours, whose fleshy nose was bloodhound twitching hot on a scent asked, "Look, if I lay a few bucks on you, can you buy some nose cleaner from a guy called Shifty?"

Not in their mental context, it took a few moments for me to gather up their ideas, reject and then correct them.

A disappointed Mohammed said, "Yeah, let's go to the cafeteria, but always remember, our education system and our society is all about brotherhood, peace, love, and acceptance."

The cavernous cafeteria was filled with students, noise, and movement. Cherry Blossom told me all the food served was approved:

it was fat free, sugar free, and bursting with fiber, vitamins, energy, and health. Bad food was not allowed in Acceptance Land.

With pride, Mohammed, pointing out a series of separate labeled food stations, said, "You can have native African food."

The hamburger entrée, a hamburger covered with something called Zambia sauce, was referred to as being cooked in the Botswana tradition. The roll, baked in the form of a spear, was referred to Niger bread. I declined and said, "Doesn't hamburger contain saturated fats?"

"Not when it's cooked in the Botswana way," Up Yours told me.

"What about some Muslim foods?" Mohammed suggested.

The French fries were labeled *cous cous* and accompanied by a frankfurter covered with a sauce suspiciously resembling the African station's Zambia sauce, but it was called Moroccan Ecstasy.

"The fries are—" I started to say.

But Mohammed quickly explained. "Not fried when cooked in the Moroccan Berber way."

"There is a vegetarian station," Cherry Blossom informed me with an attitude suggesting it was what whiney whites eat, or should eat. The veggie hamburger, liberally covered with a sauce again resembling the African sauce, was identified as Health Delight.

I decided to have a go at the Hispanic station, getting some flat bread wrapped around veggie beef covered with the ubiquitous sauce now labeled hot Montezuma. Hunger and taste buds duked it out, and after the first bite, the buds won. I didn't gag but it was close.

Sitting in a segregated area reserved for faculty, I noticed that the room, though chaotic, did have order superimposed on its inhabitants. There were black students over there, subdivided by gender, then, separated by empty tables, were white students similarly separated by gender. A group of Hispanics sat between the blacks and whites, so the flowing color contrast was not too great. Sprinkled in were separated nervous groups of Orientals, Arabs and Indians, some with turbans, some with feathers, some with saris.

While debating whether to be so obnoxious as to mention the obvious segregation of the groups, I was forestalled by Mohammed proudly swinging a hand around, telling me to notice the diversity of the cafeteria. "All nationalities are represented here."

Sitting at a table well removed from the students, not eating, I sat back looking askance at a dessert called Guatemalan Surprise. If anyone ate it, it would be surprising. I certainly didn't eat it after finding the surprise beneath the non-fat, non-sugar Zambian chocolate syrup was a crunchy looking insect embedded in the ice cream.

Cherry Blossom, noticing my lack of appetite for the dessert, patiently explained it was a good thing to try many diverse dishes as the chefs and the head nutritionists were wonderful in preparing diverse dishes from around the world.

Mohammed and Up Yours chimed in, maintaining they ate the dessert often and enjoyed, nay relished, the grand Guatemalan Surprise. They would have ordered it today but were trying different dishes to expand their culinary horizons, and in educating their taste buds, allow them the opportunity to discover different foods from around the world.

"Yeah, whatever," I said, noticing Cherry Blossom had requested apple pie a la mode called Brazilian Cake, while the other two were deep into New York Cheese Cake called Israeli Kibbutz Cake.

Noticing I wasn't forking up the insect-inhabited desert, Cherry Blossom, fearfully looking about, said, "Eat up, don't leave anything. You'll hurt people's feelings."

"Yeah man," Mohammed said. "There may be Guatemalans somewhere around here and if they see you turning your white nose up at one of the country's popular desserts, taking umbrage, they could either cry, sue or beat the shit out of you."

All three looked about, searching for possible teary eyes, hurt eyes, or angry eyes of Guatemalans, and finding none, exhaled with relief.

With finger tips gingerly picking up the dessert by the plate's rim I offered it to these three gourmets who were so volubly partial to such subtle delights. All, leaning far back, refused, declaring "I'm full," "I'm on a diet," and "I couldn't deprive you."

Tossing it, plate and all into an overflowing garbage pail I noticed some fugitives from the grand Guatemalan Surprise were moving about, happily dining on the non-fat, non-sugar chocolate.

Back at the table, relating the full garbage insect action, I asked why the garbage wasn't emptied, commenting on the health concerns regarding cockroaches in the kitchen.

"Strike," Up Yours said. "The school waste managers are on strike."

Orchard amplified. "They're illegal immigrants who feel just because they have no right to be here, they're being insultingly and unjustly forced to take low-paying, degrading jobs and their union isn't taking these insults anymore."

Mohammed maintained the guides were solidly behind the strike. "Having no right to be here doesn't mean they don't have the rights of those who have the right to be here." He finished by asking the table, "Am I right or am I right?"

"So very right," Cherry said.

"Right on," Up Yours echoed.

Trying to drink some Ivory Coast coffee, the first sip of which, slipping past the lips, was in my mouth before I could reject it, was in my mouth before I could expel it past the buds before they could expect it, down a shocked throat before I could regurgitate it, into a stomach that proceeded to be devastated. "This coffee is terrible!" I said, and again they were horrified at my comment, glancing nervously about while shushing me.

"It's an acquired taste," Mohammed said.

Fearfully I asked if it was made from insects.

"From wood bark, ground up, slow cooked, stirred with exotic herbs. It's a popular Ivory Coast beverage," Up Yours told me.

"It's prepared in the expensive, classic, primitive Mongolian way," Mohammed said.

Cherry Blossom said it was caffeine free and calorie free, and besides it was a wonderful purging agent for the upper digestive tract, sweeps cleans the lowest of the lower track, and wire brushes the colon to a pink, glossy shine.

Pushing the cup away and noticing the Starbucks' mochas they were sipping, I asked what type of person they hoped would be the end product of their educational system.

"An open-minded individual," Mohammed averred.

"A flexible-minded person," Up Yours told me.

"A person who loves and doesn't hate," Cherry Blossom whispered with a beatified smile." She added, "We should love the weak, help the oppressed, support good people, embrace all different people, hug those who are very peculiar, and support the bizarre in a non-religious, non-judgmental way."

"Yeah man," Up Yours said, adding, "We want our students to fight and punish the bad people, like destroying all bigots, crushing and ripping the racist bastards' guts apart."

Mohammed, feeling he had to put his oar in and stir the BS, said, "We want people who, when they see grotesque and disgusting things, will not notice them, will not even say to themselves, 'That's grotesque and disgusting.' Our students, upon graduation, will have a mind above making moral judgments of good or bad. He will realize the only correct judgment to make is to make no judgment, except the judgment to fight those who make judgments. They are the worst type of person."

"Yeah, man," Up Yours said, "he's got to be ready to fight against those who make judgments, people who say 'This is wrong,' 'That isn't right'—"

Mohammed agreed. "Yes, people who hurt others must be hurt in order to be made to see it's wrong to hurt people."

Cherry said, "And our educated graduates will never judge a person by the outer man, by what he says, by what he does. They will only judge a person after getting to know the real inner man."

"Yeah, and walk in his moccasins," Up Yours added.

I argued, "Inner man? Has anyone met, seen, or talked to this inner man? For years I've peered into my mind attempting to discover my inner man, only to find two façades: the wonderful person I think I am, who is continually in conflict with the person who constantly is trying to keep me alive, happy and prosperous by doing mean, nasty, selfish things. All I do is bounce from one pseudo inner man to another, trying desperately to maintain a functional unity and rationalize differences away."

I stopped short. I had said too much, or rather too personally.

Cherry Blossom, being sensitive, said I was a cynic as if that was synonymous with being evil.

Mohammed advised me to join some yoga or Hindu meditation group to find myself, and Up Yours suggested I needed to go to an Indian Reservation and, getting back to nature, find my true nature. Up Yours then modestly confessed he was not only in touch with his inner man, but they held daily conferences in which both agreed he was a damn good modest giving fellow, tolerant toward different people, a staunch fighter against white bigots and, possessing a brilliant mind, is a hell of a stud.

Mohammed thought his inner man wasn't just inner, but also was his outer man because he was so open, accepting and non-judgmental. He told me, "My inner man stands before you, guileless, innocent and honest, but definitely non-judgmental."

Professing that her inner self was endowed with extrasensory power, Cherry Blossom claimed to be not only intimate with her inner self but possessing such depth of sensitivity that it enabled her to see and communicate with other inner selves, and it was not reserved to just humans.

To stop their discussion of their manifestations of inner persons I again asked what they specifically meant by an educated person.

As Cherry Blossom and Up Yours were busy conferring with their inner selves, Mohammed's inner man, standing right outside in front of me, summed up their view of an educated person: "Well, a person who is in the know, who knows what's cool, what's not, and who goes with the flow, gets along with everyone, is never uptight nor surprised by anything. You know, a person who is open to and willing to try new ideas and most importantly, doesn't feel his values are better than anyone else's ideas, culture or background."

"An amorphous type person," I concluded.

"Hey man, not so," Mohammed said. "The archetypical educated person we strive to achieve has a definite core of beliefs. For instance, abhorring discrimination against anyone for any reason, an educated person will always fight bigots wherever they show their prejudices. In other words, an educated person is against people who are ignorant."

Returning to my prior logical contradiction, I said, "So an educated person is open, accepting, and supportive of diverse positions save to labeling as ignorant individual's positions that are committed to beliefs different from theirs."

Concluding their educational goals, an annoyed Mohammed said, "An educated person believes in everything new and novel, distrusts everything old, sees good in everyone who thinks as he does and castrates those who are blind to the truth—the truth that there is no truth. We hope our citizens will have such a high degree of sophistication they will be able to agree with a proposition while simultaneously accepting its negation."

"Love... don't forget love," Cherry Blossom whispered. "An educated person loves everyone, criticizes no one. Oh, we need more love, more giving, more caring in the world."

Just as she looked like she was going into hugging mode, Up Yours, pressing a forefinger hard on my chest, said, "Don't be judgmental. Always ask yourself if walking in his moccasins, would you not do as that poor soul did?"

"If a criminal robs a store, where's the responsibility? Didn't he do wrong?" I asked.

"Wrong, right," Mohammed yelled. "It's the capitalist system hurting people that's wrong."

Cherry Blossom spouted the 'love the sinner, hate the sin' aphorism.

Annoyed, I told her, "Without the person willing and wanting to sin there would be no sin."

She bit her lip. "That can't be right. You're wrong. I know it and more importantly I feel it here," and she patted her round stomach.

Up Yours ended the conversation. "Society is responsible for all crimes and should pay to rehabilitate the criminal. It's only right to make restitution to the sinner."

"Amen," Mohammed said.

"Oh yes, it's the caring thing to do," Cherry Blossom added.

Suddenly there were angry shouts coming from the cafeteria's black enclave. Several black students were yelling at a Hispanic who was trying to drag one of the blacks' chairs into the Barrio. The black students weren't using it, but this affront to black self-respect could not pass unanswered, so they responded by shouting hurtful—you could even go so far as to say hateful—language.

The Barrio couldn't let those racially inspired affronts to their manhood or their mother's marital status slide. Machismo demanded stronger linguistic retorts consisting of equally strong racial slurs and physical challenges. Words such as "nigger" and "greaser" were frequently exchanged, interspersed with many ubiquitous "MF"s filling the air, and a proud black individual became so irate he tossed a Niger veggie burger into the Barrio, hitting their leader in the face.

The resulting black laughter was quickly followed by more Niger burgers, and a food fight ensued. No Hollywood *Animal House* carefree 'aren't we being so outrageously naughty' type of food fight, but one carried out with anger, even hatred. Trays soon followed by chairs and then the use of fists and knives were flashed in the general melee as whites and Orientals started fighting the Arabs. A harsh chorus of loud bells, whistles, and buzzers sounded, drowning out the faculty's girlish cries of panic as school security guards came rushing in.

I was denied seeing the climactic chaos as my guides as well as the diverse faculty rushed madly from the cafeteria. The dwarf, the Bishop and transvestite were fighting for the lead.

In the mad rush and mayhem of people running pell-mell down the corridors, I was separated from my guides when a trio of older blacks—not book-carrying students, more the knife- and fist-carrying type—bumped into me.

Each pushed hard at a different part of my upper torso, accompanied by "He's a racist cracker!" and "He's a M- F- lookin' to get a beatin'!"

"I need money," the leader announced.

The second inquired, "You got money?"

The third firmly directed me to give them all my money.

I was debating whether my self-esteem would give way to self-preservation when providentially several school security guards came rushing up asking the trio where the riot was happening this time. Turning to face the security guards, the black triangular cage loosened and I escaped. Running faster than a white man can, I turned a corner and ran into my guides.

"I was mugged!" I shouted, then yelled, "Let's get the hell out of here! There's a gang of blacks just behind me and—"

A shocked Mohammed corrected me. "African Americans!"

Up Yours said I was stereotyping. After Cherry Blossom suggested profiling was not only hurtful but illegal, she advised we quickly leave as her sensitive intuition was strongly telling her we needed to quickly get outside.

As they busily corrected my semantics and subconscious racist attitudes, the blacks—er, African Americans—turned the corner and in unison shouted, "Dars the m-f white cracker!" and started for us.

Pushing Cherry Blossom aside, the last I heard was Mohammed yelling, "Yo bro!" before he went down, receiving several good kicks for blocking them. Up Yours tried to stop them with several smiling "Hows" and with upraised, greeting hand announcing he had no wampum. He was slammed hard against the wall for interfering with them. Cherry Blossom, shouting "Peace!" got nothing except a date offer from a bro to give her the opportunity to prove she wasn't a racist.

A safe distance from the school, I was finally reunited with my guides. They straight-faced lied, telling me this was the first time this had happened.

Cherry Blossom said it was caused by the tension and pressure students felt, this being a test week.

Up Yours complained that the protracted cycle of poverty caused by the capitalist system was the instigating factor.

Mohammed, peeking through a cafeteria window, happily said, "Say, the Nig—black—er, African American boys are winning."

I told them I should be leaving, having learned much about the value of diversity.

I tried not to sound sarcastic but they smelled it, and Mohammed got defensive. "Hey man, it's been a bum day. Personal physical altercations like that almost never happen here in Acceptance Land."

Thinking *BS*, I said, "Whatever," then asked Cherry Blossom if I could use the road we were currently on to go to the next country. Horrified she exclaimed, "Never! Alone? Never! That road is the boundary between the black neighborhood and the Hispanic Barrio. You, being white, would be barbecued to the delight of both. Police travel in correct diverse pairs down that road, and only in speeding police cars."

I asked my guides, seeing they were a diverse group, if they could escort me.

"Well," Cherry Blossom said, "I'd better confess. I'm not really oriental. Make-up, eye liner slanting the eyes, yellow pancake—well, under the makeup I'm really white. My name is Barbara Adams."

"Why in Heaven's name would you disguise yourself as something you're not?" I said.

She said, "Inside my head, I'm not white. In my mind, I think oriental. In my heart I feel oriental. At home I sleep with an oriental. I'm a Buddhist. Can I be hypocritical to the real me if inside I'm oriental and outside I'm not?" Then rubbing her belly she added, "Besides, I can never be accused of bigotry if I have a minority child."

Turning to the men who were aghast at her startling revelation, Up Yours complained she dishonestly got her guide job through a minority preference program. Mohammed vowed he'd see to it that a black woman, a real black woman, would get her job.

Up Yours was so incensed over Cherry Blossom's betrayal that he accused her of faking her pregnancy.

"Did I say I was pregnant? No, I never claimed to be pregnant. I'm just wearing a pillow for fashion," Cherry Blossom said.

Turning to Up Yours, I asked if he could see me safely out of the Land of Diversity and Harmony.

"No way," he said, taking the plastic feather from his hair and confessing with shame to being white; not only white but also English; not only English but Anglican; not only Anglican but a twentieth generation American on Ellis Island, his people were here busy screening the immigrants. "I know what you're thinking, that I'm a hypocrite, a phony, and ashamed of whom I am. But let me tell you, looking deep under my white skin I found nothing, but when I became adopted as a true full-blooded Sioux, in an emotional adoption ceremony at a casino, for a donation of a hundred to a dealer, I discovered the real me. On his break, the blackjack dealer, in cutting my middle finger and giving me my name, Up Yours, I finally felt fulfilled. I was now a someone and entitled to all the perks, all the courtesy society awards to us persecuted minorities. Besides, I've been told by some relative at a party I may actually be one one-hundredth Cherokee.

"Now, when I enter a room, no one dares not notice me or talk to me or laugh at my jokes, and they must apologize and feel guilty whenever I decide to arbitrarily take offense at anything they do. Well, I don't expect you, a visitor, to understand. It's a diversity thing."

Sadly understanding him all too well, looking at Mohammed, I said, "You're certainly black!"

"Proud to be black. All us blacks are proud to be black. All us blacks are proud of our great slave ancestors who made this country."

"Er," Cherry Blossom whispered, "not slave... the new correct word is enslaved."

"Shit, I forgot. The damn words keep changing. Well anyway, we're proud. So proud, when taking welfare handouts from the man we spit on him because we're—"

"Proud?"

"Yeah, well anyway I can't go down that road with you 'cause not only would the Hispanics shoot my black ass along with yours but so would my brothers, believing by working for whitey, I'm an Uncle Tom. I'm not a Muslim, but a Baptist, so the black Muslim converts will skin my ass."

Pointing to another road, I said, "What about that road? Can I safely take it?"

"Hell no, that's Oriental turf," Cherry Blossom said. "They hate blacks, Mex, and whites in that order and the Viets are the nastiest. They would make sushi out of your ass."

Wondering whether I ever would be able to escape the Land of Acceptance, I suggested a white neighborhood..

I escaped slinking through back alleys. Glad to be waving a farewell to this tortured land, I heard a tearful Cherry Blossom desperately trying to say something in Cantonese to her fellow guides, but with a hint of an Irish accent; Up Yours, feather back in place, hands folded across his chest, was yelling with a Boston accent, "Up yours!" at Mohammed while Mohammed was screaming that he was the only true minority and proud of it, and he had no respect for honkeys hiding in other cultures. He was going to report them to the Love Acceptance Action Commission Police, the LAACP. The LAACP knows how to deliver hurt to racists and get them fired and hopefully jailed.

AFTER ACCEPTANCE LAND

In the hotel bar waiting for Sunni I questioned myself and the Rob Roy standing in front of me. Was I drinking too much? After every visit I had to have more than a few drinks. Being an occasional social drinker, I had never felt the need to be sustained by drink, yet now, alone on the road, nervous about Pru and my job, depressed by what I'd been exposed to and with little hope for the future, I sat with Rob and the Brandy Alexander I had ordered for Sunni.

Unexpectedly, Sunni had called my hotel room, suggesting we meet for pre-dinner drinks. I'd like to say I agreed since her request caught me unaware, but I know it isn't true. I tried to tell myself I accepted only out of politeness and a sense of collegiality, but it isn't true. To hide my real expectations I would like to excuse myself with placing a white clean veil over my intentions. Just a drink, some casual conversation, shared impressions of Acceptance Land, leading to dinner for two and nowhere else. Viewing myself as a caring person, sensitive to the needs of others, and knowing Sunni was alone, without Hinki, needing companionship, my refusing wasn't the kind thing to do. I could justify my acquiescence to Sunni's invitation by Pru and Rudy's just-received letters. Taking the wind from me, they left me breathless with fear and suspicions of possible hurt. I told Rob and Brandy of my reasonable innocent intentions, yet neither the drinks nor I were fooled. It was Sunni's soft, shoulder-length blonde hair, her cute face, her prize-winning breasts, her trim waist disappearing into a jolly ass, and damn it I was feeling so lonely and horny.

Pru's letter stripped me naked, left me defenseless, as she again went into painful details about her dinner with Hoar. How leaving the restaurant by a side exit they missed Rudy who usually waited outside the restaurant's front door to take her home. As they drove to her apartment she mentioned her concerns over the appropriateness of it all, but Hoar overcame her reluctance mentioning they were so preoccupied sharing personal information about themselves, and how much they had in common—*Common! He's got 20 years over her!*—they hadn't sufficient time to talk about my visitations. Apparently from social politeness she had extended an after-dinner coffee invitation to Hoar. I took that as a lie, as well as her faux surprise that Hoar accepted. Sitting on the couch sharing coffee she did suspect his intentions; however, apparently her feminine instinct was wrong. Hoar was a perfect gentleman.

What crap! I editorialized. Feeling visceral hurt I continued reading how, before she could definitely ascertain Hoar's intentions, Rudy arrived. After several minutes of uncomfortable coffee sipping and cake nibbling, both left.

Beyond all understanding, she asked, "Was I wrong in being suspicious of Hoar's intentions?" *Yeah, he loves me like a son and her as a daughter, and I'm not alone in a hotel, sleeping in a jail's isolation cell.*

Mentally I tried to argue with the ugly implications I felt hidden in her words. Innocent in mind, she was naïve in not knowing the pain her letter inflicted on me. She was unconscious of the sexual context of her actions and unaware of the sexual implications of Hoar's actions. Needing her, I thought of these and other justifications for her actions, but each newborn justification, in its turn, died. I realized Pru as a woman had innate knowledge of the ephemeral world of sexual signals. If I knew Hoar's intentions, certainly she must know them. If she knew his intentions, why is she acting as if they were unsubstantiated? And more to the point of my discomfort, why with me share her ambiguity toward another's obvious sexual advances? Was it to incite jealousy? Was it sexual braggadocio? Was it to extract a marriage proposal from me? I tried mightily to save her innocence, but it always came back to the solar plexus blow expelling hope, joy, pride, self-esteem and confidence: her infidelities in conduct, and her meanness in writing about her infidelities.

Rudy's letter continued my pain in relating how, after missing them at the restaurant, he went to Pru's place. According to his impressions he arrived just in time to stop Hoar from making a play for Pru. He assured me Pru would have been insulted by any such advances by Hoar and would have immediately repulsed him.

There was a disquieting last paragraph relating his staying for a little time after Hoar left to make sure Pru was all right.

Ah, so they didn't leave together.

All right? My Lord, what in the hell nonsense is he referring to? Was she assaulted, ravished, suffering a fate worse than death? He needn't have stayed behind, and why didn't Pru mention his staying behind? But most important why the hell were the two of them in her apartment? Why were any men in her apartment?

While I was in such a forlorn mood, Sunni called, inviting me for drinks at the bar. Using the hurt the letters had inflicted, I accepted, because like Hoar, I had hopes.

Sunni came and after telling me how sweet I was to order her the Alexander, which she had told me over the phone to order, she gave me a hug and a cheek kiss I actually felt. During our imbibing we moved words about nothing, moving from bland social appetizers and mouthing some beef. She began serving the beef with her astonishment at my being unattached, to which I expressed sympathy over her tragic discovery of Hinki's duplicitous behavior. During the time the bartender took to mix and serve a second round, she ripped apart Hinki's character, intelligence and manhood to such an extent that, with no thread left attached to another, he stood naked. Since her vilification was in agreement with my opinion, and since my intention was to keep her mellow, my hardily agreeing with her unsurprisingly earned me an arm pat.

Picking up Roy and Alexander, gently kissing them and putting them down, we resumed our main beef course. Apparently she was mystified at our not being closer, not seeing more of each other during our visitations. Before I could give a yeah to her mystification and suggest we should make amends, like a cat toying with a dead mouse, again she went after Hinki. It was because of his monopolizing her time, being pathetically needy, he had evoked her sympathetic nature. However, he had misinterpreted her kindness as something more and she had to put a stop to that.

Concurring with her on how pathetic such needy men were, I agreed she was too kind and was right in dropping him before the situation became painfully embarrassing.

That BS gained me her hand being placed over my hand, a visit lasting a significant minute.

With my gaze continually dropping to her breasts, whose softness, half-exposed, squeezed and uplifted, was resting in red satin, I mentioned I felt bad we hadn't gotten to know each other better.

In going down, Rob was very optimistic about my chances tonight. Unfortunately Sunni had difficulty leaving Hinki, lamenting how she had opened her heart and exposed her innermost feelings only to be betrayed. However, she added that I shouldn't get the idea she had opened more than her heart or exposed more than her feelings. I said, "Of course not; you're not that type of woman." That last was a sexual mistake. You don't want her to see herself as not being that kind of woman. My new Rob agreed, telling me without words that I was going strong. Her new Alexander enabled her to lay the groundwork for excuses for future misconduct when she told me the drinks were going to her head.

With the 'I'm still virginal the morning after' excuse now in play, she suggested we should eat something. Rob almost had me saying, Let's go to the dining room, but Roy reigned me in with the suggestion we order dinner from room service. With her deep kissing Alexander, doing the hair thing, and patting my shoulder, Rob screamed, *You're home free!* when who should materialize but the devil in the shape of Hinki.

Pointedly ignoring Sunni he greeted me as if I had a check in his name for a million resting in my pocket. "Peoples, how about you and I get something to eat, then do some drinking? After Acceptance Land I feel the love. You've got to feel the love."

Shit, if he didn't give me a quick hug. If I was alone in the world, despised, spit upon by all, I still wouldn't eat, drink, talk with this character.

With Sunni about to dine in my or her room, I mentally wished I had the laser power to vaporize Hinki.

Sunni wasn't going to let Hinki's slight go in not recognizing her presence. She asked him how his girlfriend had reacted in finding out he was trying to cheat on her.

Hinki tried the 'didn't hear you, you're not there' defense, telling me about a fantastic steak house just down the street.

Sunni interjected her venom, asking me what I thought of guys who cheated on girlfriends.

With a slight feeling of hypocrisy I vehemently said they were worst type of men.

Sensing it was two against one, Hinki told Sunni she was just a jealous bitch, mad because he didn't want to sleep with her anymore.

Rob Roy, Alexander, the bartender, and I squirmed at that.

Hinki stating what we all knew—that they had slept together—did give me encouragement and at the same time made me feel dirty in getting his seconds. Certainly his calling her a tramp didn't help my purpose. In fact it squashed my sexual hopes like a dirty bug.

Dragging her rotund butt off the stool, shaking those two semi-cones in front, Sunni slapped Hinki, not your patty cake but a hit that snapped his head back. "You're a vile, despicable human being!" she yelled and she would never dream of letting anyone as vile as Hinki touch her. Her exit to the elevator was worthy of an Academy Award, back straight, swinging ass keeping in step with her steps.

Hinki gave up on me and went outside. I gave up on me and went to my room to order steak and a baked potato. Honestly I was tempted to give Sunni a ring but with the sobering steak taking the fight out of both Rob and Roy, I didn't. Of course knowing there was no hope didn't hurt the decision.

BEFORE FEMININE LAND

Blessed with good fortune, Hinki and Sunni decided to ignore me and each other at breakfast. I had to be thankful to be left alone and be able to eat and reread Pru's and Rudy's latest letters, which still exhibited contradictory information.

After three heartwarming ego-boosting paragraphs telling in intimate ways her love for me, her need for me, and her desire for me, at the fourth paragraph Pru related what Hoar had said during their dinner together. Apparently Hoar wanted me to continue being stringently honest but more OP in my honesty. My gut reaction was the two could be reconciled only at the cost of honesty. Still, in Feminine Land, how hard could it be to be kind, hopeful and upbeat? I faced the Land with optimism and an OP attitude.

In a brief fifth paragraph Pru enthused over how Hoar was my very good friend who, respecting me, wished for my advancement and our future happiness. A last paragraph summarized Rudy's night visit.

Rudy's letter reflected his admiration in my exhibiting the courage to be honest enough to go against bureaucratic expectations. My hard-hitting reports were being applauded in the highest levels of bureaucratic circles. He was sure if I maintained my reports' integrity on the rest of my visits I would be highly rewarded.

After work, over a drink, Pru had told him about Hoar's opinions. Rudy believed she was misreading Hoar's intentions, or Hoar, out of ill will, was giving her misinformation. Rudy stated both Sunni and Hinki's reports were received with laughter and in juxtaposition with my reports, theirs were greeted with scorn, being labeled reports of ignorance. His last line was to reassure me that Pru loved me and that he valued our friendship and that he'd watch over her.

2

Feminine Land

Women in my Land, reading glowing news reports about Feminine Land's achievements in women's rights as well as fostering a caring, empathizing population, demanded the inclusion of Feminine Land in the investigative IV tour and an extensive report on Feminine Land be submitted. As a respite from the bizarre Science Land, the mental sickness of Psychology Land, the frightening ignorance in Education Land, and the hatred in Acceptance Land, I looked forward to the genteel, nonthreatening land of women: good food, good lookers, easy conversation and soft beds were what my nerves needed.

Now well into my visits and with my discouraging reports submitted, I suspected the reason why so many men back home with superior claims and more seniority graciously yielded their preference to me: the bastards knew what I didn't know. Because I was ignorant of what was waiting for me, they screwed me with smiles and attitudes of graciously granting favors and opportunities. I hoped the worst lands were past and here in Feminine Land I might recapture the advantages of my appointment I had presupposed existed.

My optimistic hopes were initially ratcheted up three times three as my three guides greeted me: a young nubile girl of less than twenty and more than sixteen told me she was Blossom and gave me a hug; a woman of more than twenty but less than thirty, still possessing and exhibiting endearing girlish charms and ways told me she was Flower and gave me a cheek kiss; the third, somewhere between her third and fourth decade and possessing mature beauty, favored me with both a hug and a cheek kiss as well as her name, Rose. Using similar expressions, all three told of their delight and happiness at seeing me: Blossom, another Blossom, a young maiden, in excited tones bordering on a scream and accompanied by little up-down hops, said it was "absolutely fabulous" that I was visiting them; Flower, my twentyish guide, in similar animated tones continually expressing her absolute disbelief I had indeed finally arrived, loudly exclaimed how she absolutely couldn't believe I was there, right in front of her, and someone must pinch her to verify she wasn't having an absolutely fantastic dream; Rose, the good looking mature guide, in breathless tones, was shrieking that she was going to just have to scream, followed by threats she was going to faint, followed by appeals to the other guides to swear she had never been so excited.

Possessing a naturally modest and retiring disposition, being the recipient of all these effusive greetings, all unwarranted and certainly unexpected, caused me to feel uncomfortable. Was something expected of me? Such impassioned greetings hurled at me suggested expectations of unspecified accomplishments on my part. Their attire constantly interfered with my ability to construct a rational chain of thought.

Each wore a t-shirt, the youngest a size or two too small, outlining both ample and braless breasts. Her habit was to vigorously twist and turn in joyful, youthful enthusiasm, letting centrifugal forces send her perkiness violently side to side. I had to wonder why they didn't just fly off into the ether.

Rose, the eldest, had a shirt so many sizes too large that it hung low, dropping deep from her shoulders, revealing fulsome breasts to nipples' edge so when she bent over and shook, as she was often forced to do by some very troublesome shoe laces which refused to stay tied, everything was on view and certainly not as a still life.

Flower, the middle girl—er, woman—had the right size shirt, but it was cut too short, as if for a ten year old. Her shirt came up so short that her nipples' undercarriage was exposed reassuring it supported some heavy stuff, as she continually jumped up and down, raising her hands to the sky.

After Pru's downer letter, Acceptance's troubled letter, and Sunni's turn-on, turn-off signals, t respond appropriately to the blatant displays I was being favored with, feeling they were inappropriate, strange, and in a sense threatening. What was more curious, from the bellybuttons of each hung pieces of costume jewelry, for what purpose was open to interpretation. I suspected my low opinion of these vulgar displays were markedly different from the wearers' purpose, my chase opposed to their exotic.

The overriding puzzlement was why such silly girls were sent to be my guides to Feminine Land. Such wanton, unrestrained greetings and anatomical displays bruised my sense of propriety and were uncalled for, given the serious purpose of my visit. After the girls had made sure all six breasts were shown, noticed, and appreciated, in the person of the eldest asked where I wanted to visit first.

While eyeing a tattooed arrow entwined by flowers on twenty something's thigh pointing suggestively upward as if any traveler could possibly get lost and would need directions, I suggested we first visit Feminine Land's schools. I had heard their education, especially in women's studies, had been praised by the feminists of all lands.

All agreeing, we started, the younger holding my right bicep with her two hands, the older replicating the two-hand hold on my left hand, while the middle-aged walked in front, but for some reason having placed one foot directly in front of another, had to swing her hips out to the side, forcing the attached cheeks to swing and sway a foot off center on each step. Either her hips were enormously broad or she was exaggerating, because her ass moved faster than her legs and covered twice the distance. While watching the wavelike motions of her behind I noticed a tattooed butterfly high on her thigh, flying upwards.

When we'd taken fewer than one hundred paces we arrived at a plaza centered around a fifty-foot statue. Looking up I couldn't recognize the person whose accomplishments warranted such great elevation, save it was a barely covered braless woman. Hazarding a guess to avoid appearing ignorant, I suggested Madam Curie.

The younger said, "Huh?" the middle "Who?" and the oldest said, "No," it was in honor of a really fabulously important woman, a woman famed for her contributions to the advancement of mankind.

"Ah so," I said, raking my brain for another name. After all, fabulously important famous women aren't a dime a dozen.

"Jane Austin?" was my second guess.

The trio in unison said, "Who?"

"The great author," I said, and observed that my adding information, added nothing in aiding their recognition. My last guess came to mind without any deep reflection, "St. Joan of Arc?"

The youngest still was confused, but the other two recognized the name, if vague as to her accomplishments.

"A religious fanatic?" said the elder.

"An innocent witch burned," added the middle, "by evil men."

Realizing my three guesses had completely missed the mark, I asked them to put a name to the impressive marble monument above us. In one hand she held a children's book, and in the other something that looked like a torch. Thinking it might be their version of the Statue of Liberty, my fourth guess would have been a statue representing freedom.

The youngest, Blossom, vigorously twisting and jumping up and down, the mature Rose bending down in a mock bow, and Flower, the middle, jumping up and clapping her hands over her head, all in unison shouted their disbelief. Was I so ignorant? "Can't you guess? It's Madonna. The microphone she's holding is the giveaway."

So that was the torch. "Ah yes," I said, waiting for six breasts to stabilize and return to their partial coverings.

"If you've got time you absolutely must see the Brittney Spears Plaza. It's next to the Jennifer Lopez Women's Institute."

"Ah yes... unfortunately my time is short."

The youngest pleaded that I mustn't leave before gazing at the JLo thousand-ton granite statue done in the style of The Thinker. The older said, "She's wearing just as much clothing. Hundreds of people who have seen the original in the flesh swear it's an exact replica of JLo."

"Ah yes... well, I—"

"There's great speculation as to the man she's thinking about." Flower informed me. "Several books and not a few articles have been written trying to deduce who's the man she really loves."

Fearing another invitation to view another monument to nobody I asked, "Can we visit your school?"

"Yes! Yes!" they shouted and, with them repeatedly jumping, wiggling and bending in joy, we walked five hundred or so yards to a white granite building facing the Paris Hilton Plaza containing landscaped gardens seldom seen outside Versailles.

"Impressive building," I said and meant it.

"It's the NOW Institute for Advanced Women's Studies." The younger, pointing to it, gave three vigorous twists for emphasis.

"It houses the world's research leaders in advancing women's causes and issues," the oldest said, bending to tie that naughty lace.

"It's the recognized pre-eminent institute for women's education and it's co-educational," the middle one said with pride as she needlessly jumped, with two hands pointed out the roof.

"Ah yes, but I suspect there aren't many men in attendance," I maliciously said.

All agreed that was the case, and shaking their heads confessed the absence of men was a complete mystery to them.

Thinking such a learning institution was too specialized for my research purposes, I requested visits to primary or high schools. All three were adamant, I had to visit the NOW Institute for Women's Studies, for without a firm understanding of the culmination of their educational system, the schools leading up to this educational pinnacle would be unintelligible, if not confusing.

So with foreboding, which turned out to be justified, I followed the trio, asses swinging left, right in military unison.

The colors were what first assaulted my senses: pink corridor walls, baby-blue ceilings and a vibrant teak-brown floor.

Seeing my open mouth they gleefully observed, "It's so hot. Isn't the paint so very, very, absolutely hot?"

"Different," I mumbled, as we walked down a corridor devoted to NOW's past leaders and referred to as Lesbos Valley. Suddenly my attention was lassoed by screams, shouts, curses and noises of breaking dishes emanating from a classroom centered in Lesbos Valley.

Opening an electric-blue door with golden daffodils scattered about its surface I saw a huge thick panel of glass hanging low from the ceiling and at least forty female students throwing shoes, plates, cups, bras and panties at it while yelling the most obscene curses. Some hurled themselves at it, batted furiously against it with clenched fists. Suddenly the teacher, pressing a button, raised the glass 'til it disappeared into a meadow-green ceiling covered with gaily-painted butterflies hovering over violets and daisies. The class, cheering, jumping, giggling, hugging and cheek-kissing each other, was reminiscent of Germany's joy over the fall of the Berlin wall.

Sensing my confusion, Flower, the middle guide, pointing up at the ceiling in a momentous tone said, "The glass ceiling," while Blossom, the younger guide, twirling about, screamed in joy, "Women breaking through the glass ceiling!" and mature Rose stooping picking up a piece of carpet lint informed me it was a solemn but joyful class reenactment of the breaking of male barriers against successful business women. Rose said this looking up from her stooping position.

Remembering Dr. Horny's class, I saw the glass ceiling hanging over the women. Flower, the middle, stretching and up on her toes, moving her hands behind her head to correct an unnoticeable errant hair said, "Men are afraid of successful women."

"Absolutely," the youngest, Blossom, added. "It's absolutely true. Men feel threatened by powerful women," then did some vigorous turns at the waist, whipping left, right, her front two semi-attached semi-spheres threatening to send them into orbit.

The elder, Rose, still energetically picking minute pieces of floor offal, looking up, told me, "Here, in Feminine Land it's the Age of the Woman."

"Absolutely true," Flower added, clapping her hands overhead in joy, squeezing you know what together so tight they resembled rear cheeks.

Looking like they were a nanosecond away from gripping me in a joyous hug, I asked the trio and their quivering six important attachments, "In what subject areas does the school provide instruction?"

"Well, you just follow us," the elder Rose said, leading us in swaying nautical steps down a corridor with yellow walls decorated with cuddly teddy bears picking flowers, smelling honey jars, or cuddled up, sleeping. There were numerous bunnies waving at passersby with messages stating they loved us and they wanted to be our friends.

Going into a large wing of the school from which machine noises and loud, excited voices emanated, Flower, my middle guide, grandly announced, "Here is our cosmetology department."

With skipping steps, the younger Blossom, opening a classroom door, cried, "Here in the pedicure department you learn the latest techniques as well as the hottest in toe jewelry and toe painting."

Middle Flower urged me to venture forth. Shivering with disgust at people decorating their own and other's toes, I declined with thanks.

Older Rose was bending over, looking over you know what, and examining her toes, lamented the cherry red on her big toe was chipped.

"Can we see something else?" I asked, trying to escape the land of cosmetology.

"Well, you don't want to leave before you see the latest in hair coloring!" the young Blossom screamed and turning so quickly her breasts shook back and forth several times as if responding to a seven on a seismograph.

"And you have to see the great advances in hair removal—permanent, painless," the older Rose cried, bending over to see if a mischievous leg hair had dared show itself.

Middle Flower, in the cut-too-short T-shirt, was stretching a hand over her head pointing to a far room. "That's our body piercing laboratory, and next to it the body tattooing classes. We have one of the greatest practitioners of eyebrow tattooing in the world on our staff."

Bewildered I asked if there were any serious classes, like Mathematics or Physics.

"Oh no!" Three heads and six appendages shook back and forth.

"We'd like to have them," middle Flower said, standing again on tiptoe waving to someone in the distance.

"But there just isn't time in the school day," said elder Rose, bending to retie a shoe lace, while the youngest Blossom, clapping and squeezing hands, together squeezed 'you know what' and screamed, "Absolutely true! We're so absolutely swamped with our studies in fabulously important and interesting subjects!"

I asked them what classes other than those related to cosmetology are offered at their high school.

"Well," middle Flower said, "in all modesty, I'm a Master Counselor in eating disorders—you know, anorexia and bulimia. They're reaching epidemic proportions." She actually told me this without raising a hand, but she did lick her upper lip to and fro.

The elder Rose, refraining from stooping, bending, or folding in any way from the hips, said she was a Master of numerous schools of Yoga. She had trained young women in Buddha Yoga and Confucius Yoga and in the Mao advanced lotus technique. All this was said with pouting lips.

Blossom laid claim to being a graduate student at the Oprah Winfrey Institute, majoring in counseling white middle-class women in the proper way to live their lives, in what they should purchase, read, watch, eat, and think, as well as how to train their husbands and then to be forever happy. With a strange seriousness she had yet to exhibit, she informed me, "I've only got to watch twenty more Oprah Shows and I graduate. And I'm not even black. Isn't that the absolute most? And by watching her shows, shows I'm not racist."

"Ah yes," I replied, then wondered aloud where the exit was.

We were walking down a corridor consisting of a blue ceiling populated by little stars and off white walls covered with sleeping rabbits and turtle doves resting with closed or sleepy eyes in various poses of repose.

When passing another corridor, Rose suggested visiting the DeLaurente Fashion Institute. They tried to drag me to it, but mumbling "No" and keeping my head down, I continued plowing toward the exit, passing walls of infants sleeping in beds, chairs, and sofas, all accompanied by various assorted rabbits, cats, puppies, and birds cutely looking at the infants.

"Stop!" yelled middle Flower, waving her hand over head. "You absolutely must visit the absolutely greatest, the absolute crown jewel of our educational system!"

"Oh yes!" the younger Blossom shouted, underlying each word with a vigorous twist. "It's the most fantastic area in the whole world!"

Older Rose, after adjusting her shoelace, grabbed one of my hands, the middle Flower, the other hand, and the younger Blossom, my behind, and half-pulling and half-pushing, got me down a corridor painted yellow and decorated with pencil-thin women in assorted sophisticated poses in tailored dresses being admired by rugged, handsome men either dressed in business suits, suggesting success and wealth, or stripped to the waist, sweating and muscular, suggesting sexual prowess. Given my only other choice was to physically fight for my freedom, I let my legs follow my arms and butt. At the end of the corridor we entered a classroom so bizarre it boggled the mind. Reminiscent of Intellectual Land, serious women were gathered around several tables practicing various methods of putting condoms on plastic penises while an instructor was showing the latest one-hand foil tearing method.

Quickly pulling back I exclaimed, "Crap! What the hell is that?"

"Safe-sex class," they said.

Unable to even generate an 'ah yes' I just shook my head and quickly continued down the corridor.

"Stop!" they shouted, as I was passing a large lecture hall. "You have to see this class! It's one of the most important!"

Against my better judgment, curious to see what was the next absolute absurdity they viewed as most important, I peeked in. A panel of experts on a platform were answering questions from an audience of about a hundred women students. The entire proceeding was being videoed for future endless showings on public television. I hoped at last, this was a serious class, a class of some depth and serious meaning.

The moderator of the panel had just thanked one of the panelists for her astute, insightful reply to a student's question and asked the audience if there were any other questions for the experts. Hundreds of heads were bent busily finishing writing down the prior answer, when a hand shot up from the middle of the class. "Professor, could the panel give me advice on a problem?"

"Go on," the moderator encouraged.

"My boyfriend and I have intimate relations only once a week. This, after all my attempts to increase the frequency."

Some joker in the last row shouted, "For some of us, he's a wild sex machine."

Sprinkles of laughter were cut short by the moderator admonishing them. "Ladies, please... there is nothing funny about serious relationships having problems." Then, turning to the panel, she asked for their expert advice.

A man with a ponytail and matching horse face advised the troubled woman and her significant other attend his advanced sexual stimulation classes for couples experiencing difficulties. There were currently openings in his Exotic Sexual Techniques Institute if she was interested. "They're being held in the Kinsey Institute with Mandi and Randi as teaching assistants."

A woman panelist, who from a distance looked thirty but whose face didn't move when she spoke, and the liver spots on her hands suggested a closer inspection would double, if not triple, the initial estimate, said, "In my book, *One Hundred Bewitching Ways To Excite Your Mate*, I suggest you try number 46, viewing pornography together, or number 54 on the ways to make your own sex video, or number 67, having a couples party where the wives model lingerie while everyone views MTV musical videos geared for pre-teenagers."

The moderator reminded the audience, "Men are visual animals and you can't be too subtle with them. Mental finesse and gentle teasing just doesn't get the job done. Remember ladies, if you've got it, show it, parade it, rub their faces in it."

The audience let loose loud cheers, giggles and outright laughter at the last remark, indicating the audience felt they had the rubber to rub in full measure.

A male panelist of meager stature with a bald, oversized head that kept tilting to his right shoulder before he jerked it up only to have it then tilt to the left rose. "Viagra taken with massive doses of Vitamin E and my secret exclusive male stimulator capsules sold only on the Internet from my advance research laboratory located in Haiti is what your man needs." Then a pause before he added with a boyish smile from his left shoulder, "Except for your lovely, exciting selves."

Applause greeted the last phrase, suggesting universal belief they were indeed 'lovely, exciting' selves.

Finally a little old Jewish lady took the podium and with a coy smile meant to be cute and with a twinkle in the eye meant to be endearing told the audience, "Don't be afraid of your sexuality."

Loud cheers.

"Don't be embarrassed by your body."

Louder cheers.

"Don't be scared to be innovative, to explore different ways to excite your partner."

Thunderous cheers.

"I have a book that not only tells you how to have sexually fulfilling relationships, but explains step by step with numerous illustrations the 632 different intercourse positions, each more exciting than the next, each guaranteeing multiple orgasms. Try threesomes, foursomes. Remember that the main rule is there are no sexual taboos. If it feels good, it is good, so just go out and do good."

Loud cheers for the elderly Jewish grandmother talking dirty as she continued. "Don't be afraid of enjoying the sex act. It is a sacred, intimate bond between men and women, between men and men, between women and women."

Many shouts of "So true" were followed by applause as she indicated she'd be selling autographed copies after the class.

On the dais a woman rose carrying forty-two, both in years and in her bra, and began talking about the health benefits of belly dancing in the nude. That forced me to leave as my disgust reached the gagging level. So much sexual preoccupation could turn you into a eunuch.

Quickly marching out of the building I forced my three guides carrying their six prize possessions to run after me.

Out of the building, taking deep breaths, trying to clear and clean my mind from such sordidness masquerading as knowledge, I let the jiggles catch up with me.

"Don't be threatened by women's sexuality. We've become liberated," said the eldest Rose.

"Believe me, fear is not the emotion all of that evoked," I told her.

"You must face the fact that women have sexual needs. We're sexually liberated," middle Flower informed me.

"As a fact, being totally irrelevant to me, I'm disinterested in facing it, seeing it, hearing it, reading about it, or speaking of it."

Blossom said, "Too long women have been sexually passive. It's time we became just as aggressive as men. We're finally sexually equal and liberated."

All three had surrounded me, alternately pitying my intimidation by women's sexual desires and their annoyance at my cretin reaction to modern women. I reminded them of the economic law stating 'cheap money drives out dear money' and cheap money soon becomes worthless, unable to purchase what is desired, and so it is with women.

Blossom accused me of wanting to keep women down, then asked was I married.

Rose asked if I was happily married.

After accusing me of thinking women should only think of marriage and children, Flower inquired whether, if I was separated from my wife, I was planning a divorce.

"Let's visit some other place," I pleaded, "anyplace."

"If you're married, are you happy with your marriage?" Rose asked, suggesting she'd be willing to discuss with sympathetic understanding any marital difficulties I had.

Making a mistake of confessing my single status, which once known brought forth interested inquiries about why I wasn't married: if I practiced bizarre sexual perversions, they were open minded, sympathetic and therapeutic; if I was jaded, they were sure they could polish the jade 'til it glowed; if I was hesitantly bashful with women, they had the sensitivity to overcome it; if I were gay, they would gladly administer tests to verify or disprove it; if I were bisexual, they knew how to tip the balance; if I was worried about STDs, they had certifications of cleanliness; if I was worried about fatherhood, they not only had the miracle pill but were on it; if I worried about forming strong commitments, they were sophisticated career women totally committed to be uncommitted; if I was worried about being emotionally hurt, they solemnly asserted they never hurt anyone; if I was worried about expenses, they were cheap; if I had no money, they had money to lend; if I wanted intellectual, stimulating women, they were intellectually robust; if I wanted ignorance, they averred uninformed minds awaiting formation; if I wanted coy women, they were coquettes; and if aggressiveness was needed, they could push forwardness into impertinence.

Pathetically eager, worried about hypothetical objections I may have against them, they failed to realize, despite all the breast displays, I simply wasn't interested in them.

Surrounded by the most dreary, sadly uninteresting women, I was showing politeness in trying to awkwardly break their circle and to escape their overt overtures, when an excited girl came running up to us shouting at the top of her voice, "Did you hear about it? It's absolutely the most devastating news! You'll absolutely die when you hear!" Her sixteen or seventeen year old face was a violent violet color, tears pouring forth, knuckles alternately going to her mouth, then striking her breast.

Forming a circle about the terrified girl my trio expectedly cried, "What is it?"

I thought, *War? An anthrax plague? Possibly a nuclear explosion?* as she gasped, "You'll never believe it! It's absolutely the worst news!" As my guides, along with the girl, wiggled in excess agitation, the girl continued. "It's the hottest, an absolute gigantic thunderbolt out of the blue!"

I suspected we weren't talking about the Second Coming. She screamed, "Britani and Sting just separated!"

"Not Britani and Sting!" Flower cried in horror.

Misting up in the eyes, knuckles to the mouth, the youngest Blossom shouted, "Are they really separated?"

Older Rose gasped, "I don't believe it! I can't believe it! I won't believe it! They were so, so very perfect for each other."

"It's true. Britani left him, and she's now living with Billy Creep, the newest, hottest fantastic black rap singer."

Easing myself from the group I heard snippets of exclamations emitting from them.

"I've got all his records."

"She's making a mistake."

"He'll probably beat her like he did with all his past girlfriends."

"They use drugs."

"No never, not Britani."

"She's had breast enhancement."

"What about the children?"

"Well Sting will keep his, Britani's children by both lovers, Timberland and Steele will go with her. Of course her children by Sting will probably be shared."

"If she married Billy Creep, will it last? I heard they met in rehab."

Alone, I left them excited and enthralled by the separation of two people whose mediocre talent was greatly outweighed by the eminent ability of their publicist.

Mumbling "Ah, yes," I passed Feminine Land's boundary, having to wade past hawkers selling magazines and newspapers revealing the latest shocking hottest news concerning singers and actors engaged in sordid behavior while achieving insignificant accomplishments.

AFTER FEMININE LAND

My letter from Pru contained only two paragraphs carrying her love for me. It wasn't only the word numeral, but also the missing length and the paragraph's shortness that was troubling to me. I also noticed her reference to working overtime with Hoar. Apparently my report caused turmoil in various bureaus necessitating overtime for Hoar in crisis management. Pru begged me to be more optimistic, that I was disappointing Hoar and causing a lot of work for him.

The wise, the politically expedient course was to start to become a mental prostitute, saying I saw what I hadn't seen, expressing excitement over the trivial, and seeing deepness in the shadows in the meaningless— in other words, become an OP. Unfortunately the wise, the expedient, was unable to gain traction due to the visceral hurt over how my love, my Pru, my own and no one else's, has adopted another's thoughts and was transmitting them as more wise than mine, and I was to follow them as if I were a mindless puppet. To be lovers there must be one mind, and between Pru and me, it must be mine, no other.

Her last paragraph's words carried sufficient adoration to alleviate but not cure my distress. In pride I resolved to write what I saw without rubbing and blurring it with oily spin.

This resolve was buttressed by my pride, forcing my contradicting Hoar's evaluation and his advice, which Pru had hurtfully conveyed to me. From the perspective of an honest worker, I was telling it like it really was.

Pru working late with Hoar and being swayed by his negativity concerning my reports disturbed Rudi. In his letter he wrote how he tried to counter Hoar's influence with Pru over lunch, and hopefully may have won her trust sufficiently to keep her from Hoar's way of thinking. Rudi was insistent I continue reporting honestly, not to trim sails, because Hoar, a sly bastard, may be trying to hurt my career. Instead of emotionally raising my spirits, his letter placed two hands on my feelings, pushing them down to a confused, troubled area.

Two more hands contributed to my unbalanced, off-center mood when Hinki and Sunni joined me for dinner. Sunni, over salad with no dressing, enthused over the power of women in Feminine Land with special emphasis on numerous glass ceilings being broken. Hinki, over his salad with dressing (not that daring, it was fat free), was equally enthralled with women warriors. To my 'What the hell are you talking about?' he gushed, "With black belt karate classes with a chop to Adam's

Apple, a five toe strike to the groin, a girl can leave a rapist writhing in agony."

Spearing the last cherry tomato and cutting into a seared swordfish, Sunni added her esthetic impression of the feminist army doing their exercises.

"Exercises?" I repeated.

"Yes, over courses specially modified for women's physical differences, they ran zig zagging over fields, jumped over trenches, crawled under barbed wire, shot guns at targets, and some of them were as much as six months pregnant. Edmund, can't you envision our army made up solely of women warriors defending their homes?"

I tried to picture a platoon of JLos kicking a gang of armed terrorists' butts, but I couldn't.

Finishing his sushi roll of raw tuna and green seaweed—at least one hopes the green stuff was seaweed—Hinki seconded the all-woman future army, then added an account of his visit to a Conflict-Management class. "In these classes people learn how to defuse serious personal conflicts by talking about them with a trained moderator. Combative adversaries in guided conversation achieve reconciliation. I actually witnessed two women screaming and bitching at one another, one thin hair from hair grabbing, after sitting down with a group of concerned women suffering from similar group dynamic dysfunctions, and enjoying a cup of tea and chocolate chip cookies, by talking out their problems, solve them. The session ended with a group hug and kisses. It was beautiful. I'm not ashamed to confess my eyes dropped some serious salt water."

Knifing into some thin rare roast beef slices, Sunni had to relate her experiences in Feminine Land's International Studies forum. Biting into the raw meat she told how affected she was to sit in one of the Land's international conferences as an observer. "Across a large rectangular table sat female leaders of various countries, negotiating in total honesty the cause of tension between their Lands. Through frank discourse the misunderstandings were exculpated and in the end they—"I guessed. "Hugged and kissed each other?"

"Yes, and I was able to join in with hugs of my own," Sunni said.

Addressing his veal, Hinki said the smell in the Land was great.

I, into a medium-rare fillet mignon (all on your dime) that was sponge cake soft and didn't struggle against my steak knife, confessed I didn't smell much except for the BS being spread around.

Sunni told the cheese cake how she picked up some simply fantastic diet tips where just taking a miracle pill or rubbing a scientifically developed cream across your stomach and thighs, or eating nothing but lettuce and drinking red wine she could have a twenty year old body forever.

Concave chest and chinless Hinki turned to me mentioning, in his memos from his department to himself they expressed concern about my reports. Leaning over his Mocha Mousse he told me, "Your reports are dangerously PP and could hurt our Land's progress."

"Yes," Sunni put in between sips of Espresso. "From my department I've heard the same. Possibly you're ignorant of the irreparable psychological damage inflicted by pessimistic reports. Pessimism is very dangerous. No one should be a PP."

I left them debating on having an after-dinner brandy or seconds on dessert and Espresso.

3

Health and Beauty Land

Painfully shaking and squeezing my hand with strength, my guide Bob Stark, smiling with straight white teeth firmly attached to pink gums greeting me with an even mixture of warmth and vigor said, "Good health to you," and damn it, he meant it. With mutually pumping hands vigorously up and down, our eyes went up and down from toes to head. I was impressed, more than impressed. With his muscular calves, thick firm thighs merging into a flat washboard stomach showing between tight spandex shorts and half a tee shirt, it was enough to make me conscious of my scrawny thin legs and soft ample navel area. His tight tee shirt outlined pecs, shoulders and arms. The pecs, filled with sinew and vein-wrapped muscles, bulged without the need of flexing. Atop his thick neck was the bronzed, healthy, happy face of a thirty-five year old, making me feel a gray shadow of a man ten years older than my chronological age. With all this observing and admiring his fantastic physique, I became slightly concerned over my sexual nature. Shit, it wasn't natural for one guy to admire another guy's body.

His only reference to our bodies vis-à-vis each other was his slapping at his stomach, which possessed more undulations than wind-rippled waters, and saying he hoped I could prolong my visit and benefit from their vigorous health building regimen.

Silently weighing the cost in pain, sweat, time and though sincerely wishing to spend those coins, I suspected my willpower account was not sufficiently solvent. I answered, "Love to, but I've many investigational trips to various lands before I return home."

He said "Shame" with such genuine sadness I felt I had just denied myself eternal youth.

As if reading my mind he asked me how old I thought he was.

I demurred, finding such feminine games awkward at best: guessing five years younger than you believe, you wonder if your lie wasn't large enough. With girls you always guess younger than your true estimate. With men you always guess older.

"Go ahead," he insisted, and overcoming my hesitancy I slowly ventured "Thirty-six," which I suspected was probably a little older than he was. Expecting a frown of disappointment at my year or so lie, I received a gleeful smile and a renewed challenge. ""Guess again." The little man within said *Add*, so adding three I said "Thirty-nine." Instead of 'You're right,' or 'You guessed too high,' I got a broad smile of hard white enamel hanging from firm pink. "Off by five years. I'm forty four."

If he looked forty-four, I looked ninety-six.

"You don't believe me? Here, let me show you my driver's license," and he pulled from his tight shorts a plastic ID: Bob Stark, forty-four years old.

What could I say, but you sure look great, and certainly not forty-four. I was impressed, but I wondered why this was so important for him to prove.

"It's our healthy lifestyle," he boasted.

"And I'm here to gather information about your land's healthy lifestyle," I said to move the conversation from observing our bodies and how great he looked and how bad I looked.

"Great," he said. "Let's start walking. We always walk in our land. Notice how the road is divided into four distinct paths? The far right is the walking path, next the jogging and running path, followed by the bike path, and then the roller blade path. On the other side of the grass divider, the same, only going in the opposite direction. The grass divider is a golf cart path for those whose legs have suffered injury."

"No cars?" I asked.

"We breathe only the cleanest air," he said, and taking a deep breath gestured for me to do so.

Shit. Half the lands I'd visited were involved with air pride.

I did so, not as deep, and sniffed nothing special, but placating him said, "Yes, the air is wonderful." I declined his invitation switch to running or jogging paths, and we continued walking on the right path. Numerous types passed us: people power walking with weights in both hands, arms flaying the air; joggers and runners, all thin, all sinewy, all continually checking pulse rates as if worried there wasn't one, although being ecstatic if it was low and sinking toward zero; bicyclists, heads down, feet pumping, blank eyes staring intently on the black asphalt two feet in front of their handlebars; and roller bladers, smiling, performing turns, skating backwards, forwards, twirling, cast furtive glances hoping to spot people watching them and worried their neighbors were giving a better performance.

"It's a work day," I said. "How is it so many people are free to enjoy their exercises?"

"What's more important, a job or your health?" he asked, then answered himself. "Your health, right? If you lose your job you can always get another, but if you lose your health, you're dead."

"Can't argue with that," I said, feeling with a little thought, I certainly could.

Suddenly stopping, with horror Bob yelled, "You smell that?"

I sniffed. Nothing.

He sniffed a careful, tentative sniff, and mumbled, "I can't believe it. Not here, not now, not with all our education, not with all of the medical knowledge, not with all the advertisement," and swiveling his nose 90 degrees said, "Yes,! There, behind that bush!" and off he sprinted into thick shrubs some twenty feet off the multipurpose road paths.

After ten seconds of loud yells, screams, volcanic curses and vigorous shaking of branches a triumphant Bob emerged holding aloft in one hand a callow youth by his collar and in the other hand a pack of cigarettes.

"A smoker!" he yelled, as one would shout, 'A child molester!' and dragging the frightened youth to the roadway yelled to passing power walkers to call the smoke police.

A crowd gathered as power walkers, walking in place, stared;, joggers, jogging in place, glared; and skate boarders, practicing wheelies and looking disgusted at the culprit, hurled curses at him.

The youth cried he only had one puff… it was his first cigarette… he never inhaled.

Holding the still-smoking butt at arm's length as if it was a smoking gun, in reproach Bob shouted to the crowd, "Look! It's been smoked all the way down, and it has no filter. He's a hard-core user."

The culprit said, "Okay, I had more than one puff. I'll be honest. Yes I did, but I swear, it's my first cigarette and on my health I swear I'll never have another one."

"Look at the pack. It's half-empty," and Bob showed the pack to the crowd. As if it were a sign of the devil, as if the package contained the bubonic plague, the fearful crowd gasped and backed away.

"All right, you've got me. Maybe I did have a couple of cigarettes. But it's my first pack, I swear it. You have to believe me."

"First pack?" sneered Bob as he held up the youth's yellow nicotine stained fingers. "Look at the telltale tracks of a hard core smoker."

"He's an addict!" shouted a jogger. So great was his shock he momentarily stopped jogging in place.

A power walker vigorously swinging arm weights asked, "Where were his parents? It's the parents' fault."

"He deserves hard time, long prison time," a cyclist said, shaking a fist at the culprit. "He's polluting my air! He's trying to kill me! He's going to kill all of us! He's killing the world's environment," and he emitted a slight cough for emphasis.

A curveless anorexic woman runner more sympathetically suggested several years of rehabilitation in halfway houses employing extensive professional counseling.

Suddenly a blue and white golf cart drove up, disgorging a beautifully firm, well-proportioned woman and an equally sculptured male, both dressed in blue spandex tights and white tight half tee-shirts. Carefully pushing through the hostile crowd, now beginning to evolve from outrage to anger over the crime, the police threw the boy against the golf cart and did a thorough body search for anymore hidden contraband: cigarettes, cigars, pipes or chewing tobacco. Finding no further cancer sticks they proceeded to cuff the culprit, followed by lecturing the scared youth. "Smoking can kill you," the male said, flexing his biceps at an appreciative crowd.

"It's addictive. Every cigarette you smoke will shorten your life by ten minutes," the hard-bodied police woman told him, swinging sideways to give the crowd an opportunity to admire her bust outline and flat stomach.

The crowd "Ah"ed in appreciation of the view. Several of the better-developed walkers returned the compliment with flexes, twists and turns, and the runner coughed again.

Standing next to the cuffed boy, a stern Bob Stark said, "Hear that person coughing? Let's hope it's not the onslaught of emphysema or lung cancer that you inflicted on an innocent bystander."

"Oh my lungs!" the cougher shouted, and hurriedly jogged away, dripping little coughs behind him.

Hearing the coughs reminded all of the fatal consequences of second-hand smoke and the crowd, backing away, began discussing the possibility of brutal vigilante retribution. Taking deep sucks of air, seeking confirmation, an elderly woman power walking shouted, "I can still smell filthy cigarette smoke!"

"Show him the pictures," an angry voice loudly commanded. The crowd picked up the cry, "Yes, the pictures! Show him the pictures! He's old enough to see the pictures!"

Reaching into the golf cart, the smoke policeman pulled out a folder and, opening it, produced several 8x10 high-gloss pictures. "Here, son, look at this and learn."

I was able to see one of the pictures and was repulsed by its bloody gruesomeness.

"These are pictures of your lungs after smoking for forty years," the buff female officer told the quaking youth. Her male colleague shuffled the ugliness before the youth. "Son, cigarettes kill, not only you but everyone who comes near you. If you continue the way you're going, you'll be arrested as a mass murderer."

Tearfully the youth cried, "I only tried them today, and I swear I'll never smoke again."

Shoving him into the golf cart, they quickly drove him away before the ugly crowd could get out of control.

My quizzical look prompted an explanation from Bob. "It's a sad case. The smoke police will take him to a detox treatment facility where for several months smoke counselors will give him the professional help he needs.

"You know it's not the boy's fault; it's those big unscrupulous tobacco companies in other countries smuggling their unhealthy killer product into our healthy country."

With the handcuffed smoking youth driven away, the crowd dispersed, doing their power walking, running, jogging, biking, but not before thanking Bob for spotting this horrendous crime and, in getting involved, saving countless lives.

Resuming our walk, Bob murmured in a self-deprecating manner, "If the individual doesn't get involved, the addiction would become pandemic, everyone would die, and well...." He left the rest fall unsaid, but any listener could continue with the 'well' to the sentence's end.

"You take smoking very seriously," I said.

"Damn right." Then Bob suddenly started to take his pulse. "Justified anger can cause an increase in blood pressure. If your pulse rate isn't within a certain range after two hours of vigorous exercise, well, you're just unhealthy."

Being a person whose labored breath mirrors my racing heart rate after walking up two flights of stairs, I quietly promised my body a more demanding regimen when back home.

Ignorant of my thoughts, Bob suggested we jog while conversing, killing two birds with one stone.

Stone or not, knowing one bird that would be dead in less than a hundred yards, I politely but firmly declined his suggestion.

With a pitying look Bob dropped the idea and picked up another. "Here, in our land, we see good health as a two-fold endeavor; not only must one have health-giving habits, but also shun physically deleterious activities."

Showing him that even with a deteriorated body I could grasp the obvious, I said, "Hah, the reverse side of golden health's bright coin."

Bob, pointing to a white and pink building, said, "Look, there's a restaurant up ahead. Want lunch?"

All this brisk walking had generated an appetite, so I quickly said, "Certainly."

In a sterile booth, in an antiseptic dining room, knowing what I wanted I told the waitress, "A hamburger, fries on the side with a Coke, peach pie a la mode for desert with coffee, half and half and sugar."

The waitress, in a pink, tight spandex bra and shorts, stared at me in horror. The menus dropped from her white-latex gloved hands as she slapped me across the face, yelling she wouldn't tolerate such dirty, filthy language and I'd better leave before she decided to drop kick me in the karate manner.

While she was circling her foot in the air in front of me, Bob quickly intervened, explaining, as I was an official IV visitor, allowances should be made for my health ignorance.

Begrudgingly the foot came down as Bob laughingly informed me of my faux pas. "We never eat meat. It's outlawed. Do you want to see a picture of what meat does to your colon? There's a picture in the rest room over the urinal."

"No meat?"

"Illegal, as is soda—empty calories, kills the teeth. If you doubt it, in the rest room stalls are pictures of decayed teeth."

"No fries, I gather."

"Arteries and fats are a murderous combination. If you want to see fatty arteries, there's a picture of—"

"Is coffee outlawed?"

"Nervous system, kidneys, do I have to spell it out?"

"No picture?" I sarcastically asked.

"Over the cash register."

"My pie a la mode?" I prayerfully asked. "Is it forbidden?"

"Certainly—calories, fats, preservatives."

"What in Heaven's name do you eat in this country?"

"Healthy," the waitress said and shoved a menu at me.

With faint hope, a shrinking stomach and a desperately growing appetite I scanned the columns of low-calorie foods: low-fat cottage cheese and yogurt were there but labeled potentially dangerous with only one portion allowed to patrons over twenty-one, under fifty and in certifiably good health. As for salads, their variety numbered in the thirties, sans dressing. Of course, raw carrots, broccoli, cauliflower were on the menu as were wheat germ, oats, and other whole grains listed in various preparations, all unappetizing. I settled for a sliced apple sprinkled with caraway seeds and a glass of fresh squeezed tomato juice.

"Are all restaurants this healthy?" I asked.

"No," Bob said. I had fleeting hope till he added, "This restaurant was on the edge of what is permissible in a healthy society. Did you notice tea on the menu? They're pushing the envelope on that item."

"It was herbal!" I protested.

"Yeah, herbal today, Lipton's caffeine tomorrow, and then debauchery and ill health and death," he said.

It wasn't long before we were quick-marching again. I had been able to secure ten orange wedges to go, but only after washing and sanitizing my hands under Bob's supervision. Germs you know.

I eschewed wearing the latex gloves that were in the carry-out bag with the wedges. While I was eating wedges ala fingertip, Bob's sidelong glances suggested despite sanitized hands, I was challenging the world of germs to do their worst.

"I've seen your restaurants, your anti-smoking police, and your commitment to exercise, but what about your educational resources?"

"Excellent that you ask," Bob gleefully said. "We're going to visit a combined primary, junior and senior high school. They're located at our magnificent library."

Ten minutes later, out of breath and out of orange wedges, we arrived at a huge sports complex surrounding a large windowless building. Outside, children of all ages were running, sprinting, jumping, tumbling, and pushupping, all under the care of a teacher, who continually encouraged them, yelling, "No pain, no gain, no health," in between telling them all to go faster, longer, higher, and with more repetitions.

I asked, "Gym period?" observing that the children's beads of sweat, grimaces of pain, and cries of agony all spoke mightily against any recess idea.

"Yes, for fifty minute periods with ten minute rest intervals four times during a school day."

An "Ah, yes," slipped out from somewhere.

Inside the school I observed several classes of serious students studying advanced food nutrition. One class was being scared straight with a fried chicken leg slide presentation caused the students to scream in anger—no, not anger—pure hatred at that chicken's little fried leg.

My stomach, still not knowing what to do with the orange wedges, leaped with yearning. That crispy leg looked damn good. Better than any eighteen year old hottie.

"Have you ever seen anything more disgusting?" Bob asked.

"Ah, yes... er, no."

"Let's leave before they show slides of pizza with extra cheese, sausage bits, and pepperoni slices, and the students riot."

In revolt my hungry stomach was playing hardball, throwing pieces of oranges against the lining.

"We offer ten courses in nutrition," Bob said.

"Ah, yes."

"Care to see the cafeteria?"

Images of fruit slices, wheat germ, oatmeal, and bran in all varieties brought a quick, "Not necessary."

Indicating a classroom, Bob said, "Over there... you won't see what's going on there in any other school system."

Peering in I saw one half the class laying nude on mats with only a draped towel protecting their modesty, while the other half of the class were energetically pounding, twisting, and kneading the poor nudes, all the while slopping oil on everybody, everywhere.

Bob explained. "Eight different classes in massage techniques, including the Sun Yietze fist and foot pounding in the advanced manner. It's extreme, but you can only achieve healthy wellbeing through enduring good pain. Look Edmund, I see an empty table. Care for a Sun Yietze vigorous rub down?"

"No!"

"Not even with the graduate disco dancing feet technique?"

"What?"

"That's where Tony, over there, gets on top of your reclining back and does the twist to "I Will Survive." It's really a special experience."

"I'm sure it is, but definitely no way."

"Your loss. Now, we also have our huge sports-medicine educational facility just down the road."

Passing a gymnasium we heard screams, yells, and demands. "One more, give me another, don't quit. You don't want to look flabby like some foreign visitor."

Looking at us, a teacher shouted, "Look over there! You don't want to end up looking like that guy!" and a hundred pitying eyes stared at me.

I ignored the impolite comment and stares, and at another gym class Bob said, "This is our personal trainer class. Everyone has their own personal trainer. Even personal trainers have personal trainers. We have twelve classes at different levels of sophistication, leading to a doctorate in personal training."

"Ah, yes."

Peeking in I saw over a hundred children evenly spaced out, half-standing, yelling, and shouting encouragement down at the backs of the other half, who were doing pushups.

"We have over twenty-six different classes for learning how to coach team sports, as well as hundreds of classes in how to play team sports, but with absolute safely."

"Ah, yes... well now, I was wondering... er, what about Mathematics?"

"Not forgotten," Bob said. "Quick, what's ten repetitions of ten lifts ten times an hour, for three hours every other day for a month?"

Seeing my puzzled look and mistakenly interpreting it as arithmetic ignorance, after a few seconds he said with fulsome pride, "Forty thousand."

As a guest, refraining from correcting him, I asked about science.

"Definitely science. They study the physics of weight pulleys and the degrees of incline on running machines, graph the dynamics of heart, respiratory and pulse rates and— Oh yes, look. Over there is our Chemistry Department."

"The study of steroids?" I successfully guessed.

"Effects on the body, proper dosage for maximum enhancement with minimal body damage. One thing I want to caution you about: the importation and selling of steroids is illegal; however, small quantities for personal use is allowed."

"Ah, yes," I said, but was puzzled that something illegal could be tolerated in small doses, similar to weed..

"Don't forget our Biology department offers twenty-three different courses on the human body's musculature development, and our art department offers numerous and various courses in nude figure studies."

"Quite extensive," I said, hoping to put a period to his recital of the Land's subjects, and it did.

Bob, suddenly pulling down a jump rope hanging from a wall, started rope skipping at a frantic rate.

Swirling as fast as a propeller blade, the rope created a blurry cocoon, out of which Bob yelled, "Got to do some exercise every four hours or your body starts to deteriorate. Be through in thirty minutes."

To kill time I peered into a gymnasium labeled *Dance Studio*. The floor was covered with mats, and girls over nine, under sixteen, under five feet, and under sixty pounds were doing numerous running tumbles, jumps, and grotesque body twisting with legs appearing where arms should be and arms where legs should be. Dwarfish, muscular men were either running over, bouncing over, or jumping on headless, tailless horses, or throwing talcum over their bodies resembling a baby elephant's trunk tossing dirt. At least the men were attractive miniatures. Unfortunately the girls were skinny parodies of eight year old boys. I was just closing the door when Bob came up, red in the face, sweating profusely and claiming in ecstasy his pulse rate numbers, which apparently were extremely low for a half-hour of rope jumping.

"Ah, yes," I said to his numbers, wondering why anyone would expend so much physical energy to accomplish nothing outside narcissistic pride in one's body.

"How do you like our gymnastics classes? They're Olympic gymnasts."

"Impressive." What else could I or anyone say?

Quick-walking from the educational building, passing many recreation complexes containing soccer, baseball, softball, high jump, and track facilities, I was surprised all were without stands.

Responding to my commentary about this lack, Bob with no small pride told me everyone here participates.

"Ah, yes... of course." Feeling stupid for asking, shame faced I confessed I occasionally watched sports on TV.

Getting bored and exhausted watching a continuous stream of people of all ages from diaper-dragging infants to ninety year olds with varicose veins popping on the various paths jogging, running, and cycling past us in both directions, I asked Bob where was everyone rushing to.

He said, "It's not the 'to', it's the 'for.' We're rushing to nothing. We rush for our bodies."

Not comprehending, I said, "They have no goal."

"Certainly they have," he said, "but here the goal is within the individual's body, not outside it."

Making it sound mystical and spiritually profound, as a guest I said "Ah yes," as an Amen.

We reached Health Land's museum and I didn't know what to expect but I should've had an idea, seeing the fifty-foot replica of Atlas, not bent over but doing a one-hand lift of the world. Spotlighted inside the museum were busts of former athletic greats; uniforms encased in glass; sprinter sneakers that broke some time barrier; sweat-encrusted basketball shorts; and numerous bats, baseballs, basketballs, javelins, softballs accompanied by brass plaques indicating the 'why' and 'where' each piece of useless crap had achieved its sports immortality.

As we reached the far end and stood looking out at the garden, which was called The Arbor for Thoughtful Repose at the Pool of Inner Reflection, Bob said, "Impressive, isn't it?"

In the garden, some people, standing on one foot intensely studying their fingertips, were interspersed between reclining subjects twisting their feet to within an inch of their face, blissfully contemplating the profound messages transmitted by their big toes.

Bob, getting an intuitive feel that I wasn't in tune in what I was seeing, tentatively suggested we assume the upside-down butterfly lotus position and find out who we are and be at peace with who we are. He had such a puppy wistful look in his eyes, I mumbled apologetically about the lack of time.

As an alternative Bob suggested a visit to the media room where great moments in sports are shown on an Imax 80-foot screen, 360 degrees around, with a Dobie surround-sound system that I wouldn't believe till I saw and heard. "You'll hear every grunt, see every drop of sweat in slow motion. The show runs continuously, and it takes hundreds of days to see it all."

"Ah no, I don't really have the time." The man was frightening me.

"It's always open. You can see it when you need inspiration or when you feel depressed. Go in and watch a horse like Sea Biscuit win a race, and dream that you could be that horse."

"Ah yes."

"You know he's inside."

"Who?"

"The horse, Sea Biscuit, life-size and stuffed. In fact, we've got a pound of his certified manure. There's a whole wing devoted to champion horses, jockeys, trainers, owners, saddles, and horse shoes."

Before I could exhale an 'ah yes' Bob excitedly told me, "The land of beauty and health is not so self-absorbed as to only think human beings deserve recognition. There's a dog room filled with stuffed champions as well as winning dog teams that did a five-hundred mile sled race in times not seen in fifty years. Now the fish area is devoted mostly to stuffed champion dolphins, seals, otters as well as the largest fish caught of each species."

"Ah, yes," I said. "I'd love to visit each and every venue, but I'm dying to see your medical facilities."

Trying to tempt me, Bob mentioned a bird section and added enticing hints of champion homing pigeons and hunting falcons.

Taking all my strength to deny the pigeon, I firmly said, "Medical."

Refusing to give up as we quick-marched toward the Medical complex, Bob said, "Well, maybe later."

With a society so health conscious, I thought their medical facilities must be of the best.

We had barely started on our fast walk when a middle-aged jogger collapsed at our feet. Standing over him, Bob diagnosed the problem. "Heart... probably didn't warm up properly." A golf cart van quickly arrived and took the jogger away.

"We have extensive classes in proper warm-up procedures as well as proper cooling down procedures, but some never learn."

"Ah, yes."

Passing a neon lit bar called Naomi's adjacent to a walking, jogging, running, cycling path, my heart leaped and my stomach growled commands impossible to deny. It was now willing to tolerate raw cauliflower.

"Can we stop here?" I asked in a tone consisting of a mixture of begging and demanding. "I need a pick me up."

"We deny ourselves. Always say no to the body's first demand. Willpower, you know."

Just as I was wondering how a few slices off Sea Biscuit's stuffed and preserved ass would taste, we reached the hospital, which I hoped would be my last stop. Bob was trying to tempt me to extend my time to view a hockey game which was to follow the speed skating race which was to follow figure skating which would follow ice ballet, which— I cut him short. No more Mr. Nice Guy ambivalence. I gave him a plain, emphatic, "No."

To his "Are you sure?" I said, "Never in this world. No way in this life."

At the medical facility he wanted us to walk the corridors, peer into wards, talk to the staff, converse with the patients.

Faint with hunger and high on tomato juice, I was adamant. Inspecting the directory I said I could get a sense of the quantity and quality of medical care.

Suddenly Bob scared the hell out of me by falling to the floor. *Damn*, I thought, *a heart attack*, and was about to drop down to give him whatever help I could outside of mouth to mouth when, starting to do one arm pushups, he almost knocked me down. He did twenty with the right arm, twenty with the left, then repeated the procedure until, veins protruding, eyes popping, sinews taught, and muscles quivering, he finally jumped up, red faced, eyes glistening.

"My God, what a high!" he said while checking his pulse. "You were stressing me. I'm not saying deliberately, but doing a few repetitions of one-arm pushups just washes the tension away. You should try it."

"Ah yes," I said, thinking I'd rather remain tense, noting all my tension was due to missing comfort food.

Staring at the lobby directory I noted the expected departments in sports medicine with specialists in bone splints, pulled muscles, and disconnected ligaments as well as surgical departments dealing with body sculpture from tummy tucks along with butt, breast, and lip enhancements and liposuction, to mention only a few of the numerous departments specializing in adding, subtracting and rearranging the human body. Turning to Bob, apropos of nothing I asked the age expectancy in the land of exercise, fruit juice, and smoke police.

"Glad you asked. We're very proud of our advancements in life prolongation."

He didn't continue, so I prodded him. "And...?"

"Each year we are living longer."

Of course you live a little longer 'til the day you don't. That statement rattled around my hungry mind until, coming to rest, forced out a prodding, "And...?"

"A lot of lands are envious of our longevity and like your land, send IV visitors to learn our secrets. Funny, they never make any extensive follow-up visits. You have to wonder why is that?"

Thinking *Tomato juice*, lying I replied, "I have no idea."

"You'll come back, won't you?"

"Possibly," I lied, then asked again, "So the average age at death is...?"

"Morbid subject, don't like to talk about it."

"But the age number."

"You know it varies by sex."

"And what is it?"

Turning away he mumbled, "Fifty three for men, fifty seven for women."

I didn't expect three digit numbers, but certainly something rattling around ninety. Mystified, I asked, "Doesn't all this exercise, fruit juice, lettuce, and wheat germ help people's health?"

"Certainly," Bob angrily replied. "It's not people's bodies that give out. It's their minds. We have a high suicide rate. Our sports psychologists are working on it but have yet to come up with any definite conclusions. They suggest more exercise, but somehow once the body starts to age, people can't face it. It's like they've lost the meaning to their life."

"Ah yes," I said, and then saying "Goodbye," I started to leave this land to search for a steak, a baked potato with sour cream, and a beer, all preceded by a martini appetizer.

"No, you can't leave yet. You haven't seen our magnificent library, our world famous Educational Resource Center."

Omitting saying I was famished, I curtly told him I had to leave. Imaginary hamburgers were jumping over steak fry fences trying to catch laughing pig ribs; they were all playing in my mind and frolicking in my stomach's digestive juices.

"It's on your way out. We have to pass right by it." Persistently and threateningly, Bob said, "Look, your report will be incomplete without peeking in and I don't want to sound like a smoker, but if you don't inspect it, I'll have to put your omission in my report of your visit to my superior."

"Smoker?"

"Any very evil person."

"Ah yes," and not wishing to make either of us smokers, I told him I'd love to see the Educational Resource Center.

Walking to the library entrance, casting a not so covert look at me revealing his appraisal, Bob mentioned I definitely needed to work out more. "A few months with us and you'll be a new man, a man with a fantastic body fat to muscle ratio, a man who's taut, tight, well-defined body will bring a sense of pride to himself and not a little admiration and some envy from others, and not to mention fantastic pulse and blood pressure numbers. You can tell your friends with pride."

"But at what cost?" I murmured, made uncomfortable by a sense of slothfulness sneaking into my conscious.

Accompanying his, "The cost is paid in sweat coins, and just look at the gain you buy," he went into a gorilla-like posture, pumping up his biceps.

Definitely feeling treasonable to my body by giving it no pain, refusing to elevate it to buff status, I tried to defend myself to myself by challenging Bob. "After all this exercise, healthy tasteless food, living a life free of vices, what is the purpose?"

"Purpose? You ask the purpose? Lord, look at this," and literally ripping his T-shirt in two he redid his gorilla interpretation, giving me a front view, then a side view both left and right. His flexing the right leg and arm muscles made me uncomfortable as veins and arteries popped out along with sinews and muscles. After flexing the sides, he gave me the backside, even flexing his butt cheeks, one at a time. Finally unflexing, he grinned. "That's the purpose."

"I meant once you achieve your goal body wise, what do you do with it? What's the purpose?"

"You're getting me angry," he said, "and that's bad for heart rhythm and blood pressure. You've got to fight against anger and practice contemplative yoga." He paused, placing one finger on his wrist checking his pulse rate, and a palm on his chest checking, I suppose, his heart rhythms. Finally satisfied with the results, sternly, teacher to dunce, he said, "There is no such thing as the perfect physical body. That's a myth put out by those who would undermine our resolve to do all the good we're doing to and for our bodies. Slackers put forth the idea that if you reach your perfect body, you don't have to strive to be better, just maintain your regimen. Do you see the insidiousness of it? No one can just maintain. Trying to just maintain is to slide: cutting your jog by a couple of minutes, doing a few less repetitions on the weights—and then what's the result?" He paused either for an answer or for effect before announcing, "A flabby body. If you don't strive, you slide, and no one slides up hill. You slide down to a mass of fat."

"Ah, yes," I said to that little gem.

Bob continued. "What other rewards could exercise give but good health? Look at me—strong, energetic, optimistic, physically fit, a beautifully tanned body—I'm forty-four looking thirty-three. And then look at you... er, no offense."

"None taken."

I was about to press him again on the purpose of all this hard exercise and noxious-tasting food, when someone shouted, "Bob Stark, damn you! Are you walking?"

His healthy rosy look fading to an ashen complexion, Bob muttered, "Oh shit," then yelled back, "Sir, it's good health to see you."

"Shove that good health to see me crap. Why do I see you walking?"

"I've got an IV visitor from another country."

"Damn it, Bob, you're walking. You're shilly shallying."

"But he's not up to our physical standards."

"Damn it, Bob, you're strolling like a cheap whore."

"He can't jog," Bob pleaded, pointing at me.

Wearing muscles as if they were clothes, the man, in his mid-fifties, looking at me as one would when espying a gross deformity, turned to Bob and demanded Bob to give him fifty.

Obediently Bob dropped and started to do pushups, when he was abruptly stopped by the stranger yelling, "Twenty-five on one hand, twenty-five on the other hand. Damn it, Bob, you're getting flabby. You're starting to slide into fat."

"No sir! Never sir!" and Bob gave a right twenty-five and then a left twenty-five.

Considering that I doubt if I could manage one-tenth the number with both hands, I was again impressed and the stranger was mollified. What surprised me was his telling Bob, who had a radish flush from his exertions, "Now give me two hundred with two hands."

Bob labored with his two hundred. The first hundred or so came quickly. The remainder were done with effort. The gap after each pushup got a little longer until at the end Bob was shakily balanced on two hands, his muscles quivering like a hula dancer's hips gone wild, his face and neck a rare-steak red.

I didn't think the poor bastard would do it, but when the stranger, lying flat on the ground, yelled into his face, "Bob, you bastard, give me one more! You can! Prove to me you're not a slider! Don't quit now! You can do it! One more! Don't be a smoker!"

The shouts, curses, pleadings, encouragements, and threats were yelled into Bob's purple face. With his popping eyes, dropping tears of pain at each pushup, between 186 and 187 I thought Bob would completely collapse, maybe even suffer a heart attack, when pounding the ground, screaming one inch from Bob's bulging, tear-filled eyes, the man questioned Bob's manhood and demanded he prove his vitality and give him one more, just one more, only one more, and after Bob went down and slowly, shakily came back up, the stranger demanded again, just one more, only one more.

Well, I'm glad to report Bob did do his two hundred, and as he lay gasping, a mass of quivering muscles, more dead than alive, weaker than a ninety year old slider, the stranger introduced himself. "Tony 'The Slammer' Albert."

"Ah, yes... I'm an IV visitor, Edmund Peoples," and I put my hand out. My hand stayed out untouched as The Slammer, looking at me as you would a leper, announced with disgust, "You're flabby, totally out of shape. What you need is a good personal trainer, someone to whip your girlish soft ass into buns of steel."

Annoyed, pulling my hand back, I said, "Buns of steel do not make seats of comfort."

It was a mistake. He said, "Men of steel don't sit down except to shit. You look like a diarrhea man to me."

I had no comeback. My repartee arsenal contained only a single shot Derringer, so obviously he could outshoot me. All I could shout to his retreating front as he jogged backwards was the spitball retort, "Screw you!"

Rising, Bob eschewed my proffered helping hand, mumbling he was okay.

Looking at his tormenter, who was now walking on his hands singing in a hearty baritone "Send In the Clowns," Bob said, "What a fantastic man!"

"Your personal trainer?" I asked, irritated at the song's words, taking them personally.

"You bet," Bob said. "He's famous. Trained last year's third runner up in the Mrs. Muscles competition."

"Ah, yes," I said as I debated whether to give the finger to the personal trainer, now tumbling away in the distance. I didn't, thinking, *What the hell? I'm in the midst of madmen.*

It didn't take Bob long to recover from his ordeal and as we proceeded on our way I again spied Naomi's flashing neon lights proclaiming an oasis to refresh the spirit and supply quick, needed pick-me-ups.

Leaning on a mahogany bar, forgetting where I was, out of habit I ordered a well-needed Guinness holding hands with a house shot of whiskey. I received a hard slap, left cheek, right cheek, by a husky, beefy woman bartender with a tattooed *Kill Smokers* on her right forearm and

Death to Sliders on her left. The solid palm slap and an equally vigorous backhand pushed me back four paces.

"My gosh, Edmund, you don't curse at a woman, at least not in our land, and especially not at Naomi. You just don't use liquor words. You're lucky she didn't close her fist."

"Don't they serve bee—"

"Don't say it! Heavens, do you want to be killed?" Bob said as *Kill Smokers* was closing up to a fist and *Death to Slackers* was grabbing the bar, ready to vault.

Needless to say I covered her with profuse abject apologies while moving behind Bob. Then I said, "But this is a bar!"

"A health bar, a milk bar, a fruit juice bar, a quick pick-me-up bar devoted to vitamin loaded drinks, fruit and vegetable smoothies, and sugarless energy bars," Bob said.

To appease her and the onlookers who were gazing at me with disgust, I ordered a tall cold one, quickly adding of milk. I was served a thin, chalky substance, more whimsically watery white than paint white, certainly a pale replica of what any healthy cow delivers. While wearily eyeing her muscular *Death to Slackers* I whispered to Bob, "Er, could I get some whole milk?"

"Shush," he whispered. "Loaded with fats. We drink tripled skim milk. Any other kind is illegal. Just last night two bootlegging slackers were caught milking a cow in the middle of the night."

"And?"

"Six months hard time working on an organic health food farm."

"Hard time on a health food farm?"

"I know it's rough, but if you can't do the time, don't do the crime."

"Ah, yes."

I passed on the milk. The barmaid crossed *Kill Smokers* and *Death to Slackers* beneath a pair of breasts, more muscular than objects of nutrition or excitement. To not drink was to face her wrath and my cheeks knew better than that, so trying to appease her I ordered a double sour cranberry juice. With feet on the bar rail, Bob, finishing his five fingers of concentrated carrot juice, slamming the glass down, shouted, "Damn, that was good and strong."

Outside, jogging backwards, Bob said, "Here we are—our Community Communications Center, the CCC. We're proud of our multi-media library and TV studios."

Inside, in the library-video section, there were Arnold's buff movies, Sly's steroid puffed up Rocky movies, and films of men and woman's body building championships from 1907 to the present as well as all the Olympics, including all the tedious fluffy commentaries. An entire wall was filled with monitors continuously playing videos extolling the virtues of this exercise machine or that exercise device, as well as musical videos playing hundreds of different tunes to exercise with. They featured stars and choruses of gyrating, laughing, joyful, buff people bouncing in unison to the music.

One long room was filled with photographs and oil portraits. On the side walls were breastless oiled body building women's bikini bodies in bizarre poses that would neuter the most extreme sexual degenerate. The oiled men's poses mirrored the women's, but with muscles magnified ten times and ten times more freakish. On the far wall were pictures of grossly fat people in skimpy briefs with rolls of fat peeking out. I felt a tsunami surge of waves of fat threatening to flow down from the pictures and drown you. Pointing to the wall of fat rolls, Bob asked rhetorically, "Do you want to look like that? Would you want to be trapped, suffocating inside all that fat?"

"Shit no."

"Right." Then pointing to a wall of muscular bodybuilders, Bob said, "You want to be peering out at the world from muscle armor like those men."

I said I'd like to look normal, just average.

Missing my point, Bob agreed and gave me a flex.

One library book section, occupying ten large rooms with shelves floor to ceiling, contained every conceivable book on dieting and nutritional eating. There were books advertising the virtues of eating grains and no vegetables, of the need to consume vegetable and avoid grains, and the health-giving benefits of eating fruit, up to twenty pieces a day, but not grain nor vegetables. There also were a great number of volumes on specific foods you could eat, and exercises you can do to enhance specific body parts, inflate your bust, flatten your stomach, tighten your ass, and so on.

"No history?" I asked.

"Certainly. We have the history of wrestling and body building as well as all sports."

"Ah, yes," I said.

Wandering into the library stacks I became curious about the large section devoted to women's sportswear, and specifically to women's swimsuit competitions. In my role as IV visitor, I was pouring over a pictorial compendium of all past years' bikini competitions when a huge man approached me, a man whose well-developed biceps precluded any arm movement save for arm curls. In fact his arm rested in an arm curl position. Having difficulty straightening his arm, he asked for my help to get a book from the top shelf. Poor guy, he was so overdeveloped, he was physically disabled. I handed him the bound *Sports Illustrated Swimsuit Editions* for the past ten years he whispered thanks, then, glancing furtively up and down the stacks' alley, continued in a whisper suggesting he had something I could use and really needed. With whispers out of the side of the mouth and sidelong glances, illegality was in the air, illegal substances in the offing.

Telling him I wasn't interested, I had started to return to Bob in the main reading room when he tried to grab my arm. Due to his monstrously huge biceps, the poor disabled guy couldn't, so he said, "Wait, I see by your development you're not into sweat and pain."

Pausing, I said, "So?" thinking *Well anyway, I can still move my arm.*

"What I got, you need. What's in my pocket, you want. What I'm selling, you'll buy."

Expecting grass, speed, nose powder, or hopefully a corned beef sandwich, I watched as he tried to whip it out of his pocket, but couldn't with his biceps, tight rump, thick muscular fingers and tight shorts. Giving up with an oath he asked me to fish it out.

Smiling at his request, I firmly declined going deep into his pocket, wondering about the guy's sexual orientation. Curious, I asked, "What are you selling?"

"The best. If you doubt it, just look at me. I'm a fantastic advertiser for my product."

"Which is?"

"Steroids. Powerful steroids. What else?"

"Ah yes... and aren't they illegal?"

"Only if you're a major dealer. If you got a little, under ten ounces, for personal use, it's no big deal. Everybody here uses, so don't feel stigmatized. It's almost legalized for health benefits. If you inject your ass every now and then, so what?"

"If I was interested, how much do you have to sell?"

"As much as you need. Besides what's in my pocket, I've also got some hidden in library books. There are ten ounces in *Jane Fonda's Exercise Book.* If you want more—and from your looks you need a lot—there are ten ounces atop Madonna's children book on sexual exercises for the pre-schooler, and another ten inside Brittany Spears' thesis on the philosophical implications of wearing tight belly jerseys without belly jewelry.

"Of course, if you're interested in some serious diet pills, I've got those hidden in the diet book section."

Telling him thanks, but no thanks, I watched him waddle away, his elephantine thighs rubbing each other so hard from crotch to knees that he had to throw his feet out to the side. He advanced in a rolling waddle only seen in five hundred pound women making for a half-price sale on pizzas.

Walking into the central room, an atrium, I noticed a strange sculptured wall thirty feet high leading to the open second floor. Facing it, trying to force sense out of what was senseless, I looked at the small protrusions from the sheer surface: a religious code, symbolic faces, abstract art.

Suddenly a woman who, through vigorous exercises, had lost all the baby fat that makes a woman a woman came up to me. "Going to the second floor?"

Looking at her unappetizing body wondering when her bust disappeared and where did it go, I said, "Possibly. Where are the elevators?"

"Are you joking? You must be a foreigner. There are no elevators in our land, except for our eighty story building containing all the sports regulations and sports administrative rulings from sports governing bodies."

"Stairs, then? Certainly there are stairs."

"To the second floor? You can't be serious. We don't have stairs in any building with fewer than ten floors," she said.

"Are there reading chairs here? I haven't sat for hours," I asked.

"Chairs? In our Land? Chairs? Are you trying to pull my leg? There are no chairs in our library. We don't tolerate giving in to the body."

Eyeing her sinuously muscular leg I thought I'd rather try pulling an ostrich's leg. "Well, anyway, how the hell do you get to the second floor?"

"Climb, of course."

"Climb?"

"Certainly. We climb the wall," and she proceeded to throw herself against the wall sculpture and quickly, expertly climbed it.

Hell, I should have known. A rock climbing wall. Tired, I desperately canvassed about for any make-do chair when a smiling forty year old woman whose body was so thin she looked inside-out approached me. All her blue arteries and white ligaments were out there for pedestrian perusal. She approached shouting, "Hey flabby, who do you think you're looking at?"

Flabby? I may not be buff but I certainly resented her aggression. Still, I decided to placate her. "Sorry, I didn't mean to stare."

Getting up in my face she continued. "You think I'm heavy?"

"No, no. On the contrary. You're looking... er, extremely trim."

"Don't lie to me!" she shouted, poking a bony finger into my chest. "I can't stand condescending flabby men talking down to women who are struggling with weight problems. We both know I put on two big fat ounces on my ass, and damn it, stop looking at those ounces."

Trying to placate her I said, "Doesn't show."

She was now slamming me hard in the chest with her fist, which given its bony nature seriously hurt. Apropos of nothing she suddenly said, "Do you do Tang Foo?"

"Tang Foo? No. What is it? Some sort of Japanese steak?"

"That does it. Throwing vile filthy meat language at me. Next you'll be calling me a lamb chop, a pig's ass. I'll show you what Tang Foo is," and jumping back she swung her right foot around and landed a hard blow to the side of my head. Staggering back I was stunned on many levels: the unexpected attack, the type of attack, the attack by a ninety-pound forty year old woman, the great hurt. *Crap, did she have steel shoes?* Before I could recover I was Tang Foo left footed to the stomach, inches from caving in my diaphragm. Rattling my rib cage, the blow almost shook a rib or two loose.

Shit, I thought, and testosterone-induced anger came to my rescue. Reflexively pulling back my head, I dodged a killer hand chop to the Adam's apple. Now prepared, knowing the right Tang Foo foot was again coming, when it came swirling around, grabbing it I made her do a pirouette on the left foot before jerking her foot straight up and hearing a hip displace itself. Down she went, all ninety disjointed pounds, screaming in pain, yelling accusations that I cheated; I wasn't fighting the Tang Foo way where holding feet was illegal.

Though I was the innocent victim, I realized a ninety-pound woman screaming in pain and a two hundred-pound not all that flabby man being the cause could result in a serious misunderstanding. Seeing no one about, I ran to the only place I could think of, the place where one could sit down in privacy and not be bothered, a men's bathroom stall, and I stayed there almost an hour.

Back on the path with Bob, making no mention of the crazy woman's attack, I asked him where next.

"We have the most modern, up-to-date medical surgery facility. You've got to see it before you leave."

On our way there I saw a long line of people of all ages jogging in place or doing pushups, pale, worried, and mumbling to each other. They were queued in front of an official-looking building. Pointing to them Bob merely said, "Licenses."

"To drive?"

"Don't be ridiculous. It's our annual health exams. Everyone needs to have three health licenses. To pass you have to be able to do a vigorous set of physical challenges. After running so far or so fast you must possess the correct heart and blood pressure numbers. Of course it's age weighted. Can't expect a one year old to achieve what a seventy year old can do. I've never received a warning ticket on my health license, and it's never been suspended."

Bob pensively stared at me for several seconds before giving me the dictum, "Tanned people look attractive, outdoor healthy and energetic, while pale skins reflect unattractive indoor pasty weakness. I suggest a quick visit to one of our franchised tanning salons. In just a half-hour we could burn you to a beautiful bronze. What about it?" and he grabbed my arm, trying to pull me into a building where smiling red and orange people were exiting.

Digging in my heels, I told him no. Pale, even pasty, I came and that's how I would leave.

Bob promised a new me. "If not really in top health, at least you would look like it, and isn't that what it's all about?"

I told him I like to get my tan the natural way via the sun.

Horrified he cried out, "Ultra violet rays, skin cancer! The only safe way is the artificial way."

It became an absurd battle of the wills where Bob's smile became a grimace as I dug my feet in deeper. Finally giving up the struggle and forcing a smile he said if I didn't care what I looked like, it was my funeral, while lamenting to himself that you can't force good health on those who don't want it. I now saw the coercive and corrosive power of people who, feeling physically superior, feeling protective, demand you behave in accordance to their edicts for your own good.

As we walked to the medical surgery facility, Bob jogging up and down next to me made any conversation difficult. After a few minutes of up and down conversation I finally gave up talking, especially when Bob started jogging backwards. Along the path were numerous exercise stations which Bob made use of while I walked ahead. It was at one of these times when I was a hundred yards ahead of him and he was having a hard time tearing himself away from a balancing bar and rope climb, when I entered a heavily wooded area. Without Bob's continuous annoying exercising I was able to enjoy the silence, the leafy trees, the singing birds, the scampering squirrels. Suddenly from the woods a group of rough looking characters burst forth and, darting across the path, entered the woods on the other side. They were barely hidden by the dense foliage when a group of armed policemen with snarling, slobbering, salivating mastiffs burst forth yelling after the toughs to stand and deliver. Suddenly a policeman shoved a pistol under my nose so close it tickled nose hairs. He shouted for me to put them up, drop down, strip down and spread my legs. The commands confused me as much as the pistol scared me and his shouting numbed my mind. Dropping my hands, standing up and spreading my legs, I asked, "Strip down?"

Angrily he shoved the gun muzzle well into my nose hairs, yelling into my eyeballs, "You trying to make fun of me?" Then inexplicably he proceeded to jog in place, while ordering me to drop and give him a hundred. Then, glancing more carefully at me, amended it to ten. Then he said, "Try five."

In confusion I started to jog in place in sync with him.

"Are you a smart aleck?" he growled. "Make that one handed, damn you!"

Just then Bob jogged up and, jogging in sync with us, asked what was the trouble.

"Smugglers," the cops answered.

"Not him," Bob said. "He's an IV Visitor."

"Yeah, a visitor, and who else but a visitor would be carrying. Make him strip," the cop said.

"Look, I vouch for him and if he allows a body search and comes up clean you've got to let him go."

At Bob's 'let him go' I stopped jogging. Bending over gasping for breath I thought I'd never be able to inhale air fast enough to feed my lungs. I have to admit it, I was in poor shape. While Bob and the cop easily jogged in place while talking, I had to sit down and listen.

The cop was telling Bob about a gang of bootleggers bringing in a large load, maybe as much as two, three hundred kilos, to which Bob said, "That much could devastate the community, ruin families and most importantly destroy bodies."

Looking up I asked the four pumping feet, "Cocaine?"

"If it was only cocaine," the cop told me. "But it's not cocaine—it's three hundred kilos of Kentucky Fried Chicken, not only wings, but dangerous, habit forming legs."

"Chicken?" I gasped in wonder.

"Hey, you know, the Colonel's fried chicken can kill," Bob said. "It starts with a wing at a party, before long it's legs and breasts as your body and taste buds become addicted and start demanding more and more, and before you know it, you're arteries are gone and your heart gives out. Just think, trans fats."

Thinking, *Damn, what I wouldn't give for a bucket right now*, I got up and let the cop search me. As his hands went here and there, he told me about the depraved human mules who shamelessly tie Shake & Bake bags filled with fried chicken around their waist or hang it from their groin. And some men disguised as women stuff their bras with fried breasts.

Given a clean bill of health after the search, I sadly shook my head at the depths of the depravity human nature can sink to.

After a warning to stay out of wooded areas after dark lest we run across the dangerous Ron McDonalds's gang, the notorious Big Mac pushers on the prowl for children, viscously preying on innocent's appetites, we made our way to the surgical hospital complex, and it certainly was a complex and more. In fact, it was more like a city. The buildings were all white, each one tall in story, each one positioned in green, manicured lawns, each one with jogging and bicycle trails like tentacles stretching from building to building.

Pointing to a twenty-story building squatting hard on a green acre Bob said, "See that large structure over there? It's the Orthopedic Institute. A lot goes on in there."

"Ah yes, no doubt."

And in quick succession Bob, proudly pointing to a series of white edifices, identified them. "There's the Botox Institute, the Collagen Institute, the Institute for Rhinoplasty, and the Liposculpture Center. And that large building in the distance is our world-famous Breast Augmentation Medical Treatment and Research Center." He paused, then said, "Oh, oh, here they come. Courtesy in the Land of Health And Beauty dictates we jog in place with bowed heads."

And so, bowed heads, knees pumping, we watched a six-passenger gold-plated golf cart driven by a liveried chauffeur carrying four men in white.

"Doctors?" I asked after they had passed and my feet stopped their dancing.

"Certainly doctors. In our land, we honor them, listen to them, and pay them both the great respect and the great money they deserve. We owe our bodies to them. They keep us healthy so we can continue to exercise to be healthy."

"But for what purpose?" I again asked.

"There is no higher goal than to be healthy, to look healthy, to have a sculptured physique, and to be bursting with a healthy, optimistic spirit, for your entire body is a shrine to nature and beauty. Now look over there. See those wondrous white edifices?" He pointed out a series of short, squat buildings. "Those buildings house the Institute for the Propagation of Straight White Teeth. Don't take offense, but your teeth aren't straight or brilliantly white; in fact they're a serious gray color. Building Number 6 could easily get you a pure white smile like mine."

As he gave me a smile as broad as an actress's accepting an Oscar, I said, "Ah yes."

"And Building Number 4 can tone up those gums. After all, you'd like them to be a vibrant pink."

"Ah yes, but I really don't have the time," I said as he was trying to nudge me closer to the Institute.

"You look like a candidate then for Building Number 6. I don't want to be too critical but that left canine is not aligned with the rest of your teeth. Possibly several years of braces. Bet your teeth aren't even capped."

To detract Bob's attention from my teeth I pointed to a rather disreputable looking building whose whiteness had gone to dirt and whose shut windows had blinds drawn. That dreary gray place in all the bright white drew my attention. "And that building, the ugly building, what purpose does it serve?"

Bob was clearly uncomfortable. "I know you think everyone here is bursting with good health, visions of startling physical beauty. Unfortunately there are other people—people too fat, people too thin, too short, too tall, too old, too disabled—in other words, ugly people, people who either genetically or from slacker behavior acquired through poor parenting cannot be made attractive and healthy."

"And they're put in there?"

"That ugly building, yes... the building for the ugly."

"Seriously?"

"Of course. Can you really have a land of beautiful healthy people if ugly and unhealthy people are allowed to walk about without shame? Wouldn't the sight of them disturb those who are physically fit? And wouldn't the sight of us, in contrast, make them feel their ugliness even more? Living with other ugly people makes ugly people feel normal. It's the most humane way to treat ugly. Now, forget ugly. Thinking about ugly makes one depressed and a pessimist. You don't want to be depressed and a PP."

"Heavens, Bob, I'm definitely not a PP. I'm certainly an OP."

"Good, Peoples. Let's jog."

In the center of the complex, towering over all the other edifices, was the Surgery Building, a spider with a web of walkways connecting all other buildings. It was so dominant that I had to point and ask what went on in it.

"Building 7—important surgery, important to the health of our Land," Bob said.

"Oncology?"

"Breast and ass enhancement or reduction, Botox, wrinkle-removal procedures, not restricted to the face but also arms, legs, and stomach. It may surprise you seeing everyone here has tight, no-wrinkled skin, skin that looks like it was washed, starched and ironed. All our women have a 36C cup and smooth round firm butts, but I have to confess a lot of our uniform healthy look is due to Building 7. I personally had several unsightly moles on my chest that I left behind in Building 7."

"You seem to have a lot of hospitals."

"Good internal health as well as a beautiful exterior requires extensive medical attention. If you're not on a first-name basis with at least five doctors, you just don't care about your health and about looking good."

"Ah yes," I said, and on that note, after declining his invitation to stay and place my body in his personal trainer's hands, I left, and on leaving my only thought was for a beer, a big Mac, another beer, a couple of the Colonel's legs, another beer accompanying three slices of pizza topped with everything, and finally ending with another ice-cold beer.

AFTER HEALTH AND BEAUTY LAND

After I read Pru's and Rudy's latest letters, confusion reigned. In my suite, while dressing for a great dinner (your dime), I carefully read and reread the letters, trying with mental gymnastics to reconcile them, to no avail.

Immediately after Pru's three paragraphs, noting their briefness in professing undying, all-encompassing love (the measure of their length is as important as their content), her fourth paragraph repeated Hoar's telling her I was becoming a PP during their morning and afternoon coffee breaks and a simple dinner at her place. His remarks, uttered to her in the strictest confidence, indicated that in his opinion, I may not be up to handling the job of visitor, lacking the ability to see the forest for the trees. I was placing the entire department in a censorial position and must quickly become an OP.

By repeating Hoar's deprecations of my abilities, she covertly opted his meanings and injured my pride and in doing so, damaged our love. A woman's beauty may instigate a man's love but her unquestioning respect for his opinions and abilities are its tap roots. From stunned pride, from deep hurt, I resolved to continue as I have always done and not subject myself to other's opinions. I'll remain constant to myself. Adopting another's contrary opinion on anything always diminishes your opinion of yourself.

To be honest I did compromise to the extent of promising to scrupulously self-examine my motives. Was I being contrary just to be contrary, and being contrary, stand apart and above others?

My sense of mistreatment by Hoar and Pru's disloyalty to me was strengthened by Rudy's letter, which contradicted Pru's. Rudy's letter was fulsome with praise of my reports' startling honesty. He maintained the enthusiasm expressed in his letters was a pale reflection of the entire bureaucracy's support of my work. He also expressed strong disapproval over Pru's informal talks with Hoar over coffee breaks and dinners, being suspicious of Hoar's ultimate goals. At her place over late-night coffee he, Rudy, had tried to warn her. Apparently the situation was becoming a subject for satirical memos passed from desk to desk at the department, much to the detriment of Pru's reputation. Promising to dissuade Pru from being too friendly with Hoar, he related that Sunni and Hinki's reports were subjects of satirical diversion.

Pru had my love captured by her attractiveness, her amiable personality, her effusive unrestricted love for me, with her intelligence—a quality still undetermined—not an essential ingredient for me. Feeling Rudy was the more perceptive and Pru more subject to manipulation, I weighed Rudy's letter as the more trustworthy. In my return letters I requested Pru to leave off having coffee with Hoar, leaving my reasons unspecified. In the letter to Rudy I asked him to encourage Pru to restrict her contact with Hoar to only departmental matters.

If the two letters' purpose was to strengthen my purpose, lighten the heaviness of our separation and raise my spirits, they failed miserably. Troubled, confused, experiencing a sense of loneliness were all the letters left after the last word was read. My confused emotions caused mental difficulty about what to trust and what to suspect, what was there, what was hidden, what was right and what wasn't, and in not being right, was it free from being wrong.

With such emotional disarray, unconsciously I sat down at Sunni and Hinki's table for dinner. Realizing my mistake it was too late to politely get up and thereby communicate my opinion of them. My punishment for such weakness was to endure their conversation, a mutual exchange between the two, allowing a few weak asides to be tossed at me.

In revenge to the world of health, to stand strong against their world I ordered a Martini, doubling up on the olives followed by a spicy Steak Quesadilla Diablo (whatever that was) with grilled pineapple salsa and Hollandaise asparagus ending with Napoleons and a brandy named for him (always the dime).

My indoctrinated two companions, energized over obtaining a good-health regimen, restricted themselves to fruit salad between an apple juice aperitif and finishing off with a large prune juice desert. Watching them eat and drink that shit enhanced my meal. They were eating for health, so words like 'succulent' and 'delicious' were interchanged with enumerations of how each mouthful added years to their lives. Each salad's resident demanded their descriptions of its benefits to the body: carrots turned eyes from normal to laser; raw cauliflower aided the pancreas; spinach steel-wooled the colon to a pink glow; peas pampered the liver; tomatoes awakened the mental processes; lettuce cured depression; and artichokes, when eaten, will end all diseases. And so my dinner companions shared with each other the specific health benefit each bite bestowed.

Sunni's sudden acquisition of cherry-toned skin made obvious her time spent entombed in an ultraviolet coffin. Munching a celery stick she told me it regulates bowel movement. I replied, "I let my bowel out whenever it wants to move."

Hinki, while gnawing on a carrot, smiled with teeth florescent white, illuminating his lack of a chin, making it obvious he had enjoyed a teeth-whitening process in Building 6... or was it 7?. His continuous bright smile was reminiscent of politicians running for office.

Before the food arrived, each pulled out with great show sanitizing wipes and proceeded to vigorously wipe hands and utensils and did additional hand wipes after each fruit and vegetable course.

When their fruit drinks arrived they produced an unending parade of pill bottles and vials of liquid to take along with prune and carrot juice. Pills for hair loss, pills for feet calluses, different pills to give robust health to every body part between hair loss and dirty toes. Different colored liquids to promote the youthful functioning of blood, digestion, and kidneys were consumed.

Just before the prune juice desert arrived, Sunni, inspecting Hinki with a predatory eye, brought out a quart-size bottle filled with green jelly tablets and suggested he may want to try one or two, mentioning they were sex-drive enhancements combined with freeing the libido. Health and Beauty Land guaranteed the results would be fantastic, but warned her and her partner to take them only when she and her partner or partners felt the time was right.

Maliciously I asked Sunni what was the time. It took her a full two seconds to say nine o'clock and another two seconds to glare at me. "Very funny, Edmund." Sliding two green capsules next to Hinki's prune juice, she slyly suggested they should take them to see if they work.

I'm proud to say I resisted asking for a couple of libido stimulators. It was touch and go, but with Sunni keeping the bottle firmly between herself and Hinki allowed me to stay aloft from their sex play as they shared leering smiles. Hinki took the proffered pills. What in heaven did she see in the chinless, chestless, scroungy oddity was beyond my comprehension. Hinki was getting the dessert I would have liked to have sampled. *Damn him, damn her, damn everything and everyone.* I was bisecting my Napoleon when Sunni asked if I was able to visit Health and Beauty Land's health store. Receiving my negative response, both commiserated with my missing the store, like I had been busy pissing behind a boulder and missed Moses' arrival with the tablets.

With all the wonderment of someone getting welfare for the first time, Hinki explained, "We got all these health aids free."

Holding Hinki's hand down as if he was going to raise it, Sunni gushed. "It was as large as a giant Wal-Mart filled with all the health aids and organic food supplements you'll ever want."

Hinki asked if I missed out on the hot seaweed wrap after the mud bath, all ending with a dip in an ice-cold spring. "Look how tight, how glowing with health my skin is." After freeing his arm from Sunni's grasp he actually held out his forearm for inspection.

Screaming as if the Hope Diamond was in her prune juice, Sunni asked, "Hinki, was that you under the mud next to me? Instead of the seaweed wrap I got a pedicure," and she pulled her toes out for inspection. They were purple with smiling faces looking up.

After the two letters I received from home, after these two happily talking nonsense, knowing Hinki was going to get a great undeserved dessert, even a Napoleon and his brandy couldn't revive my spirits. Retiring, looking back, I saw them deep into each other's eyes, popping purple pills and washing them down with prune juice.

4

Compassion Land

My first introduction to the land of Compassion was a speeding car filled with laughing juveniles coming at me with murderous intent. Only by jumping into a ditch was my life saved, and it was saved by inches, not feet. The bastards, seeing me, a visitor, as a target of opportunity and taking deliberate aim, tried to run me down. For half the distance I thought they'd swerve; for the other half I was scared witless realizing swerving wasn't happening. More out of reflex than thought, at the last possible moment, I jumped into the ditch as their car careened over the curb and raced down the sidewalk before regaining the road.

As I brushed myself off, contemplating the justified mayhem I'd love to inflict on them, turning their stupid smiley faces upside down, a chauffeured limousine drove up and my guide stepped out. Wearing pink slacks and a Palm Beach shirt with smiling dolphins jumping over palms, after introducing himself as Major Drypus he asked what happened.

I told him a group of youths doing at least ninety had deliberately tried to kill me and almost succeeded.

He, being so vocal in sharing my anger and emotionally and effusively thankful of my near escape from such an accident, gave all he said the definite feeling of insincerity. After venting, emotionally satisfied, I joined him in his limo and we drove to the country's Justice building. On the way he told me he was a Major in Compassionate Land's Public Relations Division, adding, apropos of nothing, Public Relations with the most important division in Compassion Land. Noting my appraisal of his casual attire, he explained. "Uniforms for officers in Compassion Land are frowned upon as being too militaristic and threatening to the public." He actually smiled at this accomplishment. I smiled with surprise.

At the steps of Compassion Land's huge Justice Administration Building, a building surrounded by freestanding ornate columns meaning nothing interspersed with oversized statues of people who meant nothing, was a group of fifty or so carry people carrying placards and loudly, vociferously complaining. As Major Drypus exchanged hellos with them, to my surprise I discovered their anger wasn't directed at some perceived social injustice but at TV news crews who were an hour late for videoing their demonstration. Feeling imposed upon, they complained about TV news people's arrogance; after all, demonstrations without TV coverage aren't real demonstrations, in fact, they never really happened. TV people feel superior to the demonstrating participants. Besides, the demonstrators had more important things in their lives than standing around waiting for the cameras to record the group acting out their social grievances.

As we passed through them and entering the building on the way to the Compassionate Police Internal Affairs Department (after Public Relations, the second most important) I asked Major Drypus who the demonstrators are.

"Oh them... they're the usual Thursday group, a mixed bag of blacks, a few little old white ladies, a couple of scrawny community activists and several rich college students cutting classes to be part of this demonstration for social compassion. They fight injustice."

"Injustice against whom?"

"It varies, but on Thursdays they're usually angry at police brutality. Now the Saturday demonstration, you get a much bigger crowd fighting racism in hiring, racism in firing, racism in arresting, and racism in sentencing. They really bring their A game to be on the Sunday TV news." His voice quieted to a whisper. "Ah, here we are, and in time to sit in on a Compassionate Internal Affairs hearing on a police brutality case. An officer is accused of using unnecessary and unjustifiable force in arresting a black teenage boy. The defendant, Officer Patrick McManus—an old-time cop—can't adjust to our new system of compassionate justice. He's a dinosaur who simply refuses to die. The kindest thing to do is just put him down."

The three trial judges were led by elderly General Hillary, trying hard to look like a man and surprisingly quite successfully, ably assisted on either side by a black Colonel Roland and an intense white guy sporting a long silver and pepper ponytail who was merely a captain. The prosecutor was a Hispanic woman of uncertain rank but definitely above the rank and file. The defendant was testifying.

The Hispanic asked Officer McManus if he tazered the youth.

"I had to in order to—"

"Just answer yes or no."

"Yes."

"Before shooting the poor black youth with thousands of volts of electricity, what more-humane, less-drastic methods did you first employ to subdue him?"

"I yelled 'Police. Stop!'"

A surprised General Hillary said, "Just that? No warning telling the poor youth you were about to zap him with thousands of volts of electricity?"

"Wasn't time. He was about to smash the old lady's head in."

The black Colonel Roland interrupted. "Let's not get bogged down with irrelevant details. The old lady's head is not pertinent to this inquiry."

The prosecutor said, "Didn't you see he had a steel pipe in his hand and he was standing on wet pavement?"

"Yes, but the old lady—"

"Forget the old lady. We're not talking about old ladies. We're talking about how you electrocuted a black teenage boy. Knowing he was holding an iron pipe and had his feet in water, those two conditions making the use of electricity twice as dangerous, you still deliberately used excessive force to subdue and risked the lad's life."

"It was a life or death situation."

The prosecutor, rolling her eyes, said, "Yes, for the poor black boy. One could only wonder, if he was white and the victim black, would you still have been so fast to resort to such potentially deadly force?"

The three judges in unison nodded. General Hillary, the old woman like an old man, asked the red-faced defendant, McManus, if he knew all the proper humane compassionate procedures when encountering an alleged crime in progress.

As McManus gave no intention of answering, the ponytailed captain enumerated. "First, you are to identify yourself, then secondly ask all parties present to tell you what's happening and write their responses on form eighty-six. Then you are to—" "But the little bastard had her down on the concrete, standing over her with a pipe in his hand, about to—"

The ponytailed captain screamed, "Bastard? You used a hateful word! Tell us, how can you know he was... er, a fatherless boy, the son of a courageous single mother?"

"More to the point, you just made a racist stereotypical judgment about the poor black boy's parents," accused General Hillary.

The colonel, swearing he could hear someone in the room thinking the 'n' word, said he felt faint.

The captain told the prosecutor to continue, as they had a huge backlog of police brutality cases to hear.

The Hispanic prosecutor, turning to McManus, said, "As a policeman you're required to go to the next compassionate investigative step. After ascertaining that a possible crime may have been committed, you must warn everyone in sight that, because a possible crime has been committed, they are not to say anything or do anything without a lawyer present. Once those critical steps are completed, you as the officer on the scene are allowed to go to the last step and stop the crime by nonthreateningly placing yourself between possible antagonistic people. If your presence isn't enough to calm the situation, and your warnings are not sufficient to defuse the situation, you're to go to the next step." She paused. "Er, are we at step seven or eight?"

"You're at step seven," the black Colonel said.

"Definitely step nine," General Hillary unequivocally said.

"The hell with the number," the white ponytail captain said. "Just get on with it."

The General said, "The steps are very important. Each, in proper sequence must be firmly tread upon or compassionate law enforcement will be violated."

Humbly the captain backtracked, saying he was not referring to the steps themselves, but solely to the difficulty as to ascertaining their specific numeration.

The prosecutor continued. "After step seven—or it could be nine— the compassionate officer may threaten participants with arrest. If this doesn't defuse the situation, he may ask the chief suspects to hold out their hands to be temporarily restrained."

"But never threaten the use of aggressive force," said Colonel Roland. "If the citizen refuses your demands you cannot just grab them and, tossing them to the ground, inflict bodily harm."

"Possibly serious bodily harm," Captain Ponytail added more to put in his two cents than add any clarification to the discussion.

"Bodily harm! Certainly not," the prosecutor echoed, adding, "and you can't search them unless you have a judge's order."

An angry McManus was drumming his fingers on his seat's arms.

"Now," continued General Hillary, "if all appeals to reason don't prevail, the officer may take out his regulation police notebook and warn people he's going to write down names."

Captain Ponytail said, "And after names are taken, the officer may show his tazer gun and proceed issuing the necessary warning that he may have to tazer someone, but only if an immediate, life-threatening situation is present."

For no reason General Hillary began reminiscing about when she was just a police lieutenant and came upon an alleged burglary in progress at three in the morning. "I just went up to this brute of a man dressed in black carrying an awful heavy plasma TV. After I went through all the investigative steps and issued four stern warnings all the way to showing my tazer gun, he carefully put down the TV and apologized for any inconvenience. After a brief but intensely personal conversation during which I discovered he had suffered a childhood trauma of a sexual nature, we connected and hugged. Then peacefully he walked away without anyone getting hurt. By following humane police procedure I stopped the crime, returned stolen property, and reformed a troubled person with my feminine insight, and for my sensitive police work I received a deserved commendation and a promotion.

"As a post script, four nights later, at one in the morning I met the same gentleman walking between houses inexplicably taking night video pictures with expensive equipment while balancing an expensive sound system in his other hand. We had a pleasant conversation, a parting hug, and he even filmed me walking my beat."

Suddenly, in a display of emotion, standing up, McManus roared, "Enough! I can't stand all this bullshit! Enough is enough! The teenager was nineteen! The pipe he had in his hand was about to split open an old lady's head, and I tazered the creep! End of story!"

The outburst had no effect on anyone, save General Hillary who whispered, "Oh my dear! Is he going to get physical?"

The prosecutor said, "Nineteen is still a teen, a teen is a young boy, a young boy is practically a child and certainly no one can think it's an age of sufficient maturity to fully realize the consequences of his childish action." Then the prosecutor continued with a series of rhetorical questions: "Did you know the black youth was so injured he had to be hospitalized? Did you know he was going to high school to get his GED and had to miss over three weeks of his education because of this incident? Did you know the black youth's parents, on hearing of the physical assault on their son, in experiencing lifelong psychological damages are suing the City for a million and additionally citing the psychological damage and the possible brain damage to their son are after another million? Did you know—"

"Damn it, I quit! Screw you all!" and with that said McManus threw his badge at Colonel Roland and stormed out the door.

"Well," said the ponytail captain, "that certainly proves McManus was guilty."

"Well," said General Hillary. "That rids the Department of one more hot headed insensitive masculine sexist, racist ape."

"Well," said Colonel Roland, "did everyone notice he threw his badge at me, the only black here? Definitely a racist."

Apologizing to me for having to witness the ugly side of compassionate justice, Major Drypus suggested I ride in a police car for a few hours to get the feel of compassionate policing on the mean streets from an officer who is steeped in compassion.

Leaving the building we passed TV cameras busily videoing the now-happy shouting demonstrators holding up hate signs with McManus' name prominent.

Major Drypus was able to secure a squad car for me. I was to ride next to a female officer, Apple Strong. Officer Strong was a very attractive, petite blonde whose face, bust, waist, hips and legs had me looking and thinking beyond the uniform. Needlessly she told me she loved her work helping people in trouble, and being a single mother as a policewoman, working days, she was able to put her one year old daughter in daycare and see her at night. Then needlessly added her daughter was proud her mother was a policewoman as were Apple's parents, friends, and the bag boy at the supermarket who was a very special friend.

I couldn't resist asking whether the ruffled white blouse she wore (showing excellent cleavage) was the standard uniform.

"Only for policewomen," she laughingly said. "It allows us to keep our femininity while doing a man's job, just like a man, even better than a man. Besides, it's less threatening when we make an arrest. In fact, police women are demanding the right to wear pink blouses as well as tight T-shirts; it certainly would help with recruiting more women into the force."

Finally, smiling and parting her inviting, full, glistening lips, in tones suggesting there could be no doubt as to the answer, she asked what I thought of her being both a single mother and a policewoman. I didn't disappoint her. After all, could I tell her truthfully what I actually thought? Politely, I said I thought it was great, that I was impressed that she was a law enforcement officer and a single mother. She then asked what my wife did, or was she just a stay at home mother. She said the latter as if any woman taking care of her children at home was the worst kind of slacker. I told her I wasn't married, which seemed to make her happy. She looked at herself in the rear-view mirror, she patted down a mischievous hair.

Passing a bank, we heard shots from inside. Carefully pulling to the curb she pulled out several laminated cards with compassionate procedural steps to be followed if shots had been fired.

On the car's megaphone in the sweetest little girl voice she performed step one, announcing she was a policewoman and added her single mother status at three nasty, mean-looking characters waving guns and carrying duffel bags dripping green, who were exiting the bank.

One of the bank robbers gave her the finger. Another suggestively blew her a kiss while the third loudly yelled that he thought she, being a working single mother, was just the greatest.

Unfortunately by the time she unbuckled her seat belt and checked step two on her card, the robbers were in their car speeding away.

As she laboriously rebuckled her seatbelt and modestly adjusted her ruffled blouse and bra, she reported to headquarters that the alleged bank robber suspects, refusing to listen to her, were leaving the alleged crime scene before she was able to complete step two of the procedure.

The robbers' car was disappearing.

Tightening my seat belt, grabbing the dashboard, telling her to let it rip and not be concerned about civilian me, I watched as she checked to see if my seat belt was secured. "In Compassion Land it's a serious crime not to wear your seat belt. You could get hurt."

Impatient to start the pursuit I cried, "They're getting away!"

After checking for traffic in the rear and side mirrors, she pulled out and revved the police car up to thirty-five miles per hour.

Stupefied, I shouted, "You'll never catch them!"

"Don't expect to. In the Compassion police manual we are forbidden to chase speeding getaway cars. We must always obey the traffic laws when in pursuit. If we break the law, what kind of example are we settling?"

"Did you see that? The getaway car almost ran over that elderly couple at the intersection!"

"Case in point. Pursuing speeding cars at high speed is just too dangerous. If we pursue them at a reckless fifty or sixty miles per hour, they'll just go seventy or eighty. We go faster, they go faster, and where does it end?"

"They get caught."

"That's not the point. Lives, innocent lives, are placed in danger. No, if we do ten miles under the speed limit, they might do the speed limit to get away, and no one gets hurt."

"And no one gets caught," I malevolently added.

"We've brought accidents involving police cars down to almost zero. The statistics—"

"Watch out!" I screamed as, driving through an intersection, we almost got hit by a car doing ninety. It looked familiar, especially as the driver gave us the finger and the ugly rear seater threw a wet suggestive kiss at us.

"Hopefully a helicopter will be able to follow them," she said as she signaled for a turn.

Pointing after the speeding car, I shouted, "Those were the bank robbers!"

"*Alleged*," she said. "Always remember, innocent 'til proven guilty. Our problem is not having enough helicopters in the air to keep speeding cars in sight, but you must understand if too many are in the sky at the same time it could be dangerous. We did have a couple of hundred in the air tracking speeding cars trying to escape until tragically three of them ran into each other and six pedestrians were killed by falling debris. What could we do but ground them all? Now helicopters can only be sent up after a six-step helicopter procedure is followed."

"My gosh!" I cried. "Did you see that? That speeding car filled with snotty laughing teenagers just missed us and after ramming a van carrying children, is now escaping. *Damn it, those were the same kids who tried to kill me before!*"

"Please, *allegedly* the van, *allegedly* had an accident, *allegedly* is speeding away, and *allegedly* tried to kill you. Remember, it hasn't been proven in a court of law."

"Damn it! Aren't you going after those kids?"

"Headquarters has informed me they have the allowed maximum helicopters in the air already. The three are currently trying to keep eighteen allegedly speeding cars, which may allegedly be getaway cars, in sight."

"So they'll get away."

"Not necessarily. There is the chance their car will run out of gas, or maybe, when we flash our lights, they'll do the right thing and stopping, give up." We drove in silence. While looking out the driver's side window I saw the bank robbers slowly passing us.

"There they are!" I excitedly cried. "They're right next to us!"

Rolling down her window she shouted, "I'm Officer Apple Strong and a single mother. I'm warning you to stop and safely park your car at the next vacant legal parking space."

That drew a smile, a finger, and a blown wet kiss. As they were doing ten miles above the speed limit, they easily passed us.

"They're getting away... very slowly."

"Don't worry. I've got their license plate number. Isn't police work great? Even though it's very dangerous, still it's great how, as a courageous single mother policewoman, I'm doing a man's job just as good as a man. Honestly, Ed, tell me, are you worried about me, a single mother, being in such a dangerous job? My family worries, my friends, my daycare provider, my one year old worries, even the bag boy worries."

"Yeah Officer Strong, I worry. Tell me, how many criminals have you tazered?"

"*Alleged*... remember, it's always *alleged* criminals, *alleged* crimes, *alleged* victims. Well, anyway, thank heavens I've never had to pull my tazer. I'm very proud of that. Most of the time in going through all the steps necessary to compassionately defuse a tense confrontational situation, the difficulty resolves itself with people becoming bored, getting in their cars and simply speeding away. Sometimes sexist men knowing I'm a single mother doing a dangerous job just like a man, turn and run away from me, knowing, even as a police woman, a single mother at twenty-three, just as good as a man, I can't run fast enough to catch them. It's just so chauvinistic; it shouldn't be allowed.

"Now Edmund... er, you don't mind being on a first name basis, do you? Call me Apple. Anyway, I'm upbeat and everyone says I'm doing a great job in this previously male-dominated organization. Even my bag boy is very supportive, as are family, friends, day care—"

"Wow! Did you see that truck speed by, almost taking out that school bus?"

"Probably an alleged high-jacked truck or it may be filled with alleged illegal drugs or alleged illegal immigrants. I can't understand why they insist on speeding since we don't chase them. I hope they'll slow down so no one will get hurt. Compassionate Police's main concern is people's safety: our safety record is stellar. We have the best record for safe driving in the world. In the past ten years we haven't had to issue a single citation for speeding. It's a statistic we take great pride in. Unfortunately despite all our public service announcements about how we aren't going to speed in chasing after alleged criminals, they still insist on speeding. But Edmund, I'm optimistic and being a single mother, I just love doing police work."

"I take it you've never had to use, never mind show, your gun."

"Gun? What gun? Compassionate Police don't carry guns. Too dangerous, too threatening, leads to the escalation of tense situations. You show a gun, then they show a gun, and before you know it, someone gets hurt. Besides, we've outlawed guns. They're illegal. No one is allowed to have a gun, not even the police. We rely on rational, compassionate discourse and sensitive persuasion to defuse dangerous situations."

"What about those bank robbers? They had guns."

"*Alleged* guns, could be water pistols. And if they're caught, if the guns are real, that will be just one more alleged serious charge against them. They could face serious jail time.

"I don't wish to brag, but I've been successful in smothering many potentially explosive situations. With sympathetic feminine understanding, I caused many alleged perpetrators to just smile and calmly walk away."

"Wow, did you see that speeding car run over that woman?"

"*Allegedly* run over, and she was crossing against the light; however, I won't write her up for that *alleged* violation. I like to use my feminine single mother judgment in appraising the situation."

A squad car, lights flashing, sirens blasting, going a safe twenty-five miles an hour pulled up next to the woman's body. As one policewoman was reading the six procedural steps necessary for issuing a jay walking ticket, her partner was standing over the inert body, putting on latex gloves preparatory to gently touching the victim in an non-threatening manner.

Suddenly a speeding car rammed into the squad car, and my familiar gang of teenagers exited waving guns. The ticketing officer immediately started writing new citations for the teenagers as her partner started the necessary fifteen-step procedural recitation. The gun waving teenagers hijacked a passing car and, after tossing a mother and her ten year old son to the pavement, sped away.

Amazed, I blurted out, "This is ridiculous!"

"Certainly," Apple affirmed. "Notice the police car was illegally parked, blocking traffic. If the police can't obey traffic laws, how can you expect the public to do so? They're lucky the alleged criminals sped away. If they had stayed, they'd have one hell of a lawsuit against the city, and those police would have to appear before General Hillary for disciplinary action."

Officer Apple Strong had decided to break off her safe car pursuit of the bank robbers and drive back to the police building when a speeding car, passing us, threw several beer cans at us.

"Oh," Apple exclaimed. "That's so dangerous. Did you get their license number?"

"They had no license."

"You know, it's so vexing. They used to steal license plates. Now they don't bother using license plates."

I asked if she was ever tempted to speed up and catch alleged criminals.

"Regulators. All cars in Compassionate Land including police cars have regulators set to a maximum of thirty-five miles per hour. It's unfortunate how socially irresponsible citizens somehow allegedly disconnect their regulators. That's a serious offense, and if we can ever catch them, a serious fine is mandatory... of course, only after going through several different mandatory appeal processes."

Simultaneously we both spotted a drunken bum, head leaning against the building, urinating. "Oh, that's so nasty!" Apple Strong exclaimed as she exited the car. Going up to him she discretely waited for the nasty to end. The drunk turned, fly opened, everything, thank goodness remained hidden. Apple started on a preliminary fifteen steps to issuing a public urination citation. Teetering back and forth like a tapped bowling pin, at step four he asked Apple for lunch money. At step six he decided to walk away, but after a couple of steps forgot where he was going or even that he was going and, staggering back to Officer Strong, asked for dinner money as she reached step fifteen.

He gave her a toothless idiot's grin as she asked if he fully understood all fifteen steps. As an aside to me she whispered, "If he says no, I'll have to reread all fifteen."

Either he nodded yes or was looking down trying to find his fly, but Strong, taking the nod as a 'yes' put the citation in his hand, telling him in as stern a voice as only a twenty-three year old single woman policewoman could command, that on such a date, at such a time he was to appear at such a court, and if he didn't he would get a more serious citation to appear in another court on another day.

The drunk blew his nose with the citation.

Shaking her head Apple asked if I thought he would appear in court. In all honesty I said, "Not a chance."

Sadly Strong said, "People who ignore their tenth citation to appear in court to answer charges could face additional citations, even incurring serious fines. Of course, if being indigent they can't pay the fine, the police benevolent fund pays it. It's part of our outreach program, the

Caring Compassionate Connection with the Community. We call it the Four Cs Program. It's been very successful."

Back at Compassionate Justice Center, Strong mentioning she was now off duty, suggested that a nearby restaurant served excellent food. She always ate there alone, and wasn't it terrible to eat alone? After dinner she'd have to go home alone to a home she owned.

I said, "You don't say?" even though she did say it.

She said I struck her as a strong sensitive man who loves infants.

Thanking her for my strength and sensitivity and not responding to what she was really saying without saying it, with relief I spied Major Drypus coming towards us. With bad grace Office Apple Spice left me, mumbling that some men, unsure of their manhood, couldn't cope with strong single mothers doing a man's job even better than any man.

Coming up to me, Major Drypus suggested I might like to see their night court in action. Before I could respond negatively I found myself in a courtroom filled with such despicable people that their mothers would disown them, and probably had. The judge, a woman of forty, was staring down at four blacks sadly staring at a pound of cocaine in front of them. Sternly the judge asked if they were caught by an illegal police high-speed chase. Dispirited, they reluctantly admitted their engine died on them and the police caught up with them doing 25 mph.

Why didn't they run away as the fifteen steps were being read?

"What," the leader said, "and lose all that nose tickle? No way man."

"Couldn't you just take it with you?"

"Had it locked in the trunk. Just as we got it open, they reached step fifteen and took it from us."

Sadly shaking her head at their misfortune, the judge asked what was their defense.

"Shit, I... er, excuse me, Judge," the leader said.

The judge smiled. "That's all right. I pride myself on my street smarts. I can relate to street people, especially blacks, Hispanics, women, Muslims, illegals and homosexuals."

"Yeah, well, shit. It's just for personal use. You know, you divide the pound, the sixteen ounces by the four of us, you get only four ounces each."

"Still a lot."

"Don't forget girlfriends."

"Well," said the judge, "that brings it down to two ounces for each nose. Still a lot."

The youngest said, "Hell man, we're very popular with the girls. We've got two or three each, and that shrinks the pound to less than half an ounce for everyone."

"Well," the judge concluded, "we're actually dealing with a misdemeanor amount here. However Compassion Land is tough on drugs. We're waging an all-out, no-holds-barred war on drugs, so I'm afraid I'm going to have to fine you each a hundred dollars."

The shocked leader shouted, 'No way! Shit, that's outrageous! We're not giving any money to the pigs," and defiantly they all walked out of the courtroom. They were out of the building just as the judge reached the end of the seventh step in her contempt procedure and the guards were reaching for their tazers and ready to begin their fifteen steps when she reached her last step.

She said, "Well, I can understand their righteous anger because I empathize with blacks. In fact, I'm proud to say I once slept with one. Unfortunately I'll have to issue warrants for their arrest, and if caught they may get some serious jail time. It's hard to sentence anyone to jail even for a day because I empathize with the lower class. It's what makes me a compassionate judge, but if I have to, I can lower the hammer. I offer no apology."

The next case was an angry Officer Strong escorting her teetering drunk, whom she finally had arrested as he urinated in her squad car's open window, driver's side, as she was seated getting ready to drive home.

The judge said, "He appears to be allegedly drunk."

Strong told the judge that the defendant admitted to be allegedly drunk.

"Poor man. I'm going to find that the alleged drunk is indeed drunk and sentence him to two weeks stay at Compassion Land's Peaceful Valley Rehabilitation Spa to undergo their world-famous counseling treatment."

Fumbling with his fly he shouted, "Screw you! Don't want to go!"

"You'll have wonderful food, state of the art exercise equipment, cable TV, pools, hot tubs, recreation rooms and counselors everywhere, all counseling everyone in sight, including each other."

Adamantly the drunk told the judge, "Been there, done it at least ten times. It's like going to heaven and I've committed my life to going to hell."

"You mean you haven't benefited from all the good counseling?" the amazed judge said.

"Don't want to go."

"But there is booze... er, alcohol. This is a compassionate treatment center where no one undergoes a cruel cold turkey treatment. You'll start with a quart for the first day and each subsequent day your allotment is reduced by a couple of ounces, so at the end of your stay you'll be an acceptable social drinker, ready to get a job and lead a productive life just like single mother Officer Strong."

"Okay, I'll try it again. I'll stay for the first day, maybe the second, but I can't promise anymore."

"Oh, I'm so glad. You've made a hard and courageous decision. Now, are you receiving your disability check?"

"Damn it, no. I'm only getting unemployment. Compassionate politicians keep extending my unemployment. It's been seven years and in extending unemployment they're denying my right to disability money, which is more. I've got a disease, like being blind. I should be treated just the same. After all, I do get blind drunk."

"Oh you poor victim. You need a hug and a cheek kiss. Officer Strong, show him he's loved despite his gross appearance."

The drunk, going for his fly, chased Strong, who was running out of the courtroom.

Turning to Major Drypus I asked if anyone ever actually gets jail time.

"Certainly. We're a compassionate, caring, feeling society, but we're not silly. Let's look in on a parole board hearing to show you how tough we get on hardened criminals."

The officer, a chubby, gray-haired grandmother, was seated behind a long table. In front of her sat a parolee applicant. The grandmother asked, "Bruno Doggett, are you also known as Maddog?"

"Yeah!" he barked.

"You were convicted of multiple murders?"

"Had a bad lawyer. I'm innocent. I had a public defender. Damn cheap taxpayers refuse to hire decent legal help for alleged criminals."

Putting a stray hair in place, the grandmother solicitously asked if he was sorry for the six murders and four rapes, the death of two infants and the brain-damaged teen age girl.

"*Alleged* murders, rapes, deaths, brain damage because I'm innocent. Didn't have a rich man team of lawyers like OJ and certainly not his compassionate, loving black jury. Now I *am* sorry for the victims. Wouldn't be compassionate if I didn't feel their pain. We're all caring people here and all feel deeply. I—" He paused and tried to look sad, only achieving an idiot's look. He worked hard for a tear, failed. Settling for wiping away an invisible one, he apologized. "I'm sorry for breaking down at the thought of all those lives destroyed, but the emotion is just too strong even for a simple, innocent, emotionally depressed man suffering from a history of childhood abuse like me." He hid his face deep in a tissue where from it he emitted a few gasps and sighs.

A box of tissues was passed to him as Grandma Judge, making liberal use of her own box said, "It's so wonderful to see a man have the courage to express his sensitivity to other people's pain."

Peeking out from a handful of tissues, Maddog said, "And I got religion, read the Bible every day, and train dogs for the blind and give spiritual advice to the younger inmates, telling them crime doesn't pay'"

Grandma said this was indeed excellent news, a reformed sinner helping other sinners and caring for dogs and the blind.

Encouraged, balling up his tissues and tossing a three-pointer in a wastebasket, Maddog modestly admitted he didn't waste his time in prison, but learned a trade. He was now a master locksmith, got his GED and took college courses in Compassionate Law and Justice.

"Oh, you're just such a wonderful successful example of our compassionate prison system."

Realizing he was on a roll the convict continued. "When released I plan to go into education, teaching young people not to do what I've been alleged to have done. I'll tell them just say no to doing evil."

"So noble, so giving," granny said with feeling.

"Not only that but I plan to work and support my babies' mothers. All of them."

Interested granny asked how many did he have.

"Ah, I'm blessed with six."

"Six! Six children! How wonderful!" granny exclaimed.

"No, six babies' mothers. Thirteen babies. A baker's dozen," Maddog proudly said, and tossed a couple of dozen baby pictures on the table.

Looking at them, a sighing granny, saying how sweet they all looked, said she knew Maddog must be a proud father.

"And I plan to be a good father to all the little bast—er, heaven's little gifts. You know, like singing carols around a decorated Christmas tree, summer picnics, birthday parties where—"

"Stop!" cried Granny. "I can't absorb any more of these deep emotional feelings. I feel tears welling up."

Maddog had to fight off the parole officer who, standing next to him, desperately wanted to give hugs.

"How long have you been in jail?" Granny asked.

"Two long hard years."

"Oh my! That long?" granny said. "How did you stand it?"

"Prayer, hard work, good deeds," was the glib reply.

"And your sentence?" asked Baldy.

"Life without parole. Last year the parole board saw I was rehabilitated and dropped the 'without parole' part of the sentence and now, after another long, horrible year, I'm asking this board to reduce the life sentence to time served. After all, locked up here I can't help society, but released I'm sure, with my life experiences, I can make a great contribution. You know, giving back to society and all that."

On that note, after a deep three-minute contemplation, Granny joyfully told Maddog he was getting his parole. But though compassionate, she wasn't easy. He'd be on probation for ten years. That means if he kills, maims, or rapes anyone else and is caught and convicted, it's back to jail and this time it could really be for life.

A disappointed Maddog growled, "Shit!" complaining he had expected a full pardon, not an onerous, insulting, ten-year probation. It showed she didn't believe in his religious conversion, had doubts about his desire to educate children, was suspicious of his intentions to support and love his half-dozen babies' mothers and his baker's dozen babies.

"Don't say that!" Granny cried and reduced the probation to one year, asking Maddog Doggett if that was too insulting.

Mollified Maddog told them though the year was still insulting to his religious conversion and his total rehabilitation, being the bigger man he'd accept it.

Major Drypus, watching Maddog Doggitt walking out to freedom asked Edmund if he thought they were a little too hard on such a stellar example of rehabilitation. Could such a probation period send the wrong message to other inmates who are currently working hard at rehabilitation and discourage them?

With complete honesty I said, "No," that the compassionate message was explicitly clear.

He said since we were next to the Compassionate Prison we should drop in and see how the prison system takes it's rehabilitation mandate seriously.

Walking from the court building to the prison we saw paroled Maddog pull an old man from a car, grab his wallet and drive off as two grandchildren were screaming out the rear window. It was done so fast that Apple Strong, seeing it happen while drying and sanitizing her driver's seat, could barely get to step three.

"Aren't you going after him?" I asked Major Drypus.

"I'm reading the fifteen-step warning to the grandfather. He's getting a citation. The children weren't wearing seatbelts. In Compassion Land, that's serious offense. We take children's safety most seriously."

"The poor man's leg has been broken in the carjacking!"

"Possibly that's a good thing; otherwise he might run away and April Strong, though as good as any man and everyone is very proud of her being a single mother doing police work, might not be able to catch up to him."

Inside the prison we attended a conference between the warden and his senior staff. Warden Harold Musk, holding an advanced degree in Compassionate Rehabilitation Penology, was addressing his senior staff, a mixed bag of social workers, psychiatrists, counselors, therapists and sectarian people wearing religious clothing. The topic under discussion was the revolt in segregated D Block. Apparently the inmates were having such a good time in rehabilitation they were refusing parole offers, and some prisoners whose time was up were hiding in the movie theater.

Puzzled, I asked the Major what was going on in D Block to instigate such odd behavior.

"Gays being assaulted in the general population are sent to D Block to be with other gays and suffer from segregation. Now please be quiet and listen and learn."

Warden Musk defended the segregation for prisoners' safety.

A woman psychologist argued that grouping prisoners by lifestyle was hurtful, that stereotyping makes inappropriate moral judgments concerning the individual's life choices and does irreparable psychic damage.

"Still," an intense, mustached prison social counselor said, defending segregation, "bouncing back from any psychic damage from segregation, they're currently organizing a May Dance and have invited the staff. Now doesn't that indicate D block's excellent psychological therapeutic results?"

A female corrections officer, a general with eight stars running across shoulders wide enough to accommodate addition stars if they were discovered to be warranted, put in her thoughts. "I still believe letting them wear women's clothing and bizarre leather outfits may not promote good prison discipline."

A plump member easily identified by his scrubby, unshaven look as a social worker said, "It gives them identity and makes them feel good about themselves, and isn't making judgments about their attire morally unacceptable in Compassion Land? Next you'll want them to wear uniforms."

Everyone laughed at that absurdity.

"Forget about D Block; what about the riot in A Block?" Warden Musk asked. "Apparently the giant plasma TV in A Block's recreation room went out just as the Playboy Channel was in the middle of its very popular teen daughters and their hot thirty-five year old hot mothers doing their annual nude mother-daughter survival show. Of course it's artistically done with nudity as an integral part of the plot. Unfortunately the screen went blank just as the teams were starting the mud wrestling team competition."

With advanced degrees, a professional sex counselor bragged how after the Playboy TV Shows, his clients were very open to an in-depth exploration of their sexual interests and problems. This type of educational TV is a great help in addressing his clients' sexual dysfunctions.

"Riots come and go," the prison nutritionist complained, "but good nutrition is basic, and where else can criminals learn good nutritional habits if not in jail? But they aren't eating their vegetables. There are too many hamburgers and fries at lunch meals, and in their nutritional ignorance the clients are now demanding Ruebens and hot roast beef sandwiches to be on the lunch menu. What I'd like to see are more salads and low-fat cottage cheese, but the Prisoners Food Board keeps vetoing any sensible diet reforms. They're just getting too fat. It starts in the schools. They learn bad eating habits from school lunch programs and what's the result? Eighty percent of prison clients are obese."

Raising her eyes to heaven and spreading her hands in supplication, she shouted, "Why, why? I ask again, why do people not love cauliflower and broccoli? It's because of bad nutritional habits in the elementary school cafeterias."

"You must see both sides," the warden said. "Wasn't the Clients Food Board willing to compromise, agreeing to a salad with dinner if they got some dinner wine? Many clients feel they are being stigmatized as palate barbarians with just iced tea and coffee for a dinner beverage."

"Well, what about the clients' bodies?" a recreation specialist, a former football player with advanced degrees in playground games and kinesiology. "If the clients don't exercise... well, good nutrition is just half the story. I'll need to double my staff if I'm going to provide the additional ten sports programs the clients' sports committee has demanded. Especially in light of the synchronized swimming program Cellblock D wants in addition to their swimsuit competition."

"Crap!" yelled the college coordinator, looking suspiciously like my blowing wet kisses bank robber. "Too much money is spent on the clients' bodies and not enough on their minds. If we're serious about rehabilitation and not just serving as a warehouse facility, my budget has to be tripled. The clients' educational committee wants more laptops and cell phones. My prison clients are strongly motivated academically and the prison's refusal to back their critical scholastic needs is a serious roadblock to rehabilitation."

To change the topic the warden queried the wet kiss college coordinator about complaints of widespread test cheating, adding that possibly the prison school's honor system may not be functioning properly.

"Not working? On the contrary, given that no one has been turned in for cheating, you're forced to logically conclude there is no cheating. Besides, given everyone's absolute perfect test results, it's also logically obvious the clients don't need to cheat. Do 'A' students need to cheat? I think not. Besides the Client Educational Committee is adamant in refusing to even consider staff proctoring the tests, considering it a negative stereotypical judgment that the clients and alleged criminals can't be trusted. And I'd like to say it would be a serious mistake to change a system that's working beautifully. We had 100% graduation rate, all summa cum laude, some graduating with a doctorate after only a semester of intense study."

"Bullshit," someone in the back yelled, who then went on to loudly doubt the probability of clients getting A's in courses like an Appreciation of Shakespeare's Sonnets, especially since the class couldn't read at the fifth grade level.

From personal experience I knew back room voices were universally negative, universally right, universally ignored, and always frowned upon and argued down.

The champion for the front was the female head chaplain of the secular Universal All Denominational Compassionate House of Embracing Love. She felt it imperative to put down this example of the back row's negativity as one would do a rabid dog. Standing she said with secular's absolute faith never would any of her congregation cheat, and she wouldn't tolerate hearing such calumny spoken against her parishioners, all of whom responded to her ministrations with love, fellowship, and had experienced personal life-changing spiritual renewal from her sermons. Pulling a stack of white cards from a voluminous black bag with embroidered pink peace signs on each side, she cried, "Here are the proofs of my ministry's success. These are pledge cards clients have voluntarily signed indicating they're experiencing life-changing catharses from attending my ministry. Having found piety in the cleansing of their selves, they now discovered a caring self, a giving self, a righteous self, and a loving self."

The front, the middle, and even most of the back gave their loud assent, crying aloud, "You can't argue with those signed cards!" and "They can't be cheating if they found spiritual renewal and love!"

Sex counselor Ms. Purity Perry, a looker, just shy of thirty, not to be overshadowed. pulling out a thick stack of purple index cards, shouted, "Here! Here I've signed pledges from all our clients, especially Block D, vowing never to have unprotected sex, and my former rapist clients are pledging to respect women and understand that when she says no, she means no, even if she whispers it."

"Wonderful, Miss Perry," Warden Musk said. "These are the kind of fantastic results I expected when hiring Ms. Perry as sex adviser to the clients and to head up our sex advice program. If the staff doesn't know, she has advanced degrees from NOW University's Hollywood Campus in Exploring Diverse Sexual Practices. She's so popular with the A Block clients there's a year's waiting list for up close, intense, individual therapeutic counseling.

"Now," the Warden continued, "I want to stress how words can mold behavior. By talking, with caring, sensitivity, understanding, and nonjudgmental counseling you can change the most depraved drug-dependent predator into a sensitive, responsible, hard-working man.

"Let us educate the public and remind the politicians that counseling and rehabilitating our clients is cheaper than expensive long, hard prison confinement. Always remember, talk is cheap. Yet even in Compassion Land we're being cheap on talk as we have only one career advisor for every five clients."

Cries of outrage came from the career counselors.

"Only one drug counselor for every three clients."

Cries of pain emanate from a large contingent of drug counselors.

"Only one sex counselor for every two clients. Tell me, how can our clients know how to have good safe sex and respect women without a sex counselor?"

"Oh the shame of it all!" came from the numerous sex counselors, led by Miss Perry.

Finally the warden came to the most important shortage. "We have only one administrator for every three counselors. It is only by the exhaustive, dedicated work by this administration that we have been able to keep all the prison's counseling services functioning smoothly."

After the applause from the mob of administrators greeting this statement died a slow, lingering death did the Warden tell the assembly, "We have one last item on our agenda: Mr. Wolf Larsen, head of the prisoner's union, wishes to address us concerning some important concerns of our clients."

Mr. Wolf Larsen, with his muscles, tattoos and a shaven head, rose and his first word was "Shit." The second and third were, "Damn shit." The fourth through the twentieth were similar in content. Eventually he reached the substance of his oration. "There are only two choices of meat at dinner: chicken and beef. What about lamb, pork, ham, a little veal?" He suspected the prison staff was gorging on what the clients weren't getting.

"And drugs. Many prisoners, suffering migraines, eye problems, back problems, or joint problems, need weed, lots of weed, for relief. Not to get high, heaven forbid, never. It's only for medical purposes. Also mental depression is widespread and uppers are needed. Lots of uppers. And what about the anxiety sufferers? They need downers, lots of downers."

"Well, let me make a note of that Mr. Wolf Larsen," the warden said as he wrote in a notebook.

"Damn it. It's not Mr. Wolf, it's *Doctor* Wolf. I attended the prison's college education program. I just got my degree in advanced Chaos Theory and it took me almost a full year. I'm demanding you respect my achievement. And on the subject of education, seeing how most of us clients have advanced academic credentials, I think career placement counselors should consider placing paroled clients in meaningful jobs. You can't expect MBAs to flip hamburgers."

"Case in point. Now, Dr. Wolf, I now know why you were insulted with the career counselors' suggestion that you be employed at a waste management company."

"It was a personally despicable suggestion. He should have known my life interest is in helping teenagers, especially teenage girls, and running a teen age girls after school daycare sports facility is a perfect fit for me.

"Now one last item, and it's important. Given the Playboy Channel fiasco, I can't go back to my membership without individual plasma TVs. That, along with the lamb chops and pigs ribs, is not negotiable."

The meeting broke up with Warden Musk appointing an ad hoc committee of administrators on plasma TV's, another group of administrators on veal, an ad hoc committee to address concerns of prisoners who are sensitive to animal rights, and ad hoc pork committee to address any client's dietary pork restrictions, as well as an ad hoc committee to satisfy vegetarian concerns. Finally he assigned a fifteen-man super ad hoc committee to oversee and coordinate all the ad hoc nutritional committees. All of this additional administrative work necessarily entailed the hiring of twenty more administrators and the employment of outside consulting firms.

Outside the prison Major Drypus asked me about the conference. "Was that a something or was that a great something?"

"It was something, definitely a something," I said.

Major Drypus pointed out, "In all tests administered by Compassion Land testing and measuring of prisoner contentment, Compassion Land scored the highest of all other lands. And note there are no escape attempts. In fact some clients have to be physically forced to leave. Now tell me isn't that a tribute to our compassionate penal system."

I asked how many murderers given a death sentence were put to death.

A horrified Major Drypus, backing away a few feet, cried, "Death? You mean killing someone? Mr. Peoples how can you even ask that question? We're not barbarians in Compassion Land."

I said, "Sentenced to prison in Compassion Land is a life of free food, TV, rooms, library, exercise equipment and sports facilities."

"We try to make clients' incarceration as pleasurable as possible. Remember, Mr. Peoples, you have no idea how many innocent men have been wrongfully convicted, one out of ten, even two out of ten, even—"

Annoyed, I finished for him. "Nine out of ten are innocent and unjustly convicted." I added, "What if they confess to their crimes?"

Major brightened up. "It's a conundrum. To gain parole the clients must confess and express sorrow for their crime. The guilty, having no difficulty in confessing and apologizing, get paroled. The innocent, being guiltless, have difficulty confessing and apologizing to doing what they didn't do and so often are refused parole. The net effect of the parole board is that only the innocent are denied release."

Walking away from the prison I was almost run over by a silver Lamborghini driven by Wolf Larson. I dived for safety as Wolf waved.

"What the hell?" I shouted. "Major, did you see that? Wolf is escaping, escaping in a Lamborghini, escaping wearing a Scottish Tweed sports coat, leather driving gloves, a plaid cap and designer sunglasses!"

"If he doesn't slow down he'll certainly get a citation," the Major said.

I said, "No, he'll get a citation if he slows down. How the hell did he escape?"

"He's on a work release program; clients are allowed outside their prison residence at paying jobs."

"But the Lamborghini? How—"

"Saved his money from his outside job."

"What job?"

"He's working as a security guard at some financial institution. Now I suspect you, from a money driven land, think he's stealing. Let me remove such negative judgment. I happen to know he's meticulous in filling out the self-evaluating resident report cards showing he's a valued, honest employee."

As I crossed the border to Kumbia Land, Major Drypus' last words were warning me not to be negative. "Cynicism is a corrosive disease."

He was about to say more but a car filled with suspiciously familiar teenagers came driving at him, forcing an undignified dive into a ditch.

AFTER COMPASSION LAND

There was no letter from Pru. Rudy's letter, written between visits to Pru's apartment to keep Hoar at bay, was unstinted in his advice for me not to be afraid of being a PP if the visits warranted it. I was gaining tremendous success and a reputation for being a courageous IV.

That I was gaining a PP reputation at the office soured me, as did Rudy's reports of Hoar trying to seduce my Pru. His fighting to save Pru's love for me on late-night scrimmages at her apartment raised a red flag. Shit, did I want him to protect my Pru from Hoar or not?

At dinner, Sunni's eyes glistened with excitement as she related her experiences visiting Compassion Land's Marine woman's home. She commented on how precious she looked in her camouflage uniform. "Oh Peoples, I felt so proud of her and proud of myself being a woman."

Sunni ordered a shot, straight up, just like the Marines do

Hoping to go to bed with her, I told her about Officer Apple Spice and her courageous arrest of the pisser. As soon as I said pisser, I cursed myself for being too honest. In the battle of the sexes, disinformation is a powerful weapon. I quick expanded on pisser with "man, vicious," ending with "he was armed, and had drawn his gun."

Sunni was asking the bartender for some ginger ale to mix with her straight up. Apparently giving up on her hard bodied Marine, she went to motherhood, mentioning that Happy, the strong Marine, was the mother of two cute girls, a four and seven year old named Precious and Love. Both girls were bursting with pride over their mother being a Marine. "While I played with the children, the seven year old girl was playing house with toy women soldiers. Happy changed into Marine dress uniform. We took selfies of us together. Here, you want to see them?"

It was said as a question, but with the pictures placed before my eyes, obviously the question was rhetorical.

Looking at the two, arms about each other, I noted Happy was showing a six or seven month pregnancy. "Happy's pregnant," I said.

"Does it show? She had the uniform adjusted so it wouldn't show," Sunni said.

"She's showing a belly; she's got the last four buttons undone."

Sunni explained, "In Compassion Land when women Marines reach their third month, they are on paid leave 'til the child is five years old."

"Let me get this straight. She's got a seven year old, another four, and she's expecting. She hasn't been on active duty for at least ten years, and with one in the oven it'll be another five years? Hell, can't her husband take care of the kids?"

Hinki joined us as Sunni expressed surprise at the husband word. "Husband? Husband?" she repeated. "Peoples— Oh, hi Hinki— Peoples, you must realize she's a Marine. She doesn't need a man."

After I ordered a dry Martini, and Hinki some white wine, he hopped on Sunni's train of thought just as it left the station. "Yeah, Peoples, in Compassion Land single mothers are celebrated as strong, courageous women who shun the weakness of needing a man."

"Hinki, dear, you know, just what I'm saying; women don't need men's protection," Sunni said.

Hell, he just comes in and with a few words devastates my sex war plans.

Hinki continued. "What really impressed me was their justice system. Rather than the unproductive punishment penal system, they have installed a prison system that shows compassion to and respect for the inmates.

"Look, I met a Dr. Wolf Larson standing outside a bank so very fearful of entering and applying for a loan. He explained to me that, as a successfully rehabilitated bank robber and child molester he desperately needed a loan to start a child care center.

"Now Sunni, what's really amazed me was his pride. The Compassion Land penal system didn't destroy his spirit. On the contrary, it made him strong in his belief in himself."

"I'm sure he was a great example of compassionate justice," Sunni said, merely to get back to her Marine strong single mother. "Still, he can't compare with Happy, my Marine. She showed me all her guns. I had to help her carry the AK-40 to the living room so we could take a selfie of us holding the rifle. Here Hinki, People, is the picture. Don't we look strong but still feminine?"

Tossing the picture over to me, Hinki said, "Yeah, yeah... now I have to tell you, this Dr. Wolf Larson was so self-confident, so proud, and yet self-effacing that I had to force some money on him as a loan. Let me tell you, I really had to insist he take my money, and only on the condition it was to be considered strictly a loan. After hugging each other we_"

Sunni said, "Do you know, Marine women have military underwear, camouflaged panties and bras? Now just between us, Happy gave me a set. I'm dying to take a selfie of myself in them."

She sipped her shot, which was looking like a weak highball after she got the bartender to weaken it with more ginger ale.

Being compassionate as well as helpful, I quickly volunteered to take the picture, mumbling about minoring in photography in college.

"Would you?" Sunni asked, as if I had offered to pay for a *Cover Girl* pictorial layout. But only tastefully done and only for My Space.

Before I could finalize the deal, Hinki dragged Dr. Wolf back into the conversation, mentioning how with pride going into the bank he was able to talk Dr. Wolf into letting him cosign for a loan to get his child care center started. "In Compassion Land, children come first," ended Hinki's stupidity. Unfortunately, military-issued bra and panty pictures disappeared with the mention of children, as Sunni had to pass about selfies of herself compassionately hugging her children.

With bedroom plans, I studied each picture, expressing my wonderment and joy over how each child looked adorable, how Sunni looked radiant, how—when Hinki, more attuned to bedding Sunni, harshly announced the pictures' faults: too small, too close, camera out of range, too far, too much head, too little head, background was all wrong.

You'd think Sunni would get mad at Hinki and reward me with an invite to see her in camouflage undies, but the opposite developed. Wide-eyed, Sunni asked Hinki if he really thought her selfies were that bad.

With the assurance of a camera Picasso, Hinki took off. "Look, the only way to get a great picture is with the blah, blah tablet, equipped with blah blah zoom, at blah blah pixel resolution, with the blah blah lighting." And he told Sunni he had just that blah blah tablet, with the latest blah blah accessories and apps in his room.

With Sunni gripping his hand in expectation, I knew my hope was finished, especially when Sunni was debating aloud how daring she should go.

Hinki was busy telling the bored bartender about Dr. Wolf asking the bank manager about his security system. Apparently besides the child care center Dr. Wolf was going to open a high-tech security outfit specializing in bank security.

Signaling for another round, Hinki told the uninterested bartender, thanks to Compassion Land's justice system, Dr. Wolf was in a position to offer professional evaluation of the bank's security system free of charge. "Where else but in the Land of Compassion do you find such unselfish caring and giving?"

I left as Sunni was discussing with herself where the pictures should be taken—bedroom, living room, on a throw rug—and the lighting and her poses. Should she look like she was putting on the bra or taking it off? Should she look wide-eyed and surprised at being caught in her underwear, or seductively sloe eyed, or unaware of a photographer was in the room?

Picking up on the last things said, Hinki magnanimously said he wouldn't charge her for his expertise and the tablet's use and suggested back lighting to get powerful shadows..

Damn it, to get a woman you just need a lot of hot air and the ability to deliver it with confidence. I left to go to an empty room, to an empty bed, to turn my TV on, but it was actually just as empty as I was, to kill time.

5

Kumbia Land

I was out of sorts. Blame it on Pru's aggravating non-letter, Rudy's irritating letter, Sunni's sudden acquisition of military underwear, the growing suspicion that my reports weren't being well received, or on my irregularity.

Whatever the cause, my initial mood upon greeting my Kumbia Land guides was a 'just don't give a shit' attitude. A chauffeured extended limo whose nesting took four parking slots arrived carrying my guides. Only after the door was opened by the driver did they alight, jangling more large gold ornaments from more places than any successful Caribbean pirate. Their tailored suits, silk dresses and flamboyant scarves made me straighten my tie and curse the wrinkles in my cheap pants.

Being greeted by my three women guides, my sour mood did suffer a modification to the extent of a surface smile that didn't originate from my insides. It was almost impossible to inflict a morose greeting to three stout motherly types in transit from mildly sexual to grandmotherly comfortable. Each between 40 and 50 years old, they fell on me as if discovering a long lost son.

"Oh Mr. Peoples, I'm Faith, one of your guides, and I am so happy to see you." She punctuated her happiness with a hug having some umph behind it.

"Oh Mr. Peoples, I'm Hope and I am so excited to guide you through Kumbia Land." She underlined her excitement with a hug having real muscle behind it.

The third guide gushed. "Oh Mr. Peoples, I'm Charity and I can't believe you're finally here," and gave me a hug to reassure herself of my substantiality.

My comment on the appropriateness of their names, Faith, Hope and Charity, for Kumbia Land evoked giggles from all, followed by Faith worrying about my exhausting trip, Hope fearing I was hungry, and Charity demanding I come with them for breakfast.

I told them I'd skipped breakfast and could use some food.

Hearing of my skipping breakfast, Faith worried over my health, repeating that I needed sustenance, Hope expressed the bromide— breakfast is the most important meal of the day—as if it were a newly discovered fact, and Charity, with a no-nonsense grip, took my arm, saying I had to quickly get to a restaurant as if serious malnutrition was seconds away.

Before I could mumble a thanks, surrounding me like sheep dogs herding a recalcitrant sheep, they shepherded me to a restaurant. On the way, between them I was peppered with, smothered with, and irritated with their continual concern over my wellbeing: they gasped over my unbelievable ignorance of the dangers in skipping breakfast, were concerned over the walk being too tiring for one not carrying a breakfast, asked whether my mother, grandmother, aunt, and nieces were alive, healthy and happy, asked whether I had enough money for the visitation, whether the sun was too strong, and whether I had suntan lotion with me.

This sampling of the intrusive caring questions, delivered with such rapidity, gave me no time answer questions I didn't expect or want.

At the restaurant I tried to order orange juice, bacon and eggs and coffee drenched with half and half and sugar.

The three, as one, refused to sanction such a dangerous meal to enter my digestive system.

Faith expressed horror at all the fat and cholesterol hidden in eggs and bacon, ready to create cholesterol arterial chaos.

Hope worried about my heart getting clogged up.

Charity felt I was a yolk away from a heart attack.

With the strength of numbers they killed my appetite's desire and without my consent substituted oatmeal, extolling oats' benefit for regularity.

Out of pique, saying I was as regular as I wished had no effect on their irritating caring.

I commented on the appropriateness of their names for Kumbia Land. "Faith, your name suggests a belief in the goodness of mankind."

"No, no Edmund our faith is in mankind always needing our assistance. The faith we have is in people being eternally in need, so we can show our love."

Turning to Hope I asked if her name reflected the hope that people can overcome their needs and be free from others' charity.

"Never," she said. "Our hope is that the hopelessly in need, staying hopeless, necessitates the continuation of our caring aid."

"Charity, you can't say your name doesn't refer to giving charity to the poor, can you?"

Smiling she corrected my error. "My name refers to the giver of assistance. In giving charity the giver feels elevated. Charity is not about helping the recipient but making the giver feel good about herself and achieve elevated self-esteem. Charity by the giver is not to help the poor but to allow the charitable person to feel good about the charity. When I help you, I help myself to feel good about myself."

In disbelief I said, "Faith, Hope and Charity, certainly you want the poor to be helped, to be relieved of their strained circumstances and eventually become productive citizens."

With patience Faith said, "If there are no needy persons, there can be no feelings of sorrow, no emotional compassion to fill our emotional selves. We need the needy so that in feeling their need, we're able to feel our compassionate humanitarian selves making manifest our inner goodness."

Hope added, "If there aren't any in need, can there be hope of a better tomorrow? Without today's need, tomorrow's hope is empty."

Charity concluded, "Without the needy can there exist expressions of charitable giving?"

All affirmed, in Kumbia Land the needy were the Land's most essential people and the most important resource. They all agreed it's not about meeting the needs of the needy, it's about the feelings of compassionate people feeling good about themselves as they worry about the needy.

Bewildered, I looked above. Was the sky still there? Below, were my feet on the earth? To gain stability, I asked where we were going.

Faith asked if I wanted a good 'feel good' cry. Hope expressed her hope I'd enjoy a good cry. Charity, confessing her need for a good 'feel good' cry, demanded we go to the 'feel good' cry neighborhood.

We first encountered a fat, on the cusp of morbidly obese, boy happily munching a Big Mac. The trio surrounded him, one slapping the meat to the street, one shouting that he shouldn't eat fatty foods, the last stating fatty foods will turn him into a fatty, and fat is a deadly killer. Did he want to grow up fat and die young?

The fat ten year old returned a few choice words, whether at being called a fatty or losing his Big Mac was moot. With the youngster howling, his mother magically materialized, screaming words more original than the child's and demanding to know who was beating her baby, promising a bloody retaliation.

With compassionate faces, in caring words, the trio explained to the mother, who could balance a weight scale against a cow, the child was eating dangerous fat, dangerous to her child's health. They had to intervene to save the youngster from an early horrible death.

Watching the scene unfold I couldn't help thinking, *Damn, that Mac looks juicy. I've got to ask the kid where he bought it.*

Faith told the mother that Mac, Burger King, Wendy, the Colonel, and all their brothers foisting poison on innocent children were outlawed.

Interrogating the kid, Hope asked where he had purchased the fat. Leaning forward I hoped to get a fix for my hunger but the damn kid dummied up.

A virtuous Charity castigated the mother for allowing her child to eat fat. Didn't she see all the Kumbia Land info ads and public service, and news programs on eating healthy and avoiding fat?

Torn between the desire to lambast these nosy do-gooders or defend her mothering skills, the mother decided to go hopeless. Apparently peas and cauliflower were too expensive for her; she couldn't afford the organic health foods everyone else could afford. What could she do if her hungry child fell victim to the street culture of the Big Mac?

Faith uttered a compassionate, "Oh you poor mother!" and gave a pantomime hug. Hope, after expressing the definite hope of a new fatless tomorrow for her children, threw air cheek kisses. Charity, acknowledging the mother's financial plight of being unable to buy broccoli and being unable to protect her youngster from the enticements of the street culture of hamburgers and fries, promised her financial aid.

Surreptitiously the kid, picking up Mac and brushing him off, slipped away to enjoy himself. He was able to do this because the trio and mother turned their attention to me saying, the only Kumbia thing for me to do is give the mother some money to buy health-giving cabbage.

Bemused by the unfolding tabloid, their sudden demand that I give Kumbia cabbage money took me by surprise. My first response was a denial of their claims on my wallet. My more considered response was "No way am I giving anyone any cabbage money."

Charity argued, "In Kumbia Land, out of love, you have to give her some food money."

Hope informed me, "It's the law in Kumbia Land to love to give money to the hungry."

Faith asked, "Don't you want to be a good person, a Kumbia feeling human being who loves to feed the hungry?"

Irritated by their importunities, I observed that the hungry starving mother and child were wearing thick coats of blubber.

"Yes," Faith continued, "it's proof of their poverty. They can't afford healthy food like carrots that will make them skinny. They're economically forced to succumb to Big Mac's seductive blandishments."

Again they demanded I show my love to the fat starving mother and equally fat child, and I repeated my refusal. Pointing to the three guides' obvious display of wealth in the form of designer clothes, garish gold ornamentation, chauffeured limo, I asked why they weren't giving the woman any carrot money.

Faith argued that devoting all her time and energy forcing selfish people with money to feel the needy's suffering was more helpful to the poor than just giving money. Her generous words of caring, her intense words of love, her numerous tears of sorrow for the needy was a greater gift to the poor than mere money

Hope, with a lot of self-pity, explained how she and the other guides go from village to village uncovering poverty, enabling the affluent greater opportunities to express their Kumbia care for the poor. "Without our selfless, tireless work, the poor would simply disappear from sight."

Charity continued the theme telling me, as if it were a psychologically profound nugget, "Even in Kumbia Land people are reluctant to substantially aid the poor, so we tirelessly work for laws to enforce Kumbia type of giving. Without our diligent efforts, goodness in the world would disappear and Kumbia Land would turn into a dark, selfish, horrible place. So you see, we give, but not in the easy way of donating money; we donate sweat, tears and love."

"You seem to be well off despite all your love, tears and sweat," I said.

Hope said, "It's the law of giving: those who write voluminously about heart-rendering depictions of the needy's plight, who cry most extravagant tears about the adversities the needy encounter, who suffer in spirit as the needy physically suffer, who deliver emotional lectures concerning the needy's unwholesome environment, who pass compassionate laws to ease the needy's poverty using someone else's money, and who on TV evoke tears for the needy's scarcity are always mysteriously made richer through unseen spiritual hands laying on earned and deserved rewards."

Faith said it was a mystery; people who care a lot get abundantly rewarded by the Kumbia spirits.

Charity, with a straight face, said it was an iron law of economics recognized by all caring people. The more you evoke caring, the greater your material rewards.

After a short ride in the stretch limo enjoying an iced Cappuccino, we alighted at a two-story, two-car garage, two thousand square foot brick home sitting on a half-acre. Inside, the furnishings were low end but quite serviceable. The woman, together with her current lover, her three children and her dog, greeted us with tears; the dog, on his hind legs just begged.

"Our home, good ladies, is being taken from us by the bank," the mother cried out, evoking a tearful response and a motherly hug from Faith.

The man boasted, "We worked hard for this home, saved, denied ourselves, and are good people, just as good as people with money."

Hope allowed his manly tears to fall before going for a hug. The children, all crying as if in a choir, said they loved their school, their neighborhood chums, their bedrooms filled with cherished toys and dolls. Going to her knees and through tears, Charity hugged the children, repeating over and over, "Oh, you poor precious dears."

After a futile attempt to lick faces, the dog, retiring to a corner and sighing, went to sleep.

I thought all this was just over the top. Observing from afar this soapy opera I could easily believe it was all a dreadful, soapy play.

My mistake, if it was a mistake, was soon revealed when Faith asked me what I wanted to do to help them.

Startled I said, "Nothing! I wish to do nothing."

Hope challenged me. "They will lose their home because they can't pay the mortgage."

I said, "If they can't pay, they must move." It was an obvious fact to me.

Charity accused me of having no empathy for this hard-working family being thrown out into the street just because they missed six house payments.

After pointing out if they were so hard working, why had they missed six payments, I again proceeded to ask how this economic plight affected me. "I pay my mortgage every month. Let them do the same."

"Oh," Faith cried, her gold bracelets jiggling in horror. "You care only for yourself."

Confused I said, "Certainly, everyone does. It's the basic law of human nature; you take care of your family. All other caring is decorative."

Hope repeated what the entire family was yelling. "They'll lose their home if no one helps them," in tones suggesting I was one of the 'ones'.

I said, "It's not their home, it's the bank's. In actual fact they didn't purchase it. The mortgage is a form of rent. Don't pay rent, don't come crying to me."

Still on her knees. gripping one young girl tight by the arm, Charity, looking up at me, cried, "They would pay, they want to pay, they desperately tried to pay, they did everything they could to pay but—"

"Did they try working harder?"

My impolitic question stopped all the crying, tears, and lamentations as quickly as a gunshot report. After recovering, my three guides were effusive with shock at how I could think, never mind say, such a hateful, prejudiced thing.

The children's father angrily told all that he had looked diligently for work, lifting every stone he peered beneath, but nary was a worm of employment discovered. Unfortunately, currently on physical disability, he had to be selective in job applications. With a ruined back, he told me, he was one beer can lift from complete paralysis.

The mother cried she'd scrub floors, clean toilets, or sweep the streets if she could but she couldn't. Due to her motherly love she had to stay home to nurture her babies. She attacked me with the accusation: "Who could be so cruel to force a mother to leave her children?" She added a monetary consideration, saying if she worked, she would have to hire a nanny and on the whole, it would be a financial trade off and not cost effective.

Faith said, "Do you see how they desperately want to work? No work is too demeaning, no work is too hard, but they can't find work through no fault of their own. To give help is the only recourse for caring, loving Kumbia people."

Hope told me I was their only hope to save them from living in filthy gutters.

Charity was sure, in my sympathetic Kumbia feeling, in my response to the Kumbia spirit, I'd love to give them money.

Without any justification, I told them no.

As we left, the children just cried except the little boy who kicked me in the shin. The dog marched out of the room, tail proud high. I was excluded from a tearful caring group hug, Kumbia Land's de rigueur method of caring people greeting and leaving each other.

In the limo, now sipping cordials, my guides were quiet, mad quiet, in expressing their disappointment in me. A horrified Faith couldn't believe I'd say such hurtful, insensitive words. Hope voiced her devastation at my lack of empathy for people in pain. An angry Charity couldn't believe the extent of my meanness in not giving my money to those deserving people. She kept repeating, "He wouldn't even give one month's mortgage payment."

With such hostility I expected to be quickly expelled, an expulsion I reverently desired. Such was not to be as Kumbia Land. If it is anything, it is caring and therefore I was given one more chance to regain my right to be called human.

We stopped the Kumbia Convention Hall. Inside were numerous booths manned by serious women of all ages. The booths were selling hard-luck stories in print, pictures and video. The most popular stalls were doing a healthy business in sick, deformed and dying children. Numerous women, most entering the grandmother years, delved into wallets and purses accompanied by their uncontrollable chest beating and tears expressing the Kumbia spirit to purchase the images of poor neglected babies, three pictures for a dollar, as well as a receipt for tax purposes. As the pictures were purchased, the purchasers were immediately engulfed by hugs lubricated with tears from the sellers, tears of such volume you had to congratulate the manufacturer.

Dragged by Charity to a stall specializing in kids, I saw pictures and videos of skinny kids reputed to be seconds away from eating with the gods, and fat kids with extended stomachs singing "Nearer to Thee My God."

To leave I had to push through several arm-entangled women group hugging, loudly crying with great gusto over the poor children. My reason for leaving was smelling the faint, meaty odor of a Big Mac hidden somewhere in the next booth.

Before I could uncover Mac I was dragged to the drug booth where numerous unshaven red-eyed cadavers were shuffling about in zombie fashion. Apparently they were merely one day from successfully finishing a rehabilitation program and entering a full, productive life become hard-working family type guys, except their program needed more money. If not injected with money, the losers would lose what they had gained, all for a few paltry dollars. I hate to report it, but the odor of roaches was present, not the insect but the smoke that never, like tobacco, hurts the lungs and makes the head happy and is not habit forming. The zombies were walking among the compassionate crowd shaking collection cans accompanied by the castanet music of their body's bones. The compassionate crowd gave each other hugs but kept the zombies at arm's length, shouting advice and shouting love, but the shaking zombies' cans remained noiseless.

Suddenly over a loudspeaker came the announcement, "Everyone please gather in the center. We're going to have a Kumbia event." Everyone ran to the hall's middle, gripped hands and began singing Kumbia with smiles, with gusto, with togetherness, with shared bonds of compassion. At the song's end the loud sounds of cheek kisses raced throughout the hall. The loudspeaker congratulated the crowd for their moving expressions of joyful love in singing Kumbia Land's national anthem.

Now the speaker challenged the crowd. "Can we now have a sad Kumbia?" Swaying with the melody, everyone crying, they sang sadly and at the end, enjoyed tears and hugs.

Crap, I thought. *I'm in a Looney Toon short and any minute the pig will say "Th-th-th-that's all folks."*

Extracting my three guides from their tears, hugs and kisses I demanded we leave.

Hope asked if I had purchased a picture of a one-eyed three-footed homeless dog to take home with me. The picture, not the dog. Charity had a three foot long picture of a whale with a couple of harpoons sticking out of it. The beast's cold eye stared at me without love. She vowed to put the picture on her bedroom wall so every night looking at it she could have a good cry before going to sleep. Holding a plush stuffed polar bear cub, with Faith hugging and kissing it, showed she loved animals. When its stomach was squeezed, it emitted a plaintive "Please save me. I'm going to die without ice."

Outside in the limo, they wanted to show me a Kumbia school where sadness is taught, tears are evoked, compassion is imprinted and love is learned and all graduates feel good about themselves because they're caring people. I declined. Begging to leave, I pleaded for some compassion from them.

Charity told me that at the school I could see children drawing pictures of the homeless.

Faith said there was an opportunity to watch the children collect pennies to feed hungry children somewhere or other. The 'where' constantly changing wasn't important.

Hope promised it was a good chance to see children waving a rainbow flag while singing "We Are the World" and vowed it was guaranteed to bring tears to my eyes.

Suddenly Faith screamed, "Edmund, you've been here all morning and haven't had a good cry! Here, hold my baby polar bear, squeeze its stomach and imagine he's without ice, dying somewhere."

In her amazement Charity asked if the cause of my dry eyes was the result of a physical problem. I said no, and she foisted the harpooned whale on me saying if I pictured it as a mother whale nursing babies and that it was about to be chopped up and eaten my tears would float an entire pod.

Pulling from her purse a picture of the one-eyed three-legged dog, Hope, demanding I look at it looking out at me, unloved, uncared for, and abandoned was guaranteed it would produce a good cry.

Remaining dry eyed even with the bear in my lap, a one-eyed dog, and a mean-looking whale in my hands, they took me to the border and pointedly gave me no hugs, no cheek pecks, not even a finger wave.

Conclusion—if you can't feel for others, if you can't cry, if you're uninterested and unaffected by manipulation, stay away from Kumbia Land. You're not wanted but you can send money. In fact you should send money, you cheap, unfeeling bastard.

AFTER KUMBIA LAND

My letter from Pru was filled with compassion. In the first four lengthy paragraphs she empathized with Hoar's past life. Did I know that when Hoar was a child of ten, his father divorced his mother? At eleven, a beloved aunt passed away? At twelve his mother remarried and his stepfather beat him? At thirteen, Toot, his only companion, his beagle, died? At fourteen he was sexually abused by Katie, his sixteen year old cousin? At twenty, he suffered an unspecified near-death medical trauma? At twenty-one his father died? And recently his mother divorced his stepfather for physically abusing her and his own marriage was loveless and sexless, and he was days away from separating given his unfaithful wife?

Pru swallowed all this whole. Philosophically summing up her conclusion, we (her and I, I suppose) like to think rich, successful people live happy lives only to be surprised to find on closer examination people live sad lives. The stupid broad didn't realize other's happiness sours ours, other's unhappiness sweetens ours.

Apparently her voyage of discovering Hoar's past occurred during another dinner in a quiet, quaint, authentic Italian restaurant where he unburdened his heart to her and she allowed and listened to him over an exquisite bottle of Chianti and cups of Espresso.

Here I am alone, writing to her about my love, my travails, my need for her nearness, my isolation from all the familiar things one needs for ballast in one's life.

In her letter she didn't say how the evening ended, but Rudy's letter filled in that omission. Over lunch with Pru, Rudy had tried to persuade her not to continue dining with Hoar, attempting to alert her to Hoar's purulent purposes and the serious dangers to her relationship with me. Apparently in my name he energetically tried to breach her naïveté regarding Hoar's dark purposes towards a beautiful trusting woman. Only after hours of discussion at her apartment late into the night was he able to make her see Hoar as he really was, and how I could misinterpret her dining so often with Hoar.

Appreciating Rudy's efforts, I still suffered almost as much with his late hours in Pru's apartment as with Hoar crying and spilling his guts all over Pru at an intimate authentic Italian dinner.

Going to the hotel dining room I felt the Kumbia spirit all around but none for me. However since Sunni and Hinki were on the outs I still had hope for Sunni's with optimistic expectations of sleeping with her. Sitting down next to her I was disturbed to discover Hinki was also sitting with her. However, I was buoyant by the obvious freeze between them.

In wooing a girl, honesty may be what girls say they want, but they hope to hear lying phrases of success, excitement, and adventure floating on a sea of money. In the love game never leave money out of the conversation. They want to believe it's there, need to believe you're a winner, and if winning you, so are they. If you're a loser, they will quickly lose you.

I felt expressing feelings was my best initial thrust, so I started to gush compassion for all the suffering I witnessed in Kumbia Land, especially a little girl who lost four fingers of her left hand. (A lie, I admit it. There was no one-fingered child and my compassion was as real as her missing fingers, but my goal justified all.)

My satisfaction with my opening gambit was short lived as Sunni, pulling out a picture of a little girl horribly disfigured by fire, slid it across the table at me. (Obviously with her one-upsmanship she wasn't trying to get me into bed.)

Looking up from his study of the menu, Hinki told the world how his heart was torn visiting a little girl who had no hands and he didn't think he could eat.

Shit. Given that my one-fingered girl was emphatically trumped, I shoved out at them how my heart broke seeing a little girl without arms and legs. In Kumbia Land there is no bottom.

First murmuring "Oh dear," to show her feminine side, Sunni said, "that's almost as sad as the blind, armless, legless orphaned infant. Seeing her, my heart just burst. I confess crying for a good hour."

With her begging for sensitivity I tried to cover her hand but her hand was in the process of elevating spirits so I had to settle for complementing her sensitive nature.

After deciding on Veal Parmesan, the house antipasto, and a cravat of red wine, Hinki mentioned how deeply affected he was in visiting a little bald headed girl suffering with terminal cancer, and who was sexually abused by her father and mother.

Sunni glared at him, then ordered Spinach Salad, Tuna Florentine and a white wine while she explained she was drained from all the emotions she experienced in Kumbia Land.

"Yea," Hinki agreed. "Being so emotionally empty I've worked up a hell of an appetite myself."

Mindful of your dime, I ordered Lobster Ravioli and a stein of imported beer. We ate with spirit and drank with gusto, going into seconds on all items. Getting emotional, draining you creates a healthy appetite.

After dinner, Hinki was hanging around, obviously having no place, no urge, no objective except to sit in the lounge with Sunni and me digesting his veal and children in horrible conditions.

Apparently oblivious of my intentions, Sunni kept reliving the worse horrors she had visited, even bringing out a picture of her smiling and holding a happy birthday balloon next to Siamese twin babies joined at the head. Despite the smile for the camera she related how emotionally devastated she was and only put up a happy front for the babies. "Their names were Robin and— Oh waiter, I'll have another Strawberry Daiquiri— Oh, the other was Sparrow. Robin and Sparrow—isn't that so cute?"

Crap, I thought, *is this what I'm trying to get into bed with?*

Going to his wallet, Hinki extracted a picture a ten year old child with the body of an eighty year old man sitting on Hinki's lap. It wasn't long before it was a picture game between them. Can my revolting picture top yours?

With no stomach for the game I said goodnight and felt very compassionate for my loneliness.

PART V

MISCELLANEOUS LANDS

1

Entertainment Land

My guide, Joan Rivet, met me at the boundary of Entertainment Land. Joan Rivet, in her 70s but looking 40, talked from an immobile face encased under a thick inch or more of makeup. Her never-blinking eyes stared at me and not in a friendly way, and her bumper-size lips were able to exude words without any motion. Greeting me with a hugging gesture and making perfunctory kissing noises three inches from my ear she dropped a large staining decoration of face goo on my lapel. Her hair was a blonde color that never escaped from a woman's womb and her ears were stretched Uganda like by large heavy silver earrings.

On our way to interview movie mogul Lance Starr, looking out the stretch limos smoke-tinted privacy windows I was amazed at Entertainment Land's opulence. In fact to say Entertainment Land was merely opulent was to refer to Versailles as a hobo shanty. Stores were palatial palaces filled with luxury items whose prices were inversely proportional to their utility: loud, colored scarves shouting even louder prices, women's shoes not meant to be walked on demanding money sufficient to feed a child for a year, cars so expensive they demanded more attention and care than newborn babies, dresses and gowns so ashamed of their astronomical cost they could only be worn at night, men's ties costing a worker's suit, shirts costing a workers' mortgage payments for a year, suits costing a college tuition. Just passing through these streets filled with the privileged entertainers in exclusive designer clothes, driving impressive cars, the normal individual, feeling the poorer, senses the onslaught of a communistic envy.

We passed gated palaces atop hills peering down at us and passed walled-in palaces enjoying the sun at the beach, all guarded as if golden idols resided within. I asked Joan Rivet, "Given this fantasyland of excessive opulence, where does the land's real substance reside?"

As we rode past a gatehouse guarded by several armed guards she said, "Here reside the real people. Outside our land all is insignificant and ignorant."

Lance Starr, world-renowned film and TV director and producer, sat behind a room-size desk in a room the size of a building, in a museum-size mansion, centered in a botanical garden's landscaped thirty acres. Next to him, whispering into his ear, was a forty year old man who wore a smile that never disappeared. Introduced, I found his name was Oscar White; his job was public relations.

A haughty, fiftyish man far above and miles detached from everyday realities sat on a couch astutely examining his fingernails. His name was Jason Cousin, and his sole function in life was to be Lance's personal lawyer. Since 'personal' was mentioned, I inferred there were other lawyers, only farther removed from Lance's person.

To my hello, the lawyer said nothing. To my extended hand he pulled out a gold nail clipper and snipped at a saucy pinky nail.

A twentyish woman of startling beauty sitting at a desk in the far corner was carelessly identified as Rolanda, Lance's personal secretary. Prepared to take notes, she didn't look up.

There was a gentleman touching seven feet, over 240 pounds, overly developed in a steroid manner, who was not identified but I suspect his function was to guard Lance's body lest some audacious unauthorized person try to touch it.

The final body in the room was a whippet gentleman who was introduced simply as Wily, obviously Lance's gofer and the only one who shook my hand while glancing at Lance to see if it was permissible or whether he was stepping over the line.

The visitors' chairs were placed at least five feet from Lance Starr's desk, allowing for a grand view of his desk's edge but little of the man himself.

Ploys, I thought. *Stupid upsmanship ploys* and, annoyed, picked up my chair and moved it to the side of the desk so I could see the man's eyes and talk to his mouth.

The gofer gasped at my audacity. Joan Rivet remained five feet back. The bodyguard moved a step closer to me. The secretary crossed her legs, and they were such fantastic legs that watching them could cross your eyes. The nail clipper lawyer continued his intensive work and Lance himself never looked up from signing some papers. After a few moments of silence, still looking down, Lance said, "Jason, are these the only contracts? I thought Charlie Shorn was begging for a TV renewal."

"He can wait. His FMN is down and we can buy him for only a mil per a week's episode."

Coming over, the gofer helpfully whispered in my ear, "FMN, fan mail numbers."

Paper signing continued. The room remained silent. The secretary uncrossed her legs and, uncrossing my eyes, I enjoyed watching the maneuver. Through floor to ceiling windows behind Lance, I idly watched ten illegals doing things to the topiaries, the pool—or was it a lake—and the lawn, or was it a fairway? Suddenly several peacocks pranced by flashing their tails followed by a dozen stately pink flamingos passing in the opposite direction. Neither flock said hello to the other.

"Lance is into animal rights," PR Oscar White said to remove my startled reaction.

"Yes, Mr. Starr has rescued monkeys, camels, and eagles on his estate," the gofer eagerly said.

I observed a passing parade of llamas followed by a couple of buffaloes. I said, "Quite a menagerie."

The lawyer was putting in eye drops. Rivet, robbed of expression, remained expressionless. Lance was writing, the bodyguard stood in a permanent flex, the gofer nervously hopped from one foot to another and PR White suggested I should get a copy of *Time* magazine where in an entire issue I could read about Mr. Starr's love of animals and his dedication to saving endangered species. Putting a drop in his left eye, the lawyer mentioned a tax write-off to the eye dropper. When the secretary stretched and arched her back, my eyes stretched wide and I was impressed by her. Truth be told, I was in love.

Not looking up, the man himself asked either his papers or me what he could do for me.

Thinking to toss a pleasant tidbit to start things rolling, I said, "Well, I'm here to learn the secrets of Entertainment Land. What has made this place the great, enchanting venue that creates such amusing distractions for the world?"

Things didn't roll. After a long silence, thunder spoke. Lance Starr roared at me. "Enchanting? Amusing? Distractions? Do you know who I am?"

Joan, from my back, hurriedly whispered, "The great producer, Lance Starr," as if I needed to cheat on the question.

I didn't answer because it wasn't a real question. The verbal test continued. "What do we do in Entertainment Land?" he asked the room. He then went on to the third question. "Do we entertain?"

Having recently seen several TV situation comedies that only laugh tracks found funny, or stupid idol or survival shows, I was tempted to whisper "No" and flunk the test.

Turning to me, the irate mogul asked, "Do you think we try to amuse people? Your honest answer now."

Hell, the whole atmosphere was so cheap and theatrical, I gave him honesty I suspect he rarely got. "No, I don't think you entertain anyone." I was about to say he actually bored people, but I stopped in time.

Expecting an angry outburst at my brief foray into honesty, I got the great man's smile of approval. "Exactly! You're perceptive, Mr. IV Visitor. We don't try to entertain the people." Then he put out another test question. "What do we try to do?"

Not letting his choir time to answer again, Lance answered himself, much to his satisfaction, "We free people from the onerous process of thinking. Not only that, but more importantly we keep the individual from being alone with himself. We fill people's long hours of potential self-generated boredom with desperately needed mindless entertainment. The key to success in this business is to remember people watch TV or go to the movies to escape being alone. In the past, when the work week was fifty or sixty hours, you went home, ate, briefly rediscovered the family and slept. Now you're home before the sun sets and are faced with the same faces with nothing new to say to each other. You turn to the TV to fill in painful hours with mind-numbing reassuring sameness, allowing people to sleep with their eyes open. In any TV series we make sure each character says and does what the viewer anticipates; surprises in plot or character are not allowed. People don't want surprises as it would jolt the viewer into the most hated, exhausting, vexing activity: conscious thinking. The most important axiom in Entertainment Land is Thinking Is Painful. No one likes to experience pain, so no one likes to think. Even the news, being a stealthy, silent arm of entertainment, is predictable. Now, besides stifling the public's mind with the expected, what else do we strive for in Entertainment Land?"

I almost made a fool of myself but the gofer saved me, yelling out, "We educate the people."

"Exactly," the producer said to me, as if I had given the answer.

Confused I mentioned that *The Three Stooges* didn't seem too educational.

"That was in the past. Today entertainment is too mature to engage in mere entertainment and piquant melodramas. No sir. You may take the word of Lance Starr: we do not entertain, we educate. We form the morals of people so they conform to our morals. We educate people to our correct diverse intellectual political and worldviews. We mold the world's culture. Hell, we create a culture that reflects our values and lifestyles. Entertainment? Never. Mr. Visitor, I think on behalf of people who are afraid to think or who don't know what to think or who are too tired to think and must rely on me to think for them."

Swiveling his chair to face the floor-to-ceiling window, he enabled the room an opportunity to admire the back of his hairpiece, sufficiently expensive to almost achieve the appearance of reality. Facing the window, Lance was able to check on either a busload of illegals' work ethics, or watch the monkeys fornicating in their spacious enclosure. Lance intensely looked at a couple of monkeys fighting over a banana. The reverent silence was maintained waiting for the next holy words to be issued. Lance asked himself, the monkeys, or the crowd behind him, "What is the greatest danger to Entertainment Land?"

First to answer, the lawyer pronounced with the finality lawyers always use, "Censorship advocated by closed-minded puritan bigoted idiots."

Laughing at the antics of the monkeys struggling over the banana, Lance tossed over his shoulder for his secretary to catch, "Rolanda, make a note: tell the comedy writers to work into the next comedy segment monkeys playing with a banana. Remind them not to be too subtle over the sexual innuendo. Being unsophisticated, the viewers could easily miss the sexual humor.

"Now, where was I? Oh, yeah... yes, Jason, censorship, the destroyer of all creative art.

"Rolanda, a note to the writers. In the monkey, banana, sex-play scenario, they're to have the hero previously hide an engagement ring in the banana and he and his dumb sidekick are trying to wrestle the banana from the monkeys.

"Note to writers—needn't worry about the logic of how the engagement ring got into the banana. Once the viewers see the ring, the banana, and the monkeys, they're conditioned to expect, want and be relieved at what is expected to happen, and what does happen."

Gofer Willie applauded. "Fantastic idea!"

I suspected it was more a reflex utterance than a rational evaluation.

Lance continued on censorship. "Narrow-minded, moral fascists would like to put creative and original people in a straight jacket.

"Rolanda, have the writers insert a straight jacket into the hero's struggle with the monkeys over the banana. He's trying to get it on the monkey, and the monkey, being smarter and turning the table, has the hero ending up in the jacket."

Lance's choir sang "Great idea!" and "Brilliant comic content!" The lawyer, confessing the imagery had him crying tears of laughter, was able to generate a few anemic "Ha ha's" which, like all lawyer utterances, you almost believe and never should. From a face molded in Mount Rushmore stone, Joan Rivet confessed she'd laughed so hard she'd had to pee. She didn't leave the room.

Oscar the publicist shouted, "Now we know why Lance is viewed by the industry as the greatest creative artist!"

The only indication of approval Rolanda gave was to recross her legs. Probably she had a deeper, more intimate knowledge of Lance's mind.

Emerged in watching the monkeys' antics with the banana, Lance announced to himself or to others or both, "I'll fight to the death for freedom of speech, right Jason?"

The lawyer was quick with his expected, "Right back at you, Lance."

Rivet added, "Only when we have full frontal nudity and are able to show bedroom sex explicitly will we have achieved real free speech."

Lance asked, "Oscar, didn't I get an award for expanding the boundaries of good taste in TV programming?"

Oscar, as head of public relations was forced to remind Lance, "You got the Clinton Award."

Gofer added, "It was well deserved. You certainly earned it."

Rivet, with motionless baboon lips, whispered to me, "The Clinton Award is a prestigious annual award given by the Victoria's Secret Corporation for the person who promotes women's self-esteem."

"Well Oscar, make sure I don't get the Clinton again. It was embarrassing holding the statue. They should at least glue on a fig leaf.

"Rolanda, make a note to the writers: monkey eats banana, ring and all, forcing the hero and his idiot friend to argue over how they'll be able to extract the ring from the monkey's poop, and who will be the one to dig into it."

Beating the choir, Oscar gave a loud solo, "Lance baby, you've got another Emmy segment here!"

"Yeah, whatever... now where was I? Oh yes, let's get a gorilla into the mix. It could scare and chase the two idiots up a tree. Wait—it's a girl gorilla and, falling in love with the hero, it wants to hold and kiss him."

Rivet, from unmoving lips, suggested, "Lance, we could introduce a male gorilla angry at losing her love to the hero and wants to tear him limb from limb."

The gopher suggested inserting a baby monkey. "They're so cute. We could have the baby monkey make monkeys out of the hero and the idiot friend by throwing things at them."

Unable to contain himself, an excited Oscar predicted a segment of tens of millions, whether viewers or dollars wasn't specified, but actually were equivalent.

A worried Lance, from the back of his head, asked the room whether they felt this segment idea was getting too original or whether it was dangerously unpredictable.

The room told the back of Lance's head it was exciting and hilarious and the TV audience would be able to follow the story line without difficulty.

The back of Lance's head worried. "We don't want to get ahead of the common man."

A chorus of no's led with Oscar swearing the story plot wasn't too original.

A worried Lance asked, "Now truthfully, does the story line sound too original to anyone?"

The chorus of no's put Lance's concerns to bed.

Sighing, Lance Starr said he had worked enough and needed a message. He was facing the window and I half-suspected he was talking to the monkey.

Everyone silently got up to leave. I was tempted to ask whether, when leaving, did Entertainment Land's protocol dictate walking backwards on leaving Lance Starr. Apparently only a quiet retreat from the Presence was required.

Outside, Rivet's face moved a millimeter in excitement. "Edmund, do you realize how privileged you were to be present at the birth of an original comedy episode? Tell me truthfully, does Lance's brilliance take your breath away?"

Feeling more put upon than privileged and being able to breathe, I politely uttered a tepid, "Yes."

Gaining control of her face, Rivet suggested an additional chance of a lifetime. "Down the street, in a musical studio, the musical group Happily Deceased, previously separating, has been resurrected and the group is making a new album. I'm sure we can peek in and observe timeless music being created; however, you must remain respectfully silent."

The sound room was partitioned in two: one side contained enough electronic paraphernalia to not only land a probe on Mars but have it stroll around, dig a few holes, and bring the dirt back to Earth. The mass of electronics was manned by a crew of six intense operators.

On the other side of the partition were the revered five members of the Happily Deceased. An argument was going on between the creative people and the technical operators. The Deceased complained they sounded terrible and, blaming it on the electronics, vociferously demanded the electronics people give the sound track more range, more volume, more bass, let up on the treble, smooth over the voice cracks and for heaven's sake, add more echo.

Being a novice, I asked Rivet why the need for all of the electronic paraphernalia.

Leaning close to me, dropping a few ounces of makeup on my shirt, she whispered, "Inside the industry it's well known the Deceased can't carry a tune—can't even hold a tune, never mind sing a tune—but with these advanced electronic gizmos anyone can be made into an Enrico Caruso. It's not the talent in front of the curtain, it's the talent behind the curtain. The most important thing in Entertainment Land is never peek behind the curtain; it's very ugly there."

"Do the Deceased have difficulty writing the lyrics and melodies of their songs?"

"Edmund, this isn't grand opera, nor comic opera, not Broadway musicals. The Happily Deceased's music is aimed at the buyers who want to feel like they're bad asses. To feel Gotterdammerung is now and they're part of it. It's not for dancing but for jumping, to feel excited, not to feel good, to feel chaos, not to feel uplifted. Its appeal is to teenagers, even if they and the Happy Deceased are in the social security set."

"Crap!" one of the Deceased shouted. "We've got to get into costume for the publicity shots."

To my puzzlement Rivet explained, dropping another ounce or so on my jacket, "When the group gives a concert, and their concerts draw thousands of hysterical worshippers, a hell of a lot more than a Second Coming could draw, the band dresses like zombies and between songs they eat chicken heads, smash guitars, and throw blood over the lucky few in the audience. The fans eat it up."

"Chicken heads? Blood? You're kidding!"

"It's a great ad ploy. Fan magazines and TV have heated debate over whether it's a real chicken head or just a marzipan replica, and whether the blood is human or pig or spaghetti sauce.

"They generate so much excitement that two 12 year old girls were crushed to death in the mêlée. The publicity of the girls' deaths guaranteed the next ten concerts would be sold out.

"Now, as a special treat, once they get into their Happily Deceased zombie costumes, I may be able to get a group photo with you in the middle of the band."

"I'll pass."

"Pass? Pass on this opportunity? They may even autograph it with a cute saying like, "See you in hell" or "Life is shitty" or "Drink blood" or "Eat chicken."

We left, her shaking her head in disbelief at my passing on the opportunity, and drove to a sidewalk café for lunch where we were joined by publicist Oscar White. At a table near the sidewalk, passersby could see us indulging in a champagne cocktail followed by a lobster salad, and for each salad a crustacean donated a pound of flesh, followed by strudel buried beneath a whipped cream pyramid. Oscar ordered wine for himself, so expensive the bottle had a red wax encrusted cork and a year, a year before my birth. Telling me the meal was a tax write-off,

Oscar suggested I might need a brandy to finish the meal. (Ah, the dime is always there.)

With pride and a sly wink, Joan mentioned she couldn't remember when she had a lunch or dinner that wasn't cleansed with business tax write-off wipes.

We were still sitting under an umbrella, patting our lips with linen, sipping from crystal, when a passerby shouted, "Oscar!"

Ignoring us, he told Oscar how he was forever in Oscar's debt. "Just when I wasn't getting any air or print time and about to become invisible you rolled out the idea of getting me arrested on a drug possession charges. It got me fantastic TV and print exposure. Entertainment shows, news shows, and ubiquitous women talk shows talked about me, and interviewed me about my foray into drugs, and wasn't my drug use affecting my relationship with Bunny, my live-in."

Turning to Joan he informed her of numerous offers to guest star in sitcoms and he may be dancing with stars. "Joan, Oscar here is a genius. He's got me in rehab and everyone wants to know how I'm doing, and will I be able to stay clean and I'm to be one of the judges on *Who Wants to be the Next Star.*"

I was about to ask him how someone in rehab struggling with drug dependency could be prancing down the streets when, telling Joan to give Lance his love, he gave a ta ta, a wave, a blown kiss and left.

No sooner had the real or fictitious drug user left us than a stick figure of a woman stopped by to thank Oscar for convincing her to go public in her struggles with bulimia. The tabloids featured her in bikinis, woman talk shows kept inviting her to give a first-hand account of her struggles to gain weight and to advise their audiences to eat more and love yourself. Apparently now as a TV spokesperson for a drug company, she was getting a dollar for each diet supplement pill sale she generated by appearing in their commercials.

Turning to Joan she confided, "I was disappearing in the business before this dear sweet genius got me the publicity. Now I've got TV appearance offers and speaking engagements at upscale women's groups and women's universities."

Not usually a daytime drinker, I ordered a highball as Oscar bid the bulimia goodbye. The high ball and a new passerby arrived simultaneously. Stopping, doing a double take, she screamed, "Oscar darling, is it really you?" as if it could be anyone else. Reassured it wasn't anyone else the woman told Joan how Oscar had saved her life. "Honey, I was going nowhere. With dropping out of the A list, passing through B and C list, coming to rest in the D list, a scant inch from the Fs, I was eating as if worldwide famine was only a chocolate strawberry away. I took to hiding, I was so fat. There was so much of me, in Entertainment Land I became invisible."

Looking at her I was puzzled. She was prime meat. I gave her my Grade ' seal of approval.

"Joan, Oscar here talked me into it, flaunt my fat, put on more pounds and do TV interview shows where I cried, where I suffered dejection over my binge eating, where I attempted to overcome my insecurities with ice cream, where I considered suicide, where I was doomed forever to live encased in blubber, never to walk out of my fat, always its prisoner. Well, after I went public with Oscar's publicity acumen, after taking some stupid diet pills and a little liposuction— well, not all that little—I regained my teenage body. To be honest, just between us, it was one hell of a lot of liposuction. I was almost turned inside out. After losing the blubber I'm now on TV pimping some company's stupid exercise machine along with my exercise video. Both are selling very well. I figure I made a hundred thousand for every pound I lost. Got to go, fashion shot for *Vogue*. Now Oscar, you've got to get me invited to one of Lance's awards acceptance parties. I heard he's up for another Clinton."

She was about to give the obligatory air kisses when another passerby stopped and, pushing the former fatty aside, grandly announced, "Oscar my dearest, my savior, when you came up with that publicity stunt I thought you were crazy, but I was so desperate, so near the edge of falling into a black hole of TV oblivion, I did what you suggested."

Turning to me she said, "This genius told me to shoplift some jewelry in front of security cameras and getting arrested, have a trial.

The free publicity was fantastic. The security tape of my stealing and my arrest ran non-stop for at least a week and let me tell you, for the arrest I was wearing a tight, low-cut one-piece sheer basic black Dior that cost five figures but did right by my figure. Emoting fear when arrested, I performed magnificently at my trial, doing a Joan of Arc better than Ingrid Bergman. Fans wept when I cried at my shame, applauded when I confessed my mental problems and were proud and loved me knowing how, trying to be a good person I'm now doing community service, serving meals to bums. The fans are intensely interested and supportive in my agonizing battle to overcome my kleptomania. I've got a book deal and a lecture series to women's groups, never mind appearing on hundreds of women daytime talk shows.

"Oscar, the air time, the news time has been fantastic. I'm getting offers to do a PBS special on psychological addictions and a starring role in a police drama. Then there's a good chance I could be one of the judges on TVs *Who's Got Talent*.

"Before I leave, Oscar as my dearest friend, could you introduce me to Lance? I'd do anything to meet him." The anything was said with double meaning.

Oscar said, "You know, it's just possible. Lance is developing a fantastic comedy segment about bananas, monkeys, poop and rings. You'd be a natural as the person who steals the ring and hides it in the banana."

Hesitantly she said, "I don't know. I might not want to get locked into the role of a thief."

"Trust me, it's you, maybe working in a statement of animal rights, putting it all on a moral and intellectual basis."

"I'll do it. Tell Lance I'll do anything."

What she'd do I could easily imagine.

Getting a headache, I asked Joan if we could leave, and I stood up hoping to get Rivet moving. She and Oscar remained seated, waving at a twenty-plus fabulously attractive woman across the street, walking towards us. Midway through the traffic she became a mid-thirty, somewhat attractive.

On the sidewalk standing next to our table, the forty-plus woman with a so-so face as mobile as Rivet's gushed, "Oscar darling, I'd die if I didn't come over and drop a hello on you, and you've got to tell me, how is Lance? Is he casting? If a role was right for me, not too young, but not anywhere near menopause, I'd be glad to consider it. I'd do anything to work under Lance."

It was Oscar's smirk and Joan's struggle to smirk that alerted me to the double entendre.

Smirk still evident, Oscar asked, "Brazil, how are your children?"

"Children? Oh yes, my children. Oscar, can I ever thank you for the children? It's so fulfilling to be a mother. It's a rewarding role."

Pushing out her bumper lips Joan asked, "Getting any more?"

"No, I've only six, and believe me they're quite a handful. Balancing being a mother and an actress is very hard. Still Oscar, remember if Lance has the right artistic project for me, I'm available."

Oscar told her of a project being currently developed by Lance, which was going to be a smash comedy.

"Oh Oscar dear, you must tell Lance I'm available, but only if the money and artistic control can be satisfactorily arranged."

"It's still being sketched out but I think there's a great role for you as a monkey trainer. You know, people love watching monkeys getting into all sorts of trouble."

"I'll do it. I just can't resist comedy, and working with monkeys... well, it all sounds absolutely delicious."

My having been limited to a yes to the champagne and lobster salad and a quick whisper to the server, "Whiskey," and now standing like an unoccupied server and just as visible, I felt I had to say something, so I asked Brazil her children's ages, as if I was remotely interested.

"Ages?" The question took Brazil by surprise. She pulled a lizard bound notebook from an alligator handbag and read, "Well, two are six, one's four, another just turned two, the fifth is a month from her second birthday, and the last just turned one."

The just two and almost two had me thinking as Brazil gushed over Oscar, "Oscar, dearest, how can I ever thank you. You're simply a genius.

I know it's a word used too often in Entertainment Land, but you're an actual living, breathing genius."

Annoyed at all the Brazilian words washing over Oscar, Joan desperately tried to say something nasty while vigorously sending semaphore signals for the waiter's attention, and in pantomime writing a check. Through clenched lips she mouthed, "The bastard, why won't he come?"

Coming closer to me Brazil came closer to mid-fifty, asked if I knew what Oscar had done for her.

Still confused over the ages I dumbly asked, "Er, did he father a couple of your children?"

Oscar and Brazil laughed.

Standing up, waving her napkin over her head, Rivet pushed out from swollen lips, "The bastard server is looking right at me"

Brazil narrated, "I was in Brazil doing a travel log for their tourist bureau. You know, my name, the same as the country's as a tie-in, well who do I bump into but dear Oscar."

Oscar explained. "I was doing a PR for *Get a Brazilian Ass*, an exercise information show with several bikini babes."

Feeling he couldn't top several bikini babes, with a sly smile Oscar went silent.

"Anyway," Brazil continued, "knowing I wasn't getting the air time I deserved, this genius here—"

With the waiter finally arriving, with concentrated effort Joan opened her lips sufficiently wide to shout, "Damn it, we want the bill! Can you understand English?"

With a smile that told Joan to drop dead, the server left.

Brazil continued. "Anyway, Oscar tells me since I'm down there, since I've got the country's name, since I already had the film crew, why not adopt a batch of orphans? All I needed to do was to go to the grubbiest orphanage and grab a few of the most photogenic dears. We got videos of me hugging the dears, of their happy faces looking up at me as I fed them ice cream. Since Brazil is multiracial, I was able to get kids from ink black to Denmark white and all the shades between. I built a special guesthouse for them, surrounded by an army of nannies and guards to watch over them and keep them out of trouble.

"Now Oscar, how about I build a school, say in Africa, for young girls at risk? It would be great. You know, every time I need a little air time I could spend some time at the school and have all the little smiling kiddies gathered around me singing native songs. I could give the brats sage advice, like stay in school, or be all you can, or love yourself."

Still standing I asked, "Brazil, what are their names?" as if I cared.

"Names! My lord, they were in Portuguese. Oh yes... well, the new names I gave them are—" Looking down at her lizard she read off, "Regina, Prince, Queen—"

Oscar said, "Look Brazil, isn't it time one of them had a birthday? You know, clowns, donkey rides, birthday cakes, sing alongs? I think three cameras, a decent director, and some editing and you get on the evening world news shows and a lot of tabloid press. It could be the twins' birthday."

"Not the twins. One being the shade of night, the other high noon daylight would raise questions."

"Look Oscar, we have to go," Joan said, putting the bill next to his brandy. Without ceremony she pulled me away, saying she couldn't stand Brazil. "She's such a phony, adopting six orphans! And where did she get that name? How low can you go for publicity?"

I was eager to leave Entertainment Land as it was a little frightening, and you had to look in the mirror, stare hard and long to see who you really are.

AFTER ENTERTAINMENT LAND

In the hotel lounge, in a soft leather easy chair, with a chilled Martini wetting its napkin on a polished wood side table, I nervously fingered Pru and Rudy's latest letters. Taking a deep breath and a deeper Martini sip, looking about at the few fellow imbibing inhabitants talking and laughing in the lounge, I felt they were real and, feeling that, felt I was also real. You need to believe in a firm separate reality to support your belief that you are real in order to function.

Entertainment Land's citizens, believing and functioning in their self-constructed specious world, are forced to believe in other people's ignorance and unsophistication so they can believe they occupy a superior reality.

My first Martini worked wonders, dissipating my sense of dread of isolation replaced by feelings of wellbeing; the elevation was of sufficient height to give me the confidence or courage to read Pru's letter.

In a lengthy paragraph running two pages, in surprisingly lyrical mastery, she expanded on her love for me. I marveled at the passion and commitment, simultaneously pausing to marvel at the surprising play of words and her turn of a phrase.

Only arriving at page three did she discuss what had previously generated my disquiet. She related how Hoar seemed distant, not sharing coffee during the day nor suggesting an after-work dinner and drinks. Unfortunately, her explanation being awkward, created doubts in my mind as to her being relieved in not being placed in an awkward situation in regards to Hoar. Or was she put out that with no overt negative response on her part, Hoar had voluntarily stopped bothering her? I was left with the troubling thought that she would she have preferred his attentions in order to be able to rebuke him.

As far as my work, she and Rudy did have lunch and after work, over drinks, they compared notes. The lunch conference confused her as Rudy kept telling her my visitation reports were praised by all for their insightful honesty. Her impression from Hoar was just the opposite: all were horrified by my reports' negativity and the cynical tones they relentlessly emitted. (PP were the initials tossed about.) Her confusion was understandable as she was innocent in so many ways. My confusion rested on the after-work drinks.

Rudy's reading of my report's reception was more comforting. In fact Rudy's letter had pumped me up with his exaggerating praise for my report. Without mentioning his lunch or drinks with Pru, he indicated his efforts to wean her from Hoar's toxic view. Hoar had used artificial PP smear to demean me in Pru's eye.

Taking Rudy's letter as an organic whole I felt better, yet with the drinks, not completely tranquil; a breeze from somewhere was raising small mental undulations. Floating in the hotel's soft leather, ordering a second Martini to keep the elevator's 'up' button pressed, a sense of wellbeing inhabited me. Thinking a nice dinner wouldn't be amiss, I was assaulted by Sunni and Hinki, both 'penthouse high' and the penthouse was Vegas style.

True to her nature, Sunni was the first to report in a loud voice the concierge heard, how absolutely thrilled she was with her visit to Entertainment Land.

As his nature required, Hinki shoved a glossy picture into my hand asking did I see it. Since it was six inches from my face, an answer was unnecessary.

Sunni, who in her normal voice could send sound vibrations for miles, asked if I knew who had kissed her.

Hinki told me, in my hands, in my actual hands, I held an autographed picture of Kim Kikerchin in evening dress. Looking for the dress, I saw more of her and little of the dress. Bypassing the scant dress, I can honestly confess I saw at least 90% of Kim's skin, but given air brushing and cosmetics, almost 30% was actually her.

"Tom Cruiser kissed me," Sunni gushed as if it was her first kiss, not the millionth. "And you'll never guess where."

Knowing Sunni, the 'where' brought to mind frightening conjectures.

To my relief she supplied the 'where': "On the lips! He kissed me for at least two full seconds on the lips!"

"Kim gave me a hug," Hinki said, and Sunni and I didn't believe him. To add more improbability he added that he'd felt her ass. He was lying. Hinki didn't feel it, but then again who would want to feel her ass?

"Richie Gerr asked me to have lunch with him," Sunni bragged.

It was my second Martini that said, "Did you feel his ass?"

The grounder went through an excited Sunni's legs as she lamented that her guide wouldn't let her lunch with Gerr because they had to see 'the feet' and 'the knees.'

Hinki interjected. "Certainly doesn't compare with my visit to Libraci's home. It had 72 rooms, each with a bathroom and a piano. There were—"

"Excuse me, Hinki, I was telling Ed about the absolutely fabulous feet and knees in front of the Mongolian Theater.

Ed? where did that come from and where was it going?

"Ed, can you imagine as far as the eye can see, the bare feet and knee impressions of all the great Entertainment people were set in concrete. Look, I've got a picture of my bare feet inside Klark Cooney's feet. Don't my feet look so small inside Klark's?"

Looked like an almost perfect fit, but the picture being presented now elevated to Ed, I swore her tiny feet, being swallowed up by Klark's, were virtually invisible.

"No, no Ed, don't exaggerate," she purred.

"Forget the feet," Hinki said. "I was able to buy an exact replica of Boyce's personal comb," and with reverence he pulled out a glass-encased pink comb resting on black velvet.

Out of politeness I reached for it, expecting to give him a sarcastic 'wow' while examining it.

"Don't touch it!" he shouted. "And for heaven's sake, don't open the case! If you look carefully you can see the blond hair between the comb's sixth and seventh teeth."

"Yes, I see, but why am I seeing it?"

"It's Boyce's actual hair."

"But the comb is only a replica."

Hinki said, "An *exact* replica, but the hair is authentic. Upstairs in my room I've got a certificate of authenticity from the Boyce Corporation."

Sunni put in my hands a picture of her knee in Red Ford's knee indentation. "I've got several pictures of my knee in Red Ford's knee. Now Ed, how fabulous is that?"

Still being Ed, I gave her an absolute fabulous in return.

Not to be made small, Hinki related his adventures walking about the Libraci Pink Mansion. He dangled a gold piano key ring two inches from my nose.

I joked, "Exact replica of Libraci's piano?"

"Yeah, you know he has a piano in every room. This is an exact replica of a miniature one he had in his bathroom. He had gold, ivory, crystal and brass pianos. He had one twenty feet across and another, a working piano, smaller than this one." He jingled it under my nose.

Pushing aside the piano, I signaled the waiter to bring Mr. Martini the third to me.

Sunni, getting testy at Hinki's one upsmanship, told me she got an exact replica of the baby doll nighties Abdula wore in accepting the UN's Freedom Award. Teasing me with, "Now Ed, don't get any ideas that you can see me modeling them," she put the idea in my mind, and there still was Ed.

I didn't have a chance to feel deprived, challenged, just bemused or excited at the idea because Hinki shoved a photo of himself sitting on a bed. "It's Libraci's bed, solid gold, weighing ten tons. The silk sheets are imported from a silkworm farm deep in the Himalayan mountains. The covers were weaved by two hundred native Afghan women over a ten year period."

Sunni said, "Just like a man's mind, always in the bedroom."

She certainly was dragging my mind there.

"The bed cost over fifty million," he said, to keep Sunni and me from getting into bed.

Out of pictures, stories, relics and artifacts Sunni asked, "Ed, what did you do? Who did you see? Show us the souvenirs you bought."

As Hinki was head deep into a bag looking for more treasures to share, I quickly said, "Lance Starr."

"Who's he?" Sunni asked.

Reflecting on the difference between in front and in back of cameras, I added, "I also met Brazil."

Sunni screamed, "Not Brazil! Not *the* Brazil, not the wonderful woman and great actress who adopted all those poor children."

"Yeah, that Brazil."

Hinki, acquainted with Brazil's fame, challenged me. "You couldn't have met the real Brazil. It probably was her look-alike stand-in."

Sunni asked me for an in-depth analysis of Brazil's personality. "Tell me, what's she really like? Is she as beautiful and caring as they say? Is she really only twenty-eight?"

With them pouncing on Brazil I began to think more of Brazil than I did initially. However, given my initial opinion of her was level with my opinion of Hinki, the 'more' was not really a hard life.

"Brazil's having a birthday party for one of her children, the youngest," I said.

"No! A birthday party for the twins? Will we be able to see it?" Sunni asked.

"I suspect it will be on pay TV," I said.

"I don't care how much it costs, I've got to see it," Hinki said, making me wonder about him, and that was in addition to all my prior wonderments.

Expressing suicidal intentions if she were unable to see the birthday gifts being opened, Sunni claimed devastation in not being part of the party.

With all the profuse anxiety and happiness over the coming birthday, I had to mention Brazil's plan to start a school for orphaned girls at risk of rape in some third world country. Blame it on Mr. Martini three who now joined his prior two relatives.

The idea of Brazil starting a school for girls left them in a wonderful place, inhabiting a caring world, gaily dancing in a fog of love. Apparently their mutual feeling good in believing people are good brought them back together as they walked in step to the elevator. Mr. Martini the fourth joined the other three in curing my emptiness.

2

Green Land

When I first heard I would be visiting Green Land, I mistakenly thought Arctic. Hell, I thought, who'd want to go to a place tourists visit only when in desperate need of an exotic travel story. I didn't need to freeze, didn't need to see a few jaded tourists taking pictures of themselves in front of nothing.

After my visit to Green Land, Greenland had to be better. It would be better to see nothing, feel cold, talk to no one, than go to where I did: to see and hear pompous self-awarding people sanctifying and exalting themselves, but I anticipate.

At the start of my visit, my guides, a young boy and girl in the healthy bloom of their twenties, just out of Green Land University, introduced themselves.

The boy, an earnest youth named Peace (last name, first, or neither, was left in limbo) said his name as if it described his inner being. He sported green granny glasses and a sparse dark beard. Sparse beards, in their incompletion, are not only undistinguished but disconcertingly ugly, while trying to communicate some profoundly deep bullshit.

The girl was hot, and her name, Valley, was suggestive. Wearing large round black framed glasses made her librarian hot. Her t-shirt had a cute polar bear cub with *He dies, we die* written across very full breasts. If she was trying to look serious and studiously hot, she succeeded. Peeking out from behind the façade of virtuous innocence she gave the look that girls extend, while playing the asexual intellectual. Her broad smile with double row of straight whites, her constant little jumps, and her spastic hand movements said perky, and isn't it great to be alive, especially if you're twenty, hot, and in your prime.

After introductions, Peace promised a busy schedule with enjoyable trips to fabulous Green places to see lots of amazing things. Valley told me to take a deep breath, and with Peace seconding her request, easily made it sound more like a demand. Seconds after meeting people, how often do they demand you take a deep breath? Hell, did they think I'm tubercular? Granted I had some bad past visits necessitating more booze than is healthy, but I couldn't look that bad.

Stupefied I said, "Huh?"

Valley promised, "Yes, breathe in our air. It's clean, fresh, oxygen filled air."

Peace treated himself to some deep theatrical inhales.

To satisfy them, squeezing my lungs in and out, I reported the air was great. I must confess, I didn't detect any freshness, and the oxygen content seemed normal and why were all these lands so focused on air.

Valley told me the air in Green Land was so wonderful, just breathing it gave you a high. Someone definitely was high, but on what? Like a bloodhound smelling another dog's urine, Peace kept deep breathing for a good six intakes. With the three of us, noses high, smelling, I felt stupid, particularly as there wasn't any special smell wafting across the nostrils. To get our noses back to the grindstone I asked where we'd visit first.

Peace asked Valley about going to the protected beach area. A giggling Valley thought the idea fantastic. Looking at the empty street I asked, "Where's the car?"

"Car?" screamed Valley as if suddenly seeing Jack the Ripper behind her, breathing hard.

"Car?" yelled an angry Peace. "Where the hell do you think you are? Car, indeed."

"The devil's machine!" Valley screamed as she backed away from me, a synapse from running away.

With stringy beard bristling, outrage peering from green granny glasses, Peace told me there are no cars in Green Land.

Coming closer to me Valley said, "Oh yes, we've outlawed the devil's machines. They pollute the air, kill innocent little babies."

Peace suggested I take another deep breath and experience what banishment of cars had wrought. Somehow being able to breathe was an exotic experience in all the pink lands.

Passing on the deep inhale, I nervously asked again, "No cars? None?"

Coming close to me, a beard's hair separation, Peace asked, "Cars run on what? Gasoline."

Valley added, "The devil's drink."

"Where does gasoline come from?" Peace asked, then quickly answered himself, "From oil."

Valley added, "The blood of the devil."

"And what do cars breathe in and breathe out?" Peace said. "They intake nature's pure air and spew out poison from hell."

"The devil's breath," Valley said

"Take another deep breath of our pure air," Peace demanded.

Valley told me that in banishing the devil's breath, Green Land had put a stake in the devil's heart.

Obviously the mere mention of a car in this Land brings out the strangest behavior. To end their triad against the C word, I asked how we'd get to the beach sanctuary. If I'd stopped there I'd have put an end to this conversational theme, but being a big mouth I suggested an electric car.

"The devil's help mate!" Valley screamed and again backed several feet away from me.

Made of stronger stuff, Peace stood his ground to instruct me. "Mr. Peoples, where does electricity come from? It comes from coal."

"The devil's food," was Valley's description.

"And when burning to generate electricity, what does it exhale?"

"More venomous devil's breath," Valley said.

Again Peace said, "Smell our air, breathe it in, enjoy its purity."

Whether real or just a trick of hunger, I thought I smelled some bacon being fried and asked, "Well how the hell are we to get to the beach? And do they have a food stand?"

"Bicycles. You can inhale the fresh air as you pedal," Peace said.

Valley added, "There are no food stalls to ruin the beach's beauty."

"Is the beach far?" I asked.

"Only nine miles. With ten speeders we'll just fly," Peace said.

"And you can enjoy the scenery as we travel," Valley said.

"And it's so safe, not like traveling by you know what," Peace added.

After changing into bicycle outfits, multicolored skin-tight clown suits with the stupidest helmet designed by a buffoon for fools, we drove down to the beach with heads hanging down. The only scenery I saw was the monotonous asphalt moving between my two handlebars. Given the horror the word evoked, I was dumbfounded when I was almost hit by a stretch limo doing ninety. The wind it left behind had me fighting for front wheel control.

What the hell am I doing in a tight clown-colored suit, riding with two characters deadly afraid of the devil's— er, the car's exhaust, while continually searching for hints of heaven's perfume, and a stretch limo races by? Like many of my past visits this visit promises to be interesting.

Throughout our bicycling, both Peace and Valley took demonic pleasure in pedaling ahead of me, then waiting for me to catch up, giving out with the phony, insulting "Are we going too fast for you?" and "If you want we can slow down," as if it was in doubt I wanted them to do it and could say it.

Those are among the vast arrays of polite insults you can't take offense at, but having to stand and take it makes them doubly hurtful. To my "I'm doing fine," Valley promised they'd go slower as if I were in my dotage. Of course they didn't go slower, making the entire trip one of fits and starts for them and a continuous pain in the ass for me. And you can take that literally.

With me breathing heavily, and not to experience clean air, we finally arrived at the huge beach preserve. The salt air carried by gentle ocean breezes caressed the nose, and the ocean's blue, ribbed with white cresting waves, treated the eyes.

Peace came up to me, saying the obvious as the unintelligent often do, believing they have to say something and possessing nothing original to say. He observed, "Beautiful, isn't it?" The beauty was marred by numerous signs forbidding any unauthorized personnel from entering the protected beach, promising arrest, threatening a maximum of ten years in jail, and/or a fifty thousand dollar fine. This adequately explained why the beach and surf were empty, empty except for a large group of young people laughing and playing in front of an upscale beach house, the only house for miles on an otherwise deserted beach.

Pointing to the group frolicking in the sand and in the mansion's pool, I asked Peace, "How come they're allowed?"

"Oh, they're Green Land University's Environmental Scientists doing important research work."

Seeing a vigorous ongoing beach volleyball game, seeing a girl being thrown in the pool, and seeing several boys in the ocean, surf boarding, I saw a lot of fun, but I saw no research work.

"Valley, what possible research are they doing with such enjoyment?"

"Horseshoes."

Before I could ask what about horseshoes, my two guides ran over to the beach house, a building running at least a hundred feet along the beach, fronting a wooden deck and a freeform pool. Walking to the boisterous group, I joined them with as much dignity I could carry, dressed in my bike clown outfit, feeling unique and not in a pleasant way. Helmet in hand, tights getting even tighter, introductions were given: a Dawn here, a Winnie there, a Hope somewhere, and with numerous similar names unceremoniously tossed in the air for me to catch. I dropped all of them.

Most liked my name, Peoples, but had difficulty grasping it was my actual birth name, especially two nubile bikini girls called Sugar and Smiles. Seeing all the bronze bodies, muscular boys and jolly girls I felt I was at some rich Hollywood star's party celebrating a beached whale's rescue.

Invited to change into a swim suit, I used the large marble tiled bathroom: with sufficient sinks to wash a dozen hands at once and with urinating stalls to relieve another dozen. Although I marveled at the shower room with its various faucet heads aimed at head, chest, privates, and feet, but it was the wet and dry cedar sauna rooms that took my breath away. *Crap, this must be like living in Clooney's Malibu beach house.*

On my way to the beach, I passed through the mansion's living room, a long room with a fireplace at one end, a pool table at the other, and numerous easy chairs and couches between them. The central air must have been set at seventy as I felt a chill.

Not a little embarrassed at my whiteness in this tribe of gold, I sought out my guides. Damn it, talking to Peace, even standing still, his muscles rippled. Valley's bikini was such an advanced bikini, I was embarrassed to look anywhere but at her face. Occasionally my eyes did drop but guiltily were quickly yanked up to her face. From somewhere, not from her swim suit, Valley pulled out a can of sunscreen and started to spray me with something she called two hundred plus.

During the morning, in this group of Green girls, constantly losing eye control, I suffered bikini blindness. I suspected my eyes belonged to a dirty voyeur and not me. In between jumping in and out of the pool, the girls danced to music on the deck, shaking everything so vigorously I feared they were in danger of losing body parts. Walking about I heard more snippets about horseshoes, especially evening and night horseshoes, who would keep score, who'd check the scores for accuracy.

From the direction of the ocean, I suddenly heard someone on a surfboard yelling, "Intruders!" as he pointed down the beach. About a hundred yards down the beach a family of four were laying down a blanket. Everyone at the pool yelled for Serenity and Star, a girl and boy who quickly put on shirts emblazoned with POLICE jumped on their ATVs and zoomed down to investigate the unauthorized intruders. They arrived just as the two children were testing the waves and the mom was unpacking lunch.

Curious, I ran down to overhear the conversation. The girl, Serenity, was asking if the intruders realized this was a protected beach preserve and only authorized personnel were allowed. Star told the man to get his children out of the water before the situation dangerously escalated. With her notepad out, Serenity was asking for identification. The frightened man ran to the water's edge to collect the children while the mother was quickly repacking. Star sternly reminded them of the penalties while Serenity was getting angry at their not being forthcoming with their identification. She wanted to arrest the family, or at least the father. Star seemed content to give them a scare before chasing them off the beach. The terrorized family, clutching children, beach toys and blankets, ran desperately to a cut in the dunes.

"Stop them!" Serenity demanded of Star, explaining she hadn't brought her revolver. Shaking a fist at the fleeing family, she promised the pain of hell if they dared step on protected sand. Apologetically Star told Serenity he wasn't packing either.

Packing! What is this beach, a critical national defense area?

Back at the pool, all congratulated Serenity and Star for chasing away the interlopers. I now identified Serenity and Star as Green Land Beach Protection Police. The crowd's condemnation of the family was vicious, with the most humane of the group suggesting jail time for the father as the minimum for daring to desecrate a protected beach. When Valley told me horseshoes were put in danger, it dawned on me it was all about horseshoe crabs. "So Valley, these Green Land university students are studying crabs."

"Counting them, Mr. Peoples. When they come up the beach we count them."

Possessing suggestive ideas, I suggested, "Please Valley, drop the formality. I'm Edmund... er, Ed."

This tenuous outreach to establish a closer one on one relationship wasn't too successful as she said, "Yeah, whatever."

Then jumping up and down she shouted, "Here come Professor Ivory and Dr. Waters." Ivory and Waters were accompanied by a third person, an important politician named Reed.

As the youths encircled the trinity, I complained to Valley, "Those were the guys in the speeding limo that almost ran us over, and why do they have a car and I have to ride on a bike?"

"Love," she said. "They ride in love."

"But you didn't answer my question. Why can they ride in a limo?"

"It's a LOV, a Legal Official Vehicle, the only type allowed in Green Land. The LOVs are reserved for dignitaries on important missions. Unfortunately your visit wasn't considered warranting a LOV."

"So we're not allowed to ride?"

"Only bikes or roller blades. We felt a bike was more suited to your age."

Professor Ivory, drink in hand—given the crystal glass, I deduced it wasn't soda—asked how the crab count was coming along.

"We'll get to it tonight," Star said, then added, "Got a great stack of driftwood for tonight's beach barn fire and there's more than enough lobster for all."

Dr. Ivy said, "You've been here all summer. You've got to come up with some results we can show Green Land University."

Turning to Valley I said, "All these college students are partying at this beach house so they can count crabs?"

Serenity, overhearing me, said, "People are worried over the decline of horseshoe crabs. They're below nine million. Saving the horseshoe crab is one of Green Land's highest health priorities in protecting our environment." Then enticingly she added, "Can you stay here all day? We've got some serious volleyball games set up, or we could get you a surfboard. Later tonight after the lobster bake you can help us count the crabs along the shore. Just realize you'll be part of a dedicated scientific research team working to save the environment, and remember, there are the lobsters."

Knowing my itinerary called for visits to a Green Land housing complex and an environmental educational institute and if time permitted something called a self-sustaining factory, I quickly told myself, screw the housing complex, education, and factory. It's sun, sand, splash, lobster, and maybe go down the Valley or get some Serenity. I told

Serenity I'd love to be part of this important environmental endeavor, "And now I'll race you to the water." Whether we'd race together or not was left undecided when Peace, bringing Reed, the important Green Land politician, stopped us.

With his arm around a bikini babe he referred to as Eureka, Reed told me he loved nature. Between sips of single malt he told me of his enduring commitment to clean air and clear water, vowing to his last breath to protect every endangered animal, especially crabs, and was prepared to expend his last drop of blood defending the environment from evil polluters. Turning to Eureka, he asked, "Dear, who do we hate?"

She said, "Polluters."

"Who are the polluters?"

"People who drive cars."

"And why are cars bad?"

"They burn gas."

"And...?"

"Carbon pollution."

"And Eureka, who do we love?"

"People who love the environment."

"Eureka, you know your lessons and you deserve a treat. Let's go into the research building and see what we can give you."

Going towards the building, he turned and I swear he winked at me. Both Serenity and Valley giggled at Eureka's treat. I felt it was the height of ego to view the treat as belonging to Eureka and not to Reed, but I may be wrong. The treat may be a great Napoleon Éclair.

The sun was warm and the pool was there. I hated to leave my two bikinis but I jumped into the water. Damn it, it was cold. Maybe that was the reason my Valley and Serenity stayed dry.

On my way to demonstrating my devastating freestyle to the pool crowd everyone excitedly shouted, "It's the frogs! The frogs are here!"

As I climbed out of the pool everyone started running to a large multicolored bus disgorging bathing suited students.

Valley shouted to me, "It's the GTV!"

"The bus is a GTV?"

"No, it's a LOV bus from Green Technical University, the GTV."

"And the frogs?"

"They're here to count the frogs. Now watch out. Don't get hurt. Things are going to get very violent. The frog people are going to try to capture our research center building and we're not going to let them. Crabs are so much more important than frogs. It might be best if you leave. It's going to get very nasty."

I saw the professors and politician Reed sliding unobtrusively towards their limo. Grabbing Valley, I joined them. Reed started to argue that it was his LOV, and Valley and I didn't belong, didn't warrant a LOV ride. Seeing the shouting frog people and the angry crab people shoulder pushing each other and females eyeing hair, they didn't want to stay and be part of the heated discussions of who belonged on the beach and who didn't. So, in a bathing suit I found myself with Valley sitting on jump seats looking at Eureka.

Driving away, we eventually stopped at a mall resembling a medieval fortress, for the girls and me to get clothes, and everyone to get a quick bite in the food court.

Seated in the dark courtyard's fast food outlet I asked why there were no windows.

Eureka, riding high on all her previous correct test answers said that in the winter windows let in the cold and in the summer let in the heat. Best to do without them.

It was almost impossible to read the menu and people's faces were only hints of dark shadows. "Why's there no light?" I asked. Peering at a menu two inches from my eyes I complained, "I can't read the menu."

From the darkness Reed explained, at least I think it was Reed. "It was cloudy so the solar panels weren't working."

Valley, who I suspected was or hoping was sitting next to me, added, as it was a windless day the windmills weren't working.

Peering at the menu I asked why was it so hot in the mall, complaining my new shirt was already soaking wet.

Eureka, who I hope was sitting on my other side, explained in Green Land there's no air-conditioning.

Valley added, "Electricity comes from coal."

Eureka continued. "Coal is the black killer taking air from precious children and ice from polar bears."

Valley concluded. "Coal makes the sun angry."

Reed, from out of the darkness, told me to smell the air and see if I didn't believe the minor discomfort was worth it.

"But the beach house was air conditioned."

Justifying the beach house's air conditioning, Reed said it's a REC.

Valley amplified. "Research Educational Centers are exempt."

Perversely I complained how stuffy it was sitting in the dark.

Eureka again reminded me to take deep inhales of air and enjoy its purity.

Smelling of sweat and hot nothing, I mumbled "Whatever." I suggested a few table candles would be helpful, especially reading the menu.

Reed said, "As a visitor from an evil polluted land you may be ignorant of the dangers of fire. Eureka, what does fire eat?"

"Oxygen."

"And what does it exhale?"

"The devil's poisonous breath."

"Excellent. Now let's order."

Seeing I was moving the menu this way and that, one to two inches from my nose, Valley suggested, "You can go outside to read it. However, if you keep trying, your eyes will soon get used to the romantic shadows."

Since I couldn't read the menu, I said, "I can't see any meat items. Are there any listed?"

Valley said, "In Green Land there's no meat."

Out of the darkness Professor Ivory said, "You see, cattle are a prime source of—"

"They fart too much!" Eureka shouted.

I had the impression she was smug and smiling, whether for the correct answer or the vulgarity I didn't know, but probably for both.

Professor Ivory said, "Yes, they pollute the air. Mr. Peoples, please smell and enjoy our air."

From out of the darkness I smelled cauliflower and told them.

Ivory explained, "Yes, we cook all our foods the natural way."

With trepidation I asked, "The natural way?"

Valley said, "The sun... we put all our organic vegetables in the sun and let the health giving sun slow cook them. Of course we're not up tight regarding food preparation. You can have your cauliflower or any other vegetable raw, and it's healthier."

From somewhere across the darkness politician Reed told me, "Green Land's carbon footprint is smaller than a chinchilla's whisker. You just go back to your Land and amaze your people with that fact."

Someone nearby said it would certainly be a wakeup call for my Land.

I hoped it was Valley, and she added, "If your Land wanted, we could send hundreds of college research students to instruct your people so your land could also achieve the carbon footprint of a chinchilla's whisker."

Someone, who I couldn't ascertain, told me, "The FAD Corps could be sent to your country in a matter of days."

"The FAD Corps?" I tossed out into the dark for anyone to answer.

Someone, I'm sure it was Eureka, said, "FAD—Fighters Against the Devil."

Slowly getting cat's eyes I could make out a character or two from the menu. "Do they serve milk?"

From deep in the table's darkness someone said, "Milk comes from cows, and cows—"

"Fart and pollute," happily interjected Eureka.

Giving up on meat and milk, and sweating off half my body weight I asked for some ice water.

That brought out laughs from the darkness, and a hand pat from someone I hoped was Valley.

A figure in the darkness said, "Refrigeration."

Another, between laughs, said, "Electricity."

A third unknown reminded me it was a windless cloudy day.

The hand patting my arm told me I could have all the ice water I'd ever want in the winter.

Given up on eating, given up on any physical comfort in this dark dungeon, I settled for a glass of tepid water.

Hearing my gurgling sounds someone asked if I had tasted any water as delicious as Green Land's.

Out of the darkness, someone else asked if I could describe the water's purity, its fantastic taste.

Another disembodied voice asked if I didn't feel healthier, fresher in the throat, revived in the mind, drinking Green Land's unpolluted fresh water.

I barely got the tepid water down, and once it was down I had to struggle to keep it down. I remained silent as chewing sounds of raw carrots, broccoli and who knows what else being eaten filled the darkness.

Finally someone in the darkness said, "I just couldn't eat another cauliflower." Several "me too"s brought our dinner party to an end.

Rising, feeling the wall, and holding each other's hands we walked to the exit. Outside in the cloudy daylight I turned to see I was holding an elderly man's hand. Looking about I found myself in the midst of a senior citizen group.

My asking them, "Where's Valley?" was answered by an old lady complaining I had inappropriately touched her. Everyone stared at me, suspecting a pervert with a fetish for ninety year old maidens.

Was this a step into a time warp, some twilight future fantasy? Was this the same group I had come in with? The bizarre thought only dissipated when my group exited. Somehow in the darkness either I had joined the cane and walker group or they had joined me.

Seated in the limo, air conditioning blasting, in contrast with the lightless, airless hot mall I had to comment on the conspicuous difference.

With a wave of his hand, politician Reed explained away the difference by reminding me we are riding in a LOV. Then he informed me he was going to leave me at a Green Land housing project. Then the vote conscious politician decided he would stay with us.

At the housing development, with teary eyes I watched the limo, the LOV machine with its plush seats and air conditioning drive away. If the LOV door opened I'd be inside with the speed of a flick of a chinchilla's whisker. Looking about expecting the usual government boxes, and given that the mall was a windowless bunker, I was taken back way back in what I saw. As far as the eye could see, a uniform tent city was militarily laid out in a large grid, tent flaps opened, people sitting on rocks or broken tree limbs looking uncomfortable and very unhappy.

"Why are the people so uncomfortable?"

Valley said, "They're very happy and comfortable, thanks to the clean air and pure water."

Eureka argued that everyone in Green Land was bursting with pride at Green Land's whisker-size carbon footprint.

"People are living in tents!" I exclaimed.

"Certainly, better to smell the fresh air," Reed pointed out.

In disbelief I asked, "Is this Green Land's housing development? A tent city?"

Reed said, "Without air conditioning, having all the tent's flaps tied up, you get great circulation of air, fresh air. Smell that great air. Our citizens can smell and enjoy our intoxicatingly fresh air all day long and it's free."

Sadly Eureka told me how my land didn't have the high degree of freshness Green Land's air possessed.

Sensing my negativity, Valley pointed out how with tents they didn't need electricity because they had the sun's healthy rays.

Just then a man pulling a cart down the dirt street was yelling, "Fresh organic cauliflower and cabbages!"

Surprised I noted, "The streets are not paved."

"You noticed. With no autos, there's no need for asphalt," Reed tersely responded.

Valley added something about asphalt being made from oil, and it was the devil's skin.

My commenting on the total lack of furniture in the tents prodded Reed to proudly proclaim, "Yes, we sit on stones, eat off boulders, sleep on mother earth's bosom."

"Why in heaven's name do you force people to live like that?"

"We have no furniture because we respect, love and protect our forests. A tree cut down is a murdered tree. Eureka, what does a tree breath in?"

"Carbon, the devil's breath."

"And out, Eureka, what do our beloved trees exhale?"

"Angel's breath, oxygen."

Remembering my passing up of sun cooked cauliflower in the mall, Valley asked if I wanted to buy some from the vendor. I told her no.

"They're organic," she said, coaxing me.

Reed lectured me. "People grow their own vegetables in community farms, working the soil, seeing cauliflower grow brings people together, fosters a democratic togetherness. It take a village to raise organic cauliflower."

Letting that BS go by for idiots to digest, I asked, "Why are the people so dirty?"

"Because of the SWFG Project, the Save Water for Grass Project," was the uninformative answer Eureka gave me.

Valley explained. "To save scarce water, we've limited the amount of water each tent is allotted."

"You ration water?"

Reed said, "We don't like to use the word rationing. We call it water conservation. Every tent occupant is allowed a full quart of the freshest purest water to use as they see fit. We're completely committed to protecting the individual's free choice. People can't resist the enticing intoxicating taste of our pure water and drink the quart rather than bathe in it."

Eureka mentioned that at the mall I swallowed a half-day's water allotment.

All this talk of water brought toilets to mind and I asked what about all the flushing toilets, and what about the shower rooms at the beach house..

"The beach houses are exempt from water restrictions," Valley said.

With delicacy Reed silently pointed to a small tent behind the larger family tent suggest if I had to go, that was the tent to go to, to go. Beginning to feel my half day's supply of tepid water trying to escape, I wished it could escape, I wished I could let it escape, but not to a tent outhouse.

Noticing a tent was selling second hand clothing resembling rags more than garments, to be nasty I told Reed, "Do your people have to buy used clothing?"

Reed said, "Not used, not second hand, here in Green Land we refer to such places as recycling outlets. It's all in how you call it. We employ comforting green language, more pleasant to the ear, doesn't unsettle the mind, and doesn't obfuscate the reality."

"Whatever," I said.

Valley asked if I wanted to visit their recycling center.

"Recycling center—is that a comfort word for garbage dump?" I asked. Being in bladder discomfort my malicious self was coming to the fore; when in physical discomfort I drop politeness.

Ignoring my comment as if I hadn't made it, Eureka suggested I'd be enthralled visiting the Sun Institute where there are pictures of the sun, marble replicas of the sun, and at high noon a gallon of pure water is sacrificed to the sun using spray bottles. Being a visitor, as a special treat I could participate in the noon dance to the sun.

Crap, dancing would burst my bladder. I told them it all sounded like one hell of a great spiritual experience but my interest was strongly focused on crabs. In truth it was focused on the beach house's luxurious bathrooms.

A disappointed Reed was hoping we'd visit Green Land's legislature where I'd have an opportunity to witness the current spirited debates on how best to save the world's jellyfish population.

A worried Eureka added, "They're near extinction."

Valley said there were only ten thousand giant jellies in existence.

Blame it on the bladder, but I asked who counted them. I should have asked how.

In all seriousness Valley said, "The Green Land's scientists who are in charge of saving the jellyfish are currently counting them on the beaches of Tahiti. Do you know the jellies are a critical factor in balancing the ocean's ecological system?"

Reed said they were passing a law making catching, killing and eating jellyfish a death penalty crime.

Valley asked me if I thought the penalty was too severe.

Blame it on the bladder, but I told her, "Where saving the ocean's jellyfish is concerned, you can't be too lenient."

Reed complained that some types of sea life feed on jellyfish. "The Green Land legislature is holding meetings on developing laws to stop other fish from devouring jellyfish." He suggested he might be able to sneak me into one of these meetings even though they were closed to the public.

"Crabs." My bladder and I stood firm for the crabs and couldn't be enticed away from the horseshoes.

Reluctantly, Valley agreed to escort me to the beach house with Reed and Eureka promising to join us later.

Blame it on the bladder making me irrational, but when Reed went to his cell phone I expected a LOV limo ride back to the beach.

The limo arrived; Reed and Eureka jumped in, waved and disappeared up tent city's main dirt road.

"What about us?" I asked Valley. My frightened self prayed, *Not the bike! Not the clown tights and the wind-tunnel shaped helmet!*

Valley whispered, "I've got us sixteen speeders. They're outlawed, so if we get stopped, play innocent and ignorant. We may get off with a citation for driving illegal bikes."

The bike ride back to the crab counting beach party was an ordeal; I'll merely say that I can now offer heartfelt sympathy to hemorrhoid sufferers. The trip was again one of endless ride, stop, rest, and ride. Do I have to mention, at the first bushy area I dropped the bike and ran into the bushes to get close to nature? Valley questioned what I was doing in the bushes.

I shouted, "Admiring the flowering shrubs!" I gave them a good watering.

"Don't pick any of its flowers and harm them. All things green are sacred living things," she yelled back.

The fear of her wandering back to check on what harm I was doing interrupted what I was doing, but finally lighter by at least a quart we resumed our biking progress to the beach. Along the way I tossed the helmet, deciding it was worth paying the fine for not wearing it. (Actually, your dime.)

Finally at the beach I was surprised to see the frog counters still there, being they were outnumbered by the crab people. When we left everyone seemed to be seconds from spilling blood. Now everyone, in good friendship, was sharing the joys of the beach, the satisfaction of saving the world, and getting a great tan and college credit in environmental studies as well.

Changing once again from the clown suit to swimming trunks, I located Valley barely attired in one ounce of cloth divided in two. Answering my comment on the lack of blood and gore on the beach she told me the professors in charge of the two scientific research teams, in light of their mutually important green missions, agreed to a truce and allowed both teams to enjoy the research facilities while working to save the environment. The frog people, in friendship, agreed to share their coolers filled with jumbo shrimp and imported beer. Harmony established, the conjoined research party was enjoying jubilant comradeship with beer in hands, empty cans scattered about, franks on the outdoor grill, pool water splashing, ongoing volleyball games and surfboard riding the waves. Standing next to the grill I had two franks, then strolling away with an additional two, one for each hand, I made for an ice-filled tub floating countless cans of soda, beer, and spring water in plastic bottles.

I spent the rest of the day eating, drinking and eyeing the research science girls jumping in and out of the pool, sunbathing on the apron, or engaged in vigorous volleyball games. Finally, as the sun decided it was time to dip its toes in the ocean, I walked down the beach alone. With stomach satisfied, thirst quenched, muscles relaxed, bike ass quiet, bladder empty, my mind free from physical pain, I was able to find sufficient cause to be melancholy, to accompany my sense of loneliness. Unlike the boisterous young research counters, I was alone walking the beach noting groups of sand pipers running on stick legs or a flock of seagulls sitting on the beach, heads to the breeze, at peace with themselves and their world. They all underlined how alone I was. My thoughts went to Pru and my love for her and my anger at her betrayal in eating and consorting with Hoar, in listening to his lies, in repeating them to me as if true. Damn it, I needed her, needed her love, her closeness, and needed it now. Accompanying my sense of isolation or causing it, I was growing aware of getting horny.

Back at the party I was able to corner Valley between the beer tub and the grilling franks. I gave her mind an aromatic oil massage: it was great what they were doing, the sacrifices they were making to help save the environment were heroic, people had to be impressed with their commitment despite their personal sacrifices to save the world. I believe I threw a baby polar bear at her and to my shame went on to curse the whale hunters. Horny men are blind to all honor.

Smiling, nodding, enjoying the word oil, she liked my applying it and didn't want me to stop rubbing it in.

Given the beers, the moonlight, the rhythmic sound of waves, and the ounce of cloth, I was an inch away from making physical contact when from somewhere Peace yelled, "Valley, over here. We're going to light the fire and the lobsters are almost done. Bring a six pack."

Excusing herself, she left, leaving my mind dripping massage oil on the sand.

Watching her and her ounce of cloth bouncing away, I spotted Sunni and Hinki. Sunni was holding a beer can, and Hinki was holding a sausage in one hand, a highball in the other. Feeling alone and knowing them, though definitely not liking them, I joined them. I was that desperate.

Sunni was in a bikini with a lot of her coming out over the top and from behind, even more from behind, with her cheeks squeezing the cloth into a string. She looked as good as were her spirits and they were both feeling great. Hinki had on a shirt to hide his concave chest. I was surprised he wore a string of tattooed Chinese symbols running up his calf. I suspected they translated to 'I'm a born loser.' Sunni's heart tattoo above her ass cheek was cute, no was cheap, no was hot cheap cute.

They sat on a picnic table by the pool, asses on the table, feet on the seats, watching the activity about the fire.

Hinki, damn him, managed to sit next to Sunni, forcing me to stand to get face to face time with her. She was lamenting how sad she was that all our visitations were over. I didn't honestly comment "Thank heaven." Did I mention I was horny? Well, that justified my sighing at Sunni, "Yes, this may be the last time we'll be together."

Predictably, Hinki said we should get together when we get back home.

"Yes," I quickly said. "We must have a drink together. Let's exchange cell phone numbers."

We wrote them on frankfurter napkins and I promised myself Hinki's number would quickly see the workings of a toilet bowl from the inside.

When someone on the beach announced the lobsters were ready, in the general stampede we became separated. To my shame I'll confess out of gluttony with vigorous hip maneuvers and shoulder bumps I quickly navigated my way to the lobsters, then to the butter, then to the beer tub. It was good, better than good, certainly worth taking a second voyage to catch additional buttered lobsters. As previously claimed there was plenty for all and I got two more by artifice, claiming they were for professors at the house.

Did I feel I was a greedy pig? Definitely. When anything is offered free, I lose my shame and self-respect and grab with both hands, waiting to later justify myself.

Down to my last lobster, Valley joined me. The conversation started with her explaining how exciting it was to be part of an important scientific research project. "Counting horseshoe crabs is an important step in saving the environment."

Opening a new bottle of mental massage oil I said it was indeed a great honor but certainly one she deserved as a Green person. Did I say I was lonely and horny and now she had a lacy white jacket over her shoulders suggesting more a piece of lingerie than protection from the night's chill? To show she was tough she left the lace unbuttoned, throwing it open, freeing the bikini bra to the night's eyes. All she had to protect her softness was the bikini's top half-ounce. I'm sure I didn't stare but I did note five goose bumps just above the top's half-ounce.

She asked what I thought of Green Land's greenness.

I could have mentioned the forced biking, lack of air conditioning, dust and dirt, lack of water, raw organic vegetables, the tents, the flushless outhouse, communal farm lots—they all came easily to mind—but I shoved them to my mind's rear. Up front, the driver of my mind's bus was loneliness and named horny. Unfortunately when the driver was reaching to inject oil to smooth out the ride, some idiot from the bus' back tossed out, "I can't understand the contrasts in Green Land. Here we are drinking beer and eating lobster in front of a beautiful air-conditioned furnished mansion complete with floor to ceiling windows and in the city there are only squalid tents. The horny bus driver, seeing we were heading for a crash stepped on the brakes and squirted oil. "But I'm sure the salvation of the environment justifies the contrast."

Turning her goose bumps full face towards me she told me the observed differences are necessary, it has to do with the difference between PP people and OP people.

I guessed. "Pessimistic and optimistic people?"

"No. What are you talking about? PPs are the passive people and OPs are the outraged people."

"Valley, I don't get it," I said.

Moving a little closer, enabling me to get an accurate goose bump count of seven, Valley patiently explained, "Passive people are those who, because of ignorance, are not overly concerned with the environment and must be educated to conserve, recycle, and do with less. They're unable to fully grasp the dangers pollution poses for mother earth, the only mother we have."

Someone from the rear of my bus yelled out, "So they have to have waterless toilets?" *Damn him, whoever he is, he's a killjoy and he should shut up.*

Valley, looking sad, sipping some cold beer, said, "To save our mother who nurtures us all, we have to do what is necessary no matter how hard the sacrifices. Without us, the OP, the outraged people, do you realize the tent people would be flushing every time they go, drinking water all day long, sitting and sleeping on murdered tree's skeletons? They would be squandering energy, spewing poison gases and—"

"But what about the privileges the OPs enjoy?" *Damn it! Who the hell is sitting in the back of the bus shouting out anti-horny comments?*

Noticing the goose bumps were down to three I realized, *Shit, she's getting hot and not in a nice way, at least not for me, but hot in a religious cause way. Damn it, when will the bus driver take control? We're driving to disaster unless we get some focused direction.*

"Oh, the OPs are outraged at the ravaging and raping of mother nature, and her suffering from uneducated PPs' prolific abuse of nature's resources. The OPs, being outraged, being in the vanguard of the war in the struggle to save mother earth from those who wish to rape and pillage our resources, need all the support they can get. That's the reason for the beach house."

Damn it, all this ravaging, raping, and pillaging was getting me hot—well, hotter—and she was down to two righteous goose bumps.

She continued. "As the soldiers and leaders in all the difficult struggles to save the environment, we have to have the best of supplies."

Still horny, between sips of cold beer I gave her some oil. "You and your friends are so courageous."

Pointing to Politician Reed, hands around Eureka and a highball, singing with a group of students "If I had a Hammer," Valley said, "Without courageous leaders like Senator Reed, willing to sacrifice their all, even their lives to save mother earth, the PPs would be putting knives into baby polar bears or ripping the hearts out of majestic eagles, and future generations would never be able to see great white sharks."

The bus driver ventured, "It's a beautiful night... the full moon is so bright you can really appreciate the ocean's dark beauty," in the hope of floating the conversation towards more romantic moorings. Unfortunately once launched on their theme you can't move an OP from enjoying the imminent universe's death and the immediate emergency measures the obdurate PPs must be forced to accept to avert everyone's death, including cute baby whales.

Jumping on the beautiful ocean, she declared its death was a scant year away. "Our mother earth's life blood is in imminent danger of becoming a huge sewer spewing up dead fish, plastic and tar balls with equal abundance." Shit, she even brought up tar covered pelicans and from the heat of her outrage, her chest was goose bump free. She was getting hot for the cause. I was hot myself but not from any secular self-righteous beliefs.

I wanted to say something green, anything green, sexy green. What I didn't want to come out with, popped out anyway. "How is the ongoing lobster and beer party the OPs are having saving the world?" *Who the hell is driving this bus?*

Turning to the bus's back, the bus driver said, *Edmund, you're cutting your own throat. Shut up.*

Taking my comment as an indictment, which it was, it naturally placed me on the enemy list, forcing Valley to defend herself and her OP partners. "We are in the forefront of the dangerous struggle to save the world from pollution and are ready to sacrifice everything."

In absolute desperation I suggested, "Look Valley, you're getting cold, let's get some beer and a couple of sausages and continue our conversation in the house."

"People don't realize how much OPs personally sacrifice in defending Mother Nature."

When horny drives the bus it should travel on a direct route, ignoring the speed limit "I do, and I admire you for all the sacrifices you're making. It's a noble cause."

Making no movement towards the house, she said, "Can you possibly understand how much the students and professors are unselfishly giving up?" Waving at the dancing, singing, drinking, lobster-eating, kissing students near the beach fire she said, "They've given up their summer vacations to come down to the beach and count horseshoe crabs. We need to be on the beach all summer if our urgent research is to be successfully completed."

Shit, no goose bumps in sight, only red splotches. Soaring away in her hot air balloon, she was leaving me. However, excited broads in the grip of religious experiences often can get sexually hot. This was my driver's last hope.

Desperately I suggested a quick dip in the pool.

Finishing her beer, Valley took off her lacy nothing jacket. "I'm feeling hot; maybe a swim would be nice."

Finally with the striptease beginning, the mind's bus driver, jumping up from his seat shouted, *Last one off the bus stays horny!* But before he could get out the door, the bus crashed.

Somehow, talking to me in the darkness, she spotted Star on the beach. Waving, she shouted, "Star, I'm over here!"

Obviously not being driven by a desperate bus driver, Star continued talking to the beach police guardian, Serenity, who was almost out of the one ounce. He had his arm around her waist.

Seeing Valley getting up and grabbing her lacy cover, from the wrecked bus I told her, "I don't see how counting crabs and frogs is critical to saving the world. In fact, all the lobster and shrimp you consumed tonight will definitely put a good-size dent in the ocean's marine life."

It didn't really surprise me that Valley didn't hear me. No one really hears me.

Running away she said, "Excuse me, I've got to talk to Star about our next assignment."

With considerable lack of fellowship and love, I glared at Star. The beefcake was now sandwiched between two thin soft white slices.

Finishing my beer I switched to Jack Daniels as a consolation prize; it's a role Jack plays and he does it well. Sitting on the bench, again alone, I watched students by the fire, hearing the laughter, suspecting copulation in the darkness. Jack, he doesn't say much in the glass, but once swallowed and inside he says a lot and it's the nasty self-pity I always enjoy.

Peering over Jack's glass I spotted Sunni alone, looking forlorn and in need of companionship, possibly vulnerable. My bus driver, hopping back into the seat, drove me down to her. I didn't really want to stand next to her but I did. I didn't really want to talk to her but I did. I didn't want to listen to her but I did. I didn't want to be friendly to her but I was. What I really wanted to do— Well, we know the horny bus driver always drives straight to the same location. I had just started talking to Sunni when Hinki came out of the darkness munching a sausage and handed Sunni a beer. Might be knowledge gained from past experience, might be Jack's influence, but the driver put the bus in neutral and, standing still, with the door open, hoped for a passenger to climb aboard. For politeness, Sunni tossed a few word coins at me to keep me in her circle. Hinki, ignoring me, spent all his coinage on Sunni hoping she'd go for a quick ride..

In exaggerated enthusiasm Sunni expressed her admiration for all of Green Land's green projects. Leaning back, my horny driver mumbled, *Shit, here it comes... more shit.*

Sunni bemoaned her lack of a camera to capture the woodland streams with flowing crystal clear water, water so pure you wanted to just scoop it up and drink it.

Sitting up straight, my horny bus driver said, "How did it taste?"

"Oh, you're not allowed to drink it. It's being conserved for the forest animals," she said.

"Yeah Edmund, you've got to get into the Green Land's ethos," Hinki added. I was beginning to suspect he had a better bus driver than I did.

Sunni continued. "We visited an organic pea farm and were allowed to join the field workers picking insects off the plants. They don't use chemicals. I got two, but you're not allowed to kill the insects. You put them into jars to be released later."

Someone in the back of the bus shouted, "Bet there weren't many students there! They're all here at the beach counting frogs and crabs!" Hopefully the driver will throw the party pooper off the bus.

Hinki asked if she had tasted some of the peas.

"No. After seeing the insects crawling all over the peas, I didn't want to risk it."

I said, "Well, I visited an airless, lightless mall food court to have a glass of tepid—"

Hinki asked, "Sunni, did you visit the cafeteria for legislators at the capitol?" Not waiting for her response he launched into the abundant free buffet served there, with emphasis on the free. He described all the fantastic meat, fish, and desserts available, and it was all free. The free part outweighed the food part.

Jack Daniels and I were regaining an appetite, so I put all of Jack inside me.

As Sunni and Hinki always did, it soon became a 'can you top this,' with each story describing a piece of heaven, and each story a cause to doubt your reality. *Did I dream what I saw today?*

From my insides Jack told me it was all over. It was time to park the bus, leave the fire and go to the beach house and, with his companionship, wait to go home, home to Pru and her love.

Inside the house, Jack and I discovered couples copulating on the couch, in chairs, in the kitchen, on floors. Didn't bother to check the bedrooms. Shit, wouldn't be surprised at what I'd discover happening in the toilets. From a high sense of morality that only those without the opportunity to sin can achieve, Jack and I agreed it was all disgusting.

Refortifying Jack, I checked the TV room. There were two giant stadium-size sets on opposite walls. One had a dozen or so couples on the floor watching birds fly, fish swim, baby kangaroos hopping, children playing, and young maidens dancing in fields of daisies, all under a beautiful blue sky. With murmurs of "Oh how nice" and "Isn't the world beautiful!" and "I'm just so happy" coming from the coeds

I knew their companions were going to get lucky and get happy. The opposite screen showed scenes of horror and death. They watched birds staggering in tar, whales belly up on beaches, cute polar bear cubs desperately searching for ice, numerous seals dead and floating next to plastic bottles, and stagnant algae-filled ponds followed by torrential rains, followed by tsunamis, followed by the top of the Empire State Building peeking out from garbage-strewn ocean. The coeds, gripping their companion tightly, exclaimed, "Oh, the inhumanity! Oh I'm so scared! Oh we can't let it happen!" With all the coed fear needing reassurance I knew there'd be a hell of a lot of lucky guys here, except for me. Shit, did I just see on TV a picture of Godzilla using a giant redwood as an after-dinner toothpick?

Jack suggested, and I agreed, we really needed Pru and fresh air. I must acknowledge, after Jack and I made an intense extensive survey for unattached OP coeds and finding none, that could be the reason Pru came to mind.

Firing my horny bus driver, my thoughts were of what Pru and I would do on my return and were all romantic, not prurient. In my caring sentiment, I felt myself the good person I knew I always was and Jack and I wholeheartedly agreed we were above all this sordid bestial behavior surrounding us.

Suddenly from the beach blackness, someone shouted, "Crap! Watch out for the frogs! You're going to step on them, and I've got to count them!"

A horrified co-ed screamed, "Oh no, you squashed a living frog! A fat one, probably a pregnant one!"

Someone else yelled just as loud, "Shit! I've got its guts all over my feet!"

Someone with an unknown, reasonable voice seeking advice inquired whether the stepped-on frog should be counted.

Someone, most likely the crab counter with frog's guts on his foot cursed the frogs and tossed a frog in the direction of the reasonable voice. From the squishing sound, it was right on target, juicy and alive.

In response, a frog warrior, grabbing a horse crab by its tail and swinging it overhead with force, tossed it into the fire.

Several crab girls near the pot of boiling lobsters shrieked, "He's alive! The frogs are burning crabs alive!"

Shocked to believe the frog people could be so cruel to one of nature's noble creatures, to show their deeply outraged green sensibilities, the crab people started to toss live frogs onto the fire to the horror of frog counters.

Maddened to the edge of insanity, the frog counters obviously believed forceful retaliation was necessary in defense of the frogs' lives, and began hurling crabs at the inhuman frog killers. Justifying the noble purpose of saving frogs, especially pregnant and baby frogs, they felt righteous in going against their pacifist green principles.

Assaulted by the onslaught of thrown horseshoe crabs, the crab counters countered with a barrage of fat juicy frogs.

Jack Daniels, resting in my hand, and I calmly observed, in defense of animals, that Green people acknowledge no limitations. As the prolific abundance of thrown frogs and crabs flew over the fire at opposing animal murderers, given the war's ferocity it was only logical to expect the animal ammunition to run low leading to driftwood, empty beer cans, and stones to be employed.

Standing just outside the beach house, Jack and I had a panoramic view of what became known in Green Land as the Great Frog and Crab War. Holding Jack tight by hand, I noted Sunni, in support of the crab people, had suffered numerous frog gut-smear wounds and was tossing stones and clam shells accurately, lacking only the velocity to be effective in achieving drawing blood.

Somehow finding himself in the frog camp, Hinki had a two inch arm cut from the tail of a tossed lobster claw. With pride he hurried to each frog defender, showing his wound and reassuring them that he was all right, even though no one was interested enough to ask.

Hearing the bedlam, the screams, the curses, the previous loving beach house couples charged out to join in the fray in support of their respective animals.

Jack tried to talk me into joining the battle. It looked like a hell of a brawl and in the ensuing peace talks one could discover some serious love. Unfortunately, spending the day alone, rejected and disrespected, enabled me to assume the sacred reporter's role. From safety, I watched and critiqued the action.

With rocks, beer cans, and clam shells depleted, the combatants progressed to hand to hand combat; the girls playing tug a war with each other's hair, the boys in bear hugs dancing together.

I pointed out to Jack, "Shit, look at Hinki and Sunni going at each other! And Sunni's winning!"

Rushing into the beach house, Serenity and Star quickly exited in full uniform. Star, holding up his badge of authority, slipped between two girls and ordered them to stop and let go of each other's hair. One giving him a fist in the nose and the other groining him, he went down for the count.

As a police woman, Serenity, believing she was as good if not better than a policeman, tried to stop two men. One was trying to squash a frog in his opponent's face, the other trying to administer a serious crab tail throat cut. Serenity kept trying to get between them only to be unceremoniously tossed aside. Going below the swinging arms, she came up between them only to receive crab cuts to her uniform and frog guts pushed up her nose. Deciding a refereeing position was best she stood outside the combatants telling them to stop, ordering them not to hurt each other, lecturing them about the futility of combat to settle differences, to learn from the peaceful coexistence of crabs and frogs how to behave, finally warning them she'd have to issue citations for mass murder of frogs and crabs, two of nature's noblest creatures.

Ignoring her, the two continued grappling with each other. Turning, Serenity next approached females in combat. Learning from previous experience, from an external position she told them, ordered them, and lectured them, ending with writing out more beach citations. She left the combatants in order to nurse an injured horseshoe crab that had lost its tail.

It was all very amusing, but noticing Jack was empty and in need of replenishment I left the ongoing theater and entered the beach house. Pouring Jack into a highball glass 'til he touched the rim, I noted the professors, being too learned to resort to crab and frog tossing, were worriedly seated at a kitchen table, a multitude of forms spread before them.

The frog professor bemoaned that, with all the frog casualties his count would be down and Green Land authorities would be terrified at the possibility of extinction.

The crab professor bemoaned that, given the chaos outside, it would be impossible to count the horseshoe crabs.

"We have a problem," observed the frog professor.

"Indeed. We must cooperate," suggested the crab professor.

"I agree, and in the collegiate spirit of cooperation, if you say your research students counted a couple of thousand crabs, out of respect I'd counter sign your frog count report as accurate."

The crab man said, "In the spirit of scientific cooperation, in the advancement of Green Land agenda, I couldn't do less for you. A submitted report by you of a few thousand frogs counted based on your objective scientific authority, I'll accept without question."

And so each filled out their scientific research forms, cheating only to the extent of each asking the other how many was he putting down.

"Five thousand," said the frog man.

"That many? I've only got two thousand crabs." Quickly the crab man said, "I'll put down six thousand."

Frog man said, "That's a lot of crab. Maybe I'll put down sixty five hundred frogs."

They went on playing 'can you top this' 'til they agreed on a mutual number: ten thousand five hundred and seventy two frogs and the identical number for crabs. Signing each other's count as accurate, they mutually expressed the hope the other's scientific article will be soon published in a Green Land scientific journal and lead to tremendous advances in environmental knowledge and most important, increased research funding.

Frog man voiced his expectation of receiving funding for an in-depth scientific project researching the octopus population on the Isle of Capri over the winter break. "Already got a hundred students willing to sacrifice their Xmas vacation to scuba dive off Capri," he said.

Crabman said, "If environmental funding is available, and in Green Land it always is, I'm putting in for a couple of hundred thousand dollars to do a count of flying fish off Pago Pago, and I've got more student volunteers than I can use."

I left them and tried to find solace in the TV room watching a couple of baboons happily copulating in the Ivory Coast. Jack and I couldn't take the additional sexual tension when hippos began going at it on the Congo River. Jack suggested another channel, another Green program showing two lizards copulating, followed by the egg laying, all close up and personal. Can you possibly feel lonely watching that?

AFTER GREEN LAND

Dispirited as usual, I sought refuge in the hotel lounge with a Manhattan. I was looking for solitude, so of course Hinki joined me. His presence buried my spirits six feet down as he angrily complained that Sunni was using him.

"Peoples, she was manipulating me!" he cried and he was so angry he ordered red wine.

Amazed anyone would want to manipulate him in any way, I asked how.

"Sex!" he said, like it was the first time since Eve a woman used sex to manipulate a man. Given Hinki's sexual appeal, I easily believed in Sunni's fabrication of sexual interest for her own ulterior motives. Then again, isn't that the reason for the battle of the sexes?

Crap, the fleeting thought of Sunni and Hinki making love had me driving deeper into Manhattan 'til I hit the Battery.

Ordering a renewal, I asked Hinki for what possible purpose Sunni would employ her feminine wiles on him. I did say 'possible' like it couldn't be possible.

After a long, splashing about in his red wine, Hinki complained Sunni was stealing his ideas. "I had shown her my reports, and now I find out from a friend in my department she was paraphrasing my ideas in her reports!"

Thank goodness Manhattan was again at hand to help me digest the idea of Hinki having an idea.

"She plagiarized my stuff! Damn it, Peoples, that's illegal and she must be brought to account, made to pay for such breeches in confidence, ethics and law!"

I traveled to mid-Manhattan, and resting at 42nd Street felt the need to give him something. "Well, thanks for telling me, but I haven't shown her any of my reports."

The sudden thought that Sunni didn't bother to try to steal my ideas but stole Hinki's so upset me, I again drove down to the Battery. I wouldn't be human if I didn't enjoy Hinki's misfortune, though it added nothing to my life.

Satisfied with his pain, I worried whether the poor slob was expecting me to spend the whole dinner sympathetically listening to his audio loop of crying over his betrayal. *May have to eat in my room again.* The 'again' made me feel a social pariah, even if my reasoning mind tried to vigorously argue against such feelings as if the feelings could be talked away. Fat chance.

I was about to make an excuse to rid myself of the pathetic character when he treated me to another visit to Manhattan, and Sunni arrived, flushed red with anger. Her first words expressed her outrage over Hinki daring to think she'd want to steal his stupid ideas, followed quickly with anger at his reporting the outrageous lie to his department in an attempt to ruin her reputation. With all my serious up/down Manhattan travels, my hopes for filling my evening's void suddenly looked promising with Sunni's anger.

In my Manhattan perambulations, had I found a possible avenue for sexual success? Hoping to escape my evening's void, I murmured, "Sunni, let me buy you a drink. What will you have?"

After quickly tossing, "Brandy Alexander" at the bartender, Sunni continued gnawing on Hinki's character, ripping away at his manhood. It was obvious she had spent hours rehearsing her oration by her lack of pauses between sentences, her expressing diverse concepts, and her swift short inhalations.

As Sunni viscously rocked and rolled Hinki's mind, character, and talent, he had no chance to slip even a microscopic 'but' into the verbal onslaught, never mind easing in a cohesive sentence. After a few minutes of onslaught, Hinki turned to me and gave me a 'see you later,' as if we actually had plans for later.

I sat for a good half-hour listening to Sunni replay her rants, and at every pause I said something like, "Sunni, you're so right." Eventually, in fatigue, my replies trickled down to a slathering of yeas. Hinki was boring, but man to man I could relate to his pain. With Sunni, my hope was for an intimate relationship that would last 'til the end of our visitations the next morning.

As she was finishing her Alexander I took the pause in her spate of anger to suggest continuing our conversation in my room over room service, drinks, and dinner. Hopefully she'd eventually run down; then I could make my move to further tarnish her reputation.

"Edmund, I'm just so upset over Hinki's malicious lies, I can't think of eating anything."

Crap, reefs ahead. But having invested so much time and energy sympathetically listening to her fuming over the horrendous suffering the beast had inflicted on her, I felt justified in seeking my reward, possibly the only reward for listening to women. I showed my weak hand by suggesting (it felt like begging) we could just have a few drinks and brainstorm ideas on how to save her reputation and trash Hinki's.

She said, "Well," in such a wavering, tearing voice. It suggested if I pushed hard she might cave in. Before I could start my hard press, she confessed to having had too many Alexanders and said she had an appointment to meet someone in a few minutes.

Someone? I had invested real pain, tossed in my pride, exposed my needs and revealed my interest, only to have the 'someone' hit me hard.

I knew, you knew, the bartender knew, Alexander knew, the 'someone' was a male, a male she had picked up in a day, or was it in a night, for a night.

Afraid I didn't fathom the sex of the 'someone,' she described him. "Alex is a legal advocate for the environment."

Shit, her saying he was a 'legal advocate for the environment' slapped me where you suspect, below the navel, above the knees and I'm not talking thighs. Stupidly I stayed to finish my third trip to Manhattan, and thus was there to be introduced to the environment's legal advocate, Alex something. He smiled, as well he should, seeing he was getting what I was after. Suspecting my plans, plans he had demolished without trying, brought his good humor to a smiling offer of handshakes, offers to buy a round, while wrapping a possessive arm around Sunni's trim waist. Now with Sunni smiling, after giving me sour looks during her boring harangue, I felt stupid and cheated.

So sure he would be able to tarnish Sunni's reputation tonight, Alex was in no rush to do it. In fact he didn't speak to Sunni but to me, asking, did I like their environmental laws, and how about Green Land's rehabilitation and reforestation programs, and did I hear about Green Land's successful efforts in saving jellyfish barely a few months from extinction. "I don't want to brag" (but of course he did and of course he wanted to) "but I've been appointed to sail around the world on a private Green Land LOV ship looking for species in danger of extinction. Once identified I'm to organize university professors and students to do an intervention and save... er... er...."

"Jellyfish!" I said.

"Yeah, them, and lots of other living organisms. You don't want to hear me talk about seaweed and how fast it's being destroyed. Never mind the sea turtles."

Busy with her Alexander Brandy and snuggling tight against Alex, Sunni only picked up on the LOV boat, asking her new love if she could go with him.

"Shit, I don't know. Look Sunni, let's say we discuss it later at my place where we can resolve our sailing difficulties."

With hope, but little expectation, Sunni said she'd love to learn more about seaweed.

"And sea turtles," Alex said to cinch the deal. "Senator Reed and some of his female staff will be sailing with us. Should be a blast."

Lest anyone think this was going to be a free round the world party cruise, Alex solemnly said, "The trip will entail hard work in collecting samples, filling out index cards, and—"

"Ooh, I'm proficient in filling out index cards," Sunni said. "I'd love to work on saving jellyfish and learn about seaweed, and as for sea turtles, they're my favorite animal!"

"Great, Sunni. If I can get you on board I know you'll have a great time. No land can match us for caring for the environment with so much sensitive heart and love," Alex said as he squeezed Sunni's waist hard enough to squeeze out a giggle.

Hopping off the bar stool like a trained seal, throwing a quick goodbye at me as if it was a piece of liter, Sunni eagerly asked Alex where they were going. Sunni may have in mind the world, but Alex and I knew very well where Sunni was going.

Leaving, Alex turned to me, and damn it, winked at me, then gave her a wet kiss.

My only joy was knowing Sunni's hope of seeing the world on Green Land's LOV boat will end up like my hope of ending up on her. The only joy was Alex's, and he didn't deserve it, didn't earn it, and didn't appreciate it.

Alone, deciding I was too alone to eat, I stayed put and switched to beer to get the taste of Manhattan's dirty streets out of my mouth. After the second beer, in ordering the third, I said to hell with it all and ordered a shot of rye to keep Bud company.

PART VI

THE IV ENDS

1

Back Home

Arriving home late at night, after hurriedly unpacking, being both horny and lonely, I phoned Pru, hoping, no needing, to see her, but her cell phone was turned off. Looking forward to being with her, disappointed not being able to see her tonight and troubled she wasn't home despite it being past eleven, I left a message to meet me for drinks at the Restful Inn tomorrow night. Alone with my apartment's stale, dusty, forlorn appearance, deep into the night, I was peevish with her, myself, my room, and my life.

Desperate, I tried Rudy but he wasn't answering. I left him a message to meet up at the Restful Inn tomorrow evening as well.

Of all my homecoming welcome scenarios played out in my mind, sitting alone in a cold dark bedroom on an unmade bed wasn't one of them. In the land of hope I was denied citizenship. Although it's hard to give up on hope, hopelessly alone, any expectations of a better tomorrow weren't alive in that room, the definition of depression.

Next day I reported to Hoar, and it was a calamitous meeting filled with disillusionment. Despite Rudy's letters saying my reports were valued and appreciated, the contrary was true. I was not invited to sit, and Hoar showered me with abuse. My reports, showing me to be a PP, were the greatest disappointment to him. I had let him down, a wonderful man who went out on the proverbial limb to give me a chance to be successful. In failing him I had destroyed all his endeavors to bring me forward in the department. "Did you know all Sunni's and Hinki's reports were exemplary and their careers are made while your future was utterly destroyed?"

I was still standing, still not sitting, being demeaned and belittled by a shouting man whom I didn't like, a man I didn't respect. Nonetheless he was able to upset and hurt me by disparaging my work and he succeeded in diminishing my ego. The surprise, no shock at the unexpected abuse he hurled at me robbed me of the anger I deserved to feel; the righteous anger of a falsely accused man wasn't there, only silence, despondence, shock and dejection.

Even Hoar attacking Pru couldn't generate a defensive reply; listening to his abuse of her, my astonishment took all emotion from me. I thought, *What the hell is he talking about?*

He rumbled over her character: Pru was disloyal, he trusted her and by leading him on she had betrayed him. Initially left unspecified was the how. Of low character, she had used his good nature, and his innocent caring concern for her as tools to hurt him.

As he had done in criticizing me, he extolled himself as a great, sensitive, loving, giving man beset by low people who not only don't appreciate what he's done for them, but in return try to hurt him personally and professionally.

"Peoples, knowing you're interested in Pru, knowing your being away left her alone, I took it upon myself to look after her, take her mind off you— er, from feeling alone, feeling abandoned. Talking to her as a father over a few harmless dinners I tried to keep her amused 'til you returned. I cared for you two that much."

Somehow I saw their dinner and coffee klatch meetings as mostly innocent information gathering by Pru for me, with the old man's vague depraved intentions somewhere in the mix. But listening to his self-serving bullshit brought explicitly home the nastiness of their meetings from his perspective. Listening to him ranting, his now explicit attempts at sexual betrayal was a cold, hard, wakeup slap.

And he'd said all that in full self-justification of how, from pure, disinterested motives, he was deceitfully abused by Pru. In the midst of this self-serving garrulity, Hoar eventually went on to itemization.

Foremost in gravity was Pru telling others in the department personal information he had trustingly, in strictest confidence, shared with her. "Do you realize by bragging to the secretaries about having dinner with me she placed my career in jeopardy? These rumors easily ran the maze of office bureaucracy 'til they reached the top echelons and resulted in me receiving a reprimand." Of course Pru had to be promoted and transferred to another department with an undeserved pay raise in order to buy her silence and escape sexual harassment talk."

Not finished with the injuries he suffered, he continued telling how 'she' (which he pronounced with a venomous bite), misinterpreting his caring actions, turned them into attempts to establish a personal intimate relationship with her. "Peoples, nothing could be further from the truth. I believe an unbreakable barrier exists between management and staff."

Somehow in moving to Pru's perfidious conduct, he had moved away from me and was talking to, no lecturing, the world about himself. "It's so true that good deeds never go unpunished. You try to do good, to help people, and you're always let down and hurt. There's no appreciation, no gratitude for a person doing disinterested good deeds for others."

Eyes refocusing on me, Hoar stared for a moment before lamenting, "Peoples, you let me down. With our country and our department bursting with the OP spirit, you can't be a PP here. I specifically warned you not to go PP. No one wants to read your reports about the king going bare ass with you and then you go on to throw mud on him. You've got to wrap him up in a golden haze. If you were smart, more like Sunni and Hinki, you could go far. No one likes seeing the unadorned truth laying out there in the noon day sun, naked. Shit, it's why we always wear clothes of soft, caring words and happy talk. Truth, if it must be paraded, must be dressed with romance, good feelings and sensitive caring."

Again his gaze left me as he listened with approval to his own lecture.

The guy really liked himself, was a wise hero to himself. I guess the secret to being happy is having the ability to lie to yourself and without any doubt believe your own lies.

With his last "Peoples you let me down and now I must let you go," I was finally excused. Outside the office I wondered why I had bothered listening to the bastard. *What's wrong with me?*

I searched for a lie I could believe in, something that could save my self-respect and I could be happy with. I spent a lot of time trying one lie after another to save my self-esteem, but after numerous valiant attempts I was still naked and unhappy.

2

Restful Inn Again

After meeting with Hoar, now jobless, aimless, and insensible to any purpose, I returned to my apartment. In such a mental state I cleaned the apartment, took a shower, shaved and dressed in my best before sitting on my bed to watch the clock.

My only cognitive thought was a short series of simple questions: *What the hell happened? Why is it happening to me? What should I do now that it's happening?* The happening itself remained elusive; it was about the job, but not the job. There was Rudy sending me false reports about my work, but it wasn't Rudy. It was Pru dining with and gossiping about horny Hoar, but it wasn't Pru. Was it my need for someone's affection, for someone to give me definition, to define my life? My structure had left, and leaving, left behind a vacuum.

Eventually the clock got its hands around four and I moved from sitting on my bed staring out a window to sitting on a Restful Inn stool staring at the bar mirror. The biggest difference, I had a drink in my hand, Johnny Walker Red Label on ice. It was unwise to entertain Johnny on an empty stomach, but a meal I didn't feel like eating would stand in the way of Johnny helping me find elusive hope to turn a PP to an OP.

Sliding a glance left, I saw another hopeless man hunched over trying to find meaning from a frosted stein of beer. The hunched shoulders and the hypnotic staring at his beer said *Leave me alone.*

On my right a row of empty stools underlining Restful Inn's twilight emptiness underlined mine.

Shit, I told Johnny, *we've got a heavy load to carry,* and finishing him I ordered up his brother, Johnny two to help Johnny one. The Restful Inn had no clocks; time is irrelevant in the semi-darkened world of spirits. My watch said 4:45. Inside me, Johnny noticing I was holding his twin, asked where Pru was. My friend Johnny two resting in hand gave me some hope, possibly dinner with Pru and back to her place to find at least temporary solace As down as I was, up was needed for this night, and tomorrow was nowhere in sight. Taking in thought, this hope, now I wasn't so disappointed with the guy in the mirror. The Bud man took a new Bud with the same saturnine shoulder hunch. To my right the seats remained empty, unmistakably saying it's too early for her, and certainly too soon to be meeting up with Johnny two. To soothe Johnny two's feelings, to make him feel welcome, I took a polite sip and looking in the mirror began to like what I saw.

My watch announced five and a half and the arrival of four women searching for an after-work life of excitement and gaiety. The late-thirties women climbed the stools to my right. Removed by two stools I caught their laughter and giggles and orders of Daiquiris of various fruit flavors. The difference between men and women is, we can take it straight; they always need to sweeten it.

The girlish excitement over nothing filling the bar, got Bud man to look over at them as I did. Their loudness was successful in getting our attention, and in convincing themselves they were having a great time, and despite the mirror were now really teenage girls living dangerously. Knowing the flamboyant acting, an attempt to convince themselves and anyone within hearing was a put on, I was made sadder by their gaiety. I didn't realize it, but suddenly Johnny became a triplet, Johnny's third sibling standing in front of me gave out with an optimistic hello. On an empty stomach the preceding two were strumming a rather gay tune on my neurons.

Possibly if hunched over Bud man joined me we could make inroads into that quadrangle. Johnny three told me to reevaluate the girls' ages from an initial erroneous late-thirties to a more accurate mid-thirties. He even swore one may have just recently left her twenties behind. Looking at the mirror, the Johnnies swore it reflected the picture of a hell of a great guy, a guy second to none, a guy four women would love to meet. I argued the point with the Johnnies but reinforced by half of their third sibling, together they were very persuasive. I was tempted to take this very handsome guy along with Johnny three and join the merry group, all of whom were reordering. I was stopped by thoughts of Pru's expected momentary arrival, the difficulty of separating one from a herd and the fact that the herd was sending no signals they were interested in the Johnnies' friend.

Straightening up, Bud man started walking over to the boisterous foursome. *Damn, is he making moves before me? Getting the best for himself? Maybe if he successfully inserts himself into their midst I could smoothly introduce Johnny and myself to them.* On closer inspection I was sure they'd just crossed the thirty year age line and one was definitely a couple of years away from touching the line.

I'd just made the decision to finish Johnny, and then freshen him up like new, make my move and join the Bud man, when the stupid Bud man, passing them by, entered the men's room.

Frustrated I sent my third Johnny to join his brothers and, ordering a fourth, wondered where that dynamic stud guy in the mirror suddenly went. He certainly wasn't with me.

I decided I had to go and Bud man and I crossed paths. Passing the girls, noting they looked mid-thirties, a little shopworn, a little too much makeup, I felt they weren't worth my and Johnny's effort and besides, I was expecting Pru. *Wouldn't look right for her to see me mingling within a quad of women. Then again, maybe it would do me some good for her to see me in the midst of four early thirties broads; maybe I'd become valuable in her eyes.*

I told Johnny, I was a stud with a great job. *What's that Johnny? Okay, let's forget the job.* Still good looking, a hell of a lot better than that Bud guy, who resumed hunching over his beer, whispering to it, who knows what tale of woe. If he really wanted to hear a sad story, he should talk to me. *Maybe I should go over to him, and after getting acquainted we could go two on four with the girls. Why not? I've got time 'til Pru shows, and all the Johnnies got my back. Anyway, I didn't set a time with Pru, but still it's after 5 and where is she?*

Okay, risking less ego approaching a man than coming on to four women, particularly in a bar, I placed Johnny in Bud's neighborhood, and introduced myself with an offer to buy him another beer. First words out of his mouth, he tells me he's not gay. What's the country coming to? Hurriedly announcing my continuous need for feminine companionship, though not in those words I started to go back to home base. Quickly he apologized and, graciously accepting his apology, I bought him a new Bud as a token of my good will. Suit, tie, mid-thirties, I could relate to him. In the lull waiting for Bud's arrival, I told him about my problems at my job without being too specific. Holding a few Johnnies inside I was talkative but not at the bonhomie backslapping let it all hang out stage.

Whether it was really him speaking or Bud, he sympathized and shared some of his burden. Like a gambler thinking his winning hand beat mine, he turned over his ill-luck hand one card at a time.

He was ill,

I asked "Is it serious?" while thinking *Is it contagious?*

"Not really."

He took Bud in hand, I grabbed Johnny and we quietly sipped. To escape from being labeled the pathetic loser, I told him I was expecting my girlfriend at any moment.

Another of his cards was exposed. "My wife cheated on me."

Sympathetically I said, "Your wife... that's really tough."

"Well, we're not really married. We were three rings from marriage. Well, two. Gave her a promise ring, sort of promising sometime in the future she'd get an engagement ring and maybe she'd make it to the third."

Philosophically I replied, "Complicated. Women sure make it complicated, so if she cheated, you're going to dump her?"

Another card. "Certainly, she claimed it was only once with one guy who got her drunk and it just happened, and she didn't know how it happened. She says if I love her I should believe it didn't mean anything, that it really didn't happen, that I should forget the incident and trust her."

Being momentarily PP, I said, "It just happened? Like it just happened she took off her clothes, laid down—"

I was warming up to deliver a coarse recitation when he interrupted my flow and in continuation of his theme turned over another card. "An STD," he murmured.

Leaning back, moving Johnny away from Bud, I asked, "AIDS?" I was ready to get up and move Johnny and myself back to my home stool.

"No, hell, thank goodness for that. It's syphilis. She gave me the clap. Can you believe it? And tried to blame me saying I gave it to her. Hell, I know I was true to her for nearly two years and she tried to blame me for the STD."

Thinking, *Shit, he's got a hand of aces*, I nervously asked, "You got it treated?"

"Yeah, took several injections and it's better not to say where. I'm clean now."

Casting my eyes to the four girls, who were becoming younger in Johnny's opinion, and in the bar's neon twilight, looking like models, alternating between fashion and porn, I nodded to them and asked Bud, "What you say you and I try our luck with those?"

"Don't know. Sort of off women, you know what I mean?"

Half-past six. Where the hell is Pru? And I can't be caught picking up broads even though she ate with Hoar. In camaraderie I confessed, "You know, I suspect my girl of cheating on me. She dated our boss. Said it was to help me. Well, it didn't. It screwed me. That sums up my situation."

"She slept with him?" Bud half-asked, half-said. Given his experience, I couldn't blame him for being cynical.

"No, I'm pretty sure she didn't."

"Pretty sure is not being sure."

Ouch, he put a finger deep into my doubts and twisted it around. I said, "I'm sure. We're engaged. Well, almost engaged. I'm proposing tonight, and I plan to give her an engagement ring."

"Did you give her a promise ring?"

"No,"

"Take my advice. Do the three ring dance. Best make it a promise ring."

"No, I'm going for an engagement ring, and she'll get it soon. I haven't bought it yet."

"Soon isn't now," he said.

The guy was offensive, and taking offense brought Johnny and me back to our home stool. Deciding the hell with the desperate middle-aged broads, I'll patiently and desperately wait for Pru.

As the clock neared seven and I held Johnny four, definitely feeling the prior three, I suspected I should have something to eat.

The Bud man made another men's room voyage.

The four sexually promiscuous women were joined by two business men well past the forty yard line. The girls were bouncing with joy.

3

Climax

The minute hand inched past seven as Pru arrived, arrived with Rudy. For some reason dictated by internal needs, I completely forgot about Rudy. My necessity to be alone with Pru, in her arms, being comforted, being made whole, I was less than glad to see Rudy. His presence lent nothing to assuaging my confused mind and raise my depressed spirit.

I expected two happy faces glad to see me after my absence. Instead their expressions mimicked my own troubled spirit. Rudy took the lead in greeting me. "Edmund, good to see you back home." Being it was so good, he quickly took it back adding, "Heard about Hoar giving you a terrible dressing down." He was about to commiserate further, predicting it was fatal to my job when Pru jumped in with concern about what my plans were. "Will you be able to stay in the department or must you seek other job opportunities?"

Shit, I'm dying and she's worried about her future marriage plans, with me being jobless.

Rudy, still in the role of my best friend, had to observe how my opportunities, although undefined, couldn't reside in any other department. His exact sympathetic words were, "You're toast with every department." It was his gratuitous conclusion: a conclusion I knew, a conclusion he knew I knew, and still he had to stick it to me as if I didn't know, and as a friend, wanted to enjoy letting me know what I knew.

Finishing Johnny I turned to order a fourth—or was it a fifth? I didn't care enough to count, though by any count, it was a lot of

Johnnies. Rudy stood for a round of drinks, Pru standing behind his shoulder weakly smiled at me, a smile casual friends give to the terminally ill in a feeble attempt to keep up their spirits.

Where were the hugs, the kisses, the joy? They weren't here with me; they were with the quartet of girls spending their coins of celebration on the two smiling guys, guys eagerly picking up on the girls' false smiles with the expectation of more smiles for everyone to follow.

With my received restrained greetings, knowing what is not said or not gestured carries the real message, happiness wasn't sitting next to me. While Rudy and I took note of the barroom's half-dozen patrons' gaiety, Pru again asked about my plans.

Is she concerned over my iffy future? Is she concerned about her future marriage? Probably both. Taking both in hand along with Johnny, I told her the truth. "I really haven't made any plans yet. Everything has really hit me hard. Rudy, why the hell did you write me saying my reports were successful when they weren't?"

"Ed, believe me, I'm as surprised as you at the total change in the department's reaction to you. I recall I was relying on the reactions of the guys in the department and not on the higher ups."

Pru said, "I did try to tell you. Hoar was angry over your reports being so pessimistic, so absolutely PP."

Seeing her tossing the blame shawl for my situation over my shoulders, I naturally attacked her. "Pru, what the hell were you thinking of, going out with that old degenerate?"

Naturally she defended her actions. "I did it to help you. You don't think I enjoyed dining with him! And besides, nothing happened between us."

The gratuitous 'nothing happened between us' addition suggested something may have happened, could have happened, and probably did happen.

I continued my attack, "Well, according to Hoar you made out very well. Despite the 'nothing happening' between you, some very nice things did happen to you: a new job and a big raise."

"The raise was small and I was only transferred to a new department," she said.

"Hoar maintains you blackmailed the department into giving you a raise and a promotion."

Coming to Pru's defense, Rudy said, "Just a minute, Ed. Pru is totally innocent and only received what was due her. She earned her promotion and she deserved the raise."

Between sips, Johnny pointed out that I was arguing with the one person I really needed. Talk about cutting your own throat. Abruptly, quickly backstepping, I said, "Pru, I'm really glad you got the promotion and the raise, and I am grateful for all the information you provided. Honey, I never for a moment doubted you. I trust implicitly in your faithfulness." That trust, guaranteed, had a one-night life.

Johnny, what's that you're all still whispering? All this talk and swearing about nothing happening is suggestive that something could have happened? Telling my Johnnies to stop causing trouble and assuming an aggrieved attitude, I switched to Rudy. "Trusting in my friend, I believed the misinformation you gave me and I acted upon it. You told me my PP reports were being applauded as courageous."

He said, "Look Ed, I tried my best to help you. Most of the guys in the department were enthusiastic about your reports. What the higher ups thought, I didn't know. Pru got a clearer idea of the supervisor's and department heads' reaction to your reports. You should have listened to her."

The crowd of Johnnies pronounced, *Dummy, you never should have accepted the appointment in the first place*, and as usual they were right. "Well, I'm home. My career is finished. I've got to regroup and figure out what to do next. At least I have you two to help and support me."

Rudy told me I could always count on his help and friendship.

Pru held back, looking askance at Rudy and murmuring, "Edmund, we have something important to tell you."

With no dearest or darling appendage, no Ed, an outsider might easily guess what was coming, but desperately needing to find a safe harbor when she told me about Rudy and her being in love, all the

Johnnies crowded in my gut were knocked out. I had sensed what was coming. The PP guy in the bus's back knew what was coming, but the needy driver, desperate to believe, didn't hear the PP's words. Desperate to believe, fearing my apostate self, I foolishly asked for confirmation. "Pru, what are you talking about?"

"Rudy?" Pru said, prompting him.

Rudy mumbled, "Pru and I are... going together."

Not satisfied with 'going together,' Pru clarified. "Ed, Rudy and I are desperately in love and he's given me a promise ring as a sign of his commitment to our love and our future together."

Crap, not merely in love but desperately in love, not merely desperately in love, but promise rings desperate love, all in the short time I was gone.

Johnny told me, *You poor bastard, believe it.* I told my gut I still couldn't believe it.

Rudy went into justifications that justified nothing. "It just happened. Watching over and protecting Pru from Hoar, having lunch and dining at her place, I fell in love with her."

I said, "Rudy, how could you do this to me?"

Pru said, "We tried to deny our feelings, to repress them, but they were too strong for us."

The Johnny sitting on the bar and the guys in the gut concluded, *Crap, she's giving you the 'devil made me do it' BS defense.* Weakly I tried to recapture her love. "But Pru, I love you. I want to marry you, create a future together."

"Still, you didn't propose. So when Rudy and I realized we had strong feelings for each other, I felt free to be responsive to my heart. Besides, you wouldn't want to marry a girl who fell out of love with you."

Johnny, not I, asked her if they were sleeping together.

It was greeted by a public condemnation of people who say something gross. Asking about something gross is strongly censored as being gross by those engaging in the gross behavior, and they demand you don't give words to it.

Rudy looking embarrassed and Pru telling me it was none of my business told me they were doing it. The only question was how soon after I left.

Getting nasty, rolling their irresistible romantic love affair into reality's mud, I asked Pru if she also did it with Hoar and was that how she earned the raise and promotion.

Rudy told me I was going too far.

"Yeah? Given what you did to me, how far is too far?"

For some inexplicable reason, a horrified Pru announced she was crushed that I'd suspect her of such behavior.

Now knowing her, I told her it was easy.

She said she got her promotion solely for her work.

Rudy backed her up, saying I had underestimated a wonderful girl like Pru.

"Underestimated her? I did, but now I don't. Rudy, it's you who has no understanding. If she did it to me, with you, what guarantees do you possess that she won't do it to you and that she didn't do it with Hoar?"

Johnny told me, *Good point*, as did their reaction.

An outraged Pru was glad to find out in time how twisted my mind was.

A sad Rudy told me our friendship was at an end.

I and my Johnnies actually laughed. "As if you sleeping with the girl I planned to marry was somehow just a speed bump in our friendship."

With that said, Rudy finished his drink and Pru slammed hers down indicating that I had barely escaped having it thrown in my face. With a hurt attitude that only those acting innocent can assume when the recipient of their betrayed love and dishonesty unjustly spits in their face, they made for the street. *Shit, they didn't pay for their drinks. Another bill to be paid.*

4

Anti-Climax

Waving hands that were only marginally under my control over my drink, I semaphored for another Johnny. One of the gut residing Johnnies queried as to whether another Johnny was a smart move. The majority shouted, *To hell with it all! Screw everybody! Tonight I die, tomorrow the funeral!*

I noticed the half-dozen patrons still going strong were still a group; the two guys hadn't roped and branded the cows they wanted. They were having a joyous party and I wasn't invited; I was a stranger condemned to watching, not to participating.

My inside Johnnies wanted me to take them over to the group but I told them no, not a chance. Even with all the Johnnies helping me, there was no chance I'd make a go of it. Johnny and his friends yelled *Chicken!* I ignored them, concentrating on the latest Johnny.

So intense on him, I was surprised to find the STD guy standing next to me, shoulders straight, absent Bud, a hard drink in hand, smile in place, suggesting I finish Johnny so he could buy another for me.

Crap, I thought, *what the hell does he want? Shit, I hope he isn't getting chummy.*

Magnus was his name, and he said it hoping I'd believe it. Not giving a damn, I let it slide with quasi acceptance.

"Woman trouble?" he asked, as if he hadn't heard Pru and Rudy and he cared for my pain.

"What else?" I said, then waited for his next move. He hadn't come out of his personal bar fortress to join me without a reason. Eyeing the half-dozen happy people he remarked, "If thrown off a horse, best get back on as soon as possible."

Cognizant of his goal, I encouraged him. "Look, there are two free girls... what say we join them? Got nothing to lose."

"Yeah, nothing to lose, and maybe two of the free girls will be very free."

Smiling, picking up our drinks, Magnus and I joined the happy group, much to the girls' joy. Now with the sides even, the sex game, or is it the struggle, would be fair.

My Johnnies were in charge for the rest of the evening, so if I wanted to know what happened I'd have to ask them and they weren't talking, but if they did I'm sure they'd have a lot to say.

With that said, I can report that, next morning, having to piss real bad, I woke up naked in this broad's bed. She was there and from the look of the room, the bed, the scattered clothes, and how I felt, it must have been a hell of a night. Johnny knew all about it and damn him, he wasn't giving me even a hint as to what had happened and how it had happened. Unfortunately, with all the evidence strewn about and her lying naked next to me I easily deduced the night's activity, even if all the Johnnies remained dumb.

She was a mess, looking like what she was, a drunk barely worth a one-night stand. If not a bottom feeder, she was skimming the mud. If she was low, looking at her, I felt even lower. Her appearance had Magnus' STD trouble scarring a stomach already upset with allowing too many Johnnies to party down there.

As she sat up, her hair in disarray, shorn of makeup, bleary eyed, sagging jowls and breasts, I couldn't help thinking, *Shit, I've reached bottom.* Bashfully climbing into my underwear, I declined her offer of breakfast. Hastily, too hastily, I refused the suggestion I return to bed. Surmising this wasn't her first one-night service and she wanted to cuddle, maybe all in a sad attempt to convert a one nighter into at least a weekend romance. Seeing the hurt my refusal inflicted, I tried to smooth it over, despite the fact I couldn't remember her name.— "Honey, after the great time we had last night I'm totally wiped out. (That was the gospel truth.) You know what I mean." I managed to generate a half-hearted placating leer.

The indirect reference to her bed pleasure abilities mollified her. She said, "I've got the day off. What say we do something together, make a day of it?"

Thinking, *I've got to get the hell out of here*, I said, "I've got to go to work."

"Last night you said you were fired and you were screwed by your girlfriend and your best friend. I felt so sorry for you. It was so sad."

Am I that sad? Am I getting 'feel sorry for you' bed action? No it's her excuse for her bed action. For a woman there has to be a reason, certainly an excuse for the action other than wanting the action, especially if it's desperately needed action.

Dressed, my head aching, my stomach in riot, my throat parched, I told her I've got some important job interviews in the morning and need to get to my place to change.

She could read that as literal or not. Deciding to take the literal path she suggested I call her to tell her about my interview success; she was very, very concerned.

Lying like a politician on the day before the votes are cast I told her sure, I'd definitely call.

"You don't have my number. Let me give it to you."

She wouldn't let me go. Pathetic, desperate, am I the thousandth to be escaping her enchantments? She gave me her cell number and asked for mine. I told her I just got a new one and when we met again I'd give her my new number. That was a mistake. In dropping a broad you can't be subtle and gentle. Carelessly I had foolishly erected another barrier to my escape.

She quickly pounced, "When do you want to meet?"

"I really don't know," I said.

"Where do you want to meet?" she asked.

"I really don't know," I said.

She knew what I was trying to say without my saying it, but in desperation she suggested meeting at the Restful Inn tonight. "Last night we had such a wonderful time."

She might remember, but I didn't and Johnny still wasn't talking. Torn between being a nice guy and being a bastard I chose nice guy because it's who I am. I said, "Sure, Restful Inn tonight, but now I've got to go."

Closing the door on her, being a nice guy and not planning to go back to the Inn, compassionately I hoped she'd connect with someone at the bar. Walking away I left her and this phase of my life. Without hope, illogically I hoped the future would be better. It certainly couldn't be worse. I debated about going to a doctor's office to have a range of tests done for a multitude of STDs, but with no future, shrugging I told myself *Why bother?* and hoped for the best.

5

Just for the Ops

To end my IV visitation's account: jobless, girl less, friendless, aimless, hopeless, worried about STDs, knowing it's too painful for my OP readers, makes it incumbent on me to relieve their anxiety.

The next night, returning to Restful Inn, I met up with my one night stand for a second night, a night where now I respected her as a person. The awkwardness of not knowing her name was overcome when after two rounds of bad boy Johnny's injected fueled spirit of intimacy, I suggested we formally introduce ourselves.

"I'm Edmund Peoples, please call me Ed."

Suspecting my real purpose, she acted as if she were unaware. After all, I doubt she knew my name either. "I'm Michelle Clinton, call me Mikey."

With that problem solved, at dinner, after exchanging personal idiosyncrasies, we became comfortable with each other. I had her solemn word that as a teacher in an inner-city school, she loved the kids, the kids loved her, and she was confident she was making a difference in their lives. This being for OP readers, I affirmed my belief in teachers making differences all the time, and certainly Mikey succeeded inspiring the little cherubs to succeed in their pursuit of knowledge. Inspired by her selfless work among deprived students I became a lawyer fighting tirelessly for protecting the rights of the underprivileged.

Need I report, we married, honeymooned in Central America helping teach the orphans of— wait, know what? You fill in the country's name. Any will suffice; they're all the same. Whoops, that was a little PP, wasn't it?

After making a difference in the lives of the orphans and street children in Central America, returning home we made important differences in the inner-city inhabitants' lives as well. Very busy making differences, we still were able to generate two children of our own and adopt Tyrone Goodboy, a disabled black child from somewhere in Africa (insert your favorite country's name; one is as good as another). Whoops, PP again. The disabled adoptee, besides losing a leg was mentally challenged. However, with love, encouragement, tutoring, and a false leg, he is now on a soccer scholarship at MIT majoring in Chaos Theory. Mikey and I feel proud we made a difference in Tyrone's life. Being an orphan, besides not having a life, he had no name so we gave him both.

As for our biological children, our daughter Nightingale is a doctor working with Doctors Without Borders and making a difference somewhere, anywhere below the Mediterranean (you fill in the name). Our son Mandela is a banker at the UN overseeing the transfer of money from the haves of (you fill in the country) to the have nots (you fill in the usual names). The recipients' names of the gifts of money vary so it makes no sense to be specific, but he's making a big difference in the lives of many poor people made poor by rich people.

Throughout our own lives we were devoted to making a difference in pathetic people's lives and in doing so we have made enemies who are ignorant and evil, who don't want us to make a difference, or who work industriously in creating the differences that hurt people. The specter of these evil people is balanced by all of our OP friends, our wonderful supportive people, good, caring people who themselves are constantly making differences.

Retired, we didn't stop making differences. Mikey tirelessly works to save the world's animals. Her principal concern is saving pigeons. Do you know homing pigeons are in danger of extinction? I'm proud of the difference she's making in pigeons' lives. She has received numerous awards from animal rights organizations, especially from Green Land.

Talking of Green Land, I'm playing a small part in saving the world by being totally green: talking green, writing green, reading green, thinking green, buying green, eating green, supporting green causes, investing only in green companies. I'm a shining example of Green people. My friends are all green, as are our neighbors. My children, including Goodboy, our one-legged soccer player at MIT, are green. We visit only green places, like the Galapagos Islands to watch, photograph and study the lizards and turtles wandering around. I'm proud of Michelle's and my struggle to make a difference and we are made humble by the numerous awards and honors bestowed on us for making differences.

Now as our physical faculties are diminishing, Michelle feels she's ready for political office where she can give back to the country and make even greater differences in your life. I'm trying to make a difference riding the mean streets at night of the inner city in (go ahead, fill it in. Really, does it matter which one?) I'm helping drug addicts by dispensing clean needles, giving them addresses where they can get food, shelter, and if they feel ready, rehabilitation. I'm certain I've made a difference in several poor drug addicts' lives who are graduating from Ivy League Universities majoring in Law, Medicine, and of course Environmental Studies. I could supply names if concerns of confidentiality didn't inhibit me. Also the fact that I really can't recall any names does inhibit me from being more specific.

It's not only with the poor misguided drug-dependent sort either. I've also made a difference in riding the mean streets, talking to working girls, who actually don't work at jobs. I was able to help them escape their pimps and inspire them to find work through my caring, concerning and nonjudgmental lectures. Dozens of innocent girls forced by evil pimps to walk the streets instead of going to college to obtain degrees in Deviant Psychology are now self-respecting independent women working at responsible managerial jobs in banks and on the street selling derivatives. It's wonderful to look back on a life filled with giving to others, of making a difference in people's lives. Makes me feel very special, very different, a feeling saints in another age must have felt, only not having to undergo all their pain.

Michelle and I will continue making differences in people's lives 'til we retire to our Beverly Hills green mansion to entertain green friends in the green manner with organic vegetables and fruits, hormone-free beef and sugar-free deserts, next to our solar-heated pool. Hopefully, after making so many differences, saving so many lives, and creating happiness where misery resided, we'll leave this world to our posthumously earned rewards knowing our world now bathes in a golden glow and is a better place for us having lived.

POST SCRIPT FOR OPs

I was overjoyed to hear Sunni and Hinki are happily married and blessed with two wonderful, healthy children. The girl, Violet, after graduating from Annapolis, earned a promotion to be the Third Marine Division's commanding general and is currently attempting to swim from Cuba to Key West.

Hoar became the beloved president of our country and is currently mentoring several young female interns, hoping that as a surrogate father, he can protect their virtue and promote their careers.

For my bar friend Magnus, after intense marriage counseling he agreed his girlfriend had a one-night misadventure for which she is blameless and the STD could have been his from handshaking someone at a bar. He courageously traveled through the three-ring passage and is now happily married with six children, two of whom look like him.

Finally, my land has adopted all of Sunni's and Hinki's IV suggestions, and has become so highly educated, so scientifically advanced, it is committed to achieve happiness, health, saving the environment, and spreading feminine love and compassion.

THE END

Sit back and be prepared to laugh out loud as you read about the travails of the antihero as he becomes an Investigating Visitor assigned to visit various lands, each famous for some particular social advances, advances which lead him to shed his optimistic persona, OP, and become a pessimistic person, PP.

As an Investigating Visitor he is confronted with humorous social and non-political spoofs as he romps through ten lands such as Psychiatry Land, Health Land and Compassion Land, during which time he loses his girlfriend to his best friend and loses his job, but at the conclusion finds the right woman to help him lead a happy life.

In all the visits, the story material maintains a PG level, guaranteed to amuse, but not to offend readers